Three Hands for Scorpio

Tor Books by Andre Norton

Three Hands for Scorpio

Andre Norton

A TOM DOHERTY ASSOCIATES BOOK
NEW YORK

THREE HANDS FOR SCORPIO

Copyright © 2005 by Andre Norton

Edited by James Frenkel

A Tor Book
Published by Tom Doherty Associates, LLC
175 Fifth Avenue
New York, NY 10010

www.tor.com

Tor® is a registered trademark of Tom Doherty Associates, LLC.

Library of Congress Cataloging-in-Publication Data

Norton, Andre.
    Three hands for scorpio / Andre Norton.
       p.   cm.
    "A Tom Doherty Associates book."
    ISBN 0-765-30464-3 (alk. paper)
    EAN 978-0765-30464-3
       1. Sisters—Fiction.   2. Triplets—Fiction.   3. Kidnapping—Fiction.   I. Title.

PS3527.O632T47 2004
813'.52—dc22   2004059891

First Edition: April 2005

Printed in the United States of America

0 9 8 7 6 5 4 3 2 1

ACKNOWLEDGMENTS

The author is deeply indebted to Caroline Fike and Rose Wolf, whose twofold aid in preparing the saga of the Scorpys for publication was beyond all price. Additional thanks are due to Larry Kimbrough, Wizard of the Alabama Renaissance Faire, who lent his magely name and knowledge to the character of Zolan. Larry also served as scout on a fact-finding mission to the actual Dismals, a geological curiosity of Alabama possessing unusual plants and animals, though not—thankfully—spiders of Shelobian proportions.

Three Hands for Scorpio

One

This by the hand of Tamara, daughter to Earl Scorpy of Verset. Her Most Gracious Majesty, Queen Charlitta of Alsonia, commands us to chronicle our strange and remarkable adventure in Gurlyon, the North Land that has ever been to our nation as a thorn beneath the saddlecloth is to the rider of an ill-trained horse. Our sovereign believes that our story may aid and warn those who follow us. Thus we three have been supplied with quills, paper in plenty, and the carefully guarded palace library for a workplace.

We are the Scorpys, a name neither likely to set bards to plucking harp-strings in stirring song nor one honey-coated for general repeating. However, as Duty, our mother's trusted deputy, has always said, with a scornful sniff, a good name is worthy of honor.

We were three-in-one at our birthing—a cause, at that time (we have been told), for no small surprise and chatter. We were duly named Tamara, Sabina, and Drucilla, for two granddames and a great-aunt, forceful women in their day.

We were also born on the very day of the Battle of Erseway wherein our sire, Desmond Scorpy, the Earl of Verset, played a heroic role which all properly tutored Alsonian children can remember from their schooling.

That passage of arms was to have subdued the Gurlys of the North, and so it did for a short space—long enough, at least, for them to rearm and prepare wood for watch-fires along the border. It goes without saying that our own borderers, long used to raiding and thereby tweaking Gurly tails, also laid plans.

A twisted kind of law served the debated boundary areas: Border Law. Its rules were to be enforced by Warders appointed by our ruler, Lybert the Second, as well as by the King of Gurlyon. These leaders were responsible for protecting their countrymen, as well as for preventing raids from either North or South.

However, such efforts were like attempting to hold back water's downhill rush with a dam of sand. Bribery was rife, and raids continued whenever a Gurlyon clan leader or greedy Alsonian baron spied a chance to snatch cattle, horses, or material goods from his cross-border neighbor. This piratical policy continued cheerfully for years, with neither side having a leader strong enough to curb it.

Then, some six years after the battle, King Lothar died suddenly, after a feast laid to entice foreign merchants for trade with Gurlyon. His heir apparent was Gerrit, a mere lad of seven. The king's untimely demise began a bloody battle over which clan would claim his son's guardianship—a minor war that ended with the disappearance of the child king. Many believed him to have been the prey of either the Mervens or the Raghnells, while others said he had been taken South and was held in secret by enemies there.

However, Summon Fires were not lit and, though the South gathered an army, they remained on our side of the border until their commander could no longer feed them and they must needs be dismissed without drawing their swords.

We three may seem to dwell overlong upon history which must be well-known to most who read this, but in this past lies the root of our own story.

We Scorpys are among the women who possess some form of the Talent. This name is as a large money-bag holding coins of various values, but it is applied to a group of gifts from the Lords of Light that require the channeling of Power through the wielder. We inherited our Gifts through our mother, who comes of a cadet branch of the Scorpy line. We were taught early, under the sharp eyes of Mother and Wise-wife Duty, who served as our nurse, the use of healing herbs and the development of our own special endowments. We sisters not only shared blood and appearance but also thoughts, so that, when necessary, we could communicate silently, as if a single mind served the three of us. And now, in our eighteenth year, sometimes it seems we think and near act as one.

There is little of note to report from our early life. Though we suffered from enough of the physical ills of childhood to cause our elders the fidgets, our mother was well-learned in healcraft and dealt promptly with our ailments.

In conduct, we displayed the alternating arrogance, shyness, and rigid will of those of supposedly tender years. Of all behaviors, whining was regarded by Mother as the most unwelcome. She was strict but always just and loving—virtues that might be quickly sensed and appreciated by us even as tiny children.

In appearance, we are as like to one another as our birth would suggest. This likeness, we discovered very early, might profitably be used to manipulate other members of the household, save for Father, Mother, and Duty—we never tried any such trick with them. Despite the unpleasantness of this trait, we must chronicle it as part of our ability to blend personas when needed, for it figures importantly in our great adventure.

We possess our father's hair. In the normal light of the hall, it seems deeply black, but under strong sunlight, it appears burnished by threads of fiery red. This crowning glory frames ivory skin and the large green eyes we received from our mother.

In Grosper dwelt few of our rank; they were mostly visitors, and none lingered for long. Lacking much basis for comparison, we had, perhaps, too high an opinion of ourselves. However, that estimation came to be sorely tested ere our tale was complete.

Our father, in his uneasy appointment as High Warden dealing with unruly neighbors, maintained a tighter than customary hold, traveling from one fortress to another through the year, save in the months holding Year Turn and High Winter.

Having no son to "shield his back," as the country saying goes, Father gave a new twist to our education from the very month we arrived at Grosper Castle in our tenth year. He rode well, and he taught us to do so, for horsemanship was a skill greatly needed in this land of few roads, and many of those hardly more than trails. In addition, we learned to use conventional weapons. We rebelled at the training from time to time—why, was our collective thought, should we exert ourselves unduly in practicing with a sword or snaplock when our mental talents would serve nicely to bewilder any opponent? But Father lessoned us severely when we made too-easy recourse to our Gifts, on the grounds that the Gurlys held an ever-growing hatred for what they deemed the Black Arts, and it was best not to give any clansman cause to suspect we had been tutored in arcane lore. Southerners, in general, were rumored by the men of the North to be learned in dark practices; thus even a hint about the Earl of Verset and his family, kin to Her Gracious Majesty, could engender great trouble.

After the Gurly defeat at Erseway, where the Northerners had been forced to accept orders from the South, a strange and charismatic man had come forth whom the Gurlys believed to be a holy Man of Power. He descended from the Yakin Mountains, which were largely unknown territory to the nearby lowlanders. Into an ever-growing company of followers, this outland priest was able to draw commoners, clan lords, and court members alike to give ear to—and soon to enforce—his preaching.

The kidnapped king had been replaced by another child: Arvor of Clan Merven. Though now full-grown and a leader able to subdue overseas raiders, Arvor was obviously still under the orders of Yorath of Merven and appeared likely to always be so. However, the young king made the new-come religious leader welcome at court, and he himself appeared at all public services ordered by Chosen Forfind.

Thus affairs stood until the Tenth Day of Non in the year of Gorgast Six when our world began to be wrung, then wrung again as a goodwife twists new-laundered cloth in order to speed its drying. That afternoon, we sat midway between the cavernous fireplace with its still-glowing coals and a window unshuttered to freshen the room with spring breeze-breath now and again. We were working together on a new embroidery conceit that demanded great concentration.

Though deeply united, we each had individual talents. Bina's particular skill lay in working with herbal lore, and her knowledge surpassed many of greater age than hers. I liked nothing more than to ride in a stirring hunt with a fine mount beneath me, a sharp-nosed hound beside me, and a fine weapon to hand. Cilla could gaze intently at a weaving, such as the backing for embroidered tapestry and, simply by concentrating, produce markings for needlework of the most fascinating designs.

We now labored to fashion one of Cilla's creations. The cloth was tautly stretched on a frame, and a cushion spiked with threaded needles stood ready for our selection.

"This design," Bina commented as she searched for a needle with the proper-colored wool, "is quite different from any you have created before, Cilla." She did not at once thrust her needle into the cloth, but studied that small portion she had already worked, a wrinkle deepening between her eyes.

"Is this truly Raft's Tower as Father described it? It has certain features that I find"—with her left forefinger, Bina traced an unfilled guideline— "somehow disturbing."

Beside her, I poised my own needle but did not take another stitch. I, too, was studying the portion nearest my seat on the opposite side of the frame.

"Hmm—exactly what do we see?" I asked, using the point of her needle to trace a fraction of a curve.

Cilla had turned her head as if to examine the coals in the fireplace. "I dreamed," she answered after a short pause, "and the pattern I saw within the dream did not fade with waking. I felt—compelled, as if I must form it here and now."

Bina attempted to touch our minds but found the connection closed to her. She stared at her sister, as did I, tapping the edge of the frame.

"Have you shown this to anyone else?"

Cilla most often sketched a pattern to see it plainly before she readied the cloth and frame; then she would submit the motif for Mother's final approval.

"You feel it, too, Sister?" Cilla answered slowly. She turned her head again to look at the tracings.

The cluster of lights directly above us seemed to dim a little. Bina thrust her needle into the cloth and then placed fingertips on the small section I had earlier filled. She did not summon union, but our minds were now open as we faced each other across the frame. Cilla pushed away from the work.

"What—what is it?" she asked shakily as one who lifts a garden-pool stone and discovers something repugnant beneath.

I rose. *"I would say"*—my thought sped—*"that something is present here that we are unwise to meddle with further. The closer we look, the more clear that becomes."*

"*A manifestation of Power? That is Mother's concern!*" declared Bina.

"*No!*" Two of us linked to deny her statement.

"*Or*"—Cilla modified that denial—"*perhaps, but not yet.*"

She leaned forward to pull her needle from its thread, and we did likewise, returning our tools to the pillow. Taking care not to touch the pattern, we moved to loose the cloth from the frame; and, as the square came free, Cilla bundled it together. In the same moment, the chamber door opened suddenly.

The only one of the household empowered to enter any chamber without a knock, Mother entered, and we curtseyed as she faced us. She had taken only two steps into the room when she halted abruptly, head lifted and nostrils expanded, as if she caught a scent that was at once alien and threatening.

We knew that her Talent greatly overshadowed ours, and to see her respond thus made us uneasy. Her eyes narrowed as she came purposefully forward, and I was quick to push the frame out of her way. The closer our parent approached, the deeper grew the crease between her brows.

Mother pointed to the bundle Cilla had dropped. As she moved her long beringed fingers, the bundle lifted weightlessly, then wriggled and unfolded itself. We could clearly see the curious design as it remained aloft. Our mother studied the crumpled surface for a moment and turned her attention to us, though chiefly to Cilla.

"This pattern is one of yours, rash girl?"

Cilla faced her squarely, head high. "I dreamed it, nor would it go from my mind when I awoke."

Our sorceress mother's hand shot forward and closed on the designer's shoulder. "You—dabble—in—fearsome—things!" She shook Cilla to emphasize each word, then paused.

"I know that now." Our sister's voice was close to a whimper. We moved to flank her protectively, but Mother had already loosed her grip.

"You must repudiate it, Cilla, for, in a manner, you have tried to give a shadow birth."

The trailing cloth still floated. Our sister stepped forward, lips working; then she spat a droplet of moisture that landed on one of the tufts already set in brilliant wool. We followed Cilla's example in making the formal denial of ill-work.

"*Go hence,*" we declared in unison, "*our hands will not give you substance. In the name of the Great One, we dismiss you!*"

"Shall we send it to the fire?" Cilla asked after we had spat and spoken.

Our mother once more considered the crumpled square. "What was your intention?" she asked slowly, as though she had been knotting several thoughts together. "What would you have done with it when it was finished and you had brought what it might carry to full life?"

"I intended it as a hanging for the Gathering Hall."

"So." Our mother nodded. "Did that thought also accompany your dream?"

Cilla was silent for a long moment, during which we shared her sudden astonishment. "No! Yes, I believe so."

Mother clapped her hands sharply. The cloth drew itself once more into a bundle, the disturbing guidelines now hidden, then fell to the flagstones just as a scratching sounded at the door.

At that signal, Mother called, "Come, Duty. Here is a problem such as you are best equipped to deal with." Duty thrust her capped head past the corner of the slowly opening door before us. Her spare body, in the mouse gray gown she always favored, was taut as a stem of autumn-killed possweed with the tension she, too, sensed in the room. She glanced at Mother and then to the bundle on the floor.

The wise-wife snapped her fingers as she might at one of our father's sleuthhounds, and the untidy mass of cloth answered like a well-trained dog by rising and following her. Duty turned back to the door as the bundle wafted across the room in her wake and followed into the hall beyond.

"It will trouble us no more," Mother observed. "In such cases, it is best not to rely on fire alone. It would seem, my daughters, that you are still not too old for oversight. But no more about that now; we have other matters to consider."

She drew a small square of paper from the low bodice edging of her gown. "Visitors are arriving—and soon." We were acute enough to read the trouble behind her announcement. "Your father's call for a general truce has at last been answered with favor by the Gurly Lord Starkadder. In three days' time, he and his train will spend two days here, and then we shall depart with him to Losstrait to meet with the other clans and draw up terms."

"And belike stage a horserace or two, also," I commented. "Though to call these Border ponies horses belittles a noble breed."

"See that you keep such remarks and thoughts to yourselves!" Mother snapped. "No matter that you can sit a saddle as well as any man; young females of the noble clans do not make a show of riding—"

"No," interrupted Cilla, "the men would not permit a true contest." She spread her skirts, touched the fingertips of her right hand to her chin, and summoned up a simpering smile.

While clansmen and women were granted equality of rank, the important families within the heritage employed a particular set of manners in public life. What was done in private, we knew, was quite another matter. Highly placed clan ladies dressed with ribbons and lace, and they also fluttered fans and bedizened themselves with simply cut gemstones set in silver and gold from the mountains. Our preferred garb of riding habits with divided skirts met with their disdain as often as their stilted formal manners provided us much silent amusement. Having visited both northern peel castles and the Alsonian court, we opined that a servingmaid to our gracious queen could show more refinement and intelligence than many of the self-important grand dames of Gurlyon.

Mother stilled us with a stare and we, realizing we had gone beyond proper limits, curtseyed again with appropriately sober faces. She did not have to enlarge upon her displeasure, but continued on another subject.

"You," she addressed Cilla directly, "will go to the stillroom and fetch one of the hop-pillows Bina made. You are to use that tussie for your bed until I say otherwise, and I trust it will bring you dreamless sleep. We want no more trouble than we already face." Her wine-dark skirts of stiffened silk rustled softly as she swept out of the door.

"*What did she mean, 'more trouble'?*" Cilla's mental question touched each of us.

"Father may share more news with her than we are told." I answered aloud, and my opinion was echoed by Bina. "Could it be that the Border is ready to rise again?"

Two

Our mother's perfection as a chatelaine was well-known. We often lagged behind her, to be sure; still, she had trained us, even as she had the servingmaids, to do with all our might whatever needed to be done to show courtesy and provide comfort for guests. And so we were occupied for the next two days.

The part of Grosper Castle kept for the housing of visitors had been given a spring turnout several weeks early this year. Linens, smelling of the lavender and dried rose petals that had been placed in their folds, were shaken out and spread on the large, curtained beds. Any spiders surviving the chill of winter were banished, and the floors pathed with thick carpet.

While we were engaged in aiding Loosy, the maid, in her work in the largest state chamber where the Starkadder himself would be lodged, Duty came in, a basket on her arm.

"Underpillows." Duty was never free with what she considered unnecessary speech. She thumped the basket down on a carven chest to make a quick inspection of our bedmaking, including a twitch to the heavily embroidered upper spread; then she was gone.

Bina was nearest the basket. She leaned over to take an audible measure of its contents. "Lavender and hops," she announced. "We wish our chief guest good sleep, it would seem." Then she paused for a second sniff and looked puzzled. "What else?" She held the herb-holder to me as I labored at her elbow.

I performed a more thorough scent testing, then shook my head and passed the woven container along to Cilla for her guess.

But our third sister had none to offer. "Some other fragrance, neatly overlaid by the hops; I cannot put name to it. Loosy"—she summoned the maid, who was plumping pillows near as tall as she—"what say you?"

Loosy held the basket well up against her breast and took several noisy nosefuls. "I cannot tell, my lady, but no harm be in it. These Gurlys will have ridden long to get here, and the mistress may wish them a goodly rest."

A bunch of herbs from the basket, tied with a ribbon, was thus duly applied as Duty had ordered—a process that was repeated in each room we put into order.

We had been given to understand that not only the Starkadder chief himself would be arriving, probably near sundown, but that his second son would also accompany him, plus three of his most important kinsmen, their squires, and a train of armsmen and other retainers. The lodging of troopers would remain the concern of the bailiff, and one late addition had been made: a member of the party who had ridden from the court to join the Starkadders and whom my father had marked as an observer of the king's, not a warrior. He was to be given one of the rooms of state, but as yet we knew neither his name nor his rank.

Most of our tasks were behind us when our father's squire, Rogher of Helmn, arrived ahead of the party, and we were summoned to our mother's solar to hear what news he brought.

Rogher was an earnest young man who ever strove to give the best service he could, so seriously alert that he was ill at ease with any female. We believed that he was in awe of Father, yes, but something of true fear colored his dealings with our mother.

"He who joined us from the court," Rogher began at her nod, "is no man of the king's; Chosen Forfind sent him—"

As the squire hesitated, our mother prodded him. "Our visitor is one of the new priests, then?"

"Just so, my lady."

"None of those religious have ventured southward before. What is he like?"

"He looks to be a sober man of middle years, my lady, and goes clad not unlike the least of court servants. In manner he does not play the courtier, nor does he speak much. He has ever to hand a missal bound with plates of metal and mumbles under his breath now and then as if reading from it. He held services at sunrise and sunset when we lodged at Hamleysted, but unbelievers were not made welcome by him to attend."

"Odd," our mother commented. "If he would gather others to be of his following, should he not be the first to welcome those to his preachings who are as yet unpersuaded by his doctrines?"

"My lady, who can reckon how such a man might think? On our journey here"—the squire's voice dropped—"he took a whip to a farm girl who did not move out of his way quickly enough, shouting that she was fain to bespell, with the evil of her comely person, an innocent man."

"What!" Our mother was on her feet.

Rogher was quick to answer her rising anger, if only to deflect it from himself. "My lord rode at him, jerked the whip from his grasp, and broke it, shouting that no man struck a woman, and ordering him to mind himself and his manners. Then Lord Verset called Alin Longbow to ride beside him as we went on."

At that point Rogher paused, and we sensed hesitation in him, as if he was judging now whether he should voice some further news. Then he added hastily, as if he must speak before someone would deny him:

"My lady, odd doings have begun at the court of which we have heard whispers. Strange changes have come about there and are spreading among the greater clans. Ladies are openly denied the courtesy of their rank; they are set to eat at separate tables and are served the coarsest of food. Some heiresses have been denied their heritages, which are being delivered to men of the clan, and," he swallowed visibly, "the clansmen take any maids who be of lower birth to their beds without denial." His face was flushed, and he did not meet our eyes.

However, Mother's answer was mild. "Our thanks to you, Rogher, for this warning of what might be a source of trouble. Are these new beliefs held by the Starkadder clan?"

"That I cannot tell, my lady. But my lord said to me, quietly and apart, that I must speak of them to you."

It was her turn to nod and dismiss him graciously. Once he had gone she looked to us.

I spoke first. "What could be the root of this?"

"Well may you wonder," our mother returned. "Until we have better understanding, keep to yourselves when the company arrives. Your father has worked a half year to get this truce meeting arranged. Nothing must trouble it, for a conflict now would set fire among the tinder."

Our guesting duties behind us, we hurried to our own tower quarters. There Loosy and Hanna awaited us. Our court dresses were spread on the wide bed for our viewing, and behind a screen an uncovered tub and buckets of steaming water waited. Full honor was evidently to be paid the Starkadder, for the dresses were those we had worn to our own court a year earlier, and the coffer of jewels had been brought out.

Still we felt as if we were to don steel instead of silk and satin, for Rogher's report had given us much to think on. This strange priest, the new mistreatment of women—

"The Gurly females may have opened some portal to bring these changes about," I observed. "Always it has seemed best to them to flatter their men, play fools before them."

"Yes." Bina straightened one lace-trimmed petticoat, as Loosy stood ready to drop another over her head. "But that was love-play, and men and maids both knew it to be such. However, if Rogher has the truth of the matter, things have passed beyond a game. Yes, Hanna"—she interrupted her answer to me to instruct her tiring-maid—"I shall want but the silver neck chain and ear-drops. We will give them satin skirts but not too much otherwise."

The dresses were made alike—all in the first style, but that of a year past, and at our own court. Doubtless already some new fashion had changed what was lately right to what was now dowdy. Though the gowns were cut alike, they differed in color. My full skirts were of a rich maroon, the drop-shouldered bodice edged in a fall of wide lace trimming from the workroom that supplied the queen herself. Bina now stood before a long mirror, turning slowly to make sure her own swell of shot-satin, which changed with her every motion from rose to silver-gray and back again, showed to the best advantange, while Cilla had claimed a gown of bright blue.

At last, Loosy's and Hanna's well-trained hands had coiled and pinned the third cascade of long black hair, fastened the last neck chain, clasped the final bracelet, and set a massive-gemmed ring on one, two, three hands.

Our toilet complete, we made court curtseys to each other and thanked the maids for their assistance.

Hanna left, still laughing at one of Cilla's comments, but Loosy hesitated and at last emboldened herself to speak.

"Lady"—she picked up a fan and offered it to Bina—"what manner of men are these clansmen who come?"

We were all quick to catch an odd note in her voice, but Cilla was first to speak.

"They are Gurlys of a noble clan, Loosy. If they wish, they may frequent the Gurlyon court. Some of their customs may differ from ours, but not greatly. Many of their ilk, though perhaps of lower rank, have visited here over the years. You have seen them. Why think you these may be different?"

Loosy's cheeks flushed, and she looked down at the carpet.

"T'was the peddler, Lady Cilla—the one who was here two months since. He'd been to Snarlyhoe, and he said how the lord there had women whipped through the streets."

"Be sure," I snapped, "that the Lord of Snarlyhoe, no matter who he may be, does not rule here! Loosy, many tales are told from place to place by peddlers. And you are in our private service and so can keep to these quarters in the tower until you are sure there is no trouble to be faced. Now we must go—"

We were descending the curling tower stair when I paused for a moment. *"What indeed is wrong in Gurlyon?"* I demanded.

"Loosy's report must be told to Mother," Bina returned. *"The Gurlys are overfond of powerful ale, and wine will also be brought out at the feast. No servingmaids should be present, I think."*

We nodded as one at that. It was customary that the ladies of the house withdraw at the end of a feast, leaving men to their professed pleasure of tippling. Our father was an abstemious man, and so was the majority of our household. However, the far-riding, hard-living Gurlys were different.

As we reached the foot of the staircase, we heard a roll of drum, a blast of trumpet. Our visitors had been sighted from the watchtower. Raising our skirts two-handed, we hastened.

We were breathing faster as we passed swiftly through the great gate into the foreyard to take our proper places behind Mother. Our household made a fine array, the men all in their green livery-coats and the maids wearing vests with the Scorpy arms catching the sun's rays in gold-touched broidery.

The company that entered was a large one and plainly set to make a show of its own. At the fore a mount pranced, clearly no northern bred pony but a powerful black warhorse to match the cream of our father's stable. The man who besat it with easy grace was steel-bonneted as might be any Border Reiver. A socket on his helm sprouted aloft the two eagle feathers denoting a clan chieftain.

Beneath that helm showed the strong, browned countenance of a man well acquainted with wind and sun. His beard, which cloaked half his face, was not the neatly trimmed and chin-pointed one our father wore, but a wild gray bush, streaked with white. His buff coat was caped before and behind with steel, bearing at heart level the crooked device of a striking red adder in faded shades of yellow. Boots climbed to cover his legs near to his knees where butter-bright yellow breeches showed. He reined in his mount even as my father approached to join him, striding through the opened ranks of our household. Serving as his squire, Starkadder's second son followed him, swinging down to catch the chieftain's reins as he left the saddle.

My father advanced, made his bow to Mother, and introduced our principal guest. We all curtseyed as one. However, Starkadder's greeting for my mother held very little grace; he even plainly stared at her for a moment before returning a shallow bow of his own.

"Rogher had the right of it!" I mind-sent. "This one is not used to niceties."

But if Starkadder did not seem ready to follow social rules, his squire-son was even worse lessoned. The youth's clothing and armor echoed in richness that of his sire, but he was eyeing the three of us as if we were mares at the horse market.

Doubtless by the standard of the clans he was a handsome man. Tall, broad of shoulder, with red hair—and very red it was—falling from under his bonnet to touch those shoulders. He had even, well-cut features, though his skin was not tanned enough to hide his freckles. One of the mounts might have blown bran into his face.

We took time to study him, being careful not to meet him eye to eye, and our universal—albeit unspoken—decision was that we did not care for what we saw. However, our first view of the chieftain's second son was interrupted as another man rode to the fore of the waiting clansmen. His mount was one of the ponies, a tough and sturdy beast, ungroomed and mud splattered, with neck bent by far too short a rein.

Here was no steel bonnet but a hood, pushed back so that we saw the features of its owner plainly. His skin carried none of the browning the others bore; it showed, rather, the sickly grayish hue of a prisoner long pent in a lightless dungeon. And just as no hair showed under the edge of the head-covering, so was the face bare of beard.

His nose was like a sharp-edged knife bridging between dark eyes set overly close together. His mouth he held tight-lipped above a pointed chin. Altogether, it was not a face to awaken trust in another at first glimpse, nor, perhaps, even at tenth viewing.

Starkadder gave a small shrug as the fellow crowded up and glanced at my father. We sensed, and exchanged the thought, that in some way the clan chief was waiting for the Lord Warden of the South to make the first move.

The pause that followed was evidently disapproved of by the ascetic scarecrow, for he pulled his bowstring mouth even more taut, if such a gesture were possible. Then the Gurly chieftain spoke directly to our father.

"His Majesty craves your grace, Lord Verset, for this follower of Chosen Forfind. His name is Udo Chosen."

My father, in no way seeming to note such an unusual introduction, looked to the stranger.

"As one come guesting, you are welcome." But he did not expand that grudging greeting to include any introduction of our mother or us.

"Be all here unbelievers?" demanded Udo Chosen.

My father touched the wide brim of his hat, but for only a brief instant, making his recognition tremble on the thinnest border of courtesy—a response far from his usual treatment of any honest man.

"Under this roof," he returned curtly, "we are followers of the Established Church of which Her Majesty is the Reverend Head."

The thin grayish face seemed to swell, portending a forthcoming roar. However, the Starkadder now took a hand, or rather a foot, in the matter as, with a stride, he stepped between the seemingly wit-scrambled Chosen and our father.

"Clan greetings, Lord Verset, and also a salutation of goodwill from His Majesty." Starkadder tapped the hilt of his sword, and we saw it was tightly bound round with the gold, blue, and green plaid ribbons of a declared truce.

Our mother came down the last step into the courtyard. Once more she curtseyed. Father extended his arm a little, and she curtseyed again and laid her fingers on his wrist.

"May this house shelter you well, my lord. Let us show you to the chambers prepared for you and your kinsmen."

Thus, the proper ritual being reestablished, she and our father led the Gurlys within. Privately, we three remained astounded at the lack of manners shown by this Udo Chosen, who was said to be a representative of the king.

His horse now being taken in charge by a guard, Lord Starkadder and his son followed our parents. Several others of those dressed like noblemen moved forward as though to come next, but the priest slid from his pony and cut in ahead of them. Nor, to our surprise, did they deny him, though anger was plain to see on a number of faces.

As he clumped by us, he halted and stared, his face drawn up in a scowl. Clasping the metal-bound book Rogher had spoken of tightly to his breast with his left hand, he extended the right, folded into a fist, save the first and second fingers. Then he pointed directly at us.

"Take shame how you show your bodies to tempt the believers. Whores you are, for all your draggle of silks!" Having hurled that verbal gauntlet at our feet, the Chosen was quick to make up the gap that had opened between him and the Starkadder before him.

"*No!*" Cilla's thought was quick. "*We must make nothing of this. The creature is truly mad!*" Agreeing with her assessment, we schooled our faces so that any watching beyond earshot might think he had delivered a compliment.

Though we all desired some instruction from our mother as to how to handle such outright insult, that we could not get, for she, having done hostess duty, was now chambered with our father for a private talk of their own. We knew that it would be foolish to invite more trouble with any of the Gurly party. Yet we would have done well to remember the old adage that a serpent has more than one dose of vicious poison. Only too soon came the summons to the feast.

We had reached the second course of the banquet before the adder struck. A forest of candles and lamps gave us good sight of all persons present in the large chamber. Our full state use of plate made a treasure display on the table in honor of the guests. After the fashion of our own country, those of noble blood sat at midboard, the company descending in rank at either side of them. We also followed court custom in that we were seated woman and man, woman and man.

At the far side of our assembly, a table had been hastily prepared for one diner alone, and the disruptive stranger had been seated there. One of the household squires was busy gathering plate and food from the floor, Udo Chosen having swept all away as he had seated himself, declaiming loudly that the richness of both was an insult, for a believer ate not from silver, nor took more than hard bread and broth.

Our parents evidently meant to take the course of refusing to answer any of his slurs, allowing the serving lads to bring him what he wanted. But we knew that this shameful conduct must be angering both Father and Mother. We shared scathing thoughts, even though we kept a smile on our collective face and pretended not to hear.

Our escorts in the seating arrangement were the younger Starkadder and two kinsmen near his age. They did not appear to wish to carry on any conversation, even though we attempted to find a subject to interest them. Moreover, their table manners were so boorish as to set Bina mentally repeating excerpts from Duty's instructions when we were still in guide-reins, until we had to stifle our laughter. She had just finished repeating the suggestion that one should use the napkins provided instead of wiping fingers on the tablecloth when far more coarse behavior turned our amused communication into quite another mood and message.

The Starkadder heir leaned a little closer to me, by chance assigned as his partner.

"Your lord knows well how to bedeck his hall with fair flowers, sweetling. Give a kiss to my glass, now." He held out his goblet.

"You are ready to be welcoming, are you not?" he continued wheedlingly, leering at my low-cut bodice. "Such a toothsome bedwarmer! Yes, indeed, your lord knows how to make a guest truly at home."

He got no further with his insults. I rose, pushing back my chair to face him more directly. Sudden silence fell along the feast table, except for the sound of two more chairs in motion. All three of us were standing now.

The Starkadder scion stared, a flush rising beneath his veil of freckles.

I still fronted the Gurly, but I turned my head first toward our father and then in the direction of our mother, bowing it a fraction as I made my explanations to each. "Since this one, welcomed in friendship, gives great insult to your daughter, Lord Verset—Lady Altha—I must ask permission to withdraw. I am no lightskirt, such as I have just been named, but a Scorpy by blood and birth, and it is not meet that I draw steel in this place to bring blood in exchange."

My hand had gone to my breast while I spoke. Now I drew into plain sight the scissor-knife that a gentlewoman always wore.

The chief's son was already on his feet, breathing rapidly, plainly angered to the edge of control. His hands were curled into fists as if he readied himself to aim a blow.

"I do not call you beast," I continued in the same calm voice, "for most beasts act cleanly among the females of their kind; in field or fold none talk of 'bedwarmers.' But I advise you to watch that tongue of yours, Northling. It is a weapon that may turn on you in the end."

Now I pushed past my chair and started toward the door, Bina and Cilla following. Thus the three of us left the feast in silence; and in us such a white fury was fired that we had to summon our combined strength to contain our wrath.

Three

S et faced, our hands curled into fists, we ascended the curved tower
stair. Grosper seemed deserted; we met no one until the door of our
chamber closed behind us. Loosy and Hanna, beholding our unexpected
return by the light of the two lamps that had been left burning, scrambled
from their truckle beds to curtsey in open surprise.

I waved them back to their comfort, and we went to our three stools beneath the window which, when unshuttered during daylight hours, looked
out upon our world.

"We have done exactly what our mother warned against." Bina smoothed
the fine silk across her knees. "We have, perhaps, put an end to all our father
is seeking to do."

Each was occupied with her own thoughts for a time. By the custom of
our own land, a challenge should have been given the Gurly lout; and it was
but paradoxical comfort that that had not been done.

"*I do not think*"—Cilla mind-spoke—"*that our mother herself would
have sat silent to such insult. For a Gurly to speak so freely—!*"

"Remember," Bina spoke aloud as if to give her words double import,
"what Rogher reported of the teachings of the new religion, and also the
actions of that so-called emissary of King Arvor. It might be that these
Starkadders and he who travels with them are deliberately seeking to
make trouble."

"If so," I said ruefully, "they have succeeded, and it is the three of us who have provided them with cause and means."

We offered no denial to that. Anger still warmed us, but it had cooled enough that we now also felt the prick of guilt. Too well we knew that no apology could cover this incident, the Gurlys being ever quick to take offense for far less than had just occurred.

Our door opened to reveal Duty. Our erstwhile nurse advanced only a little way into the room and regarded us with the shut face that could still bring us to order.

"Well, a pretty tangle we have before us now," she observed.

I made answer. "And you will say it is of our doing!"

"Put no words into my mouth, my lady Tamara."

We stared at each other for a long moment; then Duty continued. "Your lady mother—perhaps my lord also—will have words for you. If you are wise, you will do some careful thinking before they come. The feast is near over—as it would be after the offense given by that sty-minded clansman and your offense taken. You all are to remain here and await the coming of my lady."

Await her we did, speaking no more for other ears to hear. Loosy and Hanna, on their beds at the far side of the room behind a tapestry-covered screen, made no sound.

"Think of this," I mind-spoke. *"Perhaps what has happened was a planned ploy. King Arvor has but little power—the noble clans keep him on a tight rein. It could be that he is about to use this Chosen Forfind and what he teaches, to stir up his own form of trouble. He might wish to kindle anger between Starkadder and our father, and this Udo could have been especially selected for his nasty tongue and sent with our Gurly guests for that purpose."*

"Yes!" Bina nodded at her own impatient thought. *"Someone does seem to have a need to make trouble between Starkadder and the High Warden of Alsonia."*

Once set into words, the possibility seemed very clear to us. Cilla added a thought which at first appeared far from our musings over court intrigue until we realized that her suggestion gave a deeper and more sinister turn to the case.

"My dream—" she said aloud, very softly.

Yes—that dream which had led her to design a pattern we now knew to have been of the Dark.

"Yet King Arvor is not known to meddle with Inner Matters." Bina said slowly. "If his court holds one with Talent, it has never been reported."

Suddenly we heard a sound at the door that meant someone outside was turning a key. The scrape of it startled us to our feet. Were we being locked in?

However, the key was being used for unlocking (had Duty's visit, was our joint thought, been made to assure that we would be present?), and a moment later our mother swept in bearing her guise of great lady, seldom used when we were alone. Upon occasion she could summon such an aura of power as daunted most persons involved in her dealings.

We curtseyed as she came into the full light of the lamps and seated herself in the chair Cilla had hurriedly placed to face us. We did not dare to re-seat ourselves until she pointed with her closed fan to the chest by the bed. There we settled, one squeezed against the other, like three errant children awaiting a knuckle-rapping for shared mischief.

"You know what you have done," she began. "Your father's plans are now in such a snarl-up as he may not be able to untangle. These Gurlys are hot-heads, either by temperament or choice, to further matters of intrigue. So far, at least, Starkadder has not summoned his men and ridden forth, vow-ing dire retribution for insult, but who can say what will chance in the next days—even hours?"

It was Bina, usually the most prudent of us, who replied: "My lady Mother, would you have a Scorpy so insolently bespoken and make no proper answer?"

Surprisingly, Mother shook her head. "Yes, that brutish boy should take the first blame. I must be honest with you: he is fit meat for steel. And"—she paused—"our blood never takes kindly to insolence."

"Was he"—I leaned forward a little to center our mother's attention—"perhaps ordered to do what he did?"

To our amazement, we were favored with a slight smile. "You show well your training, Tamara. Am I right in believing that you also, Drucilla, Sabina, share this astute guess?"

We nodded, daring to feel slight relief. Surely we had been summoned for punishment, as we had gone directly against her orders. However, the tone in which she addressed her last question was the one she had always used at lesson time when she was pleased with how well a particular subject of instruction had been absorbed. But before she spoke again, our father was with us. Once more we rose to pay him full honor.

He bowed slightly in return and pulled up another chair to join our mother. Perhaps he had been appointed to be our judge in this matter.

"Tamara," our mother ordered, "give us again this suspicion you hold."

I repeated my words as Father listened.

"So," he commented when I had finished, "you have concerned yourselves with peering behind outward action to find causes. Indeed, it well becomes Scorpy minds to interest themselves with strange ways that may lead into the Dark."

"First," he held up his right hand, turning the fingers under and using only the thumb to keep record, "Lord Starkadder remains under this roof. Two or three of his major kin have argued with him, and he told them to ride out if they wished, but he was not calling for his mount."

"Second"—forefinger arose beside thumb—"that graceless son of his sought out the king's man, Udo, but the Chosen did not appear to welcome him with either trumpet or drum. It was also plain that Starkadder himself did not find his whelp's action acceptable. One of his lesser retainers was sent with an order which, like a hound's leash, brought the cub back to his sire fast enough."

"Third"—Father's middle finger added to the tally—"such musing as you have just voiced, my daughters, is given greater strength by what I have heard during the past months of my striving to arrange a Border court. Rumors are flying, some of them outside belief, but others easily latched to the actions here."

"Fourth," and his ring finger straightened, "Starkadder has continued to agree to the court. I voiced a way to save face—I suggested that his son had perhaps been overcome by our potent Southern wines and forgot where he was, and the chief accepted that calmly. Never believe, daughters, that these clan leaders are slow-wits. Their underlings and close kin may sometimes be judged so, but one such as Starkadder, who has led the largest clan in Gurlyon for near thirty years, is as wily and shrewd as our Chancellor Yan of Kork. I therefore gravely doubt that this play was of his planning; it was too crude and ill-timed. No, I believe he was left ignorant of it by some courtier, or"—Father paused for a moment, enabling us all to fill the gap with the name of another type of hanger-on with equal reasons for starting an intrigue—"someone who did not understand how clever his country-man really is."

"It is true," he continued, after a pause, "that King Arvor wishes his throne free of any Merven standing behind it to whisper orders. He had a taste of war when he defeated the Harsorean Fleet two years gone, and he then showed himself capable of the strategy a true leader needs. His victory was followed by the prompt arrival of the Chosen from out of the mountains. I think the timing not lacking in significance."

As Father raised his little finger, then lowered his whole hand, his Scorpy signet caught the lamplight with a fiery blaze of red-gold.

"I do not," he said in a quiet voice that sounded even more dangerous than his earlier tone, "like this hint of greater powers somehow controlling us and belaboring men and women for so-called 'sins.' However, it is said that the king has welcomed this Voice from the mountains, and perhaps he has. If that is so, I foresee war—such conflict as could blast this poor country out of existence. Few of the Gurlys have visited Alsonia—they can only guess at what strength we can summon. That fiasco in the Year of Nar, wherein our army remained here at the Border without invading, might well induce the gullible to believe we cannot summon the wherewithal to defend the South from invasion. The men of the Border on both sides are used to raiding. To force blackrent, by which a landowner must pay two taxes—one rightfully to the Crown and the other, outright theft, to a neighbor stronger than himself—is common practice. The Northerners look South and lick their lips at the feast of our riches. At present, they are unable to raise a force great enough to invade—the memory of Erseway remains too fresh to permit this. But should the king pledge all his own army to such an attempt—" Father pursed his lips.

"War?" asked our mother.

"Who can guess? However, now we know that they would involve us, the House of Scorpio, in their intrigues. Perhaps they even hope to besmirch our name before the queen. Her Majesty is known to loathe war, though she does not hamper plans for the assembling of defense.

"Of this much I am sure: you must *not* allow personal concerns to override the order I now give. You will not accompany us to the Truce—in fact, it will be suggested that this is a punishment given you—" He paused and favored us with a warm smile; thus he had ever been able to charm us out of the sullens. "A punishment given you," he repeated, "for your improper forwardness of bearing. I trust you each to don the face of maids who have been well chastised when you appear in public."

Then he was wholly serious, and again he held each of us in turn, eye to eye, for the space of a breath or two. "Be also aware that you may still be marked as proper prey to incite your family—even Her Majesty, with whom we share a bloodline—into some wrong move. From now on, you must be very careful of speech, thinking twice, even thrice, before you speak anything of moment. I would, if I could, leave Tweder with you, but I must show my Captain of the Guard with me at the Truce. Your mother will also accompany me, for our appearance should be as always. Do not at any time ride out—you cannot do so safely without more guards than I dare leave at Grosper. Lock your chamber at night, and see that your bosom knives and snaplocks, as well, are ever with you."

He stood up, his hand raised in salute, as if we were men of a squadron he commanded, and—better still—considered crucial to his strategy. We echoed the gesture, warmed by the knowledge that he thought us worthy to be taken so far into his confidence.

So it was that we did not appear in the lower halls of Grosper again while the clansmen were guests. Instead, we were supplied certain books and papers. Those we studied diligently, realizing that, by means of their information, we were being made privy to the tangle of men and motives that required all our father's efforts to bring peace to this ever-troubled, blood-soaked Border country.

I drew from between two thin wooden protectors a map, linen-backed and badly worn by time and usage, to spread it out on the bed, and lay, propped on elbows, my nose nearly touching the faded paper as I studied it.

"The Yakins," I read. "Look you here—"

Look they did, laying aside their own materials of study. The surface of the map I was examining was so rubbed and dulled that we could scarcely determine anything but age damage.

I sat up, freeing my left hand to tap with a fingernail at three spots set close together.

"What do you see?" I demanded.

Both answered, "Nothing."

"But that is what matters—there *are* no markings! Look here—and here—and here—" My fingertip moved swiftly to other areas.

Oh, certain features were present, right enough, some indicating trails, one a warn tower. But the area I had first indicated, save for a stain and slight crease or two, held naught but emptiness.

Bina sat farther back on the bed, no longer peering at the map. "Wool from the highland pastures is prized—was not a cloak of it sent to the queen as a New Year gift, a season agone? Goodly trade comes in from that territory. But mere pastureland would not be marked on a ranger's map such as this—"

I glanced from her to Cilla. As if in response to some silent order, she once more bent over the map. It was her turn to point and call out what she saw scribed thereon.

"Here be the hunting land which is the king's own. Then here is a holding marked 'Langrun,' and here one 'Slagenforth.' But see—the Cursed Land lies beyond—the Lair of Baltiwaight!"

"Many tales of evil are told of that place," supplied Bina. "No proof of their truth was ever offered, at least not since the time of the Loathy King—he who became the Demon of Gurlyon's past. He reigned five hundred years ago and, even though his sins may have mountained in the telling, it is known that he ruled long and wickedly. It could well be true that the country folk nurse a dislike for a strip of country darkened by such history."

"In the Yakins, this Chosen Forfind lived a hermit," I added.

They were immediately at the map again, pulling it a little away from me to examine it the better. However, at that moment a trumpet call sounded. We slid from the bed and crowded to the window to peer below, in time to see the combined parties of the clan chief and the High Lord Warden ride out together. We had said farewell to our parents earlier, and the fact that we did not appear in public to wish them safe travel would surely prove we were in disgrace.

I hammered my right fist against the windowsill. Bina and Cilla shared my anger, needing no words. It was a feeling that arose not from disappointment or humiliation but from the constraint that would now lie upon us for future wariness of action.

Now that the visitors had gone, though, we were free of our section of Grosper. Our study materials, the books and papers, were again properly housed in the library, and for a time the subject of the Cursed Lands was half forgot.

However, the perusal of ancient records was not all that busied us. Each morning we went to the exercise hall, which had been set aside for us by our father when he had first accepted the keys of Grosper. There we worked at the ritual of swordplay he had taught us, used snaplocks to chip stone from the circled target painted on the wall, and honed our skills with the common spears of the North. We might not ride out for the present, but we could maintain our training in the meanwhile.

From the wielding of steel, we turned to another art of defense. This was the warfare against bodily ills which was our mother's Gift, the distilling and mixing of various herbal potions against fever, sepsis, and all wounds and sicknesses that might afflict the people of a land on the brink of war.

On the seventh day after the party for the Truce Meeting had ridden forth, Loosy came to us.

" 'Tis a peddler from the North, my ladies," she announced.

I placed my sword in the rack. I had been fencing with Cilla, trying to break through her long-perfected guard. Bina laid aside the snaplock she had been loading.

"Do we, or do we not?" I asked.

Peddlers had many uses beside the mere transport and supply of unusual and needful wares. They were also, by tradition, accepted as the purveyors of news. Sometimes they bore specific messages and warnings.

Both Bina and Cilla shook their heads. At that dissent, I turned to Loosy.

"Listen well." I deliberately drew myself up to my full Scorpy height to look down at the maid, a posture I believed would give my words additional force. "We will not see this peddler. However, get you Hanna, and bring her here quickly."

Hanna must have been waiting just without the door, for Loosy had only to go to the portal to return with her.

"Now, then." Bina took the lead. "You will say that we are keeping to the tower as our father ordered—you may, indeed, let it be known that we rest under his deep displeasure. Do you know what this wanderer offers for sale?"

"Yes," the maid was quick to answer, "he has pomanders and ribbons, sleeve- and bodice-knives, combs for the hair, some laces, and the like."

"Trifles," Cilla commented, "but such as are well chosen to catch a lady's eye."

In the exercise gallery, we wore breeches and shirts for freedom of movement. I now picked up the cloak I had brought to cover this mannish garb, for we all paid tribute to Dame Modesty on our journeys through the halls. From the inner pocket, I brought out a purse.

None of us had been moved as yet to spend any of the pin-money granted us upon our latest birthing date, which had fallen some weeks before. I shook a few coins from the bag into my cupped hand.

"Take these, and select what pleasures you desire. For us, procure the answers to some questions. Why does this peddler bring his business to Grosper when he would surely find better custom at the Truce grounds? Where does he come from? Does he sell for himself, or is he one of those trusted ones who serve a greater merchant and goes about on his master's purpose?"

"Also," Bina added, "mark well any question he asks *you*. If he wants guesting rights for the night, send him to—Heddrick." She paused as she swiftly mind-touched each of us. Wordlessly we agreed.

When Cilla offered a last suggestion, she startled the serving-girls but not their ladies. "'Twould be best were you to put on some of Appy's ways."

Loosy grinned, and Hanna's look of surprise changed even more noticeably. Rolling her eyes, the maid pressed her plump hands together and exclaimed, in the broad speech of the country folk, "Lawks, m' lady, I ne'er did see sich pretties afore!" Then she turned in a slow circle, mouth agape, as she expressed the amazement of a beggar newly introduced to the contents of a safe room.

We laughed at the contrast between the normally quiet Hanna we knew and this one suddenly stirred to such volubility. Loosy now also showed the wide-eyed stare of a simple backcountry maid bedazzled by hitherto unknown delights.

"You do properly," I noted. "Hunt well, sleuthhounds."

We separated as we went into the hall. Loosy and Hanna, at a pace near running, scurried to find the peddler, and we went our way to our mother's solar.

"Heddrick?" Bina made a question of the name.

At our nods, she stepped to the wall and, catching the wide, embroidered ribbon bell pull, gave it a sturdy yank. Her tug was answered by a clangor far louder than our mother had ever wakened. We had a very short wait before a scratching sounded at the door.

The man who answered our summons was tall and spare, and even under this roof he wore a helm and jack-coat, laced ready to ride out. Heddrick had been our father's man before our birth, and he would continue to serve Desmond Scorpy as long as his lungs drew breath. The order that bade him remain at Grosper had come as a bitter blow, for he had no desire to shuffle about its halls and chambers when our father rode out these days. Yet below his right knee the old campaigner no longer bore flesh and bone, but wore a wooden leg strapped on, and that maiming sealed him just as surely as Father's command to this exile from the life that had been so long his meed. However, his new post was not without its own power, for no bailiff in our father's absence ruled here without Heddrick's assent, nor ever would, not while Desmond Scorpy was in command.

Like Duty, the crippled soldier was a man of few words. Now he simply stood, asking nothing, awaiting our orders in place of his lord's. I spoke first, as was customary.

"A peddler has come," I began. Heddrick gave a slight nod.

"We wish to know more concerning him. Loosy and Hanna have started the game, but it needs further players. Nothing is of greater worth than the truth." I was quoting now, repeating words we had heard the present Lord Verset speak from time to time.

Heddrick returned at once. "M'ladies, the gallows-clapper will be ever under my eye. Should he be kicked out the gate now?"

"Not yet," I cautioned. "Peddlers learn things—they bring and they take. Might one bring solid substance and take smoke?"

"If that be the way of it, yea." The salute offered us was not quite that which he would give our father, yet it meant firm agreement.

We did not reach for any chore to occupy us as we waited. For the first time we were launching ourselves into such matters as had always been our elders' concern. I think we were all breathing a little faster but we did not mind-touch.

Bina startled us by a sudden recitation of places: "Murderers' Rock, Hell Cauldron, Killdeer Edge, Traitor Tod—this is a land of unseemly names. Was no place famed for good deeds, or loved for happy frolics? To hear that sorry list, an outlander might believe that nothing befell in this country save sin or sorrow."

In contrast to Bina's grim mood, Cilla was beating out a rhythm on the arm of her chair with light-tripping fingertips. Her eyes were half-closed as if her memory had withdrawn to another time and place.

I sniffed. "Come away from the dance, dear sister. It will be another year before you tread to that tune again."

Bina nodded. "*Unless—*" What she would say was clearer in her mind than on her lips.

As one, we tensed. Already at our last birthing-day we had been two years past the usual age for betrothal. However, due to the isolation of our life in Grosper we were set apart from the social ways our peers in the South had known since they were hardly more than infants. We were also well aware that Scorpy women were never sought after by many, for it was the custom that the married ones drew their lords into our clan line rather than departed from it.

It was a subject we never dwelt upon, even among ourselves. What comments Bina might have awaited did not come. Then, once more, a scratching at the door came; this time it preceded Loosy and Hanna's arrival. They made profound curtseys as if being presented to a lady of the castle. Cupping Loosy's brown hair was a cap of netting that glittered with her slightest movement. Dangling from each side just above the ear were several cords of differing lengths, each ending in a bead of shining metal, the style a type of headgear altogether unknown to us. Her usual cap hung all but disowned from one hand. Hanna's well-washed (and somewhat work-worn) blue homespun gown had been gaily refurbished at the neck by a wide lace scarf whose ends were tied in front.

Cilla shaded her eyes. "Lawk"—she used her own country voice—"this be a brave sight!"

Loosy giggled and pushed away one of the weighted strings tapping against her cheek, while Hanna smoothed her lace with obvious pride. Bina, however, was frowning.

"These fripperies are not usual wares," was her comment.

Loosy nodded. "I think, m'lady, that he did want you to see these, so you might wish him to show other things he has. He even had one case he did not open, but kept ever close to his hand."

I saw fit to call them to order. "What have you learned? Sit and tell us." I waved them to the footstools that served our chairs, and sit they did.

Four

He names himself Hal Shoan, my ladies," Loosy began the servants' report, "and he boasts that he is his own man and comes from Kingsburke. This be his first trip to the Border—he is testing how trade is hereabouts. All this he told without our asking." Loosy twisted one of her dangling cap strings about her finger.

"Surely he must have heard of the truce gathering, which would be a better place for trade," Bina commented as the maid paused.

"He said, Lady Sabina"—Hanna nervously smoothed the lace across her breast—"as how he did not hear of that till he was well along this way. Now that he knows, he will go there directly. He is very pleasant of speech, m'ladies, and seemed quite downcast when you could not receive him."

"Aye," Loosy nearly interrupted, "he is like no Border man, rough of manner or mien—he is more like one of the servingmen at the queen's own court. He is tall, with a chin-pointy beard such as his lordship wears, and his coat and breeks are well kept, dusty as he's been on the road, but with no patchin' you can see."

The thoughts shared by us three were knitting together rapidly. Every fact the girl added to her account set this Shoan further apart from most peddlers we had known in the past.

"Did he ask questions?" I asked a little sharply.

"No, m'lady. Master Heddrick, he came by and heard him. Said he could eat with those of the guard as stayed here and get him a straw pallet in the gatehouse. Told him to come right along if he wanted his vittles hot. Then he gave us a smile and went."

"But not afore he said something else, m'lady," added Hanna. "Told us to show our ladies what we had bought, he did. He said to say, too, that he took orders for the best as could be got from Kingsburke, and he thought he would be traveling special from there to here from now on."

"Well done," I gave credit where due. "You're the best scouts we could ask for. Get you to the kitchen now and have your Sundown. You can bring ours here later."

After they were gone and the door had shut behind them, our thoughts were open as always when a matter of importance was to be considered.

"From Kingsburke . . ." Bina spoke first.

"He must think us fools!" flared Cilla. "All folk in Kingsburke would know of a Truce Meet, for peace councils are always reported to the king."

"Yes, and no one can cap merchants and peddlers when it comes to news—they have their own ways of learning such things," Bina agreed.

"A peddler who is a little too polished for his calling," I mused. "First comes that Chosen, who is like gravel in a boot, and now a peddler, smooth as a court servant, both from Kingsburke—both from the king? What game is being played now?"

"One that bodes no good for us," Bina declared. "I tell you, sisters, this is like being handed the end of a strand of wool from a ball all knotted together. We shall see what Heddrick has to add. Loosy and Hanna are sharp of wit in homely concerns, but Heddrick is wise in affairs of a much larger world, and he has never accepted matters as they appear on the surface."

The maids brought us our simple meal of cheese and same-day-baked bread with dried cherries added to the dough, a goodly treat Cook Mattie had devised this season.

With the light supper came a bottle of wine and a pitcher of milk. As usual, we drank more of the latter than the former. Loosy reported as she served us that the peddler was in the gatehouse with his wares but that he was to be at dice later with Heddrick and the stable master.

We had exhausted all our guesses concerning what Shoan was or would do. We therefore occupied the hours remaining before bedtime in debating what might happen at the Truce. When Cilla had yawned widely at least twice, we at last took our candles and sought our tower chamber.

"It is so quiet," Cilla near whispered as she looked up at the stair curling into the darkness above. She shielded with extra care the wavering flame of her taper, as though fearful that the surrounding night would reach out and snuff it like a hand. Our sister spoke the truth; we three shared her feeling of having been almost entombed here, alone in a grim casket of stone.

We kept together as we trudged aloft. Night lamps had been lighted and set in wall niches at intervals along the rise of the stair, but somehow those shone dimmer than usual, seeming well-nigh overwhelmed.

When we reached our chamber to find Loosy and Hanna waiting, we closed and locked the door. Cilla, however, remained facing it. Slowly raising her right hand, she traced a symbol with her forefinger; chambers for family use were always warded. These Talent-born barriers against Evil had been firmly established by our uniting as one under our mother's command when we had first taken up residence here—a ceremony that was renewed each Yearsend and a ritual that promised us safety for the forthcoming twelve-month.

"Why do you make the sign of the Fear-Fend?" I asked as Cilla's hand dropped to her side. She had not yet turned from the door.

"I—I do not know," Cilla admitted. "It seemed that I must do so, as if Mother had spoken."

Bina stood by the bed and turned slowly, staring first at our familiar furniture, then to walls whose every stone we had once counted in a childhood game, and finally to the entire known, loved room. I set the bar across the last shuttered window.

Your Majesty, heretofore Tamara has had the telling of this record. But now, taking turns, each of us will report for herself what has been her portion of the tale, for from this point in our adventure we began to play different parts in this drama, with actions dictated by our individual Gifts from the Light. It is I, Sabina Scorpy, daughter to the Earl of Verset, in Your Majesty's service and that of the Lady Sorceress Altha, Countess of Verset, who will now speak, and thus we shall proceed.

Sabina

EACH OF US had retired into her own thoughts—or questions—and we did not seek to share those ideas, as we mainly do when puzzled. That in itself seemed strange. When we were at last settled within the great bed in our usual order, Tam to my right, Cilla to my left, we broke silence only to wish each other a peaceful night under the Watch of the Preserver.

The faintest of lights gleamed beyond the curtained foot of the bed; the night lamp had been newly filled to pass the dark hours. I rubbed a hand across my eyes, which seemed to burn, then closed them—only for a moment, I thought. However, when I reopened them and looked again, the lamplight had sunk far lower.

Our linens, drawn up now to our chins, smelled not only of lavender but also of other herbs that underlay that favorite. I set myself to name those faint scents, but, before I could complete this self-set task, I had fallen asleep once more.

Cilla is our acknowledged dreamer, but this time it was I in the solar, needle in my hand and rolls of colored wool beside me, from which I must choose *the* one proper shade. So heavily did this task weigh upon me that I felt fear like a physical oppression. I struggled to put the needle from me, but my motions were maddeningly slowed, as if I were besotted or—bewitched? Even my mind seemed dulled, but I held to the thought that I must *not* obey this seeming command—must *not*—

Strengthened by a last burst of resolve, I opened my eyes to find myself in our bed. It was utterly dark—no lamp now glowed beyond the bed curtains. And what was far worse, beside me, to the left, was emptiness—no sound of even-drawn breath, no warmth radiating from a body lying close beside mine.

"*Cilla!*" For some reason, I called with mind-touch.

It was as though an unbreakable shield had been slipped between us. Never had this happened before. Terror shot through me with the pain of a pike thrust by a Breaksword raider.

Surely this was a nightmare. I made a great effort to rise, but my body refused to obey; and when I would have called aloud, my tongue would not serve me, either.

Suddenly I heard movement beyond the bed-curtains. Then a coarse voice spoke aloud as if there were no need for quiet:

"Ought we t'take th' sluts now?"

"Nay, leave them!"

"They be tasty bits. One does no' waste sweetmeats—"

"Get about what ye're to do, Blubberguts, an' no more cackle."

I could not turn my head to see as the bed-curtain to my right was jerked open. Though the thick dark remained, no light having been rekindled, I was aware that Tam was being drawn from my side.

"Twa o' 'em. All right and tight," observed Blubberguts.

Once more I struggled with all my might, but again to no purpose. I might have been chain-bound as securely as any gallowsmeat.

Sounds of movement again reached me again. "She's tight, Lug-ears. Call them in for the taking," snapped the second speaker.

More noises, one the creaking of the door. Then someone must have stumbled against the bed, for it shook and I heard a blistering oath.

"These eye-things, they don't work so good namore," complained Lug-ears sullenly.

"Lug-ears?" sneered the second voice. "Lug-*head*, more like! The charm wasn't promised to last forever. Nor will the door hold itself open—Hedge witch combings don't be trusted. You want the Warden riding Hot Tod behind us and lighting balefires to bring in the others? Now *jump to,* I tell you, before they awake. That there guard be Border wise."

Covers were yanked off me. Hands groped, grasping both my bed-gown and my flesh. Helpless in the grip of the—drug? spell?—that had divided and paralyzed us, I was pulled across the bed. Hands were set on my ankles and my shoulders, but my arms were allowed to swing down limply. Then I was drawn altogether free of the bed in the cloaking dark and dropped, to land bruisingly on the floor.

A thick covering fell over me that was not the bedclothes, and rough paws now jerked me upright so that this stuff could be wrapped about me and made very tight, leaving only my head free. I was lifted again and carried out.

The darkness did not hold beyond the door, though my limp helplessness did. I was slung over the shoulder of a great ox of a man with the stench of horse sweat, clothes too long betwixt washings, and strong ale thick about him. I could see only leather and the curve of back armor. The Second Voice, who appeared to be the brain-pan behind this business, remained just that—speech with no visible speaker.

My bearer was strong enough that he seemed to have no difficulty in descending the stairway burdened with my weight. At last we came into the courtyard. I could hear the stamping of horses and, a moment or so later, was flung facedown across the back of a mount and made fast. I saw no more of my partner at pig-a-back.

It was too quiet—in spite of my present posture, which was upside down in mind as well as body, I grew more and more aware of that. The horse onto which I had been bound was moving, and I heard the motion of other animals, but no speech passed among my captors—*our* captors, if my guess was right and I shared this fate with Tam and Cilla.

Kidnapping was not unknown in the border lands. Years agone, it had been a common ploy on both sides, but it had dropped out of general favor as a means of forcing a foe's hand since my father had taken the Wardenship. However, in most of those abductions, the victim had been caught in the open. This venture into the very heart of enemy territory to take us was a brazen maneuver we had never encountered in the reports we had been combing.

Yet it would seem these Breakswords had managed to do as they wished with no difficulty. What had happened to Heddrick and the gate-guard—or to our Wards—that this villainous deed was possible? Once more I strove to mind-touch but met again with that impenetrable wall.

We were descending the slope from Grosper now. The fact that I was tightly rolled in blankets did not keep at bay the sawlike abrasion that began on my skin at the places where my body strained against the ropes lashing me to the horse. I soon passed into a haze of torment, dominated by wrenching cramps in arms and legs and punctuated by a fearful pounding behind my eyes, an anvil rhythm underscored by every thud of the horse's hooves. I would have moaned, but just as thought-send was denied me, so, it appeared, was physical voice.

Time meant nothing. My fog of pain and confusion thickened, so that only a stumble of my mount now and then roused me to full consciousness. Each time I could think, half-mazed though I was, I tried to reach my sisters.

When finally I roused with a clearer mind, it was beginning daylight. The horse had come to a halt. It stood blowing heavily as if it were winded from being used so hardly.

"Get them down, dunderheads—down and in."

Hands loosed my ropes; then, my bundling remaining tight about me, I was swung aloft to be carried on a shoulder once more. My new bearer and I passed from the predawn gray gloom into a roofed space where I again saw torchlight, felt fire-heat. I had not realized how cold I had been until I felt that warmer air.

Down I went, with a speed suggesting that my carrier had simply dropped me. I landed on my back on the floor of what seemed a hut. Though at the time the actions of my captors gave little comfort, this partial release meant that my long-bent body might straighten out, for a blessed time.

Within my limited sight stood a cloaked and hooded man, the collar of his garment pulled up so high about his ears and face that he appeared well-nigh masked. Finding that I could now move my head, I turned it a fraction, carefully, as I did not wish to attract attention. Then I could see not only the cloaked one but another man, tall, and bearing the massive shoulders and heavy head of a bull. This second ruffian was staring at me. Did he see that my eyes were open?

"Th' cub be payin' good money, right enough," observed Bull-head. "Which one is it he wants to tumble?"

High-collar shrugged. "Not our choice. They all look alike, he said, for they were born together like a litter of pups. So we take them all." Suddenly he swung in my direction and dropped to one knee. His gloved hand caught in my hair, and by that painful hold he dragged me up a little and raked me with an appraising gaze. His lips shaped a low whistle.

"So—the Chosen's not as good as he thinks he is. You're awake, slut? Want to see who snapped you out of Grosper like you were a pea in a pod?"

With his other hand, my interrogator pulled the cloak-collar away from his chin so that I might have full sight of his face. It was long and narrow. He wore his beard as did my father, trimmed evenly into a chin point; but this man's hair was fair, not dark, and the firelight glittered on golden hairs here and there.

Lancing across his right eye—or rather the shrunken socket that had once held that orb—and down his cheek was the ridge of a scar. The eye that remained was bright with a near-feverish gleam, and it kept me pinned as firmly as his hand continued to grip my hair. He gave those locks a punishing yank as if he would make sure I was listening.

"Pretty face." He smirked. "Like I had, once, before your hound of a father rent it. Would have had me off to Licking Stone, he would, but Maclan is no rabbit."

Maclan—Licking Stone! Now I knew into whose hands we had fallen; nonetheless, I held my gaze steady. In that moment, for the first time since I had awakened in the tower, my voice returned to me:

"It was a fair fight, and that you cannot deny—"

He gave a last vicious pull and, dropping my head, rose again to his feet. Then his boot flashed out and struck my shoulder to send me rolling, unable to aid myself in any way. I came to a stop only when my body struck against another in the same sort of bundling as mine.

"Cilla? Bina?"

Mind-touch, faint but true! Tam had called. I answered her swiftly and added a warning.

Five

Tamara

I, Tamara, lay in darkness. My body seemed to be swathed immovably in a length of coarse-woven stuff like a clansman's plaidie. A flap of this blanket covered my face, and I was nearly gasping from both its weight and a surrounding reek of horse sweat. This was certainly *not* the familiar, secure tower room in which I had gone to sleep. Confused and frightened, I instinctively mind-called—and was answered.

"Tam—it is Bina. We are tod-taken."

I had to struggle to understand her words, almost as if they were of some foreign language. Tod-taken? From our own bed? Yes, it must have been from there, for I could remember nothing but our settling in for the night and feeling oddly weak and tired as I had stretched out. But how could we have been seized from within Grosper?

Bina's Send sounded silently again, aimed this time at Cilla. However, she received no answer.

But we were not alone. I heard a mighty clearing of throat; then someone spat.

"Leave th' wenches so?"

"They won't be going anywhere. Any sight of that blabbermouth of a Clyde?"

Two voices, neither of which did I recognize. The speech of the second seemed that of one gentle-born, or what might pass for good birth among the Gurlys. These men were indeed clansmen of the North, for they spoke their own rough tongue and not the Border language, which was common to both Gurlyon and Alsonia. We had learned it by our father's will upon our coming to Grosper.

I wished I could move my head and somehow loose the bonds that were holding me. After a few moments of continued effort, though, I did manage to squirm free from a corner of the rough cloth that kept me blind.

"Bina, where are we?" I Sent, hoping that my sister had a better view and had gained therefrom some idea of our location.

"This is a hut," she returned, *"but where we may be, I do not know. As to our captors, I have seen but two of those who hold us, and know neither face."* Swiftly she told me of the manner in which we had been brought out of Grosper. *"How this was done, I cannot guess. It was as if the keep were deserted, save for us and our enemies. What could have happened? Where were the guards—and Heddrick? Why did our Wards fail?"*

I moistened my lips with tongue tip, though I had no intention of speaking aloud. Had the castle indeed been garrisoned only by the dead when we were drawn forth? My mind would not accept such a bloodletting. Had anyone been left to carry the lighted tod of turf tied to a spearhead and ride across country in search of vengeance—and ourselves?

But questions that concerned us three more closely had to be answered even more quickly. Why, for instance, had Bina been left with some ability to understand while Cilla and I lost our senses? Or was Cilla even with us?

I froze. Boots sounded on the floor near my head; then that sight-benighting edge of blanket was jerked fully away. I looked up into a face, and one I had seen before, for it belonged to that sour-sick Chosen who had visited Grosper. But the priest had ridden forth with those bound for the Truce!

He stared down in return. I had never seen eyes that held more menace. Had he been able to funnel his considerable will through them, the glare of those orbs alone would be able to call down a blasting curse on their luckless focus.

"She be Vitan Starkadder's meat, not a novice for your lessoning, Chosen." I could not see that speaker, but his voice was clear enough.

"This—is—vile—trash." The Chosen's teeth ground out each word, and his lips moved as if he wished to spit. "Would you have Starkadder's line destroy itself? Nay, he must be saved from such defilement! All the whores from the South deal with workers of the Dark, summoning demons to their beds if they desire."

"If demons obey such women, Chosen," inquired the wellborn voice in a reasonable tone, "then why were they not defended when we took them? Oh, we had those bags of dust and did spread them as you said, blowing the last of it 'neath their door. The lock opened at that right enough. And Prospar did carry the gore-hand as you ordered. Only 'tis ever better to trust steel, and that was our choice also. These three go to young Starkadder, for we will do as we swore."

During this speech, Udo's glittering eyes had not lifted from me. In one hand he held his board-bound missal. Now he settled that prayer book into a rope belt, then fumbled at a pouch fastened to the same cincture. Stooping a little, he threw out his fisted hand, and from the opened fingers whirled reddish sparks.

That was my last sight of him or our surroundings.

Drucilla

THIS BE DRUCILLA, third daughter of Verset. When I knew my world again, thirst had dried my throat. I had no feeling in my arms or legs, but pain rode my back in waves. At first I felt that I was fast caught in one of those dreams which had been my bane from childhood, when the world I knew had been banished and I journeyed by night where terror crept and danger threatened.

I forced myself now to try to break this dream, and indeed my feeble efforts brought the world about me into sharper focus. Unfortunately, the further I roused, the greater was my pain. I found that I was lying across a horse, for I was conscious of the shift (and smell) of an equine body beneath me. I myself, however, was unable to stir, being bound like any peddler's pack.

"That dead-faced rat ben't the one give us orders. We do as the Red Adder says—we gave word to him, not to any Chosen."

"Two bulls in the same field never brought no luck—and that dung-ball beat it right enough when Maclan stood up to 'im! But why ain't

Starkadder's cub here as he said he would be? Thought as how all this was planned out."

"Ain't nothin' ever certain, Pokeweed. The rat says as how these wenches be demon-dealers, an' Old Beck, she's a wise one, she is. I say we wait until mornin,' an' iffen Red Adder don't show, we Dismals 'em."

The first answer from Pokeweed was a grunt, but a little later he added, "These here ponies ain't goin' to do well if we leave th' sluts on 'em."

"Maybe you have the right o' that. Dump 'em off."

A moment later, dumped I was, and quickly and clumsily, too. However, the indignity and discomfort were greatly lessened by what I had heard—I was now sure that I was *not* alone and that my sisters did indeed share my captivity. I landed on my back, and though I was bundled in blankets, my head was free, and that rapped smartly against rock when I went down. I blinked watering eyes and saw that I had been loosed from a hill pony who was hardly more than a rack of bones covered with ragged, mud-matted hair. Someone caught at the edge of the top blanket about me and dragged me a short distance. This time I was dropped onto an earthen surface that sloped, so that my head and the upper part of my body were raised. From this angle, I could see better the two other bundles of blanket, bound tightly around with rope, that shared my predicament. My sister Tam, and beyond her Bina, showed white faces smudged with dark streaks. Their eyes were closed, and they breathed slowly, yet deeply, so I could see the movement of the coverings on their breasts.

"*Bina! Tam!*" I Sent. But all I met was an emptiness, and that frightened me into silence.

A splotch of sunlight lay across the lower part of the blanket bag which was my prison; dawn, then full day, had come while we had been lost in darkness or evil dreams. A man in the scruffy clothes of a Gurly farmer was leading the horse away. Since his back was to me, I did not see his face, but I could make out a stained and slotted band about his battered bonnet showing the faded colors of some clan: dust-dimmed red, sun-bleached yellow, and an edging, nearly missing from age, of black. Red, yellow, black—Yakin colors! This was of one of the mountain people who were very seldom seen as far south as the Border Land.

"Sir!" The blanket roll next to me produced a voice that was familiar, though at present cracked. The highlander turned to answer. Now I could see a great bush of wiry red beard, so full and coarse that it nearly covered a wide pug nose. Eyebrows as rank of growth as the chin whiskers did not quite cover small eyes of light blue.

He left the pony and came over to us; then he deliberately kicked the prisoner next to me. That done, he did not answer Tam but called out, "Th' wench wants t' talk." He stood, his hands on his hips, waiting.

Another man loomed behind him. This ruffian had a cloak thrown back on his shoulders to show dented steel plate protecting his chest, though he wore no accompanying steel bonnet. I could see his face clearly; it was badly scarred from a past encounter.

He moved in, his eyes sweeping over all three of us. Tam spoke again, more strongly:

"Sir, do you want your take dead? We need water!"

The armored outlaw threw back his head and laughed. "The Chosen, mayhap, has the right of it! I wanted Verset to crawl, and perhaps my wish can be granted—starting, it would seem, with his close blood-kin. Now ask for it rightly—"

"Please grant us water." Of us all, Tam found it most difficult to crave humbly for any favor.

"Now, Verset get—you can do better than that." Plate-back lowered himself to balance on the heels of his boots. The mountaineer who had summoned him stepped back and disappeared from sight for a moment while his leader sat smirking. The Yakin returned with a saddle flask in his hand, swinging it tantalizingly back and forth so that we could hear the gurgle of its contents.

When he received the water bottle, the younger man grinned even more widely, and because of his disfigurement, his mirth formed an expression of malice.

"I am Maclan, though my lord Verset saw fit to make a Breaksword of me. Me, Maclan. . . . Now, ask me as prettily as you would when you were a court wench."

Maclan Merven! Had I not been so swathed with bindings, I would have shivered. That name had been one of ill omen on the Borders these five years and more, ever since there had been a hanging and then a gallows-flit. Dead, they had said Maclan to be when they cut him down; but by some chance, after he had been borne away, he had come to life. It was well known that he had declared a blood feud against my father.

He unscrewed the flask and flicked some drops onto Tam's face.

"If it please you, sir," Tam croaked, "will you grant us water?"

Maclan swung the flask back and forth so low it almost touched her face.

"This has a price, you know. There be little water in this wilderness, and what we have we need keep for ourselves and our horses. Will you pay the price—?"

"No one bargains without a price being stated." Tam's voice was even.

"The price? Well, now." The Breaksword pulled at his well-trimmed beard while juggling the flask with his other hand, so that it slopped water even more—to no purpose except our torment.

"Hmmm . . . I would say a good tumble for you all; yet I am a man of my word. You are to be kept for him who has paid for it. But"—as though struck with a sudden inspiration, Maclan sat back and regarded his scuffed and muddy boots. "These need a brush-up, and other tasks can be found for a wench—or three."

"No!" Bina's voice rang out.

The renegade looked beyond Tam; then he leaned in my direction. "Still high-nosed, then, are you? So be it!"

He pounded the stopper into the flask and stood up.

Tam coughed from her dryness of throat, and I echoed her. Where did courage end and stupidity begin? Perhaps we were soon to discover. Meanwhile, both men moved off to our right, one towing the pony that had been my mount, until they passed out of sight.

"*Did you have a reason for that?*" My indignant Send was aimed at Bina.

"*I did indeed—give this gallowsmeat any chance, no matter how small, and your charity will buy you death!*" her reply came swiftly. "*It was he and the other Breakswords of Lammerside who took Neman's Tower.*"

The thought of that foul massacre silenced even our mind-speech, though I could feel, as did Bina, Tam's surge of rage. She had helped to bring in two wounded children who had not died when the attackers had cut them down.

We were, however, given little time to wonder if our choice had been the wrong one. A shadow was creeping from a rocky crag that overlooked the camp, and we knew it must be not too far from sunset. A few moments after the outlaws had departed, we heard the yowl of a bush-cat. The feline signal was answered, full-throated, from the direction in which Maclan and his henchmen had gone, then followed by a thud of horse hooves and a confusion of raised voices.

"—dogs on the trail—" That phrase could be picked out of the jumble of speech.

So somebody had loosed sleuthhounds! Those animals were rightly famous in the border lands. All the beasts were trained trackers, and every pack also contained dogs that would attack on order.

"I tells you th' right o' it, Maclan." One of the mountain men had swung closer to where we lay, and we could hear his speech clearly. "That up-nosed Red won't be coming. He had a slam-bang fight with the chief before he rode out last night, and his father gave him what for like he were a jus'-breeched young'un. He got such a crack on the jaw that he spit teeth an' his face swelled up till he canna but croak. He ain't a-goin' anywhere for a few days—maybe a week. The chief has got 'im a mighty hard fist."

The group that had raised the cat-cry signal was in sight now. The leader of our captors turned out to be a youngster, hardly more than a boy, who wore Starkadder's badge on his sword-scarf.

"Red?" Maclan asked. "He sent any message?"

"Nay, no message. But you had need to know. Nigh a full troop was ready to ride afore I was outta sight o' the grounds. The tod was up and alight. And I marked Gurlys as was goin' to join the Southin's too—three clan flags did be up."

Maclan had halted. He kicked the ground in frustration, and a puff of dust arose.

"Give you thanks, Jib. So we must needs find our own way out now."

Once more ponies were brought, and we were again strapped in ignominious positions on their backs. Twilight was beginning to fall as we were borne away. I find it hard to remember that night; I did not dream but was simply swallowed up in a dark pocket in which painful aches and a pounding head were my lot to bear.

Sabina

I, SABINA, SUFFERED enough that a croak, which was intended to be a full-throated scream, was forced out of me. My trailing hair, loosed earlier by Maclan, had become caught on bushes and was brutally yanked free by the man leading the pony.

No talk passed among our captors, but they kept steadily to a pace that was faster than we had held earlier. We moved ever upward, and now and then the lash of a cold wind struck. How long we traveled so through the dark, I never knew. With the blanket blindfold once more over my face, I should have had no way of seeing what lay around us, even if we had been moving by torchlight.

I held as long as I could to wilting hope, which had been briefly revived by the report that the Border had been aroused on our behalf. The horses, ridden by my father's escort, were superior to these ponies, and sleuth-hounds seldom lost the trail. But these Breakswords, who owed no allegiance to any clan chief, knew hidden ways to many strongholds; Maclan himself had been able to escape my father's well-trained men and raid during the past few years without even close pursuit. He had become, justly, something of a legend.

Soon the need for water had overpowered thought and sensation alike in my world. Never, through all those years when I had labored to hone my talent to the highest level, had I so battled with my own body, striving to set aside its demands and master such a craving. Thirst was my chief torment, but hunger shortly joined with it till both beasts claimed me as their prey and gnawed at my middle.

I did not try to Send, for I knew that my sisters suffered the same ills. In this hour, to invoke the unity we had shared for so many years would avail us nothing. Each of us alone must hold on to sanity and so to life. However, as I tried to repeat in my aching head one of the cantrips Duty had taught, my resolve faltered. For all my efforts, I could not put word to word, and what aid could an ancient wisewife's saying give us now? So I was swallowed by a dark which was more than just the night.

Then I caught a trickling sound—not for the ears to hear but for the mind. I had closed my eyes, but by some means I could still see. A crack of light opened in the dark about me, and its radiance grew broader and clearer with every thirst-savaged breath I drew until I felt I was lying in a bath of liquid sunlight. Then—oh, what a cruel mirage born of my body's need—the gold about me cooled to silver, and I rested in a stream of gently flowing water! Instinctively, I opened my mouth, and—yes, water, blessed true water, raised itself out of the flood about me, poured across and into my cracked and bleeding lips. I drank and drank.

Drucilla

WATER! TAM LAY beside me; her hands were unbound, and from each finger poured, impossibly but undeniably, a rill of water. I, Drucilla, drank deeply. For some reason, as the dryness vanished, I felt another need, not of my own but of my sister's. By mind-speech, I answered what seemed to be an unvoiced question. Then once more I scooped up and mouthed the living liquid.

Sabina

MY FACE WAS awash—*awash*? How? Whence came this water, that soothed not only the racking pain in my body but was as balm to my soul, as well? *Swallow,* I instructed myself, *then try mind-touch.* But that outflung net caught no sister in its invisible weave. A little alarmed by this silence, for it was difficult for any of us to know who we were without our two counterpart/complements, I found myself shaping the words: *I am Sabina of the Scorpys.*

Tamara

HOW LONG WE traveled on after that strange dream sharing, I cannot tell. However, when it ended, my spirit seemed to withdraw from the body that was called Tamara and rested in a place that sheltered and strengthened like loving arms supporting me.

That refuge was irreparably shattered as my physical self was again dropped to the ground, this time onto a bed of small stones. The shock and pain of the fall pulled me back into my body and the mad, random place that my world had become.

"*Bina? Cilla?*" I Sent.

"*Here,*" each answered in turn.

Then my feet were seized and, by them, I was dragged roughly over the ground. By the daylight that had, impossibly after a night of such strange doings, come again, I saw that Maclan stood above us. He held a knife in one hand, and now he stooped and grabbed up a handful of my hair as if to tear it from my scalp. Instead, he sawed the strand loose, and as he did so, he whistled.

I recognized the air; widely sung, it had not only a taunting tune but vicious words guaranteed to enrage the whole of any Border family.

"Th' Snake, he did take Ninen's Peel;
With it hardly did he deal:
Wives, maids, babes did swallow steel.
Snake? Nay, Dragon from the past—
Of him no man will see the last!"

"Should I not take up the harp as a bard, my lady?" The Breaksword brushed my shorn hair across my face, grooming me as he preened himself. "And wait till you hear the next verse, which I have just composed! We do not hang you, you see—that is not the way of the Maclan. Your father set me in a lick-stone cell, and licking is how I gathered my water, see you—my tongue to cold, bare stone. I do not think you will have even that much where you go now. We deal with you as is custom, you see. They can hunt with hounds—bring their hell-taught magic to search—it will not serve." I was puzzling over his words as he summoned his men once more.

Our captors worked quickly after that. We were dragged forth again and pushed onto a flat surface; then that platform was raised into the air. Pinioned as we were, we could see but a braiding of taut-drawn rope above. Now our temporary floor swung outward, dipping a little so that I feared we would be rolled from the rimless support it offered.

Down—they were lowering us down somewhere, and we could be sure that whatever waited us below would be no better than what we had left behind.

Six

Tamara

The support on which we rested was swinging as a brisk wind pushed at it. We had not been secured in any way onto this platform, and the possibility was very real that we might roll off before we ever reached the goal our captors had selected.

Even as I strove to brace myself against such a fate, it came upon me. I spun over, and then I was falling, falling until the blanket-roll that bound me thudded home onto another surface with force enough to drive the breath out of me. I choked out a scream, only to suffer a second hard blow from above as a weight covered my body. Then darkness took me.

Sabina

WE HAD BEEN swinging—how? why? And who—who was I? At least that knowledge returned: I was Sabina. Then I was falling, to strike a surface that moved under me. I heard a choked cry, sounding as from a far distance. Once more I lay still, on my side this time. Summoning what small strength I still possessed, I mind-Sent:

"*Tam—Cilla!*"

"*Yes*—" That was Cilla, I knew, for the variations of mental "speech" can be as individual as voices.

"*Tam!*" I called silently again. She had always been the strongest, the most assured of us three. However, she had borne the brunt of Maclan's attention at the last. . . .

Before I could thought-call a third time, my body was jerked upward by my bound feet to hang, in painful movement, upside down. The pulls continued, growing ever more vicious. I realized I must have become entangled in a rope fastened to the platform we had ridden.

A final yank, followed by further shaking; then I was free and thudding downward. My cheek scoured across a rough surface—blanket?

"*Cilla? Tam—Tam—?*" I Sent desperately.

"*Yes.*" Again Cilla answered instantly. "*Tam is close beside you—I can see her! But—is that blood on her face? Tam!*" Cilla's own message entwined with mine.

I could neither lift my head nor change position, so I could see no more than the band of darkening sky above. Then came movement against that backdrop—a square object was swinging on ropes, describing a series of irregular lifts and drops, but rising ever higher. The platform that had brought us here was returning aloft.

After I reported the departure of the flooring-square, I strove, in fashion of an eyeless worm, to edge myself backward, hoping to meet with a rocky outcrop against which I could wriggle sufficiently upright to see something of our surroundings.

Almost as if some power had read my purpose and was moved to answer an unvoiced plea, I bumped against a hard surface, nearly as wide as my shoulders, so that I was heartened to struggle onward—or at least upward. Perhaps if I continued rubbing against the unyielding support, I could hatch myself from the cocoon of rope-wound blanket. And there was a sloping shape to what I pushed against! I added another bruise to my tally, but I fought on. Then my head and shoulders reached high enough so that I could at last see.

Tam lay farthest from the wall down which we had been lowered. Her eyes were closed, and a wild lock of new-cropped hair had been glued to her forehead and right cheek by blood. Still farther from me, Cilla lay flat with her head free of wrapping.

"This—" Her lips moved now, to loose a voice that was thin and strained. "This—is—the—Dismals." She paused between each word, as though she brought the sentence forth with immense effort.

Dismals—what did she mean? The dark state of spirit to which we had been reduced?

Suddenly my memory sharpened. Those reports we had researched while alone at Grosper had mentioned a country-within-a-country in which the creatures were so terrifying that it might be the place to which all the horrors that populated men's nightmares retreated during the day. But surely that was a legend, like some imaginary monster a nurse might use to frighten an ill-behaved child: "Do such-and-so, and you will go to the Dismals."

A land that lay below the surface of the world known to man, an enclave only able to be entered by ropes, though no one in his—or her—proper senses would choose to do so. Cradled by the Yakin Mountains, the Dismals was rumored to have been delved by the Servants of the Dark, the monster-kin. No man knew its extent because no would-be explorer had ever returned.

Tam sighed, and her eyes opened. She shifted her head toward Cilla.

"What's to be done?" Her voice was hardly above a whisper.

Before either of us could answer her, a rattle of pebbles cascaded down behind me. Both Tam and Cilla looked at once to me—or what was happening at my back. I feared that, if I tried to turn and see for myself, I might lose what small advantage I had gained through my efforts.

Nonetheless, I swung my head around as far as I could, just in time to catch sight of a flow of red fur that poured itself toward us like living fire. Its owner advanced as far as my feet, then sat up, as might a cat, on its haunches. But this creature was no cat, nor was it like to any other beast I had ever seen, even among the varieties in the queen's animal-park, which was one of the great sights of the capital.

However, I still thought *cat* when I looked at the head, save the ears were not pointed but rounded. And certainly this was larger by far than any sharer-of-the-house among our people. The form possessed longer lines than seemed natural, but the tail was the most striking feature, being fully the length of the beast's body.

It opened its jaws wide now, and the teeth exposed were all pointed as if for tearing. This display concluded, it swiped its whiskers with a forepaw, arose, and trotted leisurely toward Tam.

"No!" I screamed, hopeless, helpless to protect her. The cat-thing was plainly carnivorous and was anticipating my sister as a meal it would not have to stalk.

Cilla's shriek joined mine. Tam was staring, with a certain fatality, straight at the beast. The fanged head lowered toward hers; then an elongated tongue swept out to wash my sister's face. The taste of fresh blood must surely arouse it to kill—

Cilla was struggling to heave herself up, but her frantic efforts only rolled her back and forth. I worked my own shoulders higher on my support. Suddenly I felt a loosing of one of the ropes about my breast. I channeled all my strength into forcing my arms away from my body, but no feeling answered in them. Being so bound for so long might have leached all life from my muscles, leaving them powerless.

The red-furred monster had finished its predinner dainty from Tam's face. I caught the edge of what she was trying in a final attempt at defense. She was striving to use Send—not to us, but to the animal crouching beside her. Was that possible?

I stopped my physical exertions and aimed my spirit-energy to feed hers. We had done this once or twice, experimented with projecting Power, but never for any reason. We *had* that purpose now!

At first, no joining occurred. For a moment, I feared that I might even have weakened Tam's Talent by my interference. But, even as I tried to feed Tam's strength, so I was fed—by Cilla! We were well linked; I had anchored true with Cilla's Send, and the two of us touched and held with Tam. So firmly were we bound that, when a wave of another type of Power unexpectedly washed over us, we three felt the alien surge of force as one. Then, like a stream of water, pure and heady as if leaping from a spring in the high mountains, the alien Talent flowed into ours fully!

My earlier struggles had given me a chance to see Tam more clearly. The animal had settled back on its haunches again, seeming to study our sister closely. It appeared that what we had striven to do had been pointless, for the beast was making no movement to withdraw.

That fearsomely fanged head lowered again. This time, though, it did not aim at Tam's face, but rather at her breast. I saw it lunge forward and waited, shivering, for the first of my sister's screams. My Send quivered and nearly broke; then the new Power caught it up, melded once more with ours, and held. My terror began to drain away. Was the force I had summoned—all I could raise—feeding now upon that fear?

The animal's head came up with an effort. Between its jaws dangled a strip of cloth; perhaps it preferred its prey with flesh bared for easier fanging.

Where I leaned among the rocks, I rubbed my shoulders back and forth, though I dared not concentrate too much upon such efforts, lest my part of the mind-thread snap. There seemed no danger of that, however—indeed, it felt to me stronger than I had ever known it to be. None of us had such Talent as this, even though our Gifts had been enlarged by years of practice. Who—or what—had enhanced the force we could wield, we had no way of telling.

Tam and Cilla had always claimed that I was one who mistrusted new things and always sought for an explanation of how they worked. Only my Talent for healing had I accepted without demanding proof of this and that. In this hour, however, I knew I dared not question but must simply lend all strength I could to keep our mind-link intact.

The animal continued to tear at Tam's bindings. My own were loosening also, but far from swiftly enough. Now hanging from the beast's jaws was a frayed ribbon of white; the blanket having been pierced, what the creature now mouthed was a portion of her bed robe.

Those needle-tipped teeth dipped again, settled into a firm grip. I could hear the sound of that ripping, and Tam's inert body lifted a little, only to settle back as the cat-thing spat out another mawful of the confining cloth.

However, no savaging of my sister's bared chest followed; instead, that tongue, which had cleansed her face of blood, began to sweep her body. The fact that she had not been attacked by now somehow lessened my terror, or else we had been under fear's shadow for so long that it had come to feel familiar as our own. I have read in our records that in the old days, when a depraved dynasty ruled my country and torture was accepted by law, a victim who had suffered the worst a body could endure passed to a point beyond pain. Was this happening to us?

Tamara

THE BREATH OF this dweller in the Dismals was hot and fetid as that of any carnivore. However, as its green eyes stared into mine between assaults upon my swathings, I began to understand that it meant me no harm. I did not release the Send; instead, sharpened by the force we had all felt loosed to join ours, I still tried to reach the creature. I could only trust that I had touched it, though in a way I could not yet detect.

The dark had come upon us, yet here we could still see as we might on a heavily beclouded day. My own vision was centered upon the action of the creature arching its body above me. Suddenly, a rope, which must have been a major anchor for most of those twisted about me, broke. The cat-thing now pawed at my coverings instead of using its claws, and by so doing it was able to scrape my body mostly clear of the noisome bag that held me prisoner.

I strove to sit up, but my limbs felt heavy and dead from their long confinement. Still, with what effort I could summon, I slid my right hand across the rumpled stuff of the blanket and forced my fingers to touch the paw of my rescuer. Once more we met eye to eye. In some way, our silent defense-by-mind had been the right one. Perhaps I was simply an object of curiosity to the beast; in any event, I was not prey.

At that moment, without my willing it, the Send broke and was gone. Bina had held it with me, and also Cilla, but most certainly we had been companied by a fourth. The sharing had, in fact, been as profound as that venture into the unknown when, in our extremity, we had shared spirit-born water. I had to accept as true what I thought—what I now believed as if it had been duly sworn.

"It means no harm," I said hoarsely.

Drucilla

I LAY EXHAUSTED from my attempts to win freedom. Tam's white body lay on the ruins of her constraints, but still she did not move. I drew a deep breath. Would her rescuer turn now to me, or Bina, or—on us?

However, the animal seemed content to remain with Tam, for it stretched out full length, in watchful-cat fashion, that long plume of a tail resting straight behind it.

Delivered from fear of immediate savaging, I dared to give an order. The green eyes blinked; the head lifted. Now the creature was looking beyond me—at Bina. Swiftly on its feet again, it moved toward my sister. In the meantime, I set my teeth and began, drawing on remaining rags of energy, to master my body and force arms and legs to obey me. The pain of feeling's reawakening was welcome, though it stung like a whiplash. I pulled myself up, bracing the upper part of my body with my returning-from-the-dead arms.

Sabina

THUS WE WON to freedom, as yet unthreatened by whatever fate might await us in this darkly fabled land. A wind was rising, but still we refused to assemble any makeshift garment from those foul bindings on the ground. Tam had always been our leader and, through long practice, both Cilla and I now turned to her.

She had positioned herself on a large stone, and before her was her red rescuer. It, too, was seated and now, as I watched, I saw a clawed paw reach out to rest on Tam's knee, where bruises made black shadows. Neither of us tried to catch her attention by word or gesture; we also refrained from attempting any mind-speech, for it was plain that she and the beast were engaged in some form of communication.

Cilla had come to me and we huddled together, watching, hoping against hope that our sister was finding answers that would serve us for the future.

"Look!" Cilla was no longer intent on Tam and the animal. Her arm was extended, and her forefinger pointed back toward where we had lain.

The surface of the ground where we had been dropped was rough with rocks and gravel, as our many painful bruises could testify. Now, however, small rings of light encircled some of the stones. Their glow, though soft, held back the utter dark of night and gave us limited sight.

Curiosity could not be denied. I loosed my hold on Cilla and stooped painfully, reaching for the nearest of those strangely radiant rocks. I almost dropped it again, for my fingers had closed on—warmth! I held the pebble up, turning it about. The outer casing, though against my fingers it had the roughness of stone, now appeared on closer examination to be like crystal—a drop of transparent mineral bearing a heart of fire. Cilla and I were still examining my find, Cilla leaning against me to view it better, when Tam rose abruptly and beckoned.

"Come!" That word was delivered as an order. We did not question, but followed.

Tamara

SOMEHOW I WAS not astonished when I did mind-receive from the red one. The contact was not as clear as a meld with Bina or Cilla; it was more like a humming—or a purr. But it held the Power to allay fear completely, and I accepted that we had at least a partial bond.

The creature's message held neither words nor pictures, though I think that the latter might have been intended, for through its mind I looked briefly into a strange place I could view only dimly, as through veiling. At length I understood. This more-than-animal who had freed us wished for us to follow it. Because nothing but trust now existed between us, I called my sisters and prepared to go where it would lead us.

For a very short space, the glow of the gravel gave us sight of our footing. Tall plant growth, brush or even trees, rustled about us. As we moved in the wake of the banked-ember redness that was our guide, I realized that I wanted to know his name. This was no animal, and to think of it as such was wrong. *Four-legs who speaks with two-legs, how are you called?* I projected that thought with all the strength I could.

I was answered! Into my mind came a picture of what could only be a tree, though of such girth as I had never seen in our world. Up that mighty trunk sped a streak of vivid fur—*Climber?* I ventured. The purr sound soared into a crescendo of approval.

"This is Climber," I said to Bina and Cilla.

Climber continued to lead and we followed. Our footing was solid until, after we had journeyed a short distance, the ground suddenly gave way. The three of us slipped down a bank, carrying with us chunks of clay, our guide skidding beside us, almost on his rump. I caught a flash of amusement at our shared indignity. Then he splashed into water, and a moment later the stream received us, too. Its flow was not wide, nor was it more than knee-deep; and embedded in the clay that floored it were more of the light stones, giving forth a wavering radiance.

Climber lifted his long tail, and drops flew as it struck my thigh just above the water-line. I accepted the offer and took the wet appendage into my hand. Joined to our guide by this unusual leash, I splashed ahead.

Drucilla

VERY FEW STREAMS flow straight. True to pattern, this one curved several times, until we were no longer headed toward the wall of our living dungeon but rather paralleling that barrier, or so I believed. The light of the stones reached the edges of the shallow flow, but not much farther. For safety as well as comfort against the unknown that loomed so overwhelmingly about us, Bina and I proceeded linked hand to hand.

Vegetation grew along the banks in patches, and the water had inhabitants. Many of these sported body parts that, like the pebbles, shed light. We caught glimpses of grinning heads, with teeth whitely visible, or fore- and hind-limbs flashing by in shining streaks. Fortunately, all the aquatic folk fled from our path into the shore growth. Dancing above the water's surface were winged creatures, their shapes, too, dimly alight. None of this like had we ever seen before.

Suddenly I realized something else: a warmth was present the water itself! I could almost imagine having stepped into a barrel-bath. On impulse, I paused and, loosing my fingers from my sister's, cupped my hands and raised water to ease my abraded skin. Bina followed my example, so we had to hasten to catch up with Tam and the creature she had named Climber.

All at once, the wall of rock rose directly above us—I must have been completely wrong in my reckoning. The stream ran on through an archway of stone. On the far side of that portal, its light seemed to glow the brighter.

Tam had not halted, so neither did we hesitate, but followed on. In addition to the light from underfoot, we now had more illumination. Our water passage ran on through its stony cleft, and on the right-hand wall, spiraling lines of crystal were plainly visible. It took me a few moments of observation to note that a definite pattern was described in the curving of the lines. Then Bina's hand, which had lain on my arm, turned to clutch me painfully and catch me to a halt.

"Look!" She did not touch the wall, but in the air her finger sketched one of the curling traceries of light.

Seven

Sabina

My breath caught. I knew that sweep of line, those curls that met—so—then whirled off to form an intricate maze of circles. As if the pattern had ensorcelled me, I stood still, and my heart beat rapidly.

"Come on!" Tam had half turned toward us, using mind-speech, not words.

"No!" I defied the order with the same sharpness as it had been Sent, nor did I hold her gaze any longer to see how my answer had impressed her. Instead, I pressed my hands to the sides of my forehead, digging in fingertips with no regard for the pain they awoke from my bruises.

I closed my mind to the demands of the outer life—to everything but a search through memory. The words discovered there I repeated aloud:

"Armored by the ONE I stand;
On my right is She Who Bears
The Lanthorn of the Eternal Light,
The Sword of Stars unsheathed.
To my left is Brathan,
The BOOK OF ZORTAN in His hands. . . ."

Were my words actually visible in the air, as I saw them? Suddenly, something flew against the wall—or tried to, for, as swiftly as it had arrived, it was gone. The pattern continued to curl, its involutions leading the eye ever deeper into their mystic dance—but—*no!* Those lines, which had been so sharply defined, now showed crumbled edging as if the substance that produced the light were flaking away.

Still I held my ground.

"Thus it is read from the pages of the Book:
'Light is greater than the Dark.'
The ONE said, 'Let it be so.'
Thus it was so."

I was reaching now. As far as I knew, even our mother, puissant sorceress though she was, had never had reason to perform this ritual. And to use it with Power under less than the tightest control was a peril such as I should rightly fear.

"By Yar and Yi,
By Water and Stone;
By Sky and Earth,
By the Center of all things,
And by their outward seeming—"

Hands caught at me abruptly, dragging me back, and I swayed. Then, from behind me, a hand descended over my lips in a stifling seal to silence my incantation.

"Be still!"

Never had I heard Tam's voice raised in such anger before. Her gag of flesh slipped from my chin; then her fingers bit into the flesh of my bare shoulders.

"Feel, you fool—feel!" she ordered, not loosing her hold.

Some of the strength called up by the cantrip had drained out of me. Then—yes, I felt. A foulness crawled about me, and I shivered with revulsion and fear; I felt as though a snake had wrapped a rough-scaled length around my body. The spell might be broken, but this was a backwash of Power such as I had never experienced.

"Come—" Tam kept her grip only on one shoulder. Meanwhile, Cilla had stepped up to my other side. Together they urged me away from the wall and forward. Climber stood ahead of us in the water, lips wrinkled back in a snarl, tail lashing the stream to froth. Whirling around, the creature headed onward once more.

I continued to shiver from the cold within me—the stream that washed my body seemed warmer than I felt. After a few moments, I found my voice.

"That pattern—it is of the Dark. We may be going straight into the maw of Evil!"

"Not here," Tam answered. "That pattern is very old. In its time, it had a meaning that would never have concerned us. No trap was set."

How could she be so sure? I wanted to scream the question, but the words of protest died in my throat.

We splashed on. Once more the stream changed its path and rounded a curve; there more light awaited us. I stumbled on, still the captive of my sisters and our four-footed guide, until I was dragged out of the water into a huge cave, the full extent of which was hidden.

The cat-creature halted there. Once more that long tail swung in Tam's direction, and with her free hand she again grasped the sodden fur of the appendage. Linked as I now was to Climber through Tam, I felt a surge of that alien Power from the not-beast course through me—and suddenly I was freed from the Dark that had settled on me back in the tunnel.

Drucilla

I CAUGHT AT Bina as tenseness and resistance faded out of her, and I continued to tightly grasp her hand. Tam and the red beast had gone ahead. We followed at a slower pace, one dictated by Bina's now-unsteady feet. Much of interest lay about us, and my head turned continually as I surveyed our new surroundings.

As this cave chamber widened out, it was plain that the stream made a path across one end that continued to a place from which, halfway up the wall, a waterfall sprang from the rock. Green festoons of plant growth hung, like back-drawn curtains, on either side of this water-gate.

However, as we trudged on after Tam, the vegetation disappeared. Opening off the central room of the cave were a number of cavelets. One such alcove, ahead to our left, had a screen that walled it off from the main chamber and rose to the height of our shoulders from the floor.

Tam had come to a stop directly before the screen, facing a ledge that lay opposite. There we joined her.

Tamara

CLIMBER HAD BROUGHT me to a halt. I accepted that decision, just as I had come to understand that we could, in a manner, communicate. By this time, I knew that he was not only male but also no animal, in spite of his shaping, and I further understood that some matter of importance had compelled him to lead us here.

At this point, the wall ledge that lay opposite the screen-panel was occupied. For one startled instant, I thought we stood face-to-face with other inhabitants of the Dismals. Then I realized that we faced artifacts of mortal make, not flesh and blood.

A low, baked-clay bench, into which had been pressed a number of the light-bearing crystals, balanced there. Seated firmly upon it were two small statues. They had clearly not been meant to resemble humans such as ourselves. They possessed arms, legs, and bodies not unlike my own; on their square-set shoulders, however, were mounted truly alien heads. One possessed a round ball with no features marked upon it, though the substance from which it had been molded showed incised lines not unlike scars. The other towered a little above its peer, for its head was shaped in the form of a solid drop whose narrow point reached well above the ball. This figure also bore no face.

Yet, as I continued to study the pair, I felt no aversion to their oddity; rather, I was certain that they, and this place, held peace. I knew this because none of the protective Wards that had been set at our birthing awoke.

That strength which had brought us here suddenly vanished and, just as we had thirsted, so now we hungered. Mercifully, our need was answered at once. Beneath the ledge which supported those representations of—alien beings? unknown gods?—more shelves had been cut into the cave walls. And these were burdened with an array of edibles. As one, we moved toward them.

Pottery jars, crocks, and covered baskets we explored; then, sitting by the shelves, we ate. We could recognize dried fruit, though none of us could identify the beast that had supplied the strips of preserved meat, or the grain from which lumpy cakes had been fashioned. A jug of juice served to wash down our larder-lootings, and potent stuff it was.

Drucilla

IN SPITE OF our training in herb-knowledge, I could put no name to any scent or taste I found among our new foodstuffs. However, our Wards raised no warning of poison in this unexpected feast, so I gave myself up to enjoying it. I was carefully licking satisfying jamlike stuff from one finger after another when Bina spoke:

"Tam, Cilla—where are we?"

I answered first, soberly, remembering the way we had prevented Bina from completing that dismissal of a possibly alien power.

"In the Dismals." A short answer, but the only truth I could affirm.

Tam finished feeding Climber a strip of well-cured meat and made a reply different from mine.

"That we must discover. But first"—she shook her head, yawning, and that crudely cut lock flopped across one eye again—"here we can rest."

She sounded so certain that we could not disagree. A moment later, Climber glanced at Tam; then, evidently sensing her weariness, he padded across the rock floor, his nose pointing to the screen. We did not even try to get to our feet as fatigue suddenly descended upon us. Leaving the evidence of our meal behind us, we crawled around the end of that flimsy provision for privacy.

The room beyond held a frame not unlike that of the truckle beds we knew, which were intended for personal servants or children. It was well supplied with bedclothes, showing the corners of several covers lapped one atop the other. But it was also plainly intended for a single sleeper. Following the custom we had employed from very early in our lives, we allowed luck to decide which bird would occupy this nest. The lot fell to Tam.

However, beside the truckle bed was set a basketlike chest, and we discovered that it held a wealth of other bedding, though to identify the various materials was beyond our powers at the moment. From them we mounded up two pallets, one on either side of the bed, and found them soothing indeed to bruised and weary bodies. Thus we slept.

Tamara

MY AWAKENING WAS quiet but complete. The wan light of the room had not brightened, but I could see clearly as I sat up on the bed that chance had won me. What I saw made me catch hold of the top cover and pull it up to my chin.

Climber had joined someone who stood at the foot of the bed, surveying me as if I were one of the monsters that legend caused to lair in the Dismals.

The stranger was a fraction taller than my father. His clothing had been reduced to a minimum, either by the demands of the climate or a lack of local materials, until it consisted of a sleeveless jerkin fastened by a thong, and tight legginglike breeches. There was no sign of the buff coat or defensive half-armor such as any man venturing forth in the North wore as a matter of course.

Both jerkin and breeches were fashioned of a dark material that flickered with myriad tiny sparks of light, though those flecks were arranged in no pattern. A wide belt of gleaming mesh, supporting bags and sheaths, cinctured the trim waist beneath his broad breast.

I had not dared to look directly at his face, being more embarrassed than afraid. To be found naked as the One had made me (for I had shed the tatters Climber had left me), by a male in whose bed I had slept—! This was a situation that called for diplomacy, and that quality was not my strong point under the best of circumstances. However, I knew I must make an effort; I could only hope not to appear at too great a loss. I therefore raised my eyes to regard my examiner directly.

His skin was lighter than that of the men I had known who spent their days outside, and he wore no beard. Any male I knew would have sprouted chin whiskers in some fashion or another. The hair he did possess was thick and dark red; it fell in loose waves back from his forehead and was apparently clasped into control only at the nape of his neck. Down his left cheek ran the seam of an old scar.

The eyes, regarding me with a brooding stare, were as green as my own. However, it was not his continued gaze but a shielded quality about that look that troubled me. Here was one who might be sheltered by a strong personal Ward.

I tugged my cover higher. I would have preferred to pull it completely over my head, as well, yet I knew I must assert myself.

Must there be a Naming of Names? My sisters and I might just be driven to such a revelation. But I, Tamara, would not surrender the Power bound in the sounds that meant not only my body but my very soul until I was compelled to do so.

"If this be your hall," I broke the silence at last, using the older and more formal turn of speech, "we have indeed entered without bidding. Climber found us in dire need and led us here, after Evil caught us in its toils through no fault of our own."

Climber stood on hind legs, his forepaws against the stranger's thigh. Now he actually nodded his head as if testifying in his own way that I spoke truth.

"Who—" The newcomer began to speak, but he was interrupted by a choked cry. Bina sat up, then scrambled awkwardly to her feet, dragging her top cover about her—a pose in which Cilla speedily joined her.

He stared intently, turning his head to survey each of us. Cilla dropped a curtsey, then hurriedly pulled her covering tighter. Bina came to stand against the bed as if on guard.

"Who," he began again after a sweeping appraisal, "are you three, so alike one unto the other, seeking sanctuary here?"

Our unwitting host was, indeed, questing for the names of his uninvited guests. However, I dared not even probe to find if my suspicions were correct that this stranger possessed a Talent not unlike ours.

His garb, as I had noted before, was utterly unlike that of the surface Northers. Now I noted another detail about his accessories: though a sheath resembling that of a short sword hung at his belt, it contained no sword— not even a hunting knife.

But the fact that the scabbard did not hold a weapon of bone or honed steel did not mean that it was empty.

My training had never brought me into an encounter with any adept save for the women of my own family. Yet I had long ago learned that else- where in the world, beyond this island continent where we had been birthed, dwelt others who dealt with the Light or the Darkness, and even with different Powers.

The intruder—no, it was *we* who deserved that title—was scowling now, his emerald eyes continuing to hold me. Yes, this man had Talent, but none that I could measure; it did not feel akin to the Gifts that the House of Scorpio held with pride.

Cilla and Bina risked a unison Send to me. *"Tam, you must Name or otherwise explain us, or this one might force what he seeks from us by hurtful means."*

Reluctantly, I yielded. "We are Scorpys, daughters to the Earl of Verset, Alsonia's Lord Warden on the Border, and we are come by the queen's own choosing."

"You are well north of the Border," he returned. "Who—or what—brought you here in such a state?"

I was not going to allow him to scant me of the information due me in kind. "Under what clan banner do we now rest?"

He appeared to give that question some consideration. Again he studied us for a time; then at last he smiled. That expression laid to rest the greater portion of my uneasiness.

"The banner of my house no longer flies, my lady—not since Erseway. I am a man without kin or name."

"All creatures bear names," I objected, pointing to Climber, "even animals. Therefore you, too, must be called in some way."

I did not miss the sudden tension of his body, or the fact that Climber looked at me and snarled.

"The Battle of Erseway was fought the day we entered the world," I added. "To judge by your appearance, you were too young to have borne sword at that time."

The stranger said nothing, but Cilla spoke after a moment. "That war is long ended, though the land suffers, as ever, from raiding and plundering along the Border. Our father has arranged a Truce meeting. He was at that council when we were taken."

"Any hoped-for truce has surely been broken now," I put in. "The last I heard, a hot tod was riding on the trail of those who took us, with sleuthhounds to lead them. The Starkadders will have much to answer for to their king in Kingsburke."

Again our host allowed the silence to stretch, but at length he said, "I think perhaps it would be well to tell me the whole story, ladies—if I do, indeed, behold three of you and am not completely bemused."

I was so far from the mood in which one tells such a tale that I answered shortly, moistening my lips before I spoke. "We have, sir, been left without proper clothing—"

He did not laugh, as I had half expected. The only emotion he continued to display was interest.

"Perhaps that is a lack which my stores can answer also." He turned before I could answer, to disappear beyond the screen, leaving us to guess what his next move might be.

We learned soon enough. From the cave beyond we could hear movements. Our nameless host appeared again very shortly, holding a bundle against him. This he tossed onto the bed, nearly striking me.

"Use what you can. I have not fashioned garments for any but myself." Then he took from his belt a bulging pouch, which gave forth a jangling as it, too, was flung to land on the sleeping-place. "When you will," he concluded, "give me your story." Before we could utter any thanks, he was gone once more.

We turned our attention to what he had brought. The more quickly we could garb ourselves, the faster we might be able to confront him again to learn what we must know in order to face the future.

I unrolled the bundle of clothing and spread it out on the bed for inspection. It proved to hold three sets of the long breeches, three of the jerkins, and three pairs of soft foot coverings, for each of which at least four layers of thick, close-furred hide had been used.

Cilla looked up after one appalled examination. Of us all, she had always delighted the most in attire that was attractively fashioned. " 'Tis far from court dress, to be sure," she observed ruefully. "But at least it is better than this." She gave a disgusted snort and dropped her coverlet drapery and rags to the floor.

Bina's fingers fastened onto the pair of the legginglike garments nearest to me. She shook the breeches out. They proved to be crafted of two thicknesses of hide, and the seams were not puckered. Bina knew cloth well. I myself could sort wool, grade linen, and even gauge price on silk from overseas better than most merchants; but this stuff was far from any fabric I had ever handled.

In the first place, though the inner part, which would rest against the skin, was smooth, the outside was scaled. The color was gray, but it was brightened by a design formed of other scales, these being a light blue almost the shade of a good sword blade.

It could only have been reft from one creature, or—in what I had already begun to think of as "the Upper World"—many creatures of a kind

I knew: the serpent-kin. Still, when I once more inspected the interior, I found only two seams, not the many I expected. Nowhere could a reptile exist that would be large enough to provide such a skin as this! Still, snake-skin the material seemed; I could put no other name to it.

"Snake," I voiced my discovery, passing the garment on to Bina, who tested its flexibility to discover that it seemed not unlike heavy silk.

"No!" Cilla had been reaching for a pair of the scaly breeks, but she withdrew her hand hastily. Bina, however, carefully examined the inner part, as I had done.

"Maybe a serpent-thing this large lived once and cast a skin, and that was preserved—"

Bina interrupted me. "Do you now suggest a dragon, Tam? There are no dragons. . . ." She fell silent as she half crumpled the leggings and they yielded, as strong cloth would not do.

I refused to consider any longer what might be the source of the material I was drawing on over my legs and up my body. The garments had not been tailored for me, and they did not fit tightly as did the leggings our host wore; they also rose well above my waist. The problem of keeping these clothes anchored now confronted us until Cilla remembered the bag the Nameless One had left.

She loosed its drawing string and shook forth the contents. What poured out before our eyes made us gasp aloud: a golden rivulet sparked with jewels. It was as if the stream through which we had waded the night before, with its glowing pebbles, had been turned by some alchemy to precious metals and gems.

"Treasure!" Cilla crowded closer. "So the legends are true after all!" She caught up a large brooch, part of which was a circle of jewels. They appeared gray to the first glance, but when the piece was tilted, each stone showed in its depths a slender ribbon of red-gold light.

I pulled free a twisted belt of what I thought was gold entwined with another metal. This cincture, too, held sparks of fire that slid along as if imprisoned just beneath the surface. I made good use of it to ensure the safety of my scaled leggings.

We hastened to make further use of our host's nearly overwhelming generosity.

Eight

Sabina

Having made very sure that we would not lose some part of our covering, though there were brooches enough in the bag to assure our decency, we eyed each other. Tam had used a chain of tiny links, each dotted with a gem, to anchor that errant lock of hair over her forehead.

In truth we made an odd appearance. "Hardly court garb," I commented. "Did you look closely at any of these?" I indicated three of the brooches that latched the jerkin across my breast.

"If they were fashioned by any goldsmith of Alsonia," Tam observed, "it was long ago."

"They are lettered," I returned. For I was indeed certain that some of the odd embossed turns and curves had meaning.

I saw Cilla squinting down at her own choices. She was frowning, and I sensed that she did not want such a guess to be the truth. It might be that the less she had to consider what she wore now, the better.

A glittering pile of treasure still remained, and I swept it back into the pouch, twisting the closing cord to keep it safe.

"Ready?" I asked, thinking that I would never be truly thus.

"Ready," they affirmed, and we rounded the end of the screen, coming once more into the open part of the cave.

I had been sure that our nameless host would be waiting. He was not, however, nor was Climber to be seen. All that had befallen now seemed like a many-layered dream. As children who are unsure of new surroundings, we linked hands.

What did greet us was an aroma, more welcome than any costly fragrance from overseas: the scent of roasting meat. I looked to the graceless disorder in which we had left the food shelves; that had all been cleared away. But farther along, where we had not yet explored, a red glow shone at floor level.

We headed toward that gleam and discovered a fire-pit. Over it was suspended a cut of meat on a chain, which turned and re-turned for a different kind of roasting, needing no spit-boy to tend it. A sizzling arose now and then as a drop of grease struck the low flames.

The pit was dug very close to the cave wall, and not far away was cut another of the shelves. On that ledge lay knives and two long-shafted forks. I reached for the nearest blade, thinking it might offer some protection. Though the Nameless One had offered us no reason to feel anything but comfort from his generosity, I felt a little easier with a weapon to hand—until I was able to inspect it more closely.

"Stone!" Certainly the blade was wrought of some mineral, albeit discolored by frequent kitchen use. In my hold it was heavy and ill-balanced.

"This also!" Cilla had taken up one of the forks and held it out. The two slender prongs were indeed needles splintered from rock.

"Stone or not, these have been carefully made," I commented.

Tam had picked up the other knife and was testing the point carefully with a fingertip. "I'll wager a whole Rounder that this work is not primitive."

"Done by the Nameless One?" Cilla demanded.

I had edged closer to the pit and now thrust at the meat as if delivering a death blow. The stone tip pierced the roast easily. I held up the knife in my other hand to squint along its edge.

Tam gave an exclamation and moved closer to the shelf, reaching to pull out a bowl large enough to hold all the meat before me.

"Let us eat—" My words were a suggestion. I stabbed the dangling roast again.

"Can you cut a portion, Bina?" Tam wanted to know as she brought the bowl closer.

"We shall see," I returned. As had all of us, I had received instruction in household arts, but the handling of meat straight from the fire was usually the duty of a kitchen-man or an assistant cook.

The portion I hacked off with the stone knife—it did have a surprisingly sharp edge—we took back to where the other stores were placed, below the queer blind figures. There we ate, mainly with fingers, as we had before, with additions from the shelves.

This time we remembered our manners and carried empty containers and the like to be washed at the stream, discovering that, the nearer to the falls we approached, the warmer the water was. When we returned them to their proper places, we settled cross-legged on the floor. During this time our host had not appeared, nor had we seen Climber. Whether it was day or night in the outer world, we had no way of telling; nor could we now more than guess how long it had been since we had been taken from Grosper.

Cilla introduced a subject far from the one that I was ready to present.

"Can this stranger be one we have heard of—the Lost King? That boy— he was seven or eight, was he not? Some swore that he was killed and his body hidden. Maclan meant such a fate for us at the last, I am certain. It's common enough when a raiding party with a prisoner is hard-pressed. We would not have survived, had we not been found and freed by that beast."

"A child of seven?" Perhaps Cilla *had* made a proper guess. I brushed the scaled legging stretched across my knee. "Though this Under Land has surely been used by Breakswords in the past to get rid of victims they must conceal. Let a ransom go unpaid, or their prey be one to be disposed of— what more efficient place? The important thing is that there *were* legends. But is any account known of one who entered here ever leaving again?"

Tam, who had been oddly silent and had, as I noted, glanced regularly to the right as if expecting our host to return at any moment, seemed to be alerted by my question.

"You must have read the report from the Dackner clan—the one pre- served from the fifth year of Queen Marosa's reign. In that account, a Breaksword swore the Dismals housed monsters that fed upon men. When Black Bourne was taken after the burning of Mackiton Tower, he claimed he would have won free had it not been that near half of his men had been lured away by news of a treasure. He declared that they had descended into the Dismals, even as we were compelled to do—but none returned."

"This place," said Cilla slowly, "is neither of South or North—what do we know of it or the Nameless One?"

Tam spoke slowly. "He has Power—it is not of our kind, but it is Power."

"So—you would grant me that?"

He had appeared behind us as if summoning a body from the shadows to serve him. Even as my thoughts provided this suggestion, he turned toward me.

His Send struck as a strongly thrust sword. Heat—pain—! My hands covered my ears, pressed against my head as if I needs must hold my skull together. This was a mind-casting that could be used as a deadly weapon.

The personal Ward I had trusted all my life was as nothing, and this blow had found me unprepared. But I had not been taken as was planned—taken, or killed. Perhaps what saved me from instant capitulation was the fact that my Talent was not akin to his. In spite of the increasing agony as he continued to feed his Power, I was able to call—not only upon the strength I could muster, but also upon Tam and Cilla.

They speedily found my resistance, building on that. Then—I was not the attacker but Tam, who had always been the strongest among us for a sally, even as she could more skillfully wield a material weapon.

I was no longer aware of anything but the pull of Power—united Power. Before my mind's eye it was visible, writhing serpent-wise in a place of great darkness. The red-gold of our heraldic badge, a scorpion, tail upraised for a strike, while before it loomed another creature, larger, and much like a lizard, green and black.

So much I saw; then all vision was swept away, as if my mind had indeed been destroyed.

Tamara

HIS HAD BEEN a surprise attack, but we of the Talent cannot be easily taken thus. Our Ward remained, though in Bina's case the defense had seemed to crumble. However, the foundation of that protection remained: full strength in me and in Cilla. As Bina made a small mewing sound and sank forward, Cilla caught her, held her tightly. I was on my feet facing the Nameless One. Nameless indeed he must be, I thought furiously, and with his feet turned to the dark.

Our triad was gone, an emptiness gaping where Bina had been. But we could spare no time to be concerned for her—not now. We must Send, allow both anger and fear to Send, with all the force we could draw and hurl.

Though my body's sight was dimmed by that struggle, I was able to see him stagger. So—we had reached him! Fortunately, we did not have to spread our weapon, for he was but one alone. *Send—oh, Send!*

He crumpled. The attacking Power was gone, blown out as a candle is snuffed. It disappeared so suddenly that I staggered forward; I might have been beating upon a door that was suddenly flung open. One of my feet toed his body as I controlled my Talent, damped it down.

The Nameless One lay on his back. His green eyes gleamed but no life appeared in them. Had we indeed ended him?

I dropped to my knees and fingered the pulse at his throat. His heart was still beating.

"Tam! Oh, Tam!" Cilla summoned me.

Bina was still cradled against her. I ventured a small probe even as I returned to them, but nothing answered, not a mind closed by will or Ward—nothing!

Then—was she dead? Though we had not taken out our attacker, had he vanquished Bina—our level-headed, stouthearted sister, whom I always believed to be the anchor for Cilla and me? Did he for some reason hold us now enemies?

Cilla's right hand had slipped under the edge of Bina's jerkin. Now she looked up with relief dawning on her anguished face.

"She is alive?" Swiftly I knelt beside them, my arms striving to hold them both at once.

"Yes. And he—?" Cilla donned a mask of hatred as she looked toward the recumbent man.

"He lives—or his body does." That was the last great fear of all our kind: use of the Send past the point of safety could end with the destruction of the inner spirit, leaving only an empty human shell. Had we indeed turned that fate upon him?

Cilla slid out of my grasp, leaving Bina to me, and sped behind the screen once more. I watched the Nameless One. Why had he attacked, waiting until now? He could have taken us with ease, I was sure, while we were asleep. Unless he had a need to study us . . .

Talent of our sort is seldom found here in the North. It was never honed, honored, and made supple as it was in our land where, with very few exceptions down the years, it was most often the gift of women, just as martial genius was of men.

The Power wielded by the Nameless One was, I felt certain, was not our kind but a Gift totally strange to the training we had received. Our attacker was alive, yet did only an emptied body lie before us? But now our task was Bina. *By the Great Power,* I pleaded silently, *let it be my sister, full and whole, who will return to us!*

Cilla came back with bedding, and we established Bina as best we could.

"Bina knows the proper herbs better than we do." Cilla stroked our sister's hair. "Only Mother knows the Center Call—"

I nodded. We had not been deemed ready for that lessoning. It was rarely used, and then mainly for restoring the Talent to a wielder who had tried to use Power beyond her capacity, only to be immersed in the backwash of force.

"Since we cannot use that, we can only watch and wait."

I arose and so did Cilla. However, without explaining what she would do, she headed again for the supply shelves. Taking up an extra cover, one not used for Bina's comfort, I folded it. Holding it so, I moved to the side of our host and raised his head to slip it underneath.

His skin felt warm to the touch, and his eyes were now closed. Could I believe that he was recovering? Perhaps it would be best to bind him while he was helpless. Yet if he relied on Talent as his weapon, we could not render him helpless by mere physical bonds.

Cilla returned from her visit to the shelves with a netted bag in the crook of one arm, two small lidded crocks in one hand and a bottle clutched tightly in the other. She stooped to place her selections on the floor, then sat down between them and Bina.

"Herbs?" We all had special refinements of Talent peculiar to each of us alone. Cilla not only had a strong command over needlework but she had the ability to concoct certain herbal potions. Those creams and scents we used for our needs were always of her distilling and making. Bina had herb-lore also, but dealt rather with healing, sometimes rivaling the skill of Duty, the true greenwife of our household.

Cilla did not look to me but rather stared at her selection. "It is a pitiful assortment, but it is the best here. I had to select by scent, and that is guessing, but there was no other way. Bina always wishes her court fragrances to be of red lilies. Here, smell this—"

She twisted the stopper from one of the clay pots and held it out. I obeyed and lowered my head to draw in a full sniff.

"Essence of red sun lilies," I pronounced, but she shook her head.

"Not so. Look!"

Look I did. The liquid within was not the watery juice that could be pressed from the proper flowers; I had done such a task myself. This was a turgid, oily substance. Yet, when I sniffed again, it was true attar of red sun lily.

"And the others?"

Cilla pointed to the other stoppered pot. "Gascal sticks, I believe—but I cannot be sure." Then she dangled the net. It contained five lumps with a greasy glaze upon them.

"Razzel roots, fried. I am more sure of those—and this." She dropped the net and picked up the bottle. "Vorfay wine—or its close like."

"You would make a summons?"

"If I can." Cilla frowned. "One can only try."

She stepped again to the shelves, selected an empty bowl with a spouted side for the pouring of its contents, and began work. I thought it time again to visit the Nameless One and moved to do so.

He lay as I had left him, though his eyes were once more open. Only— they were lifeless orbs. I shivered. Was the stranger now a spiritless husk? We had fought for our own lives—I quieted my conscience with that. Yet to deliver this worst of fates, than which clean death was far more to be desired, was an act that would burden any wielder of Power with guilt, shadow her throughout life's length.

Could we fight for him even as Cilla was doing for Bina? One of his hands lay limply along his body, resting on the stone. I knelt and grasped it. The flesh was warm, certainly that of a living man; still he lay totally inert.

Then, into my mind, with such force that my ears might have heard a spoken order, came thought, born of a mind-pattern strangely twisted. To learn its message was akin to dealing with an intricate foreign language.

A part of me obeyed. Still holding his hand, I bent until my lips met his, and I began to suck, as though drawing poison from a wound—why, I could not have told. I knew only that this must be done—that what our Talent had laid low, I must now cherish.

I was extracting nothing tangible from him; however, that I pulled forth *something* I was sure. Pain struck, its hot irons pressing into my forehead as if I suffered branding.

Sounds began behind me, very faint and far away, but I could spare them no heed for the world had narrowed to what I must do. My agony became a barrier, and I could draw no more remaining Power to me, into me. Raising my head, I looked into those eyes once again. No longer were they shallow, without life.

"Tam! Tam!"

Slowly, moving against a great fatigue, I placed the hand I held back on his breast. I had no energy left; to rise to my feet was beyond my strength.

"Tam!"

I could not move, yet I knew that I had not been raped of spirit. I was still Tamara Scorpy, Wisedaughter.

Cilla was kneeling beside me, her face very close to mine and her eyes shadowed by fear. With a great effort, I reached for her, clung that I might not slump to the stone of the cave.

She looked at the man. Still he had not moved, and his eyes had closed.

"He—he is emptied?" she asked tonelessly.

"No, I think not, but Bina—how fares she?"

"She is ours once more," Cilla was quick to assure me. "Come—"

Tugging determinedly, she pulled and lifted and got me across to where Bina lay.

Our sister had begun to cry, heavy sobs shaking her whole body. Her hands reached out to me and I kissed her, holding her tightly, doubly aware of what we might all have lost.

Cilla had a hand on each of us, and a thick fragrance wreathed us round. We might be cloistered in a bed of blooms; and indeed our sister began to singsong those old country names of blossoms that had been known to us since we were able to crawl and pull flower-plunder from our mother's garden:

"By Star-of-glory, Petalbright, Creeping Maids,
Weaving Stems, Better-worth, and Red-Gold Lily!
Great One, to us this treasure of Glory has been given.
In Thy Name shall a garden new be tended—
In this very land of darkness and despair.
This do I swear!"

It seemed as if the perfume that encircled us was spreading out, at the same time growing stronger, richer. Without speech I voiced my thanks to that Greatest of all Powers.

Then I heard a coughing. Bina twisted a little in my hold to look to its source. He was sitting up, one hand pressed to those lips I had met, as again he loosed a cough.

It was not I who spoke but rather Bina, for Cilla's eyes were closed, and she swayed silently to some chant that she alone could hear.

"Truce?" Bina's question was loud.

He was sitting up, braced by his arms and hands against the floor. His face wore an odd expression that I could not read, but he answered firmly.

"Truce!"

Bina wriggled free from my hold and stood erect.

"Weapon peace-tied?" came her second question.

He smiled then, and it was as if some mask cracked to show us one of kin.

"Peace-tied indeed, lady. I, Zolan, swear it so."

His name—of that I was sure, though it was no usual name of the North. So did he give it freely, breaking any usual Ward by imparting it to us.

"I be Sabina of the Scorpys," she replied.

I must render trust also. "And I am Tamara of the Scorpys."

Cilla stood up. "I am Drucilla of that line," she added.

Thus, though questions in many remained unanswered, we believed that we had been given full guesting rights in this stronghold of the Dismals.

Nine

Drucilla

hat is the way of it." I licked dry lips, having finished the telling of our tale. Bina and Tam had left it to me, and neither they nor Zolan had interrupted.

"And a black way it is!" He turned his head and looked to the seated figures of the unknown beings.

"We must keep watch," Bina struck in. "If our father traces us this far—"

"I suppose," Tam said, her attention strictly on him, "no other way is known out of the Dismals?"

"None!" His answer was harshly abrupt.

"You have lived here long?" I asked. "Were you also captive dropped, as we, into this ill-omened place?"

"I have"—he spoke slowly and with an emphasis that signaled importance—"no other memories than this." His hand moved in a gesture to encompass all that lay about us.

"No others have been left here as we were?"

"Yes—five. But all had been hard-used, and they did not live long." Zolan was open enough about those facts.

A flash of red kindled behind him. Climber appeared, to stand on his hind legs, both forepaws on the man's shoulders, his head raised until he could look directly into his companion's eyes. For a long moment the two held that position; then the beast dropped to four feet again.

Zolan arose. "Tasks must now be done," he stated. "But first, let me ask something of you—for your own safety. The perils are many in this place, which is apart from your own world. I have hunted through the seasons for a way up, which I have never found, yet still will I search for one for you—this I promise. In the meantime, do not venture forth by yourselves. Now I must go."

The tone of his voice kept us from any question. Go he did, leaving us with much yet to learn.

"If Father's forces come, they will have the sleuthhounds in the lead. We have fed Bell and Swiftfoot since they were puppies, and they will know our scent well. To keep a watch where we were lowered—that is only a matter of good sense." I was on my feet. Then I stooped to take the shallow bowl from which fragrance still rose.

Curling a finger into its depths, I brought out a smearing of the slightly greasy substance. With a gob of this I touched my body, breast, both knees, and last of all my forehead. I could not rebuild our Wards by ceremony, and this anointing was far less potent, but it must serve. Was its worth not so proven when it drew Bina back to us?

I passed on the bowl to Tam and Bina, and they followed my example.

"We were warned," Bina said. "And we have no weapons."

"We were warned," Tam echoed her, then amended, "and we have no weapons of *man's* making."

The plan in their minds was as clear as if it had been scribed in words: they would return to the cliffside from which we had been lowered. The stream gurgling at the other end of the cavern would be a guide.

I had another thought to share. Twice Zolan had come without sound, seeming to materialize out of the shadows. I wanted to know a little better the extent of this stronghold of his, beginning with the seated figures. I was sure that they were of importance to our host. Also, why had he turned his Power upon us?

Tam nodded. "I think you have the right of it."

I had not put my idea into speech, yet they agreed. I moved forward, not to plunder the supply shelf this time but to approach as closely as I could those alien watchers.

Now that I had fully centered my attention on them, I began to see many more oddities. Though the bodies were stiffly human in shape, they bore no patterns to suggest clothing. However, raised lines that appeared to be ornamental scars crossed shoulders and chests, writhed down arms and legs.

Patterns—patterns had always served me well as far back as I could remember. I began to trace a certain scar-cutting down the nearest arm of the figure directly before me. That line—no, not quite—it should turn here, but it did not. Again I saw a design not unlike the one I had dreamed. And I had seen it still more recently. I caught at the massive brooch, which clipped my jerkin modestly together across my breasts. Yes, here was a plain copy of the motif in the hardened clay above.

"We see," Tam's Send came. I felt her use her probe sharply; however, no tinge of Evil answered as it had so quickly when we had dealt with thread and cloth.

"Cafthouli"—Tam lifted a hand and just avoided touching the patterned arm.

"Who?" I demanded. Certainly I had never heard that name, if name it was, before.

Without turning from her staring appraisal of the figure, as if she had not heard me, my sister suddenly put both hands up, one to each temple and bowed her head. *"Cafthoulis sanis varton, Vo, Vo, Vo!"*

I sensed that I was hearing an invocation, and I caught at Tam's arm, pulling her back against me.

"Lord of Light," I cried toward the curve of stone roofing us in, "deliver her!"

I felt Tam's body grow tense in my hold. Then she gasped—she might have been walking in peril and now saw a trap gaping open-jawed before her.

Bina had joined us, a frown between her brows.

"What would you do, Tam?" Her demand was quick, on the edge of anger.

Tam shook her head from side to side. "I do not know," her voice was scarcely above a whisper. "What have I taken on me?" She clapped both hands over her mouth, adding after a moment, "From Zolan I received— not a Send such as we know, but still a message-of-mind, and I obeyed it. I—I drew Power out of him, into me; surely it was our own Power I reclaimed. But if it had mingled with his essence, then I have a force in me I do not know how to control.

"Yet one thing I do know." She looked to me and then to Bina, a child again, seeking reassurance. "This strange Gift is not of Evil. And of this I am also sure: we stand in a very ancient place, and those who wrought it were not human as we think ourselves to be. They had Power, a force as alien as themselves. Perhaps we cannot judge in truth whether it be Light or Dark, for it cannot be measured by what we know.

"I—I may have called a Summons."

I stiffened. This day we had already been near drained of what force we had, and I feared we could not stand so well-armed again.

Bina loosed her hold on Tam and moved to front the figures. She raised her right hand, crooked her fingers so the tips pointed to the seated pair.

"By heart and hand, spirit and body,
Be you Dark, or be you Light,
Open, to the Power of the Seer of All,
And let the truth be known!"

From her fingertips shot needle-thin spears of light. They struck the figures, and a light like fire blazed up, lashed the boxlike figures, and was gone. Our tension eased. These beings held no menace. Had they ever dealt with Power, perhaps under the command of living creatures, they were harmless in the here and now.

Bina rubbed her hand across her sweat-beaded forehead.

"This is not one of those ever-lurking dangers we have been warned against," she said quietly. "Tam, if you fear a taint, we shall have a Cleansing, but such a rite cannot be held here, in this time-past stronghold of a Gift we cannot understand."

Thus we left another puzzle behind us and began to work our way around the cave walls. The stream now faced us. Tam sat down, unlaced her fur-lined footgear, and rolled up the scaled leggings. Bina suddenly left us, running back into the cavern depths; then she returned, carrying the long-handled fork and the two stone knives.

Tam, having worked her shoes into her belt, took up one of the knives, testing its edged with a careful finger.

"Little enough, but the best that fortune appears willing to grant us."

So armed, and prepared for water-traveling, we entered the stream, a return to the cliff point firmly in our minds.

As we reached the mountain door to look out, we found its greenery dappled with patches of pale sunlight, which was all the heavy growth about us would allow to reach the ground. I surveyed the opening doubtfully. So thick was that wall of dark green, cut only by the stream, that it could conceal a number of perils. My imagination was swift to suggest such threats, though mercifully not in detail.

Without words Tam took the lead, as she had before, and we splashed along behind her, causing gauzy-winged insects to rise. We halted as a raucous scream cut the air. At its second sounding, wild movement shook the vine-draped trees to our left. More cries arose, the agony in them plain. A dark shape broke through the curtain of leaves. It fought vainly to keep its hold on a vine, then landed with a thud below, hidden again.

Something like a huge, thick green stick burst out of hiding, fanning up on thin wings into the air to descend again with force enough to slash leaves, tear vines from their grip. Then the stick-creature fastened onto a tree trunk and tensed. We could sense it straining to hold. A ripple coursed along its length—hair! Hair, or a like substance, clothed its form. A second stick, in the air, lashed back and forth through the trailing ends of dislodged vine. We retreated under the arch of the cave entrance but continued to watch.

The flying thing managed to seize upon two thick vines that were still firmly attached above it. Apparently satisfied by its anchors, it strove to draw upon both. Resistance of the lower growth defeated it at first; then that pull stiffened. The sounds of more tearing leaves and snapping branches were followed by another agonized shriek of pain. Out upon the open bank of the stream plopped what seemed a vast tightly stuffed bag, covered with green bristles that stood erect save for where torn skin hung in shreds. Four more of the furred sticks now unfolded limbs to beat around the mutilated body, while the other two creatures still clung to the support of tree and vine.

Its struggle had brought the bag-beast around to where its head, a mere ball, was now visible to us. Eyes, huge—and numbering six—bulged, green as its stiff hair, staring, though I could not be sure it saw us.

Scarcely aware of what I did, I raised the toasting fork as I might a boar spear. A red and white froth was gathering about the clashing movement of—jaws? I doubted that; the thing must be equipped with different parts for the managing of food.

"*Spider!*" Tam cried. And the creature, evidently hearing her, went into an even greater frenzy.

It certainly was not a spider such as could be found in dark corners in Grosper, for it was larger than one of the sleuthhounds, which are particularly bred for size. The spiky growth it bore had the look of rank fur and equipped it well for life among the trees.

"Back!" Tam gave warning.

Tamara

WE WERE WELL under the archway of the water-path. I realized I should have sent Cilla and Bina farther back as I heard a new droning rise above the sound of the wounded spider.

Many—perhaps even most—of our species have no great liking for insects. With some pests we wage an ongoing war, but those are small enough to be destroyed in the open with various mixtures fatal to them. But this spider, still pounding the earth, could have met any armsman on equal terms.

Down dropped the thing in the vines. A goodly portion of this one was made of forelegs folded against its body, those supports being edged with a jagged series of teeth, like a saw. The head, which bore huge and bulbous eyes, aroused in me not only fear but also a feeling of revulsion. It settled on the far bank of the stream and unfurled wings that appeared too small to support it. The upper part of the long body reared aloft, while the serrated forearms stretched forward, one after another, toward the floundering spider. It was a figure of deep and menacing cruelty.

Cilla cried out in sick horror and splashed back into the stream, Bina following. I remained where I was. The winged hunter had crossed the water and was aiming the sawtoothed front legs at its prey with cruel efficiency. It was entirely intent upon action and had given no sign of noticing anything but the pulsating body now helplessly awaiting attack.

"*Know your enemy as best you can.*" Our father's words rang out from memory. Zolan told the truth—perils existed in the Dismals that we had not imagined. The stench of blood reached me, but I continued to study both victim and victor.

The spider must have been attacked while in the trees. Yet this other monster was winged. How could it have been able to hunt where its wings would have been a hindrance rather than a help? Swooping down, it could take us easily. Against such a demon, what good would be a toasting fork and stone knives for weapons?

Were both of these creatures common in this world here below? We would be the greatest of fools not to understand that we were easy prey to such nightmares. Still—we had traveled some distance from the cliff edge with Climber before he had brought us to the water trail, and I did not remember that he seemed suspicious of any attack there.

I wanted no further sight of the noisome banquet and was about to withdraw after my sisters, when movement behind the feaster drew my attention. The winged monster paid no heed; however, a growing quivering was shaking the green wall.

A flash hurtled through the air, in movement so swift that I could see only a red streak. Jaws closed upon one of the feeder's hind legs. The insect-giant reared and gave voice, and pain thrust hot needles into my ears as the cry reached a pitch beyond my ability to hear.

Climber—or one of his kin! New blood joined the crimson wash already sprayed about on leaves and muck underfoot. However, the killer could not reach its assailant easily. Attempts to fend off the attacker by scrapes from its razor-edged midlegs sent tufts of red hair flying. Still that traplike hold remained unbroken, though darker patches of rent flesh began to show as the leg raked and beat on. Drawn by the need to aid the beast, which had saved our lives, I was out in the stream again.

The stone knife in my hand was a futile weapon, I thought. One of the thin legs of the spider trembled, rose. That the creature was still alive after being so ravaged was hard to believe, but even if the motion were a death throe, fate served me. As might a war mace, that blood-smeared limb crashed down and clamped onto one of the forelegs of the killer.

Again my head rang with a cry so shrill in pitch it became a weapon in itself. The flier's body rocked, then a snap of one of its forelimbs struck at the spider's leg, severing it with quick ease. However, when aiming for this strike, the fighter had slewed around so it was now facing me.

Without realizing it, I had come well out into the open. Bulging eyes fastened on me. With Climber still clamped in its hold, the creature half threw itself forward. One of the clawed and blood-dripping forelimbs shot out. My knife was up and ready, and long training rather than conscious thought took over. My arm swung down from the force of the blow, and the knife was ripped from my grasp.

Control—command; I did not summon these Powers—they simply *came,* as weapons of steel might have been thrust into my stinging hand. Nothing remained but those eyes, and because they were not human, they could not be read for anger or fear.

I—will! I—will! There was no time for any incantation, nor did I know how words of Power could be attuned to what must be done. Something new had been aroused in me, and it took full hold of my body in that moment.

My hand went up, though now I held no knife. From my fingers burst blue fire, dispatched in separate darts. Straight at those bulbous eyes they streaked through the air.

The monster reared back then, and, even with the weight of Climber still attached, it attempted to open its wings wider. Suddenly the air filled with a burst of nearly overpowering stench. At the same moment, the head of the thing was engulfed in fire. I threw myself back as it lunged toward me and went down, falling partly over the ravaged body of the spider.

My hand, still shaking, dropped nerveless against my side into the full current of the water. What I had done, I could not accept. When Bina had wrought with Power she had not sought to kill—in fact, we had never thought to use our Gift except as a test against some rival force manifested by the Dark. That it could *kill*—!

Shaking my head, I continued to stare at the two dead creatures. Then I remembered—Climber! That scouring leg, which had attempted to scrape him away, must have left grievous wounds, and those should be tended.

I could not see any sign of scarlet fur. Had the flying creature, during its last struggle, succeeded in flinging the cat-creature off? The stream about my legs was tainted with ichor from which a stifling smell arose, and I forced myself through stinking scum that lay upon the water.

Now I felt a faint mind plea and followed it. Climber had indeed been hurled away. Coming to the clearer bank, I won up the slippery earth to see the walling brush shiver as Climber's head broke through, and he crawled on his belly to join me. Protruding from his well-toothed jaws was a portion of the flier's limb. The nightmare insect might have shaken him off, but he had taken his battle trophy with him.

He had been wounded indeed—the attacker had raked long grooves on his sides. I drew a hand gently over his head. We might not be able to communicate beyond emotions, but I Sent, as clearly as I could, a message praising the heroic deed he had done. A moment later I Sent again, this time for Bina, a call that her skill in healer's aid was needed. Being careful where and how I touched him, I strove to settle Climber's head on my knee. He spat the foul limb from his mouth and heaved a great sigh, as I sought to reassure him by mind-touch.

Ten

Tamara

We were not yet rid of danger. As I tried to do what I could for Climber, my sisters gathered from the inner cave what medicaments they could find, I began to hear rustlings in the brush coming from the other side of the stream near that dire battlefield.

Climber lifted his head a fraction to look up at me. Faintly I caught his warning. I did not even have the knife now, neither could I run for shelter.

Heads appeared, very close to the ground as if their owners advanced by belly-crawl. Dark brownish fur made a thick, spiny covering even on the sharply pointed foreportion of their heads; the same thick pelt also concealed legs—if they possessed such limbs at all. The wiry hair formed a mask wherein no sign of eyes could be detected. Yet three—no, four of the creatures had now pushed their way free of the brush and made directly for the insect bodies.

Climber's jaws parted, but he did not utter a sound. He did not need to; I could read his growing fear in other ways. I could not move him alone. Were these newcomers, now pulling and tearing at the carcasses, so intent upon food that they would not notice us? But Bina, Cilla—they must not walk into this banquet of scavengers!

Quickly I Sent a warning, but that was a wrong choice.

One of the things, which had climbed on the already near-shredded paunch of the spider, spun around to face in my direction, its head manifestly raised as high as its unseen neck could be extended.

I still could not detect any eyes, but I was sure it had sighted us. It half rolled down the blood-drenched body and turned downstream. Climber strove to sit up. Stones washed by the water lay just below us, but those were well out of my reach. And there were four of the creatures. The other three had stopped feasting to turn heads toward us.

My hands—I worked those fingers. I had been able to blast the flier with Power. Only now, as I inwardly sought the key to release that force again, my effort was in vain. It was true: the exercise of energy in the use of Talent had depleted me; never before had I reached so deep as when I slew the airborne monster. Time would be needed to carefully nurse my Gift into full strength once more.

Sabina

As CILLA AND I came into the open under the mountain arch again, I grasped the knife in one hand and held tightly with the other the tote Cilla had found. In that sack I carried what might be used for Climber's wounds, though those remedies I was accustomed to use were not to be had in this place.

As the stream ran straight here, we were able to sight Tam and Climber, his brilliant fur like a beacon fire. Between us lay two monstrous bodies so badly torn that some pieces of flesh had fallen into the water. The horrible mess exuded a putrid stench that set us coughing.

Over, in, and around the mutilated flesh other movement now showed. It appeared as if a number of balls were bouncing, gathering on the other side of the stream from Tam and Climber.

Water flowed between my sister and these new arrivals, yes, but the stream was shallow. Perhaps the ball-things could either leap it or swim.

Cilla crowded against me, and her hand closed on the fork handle.

With that implement in her hand, she struck out before me to trot along the right-hand bank towards Tam and Climber. When I would have followed her, though, my bare feet slipped on slick clay and I went down, trying to save my burden as I fell.

Midway between Tam and me, Cilla halted. Her stance was now that of one holding a hunting spear, save that the shaft of the fork was so short that she had difficulty readying her cast. Nevertheless, she hurled the improvised spear with force and, unwieldy though it was, it struck home. One of the round creatures that had indeed taken to the stream squeaked in long, drawn-out notes, then tumbled back into the reeds along the water's edge. It struggled but appeared unable to clamber out. The fork had gone with it.

Cilla had taken out one of the attackers, but she had, in turn, lost her weapon. Just as I reached her side, her Send came.

"Feed me!" She pushed against me until our shoulders touched, skin-to-skin.

I turned the Send into Power, and Cilla drew from me. We had done this sometimes in the past when a course of action demanded great strength, but never in an hour of such need. I swayed under the drain of my energy, as force flowed from me.

Her right hand was held high; however, the weapon she called upon was no spear. Each finger wore a blue flame, even as does a lighted candle. I watched my sister snap-flick that flame at each of the balls in turn.

Screeches rent the air as flames settled in the mass of hair covering the ball-beasts. The Power drain from me increased. I caught at the trunk of a sapling, fore-scout of the wood, and held desperately, dropping the sack at my feet, intent only on providing what Cilla needed.

By now I was dizzy, and only the young tree supported me as Cilla's hand fell heavily to her side. No more screeches sounded. All that remained were small fires scattered about, puffing forth nauseating smoke.

I cannot remember how we pulled ourselves to Tam and Climber, but we did and I managed to use my training in the treatment of wounds. Tam had suffered no bodily hurt, but her face was drawn and haggard, her eyes half closed. A probe told me that, as had Cilla's and mine, her normal energy had been far depleted.

She told us her tale of the battle at intervals, visibly rousing her flagging strength after each pause. Cilla held out her own hand and moved the fingers separately, crooking, then straightening them.

"How—?" She might have been asking that question of herself rather than of us.

I finished spreading a cream of herbs squeezed in oil onto Climber's cuts. Now I raised my own hands to stare at them. I considered the invocation, which I had never used before, in my own spontaneous gestures before the statues in the cave. Though I had not used any known or trained part of my Talent then, I must have awakened the same force Tam and Cilla had just used against living enemies.

Now I looked to Tam and then to Cilla.

"What have we done?" I asked. I had always kept in mind the instructions of our mother and of Duty: do not try to use Talent except in ways lawful and wholly understood. To use unwittingly Power that needs firm control may be equal to calling upon the Dark.

Still we had done this, and it had taken its toll of us. We all moved slowly, finding further action difficult.

Cilla

As BINA WORKED over Climber with Tam's help, I stirred around, gathering up two water-washed tree limbs of some girth. Then I pulled loose vines, which were clumsy to handle, but could be forced into a kind of netting between the deadwood lengths. It was a difficult task. My right hand—I stopped now and then to inspect it, still in awe of what I had unconsciously done—scarcely obeyed me.

The heavy stench of the dead monsters made it increasingly hard to breathe, while the water, now running past the bank on which we crouched, was polluted to the point that some small forms of life were rising to the thick broth on the surface belly up.

Bina sat back on her heels. Climber lay inert, his head still resting on Tam's knee where she had supported him during Bina's ministrations. His eyes were closed.

"How is he?" I asked.

Bina did not turn around as she answered, "I have done all that I could without proper materials."

Tam sat up a little straighter. "We had best get him back to safety. There well may be other scavengers."

Thus we carried him, Tam and I holding the poles of the stretcher, while Bina held up her greasy hands, being unable to rinse them in the polluted stream. To speed us on our way, we heard a rustling in the brush, undoubtedly heralding the arrival of other and perhaps even more dangerous inhabitants of the wood.

We did not enter the stream until the water ran clear, though the foul smell traveled with us. However, we were able to pass through the archway in the cliffside without any more trouble.

Climber was still limp as we carefully shifted him onto a nest of bedcovers. Feeling as if we had traveled long on a rough trail, we too sank down around him.

My hand ached and trembled. I could see that both of Tam's shook as she held them up before her, staring at her fingers while crooking and relaxing them. Bina watched both of us with growing concern.

She had washed her hands thoroughly in warm water near where the spring bubbled from the wall. Now she shifted a couple of pots and a flask. As if to reassure herself, she uncorked the flask and held it to her nose, nodding decisively.

"Let me—" It was not a request; it was an order.

Tam stretched out her hands as Bina poured one thick clot of oily substance, then another, onto them. Setting aside the flask, she began to massage them, working the rich salve into Tam's skin.

With a sigh, Tam closed her eyes until Bina was done and all the greasy ointment had vanished. At a signal, I moved near and put out my hand, ready for the same treatment.

Tam roused as though from a doze. The look of contentment she had worn a few moments earlier was gone.

"He makes his point harshly," she said, frowning.

I was startled. "You think that Zolan somehow brought about all this?"

"How better," Tam returned, "to learn the range of our powers? He doubtless knew that we would not be bound here once he had left, but that we would return to the cliff if we could. There are different traps, and some are self-concealing. How could a flier attack prey native to the treetops, where wings could not be used?"

"And if you had failed to stop the thing?"

Tam grimaced. "He might have expected us to run. We were close to his own place of safety."

"If—?" I said slowly as Bina worked her ointment into the skin between my fingers. "Was he here watching?" I demanded.

Tam shrugged. "That could well be."

"But Climber is—close to him—" However, with the thoughts Tam had aroused active in my mind, I was no longer sure of even that.

"Climber." Tam drew her hand over the round head of the creature we hoped lay in natural sleep. "The flier may be a natural enemy of his kind. Seeing it on the ground and deeply occupied, he could not perhaps have been constrained from attack."

Having completed her ministrations, Bina locked arms around raised knees. Her expression was sober.

"What game have we been pulled into? There *is* Power here, but of no kind we know. Is it centered in this Zolan, or is there another who wishes to test us?"

The faint but restorative smell of some herb I could not name arose from my now dry hand, to expel the last lingering odor of evil blood. I could well follow the logic of Tam's reasoning. Had we not yet learned to take nothing for granted—we who believed first in common safety and thereafter in not being playthings of the Dark?

"The report of Lord Quark," I said. That account had been my reading on the last day we had spent with the material our father had left for us. "It spoke of witchcraft—evil summons."

The idea was foreign to us, trained as we were in the use of Talents and the perfecting of those for the common good. Our teachers insisted that Power used for evil purposes corrupted, destroying the user's spirit, so she or he became emptied and rendered ready to be filled by all that was abhorrent to our kind.

Lord Quark had married a Gurly wife. She had suddenly lost her wits, attacking her sister with a snaplock. Afterwards she swore that she had heard spirit-voices that urged her to act. Under superstition aroused by the Hermit-priest of the new religion, she had been burnt as a follower of the Left-hand Path.

Minds are precious things. There are very strict rules for any Talent that is centered, as ours was, in the mind. My head began to ache. All this was only guessing on our part. What if there was no truth in Tam's suggestion as to what had happened? What if it had all befallen only by chance? However, one dared not accept that possibility either.

Climber's eyes opened and he whimpered. Bina went to the stream and dipped up a small basin of water, then brought it back and held it while he drank.

However, he had lapped only twice when his head came up. A moment later, from the shadowed end of the cave, where falls formed the stream, Zolan came into full view.

His eyes were centered on Climber as he came directly to us; then that intense stare shifted to the three of us. His lips were set in a hard line as he barked rather than spoke.

"*How did this happen?*"

Tam got to her feet to face him squarely, arms folded across her breast. That she would be our spokesperson was best, for the end of a battle had been hers.

"Need you ask?"

His frown grew darker. "I ask for what I do not know."

My sister met him eye to eye. "You have told us," she began, "that paths are limited here and dangerous. If you came by the stream trail, then you know well and truly what we had to face. If you got in otherwise, it was by some secret way you have not shared with us.

"We wished to seek that portion of the cliff down which we were forced. We have good reason to believe that our father will arrive there. We have no desire to linger in the Dismals—already we have seen more of what can be met here than we wish."

His cheeks were flushed, his eyes afire. "You were told—no," he changed his sentence. "You have the freedom to search what is not openly before you. But I take it you went forth and met danger. How did you draw Climber to join you in recklessness?"

Being careful not to come any closer to either Tam or Bina, he went on his knees beside the beast, setting both hands to either side of that red-furred head and raising it that he might stare into the great golden eyes.

I could sense a stir—there was a Send in progress between them. The exchange held for some time. Bina carried her various improvised medicaments back to the shelves, where she placed them together a little apart from the other stores arrayed there. Tam, still facing Climber and the man, retreated to seat herself within touching distance of me. We continued to watch and draw deep upon our store of patience.

At length he once more settled Climber's head back into the nest. Still he continued to watch the creature as he got to his feet.

Finally he gave us his attention. "Who—*what* are you?"

Tam was prepared to answer, speaking as if she must explain to some questioning child. "We are, as was told you, three daughters to the Earl of Verset. As to what we may be—we are also of the Scorpy line, and we were born with the Talent and have been lessoned in its use—though what came to us this day was greater than we have known before. Now—who and what are *you?*" She fired that query in the crisp tone of a squad commander who must be answered whether the questioned one wishes or no.

A strange look came into Zolan's face. His left hand arose, and its fingertips traced the faint path of an old scar.

"I am the Protector," he said slowly. "This is my land, and I must know what walks here. Other captives have been delivered by men of blood— even a woman and a child. But none of them lived long, and also they did not have what you claim as Talent.

"You believe that I set the urgle on you, do you not?"

He spoke to Tam grimly, hostilely, then eyed Bina and me. After a pause he continued:

"Your belief has a twisted logic: if I am what you think me to be, would I not test you openly, pitting my inner strength against yours?"

Tam did not answer him, though she continued to hold her head high so she could meet him gaze for gaze. It was Bina who spoke instead.

"Now is no time to play with questions, Protector. We started to go where we might meet with those who care for us. Instead, our path was blocked by deadly creatures already in battle. Tam finished them; Cilla dealt with the scavengers. It should certainly be plain to you that we did what must be done for our own protection." She drew her hand down the length of her scaled jerkin.

"By this stuff I am able to guess that not all perils of the Dismals are insects grown to fight on equal terms with our breed. What else do you herd here, Zolan?"

"Much which you would not understand, Lady of the Scorpys. As for meeting with your father and his armsmen—there is no hope of that."

"And why not?" I asked, still nursing my hand against my breast. I continued to feel a ripple of heat running through the flesh Bina had treated.

"Because those searchers have come—and gone."

I shrank back. Was that the truth or rather a lie intended to destroy our courage?

"You have been here," he continued, "some four days. Since you were exhausted so fully when you came, you slept. On the second day, a party of horsemen came along the clifftop. Those who left you had destroyed the ropes for lowering or climbing. This other party stayed a full day, lighting fires at night. In the evening of the second day, they rode away. Did not your 'Talent' reach to them?" he added. "They went easily enough."

"To return," Tam snapped, "with what will be needed to aid us! Scorpys care for their own. Or will it be your task, Zolan Protector, to rouse the monsters of this dark land against them if they try it?"

I shivered again. Her words created a mind-picture that sickened me.

He shrugged. "I know only that they are gone. You do not begin to understand the nature of the Dismals—compared to the life you knew, its ways are strange and dangerous. But you must accept that you are here, and here you will stay—"

Tam held up her hand as evidence. "We believe your beast has told you what I did with two of these. Our weapons are not man-made but are woman-born, honed and ready. We shall give no bond that we will remain here any longer than it takes us to find a way out."

Again he shrugged. "So be it. However, if you go searching for such a way, then I must be with you, as is my duty."

"No doubt," Bina said crushingly, "you will also make sure that we shall be made aware of the very worst of the fates awaiting us."

To my utter surprise, he laughed, not in anger but as if she had told some jest.

"Lady Scorpy, you are very adept at belittling or bad-naming me. No, this much I will say." He swung around to face the seated beings by the shelves as if to attract *their* attention. "I will see as best I can that no urgles will swoop, nor crunchers spin to web you."

There was that in his voice that made me believe him, and that trust raised in my mind another question. He announced himself as a Protector, but those with such duties were always liege to some overlord whose commands they followed. Whose orders carried weight here?

We were uneasy, yet we must needs accept his promise for the time being. We could not tell how far the Dismals stretched, but I knew, without discussing the issue with Tam and Bina, that time was going to be spent in exploring. Unless our father would return with the equipment for descent—

Our host might have caught my thought, for I had no ward up. Now he looked directly at me.

"Proof exists for them that such a search would be useless."

I called up one of those clear memories, rooted in the Talent, to picture the spot where we had literally been dumped. It was open, with gravel flooring it, and no brush spread wide enough to conceal us.

"The blankets!" Tam was on her feet.

"Yes, the blankets," he agreed. "Torn as they were by Climber to set you free, they must present from above the look of having been mauled by beasts who would also have accounted for the three of you."

So logical was that suggestion that we were forced to accept it. But the deeper truth, which we need not allow him to learn, was that Mother and Duty would know we still lived. Had we been torn out of bodily existence, they would have felt our going at once, for so does Talent link to Talent in a family line. No, they would sense that we were not dead.

Send touched me from two directions. My sisters likewise held that hope.

Thus we looked forward to uncertainty, danger, the need to stand unshaken in a strange land where we could not imagine what might await us.

Eleven

Tamara

We expected Zolan to make one of his quick vanishing moves again. He did not, however; instead, he reseated himself beside Climber, leaning forward to draw several breaths.

"Voreker berries, and groser oil—you also are healers." It was not a question but rather a statement of recognition. "Your Talent leads in several directions," he finished.

"That which beckons each the most is what we follow the first," I answered. He had given us much to think about. I was sure that presenting a calm front to him would be the most prudent course.

"My sister Sabina has healer hands and knowledge." I nodded in her direction. My recent show of anger might never have been. "And my sister Drucilla creates such needlework as people sometimes deem magic. She can also hold in her hands an artifact from a people unknown and speak of the one who fashioned it and those who used it."

Intrigue him—that was the best ploy now. He might even believe my words to be groundless boasting and underestimate me for that.

"And you?"

"If we had swords at hand, I could show you."

That was a statement of fact; I was not bepraising myself.

He smiled again. "I do not think I would choose to face any of you in anger, steel or no steel."

I relaxed a little. Keep him talking, explaining, even instructing. Having too much knowledge was impossible, and the more we could learn about the Dismals and its inhabitants, the better.

"Those things without—" I asked the first of many of my own questions, to test whether this openness would continue. "There are some like them to be found in the upper land, yet any such can be covered by a hand. The green bag-thing has small kin, weavers of webs that fill dark corners in our towers. We name it spider—it could be crushed between two fingers, if you would. How comes it about that, in the land we knew, such creatures are small and not to be feared, while here they are monsters that can kill men with ease?"

"I do not know," Zolan replied slowly. "Your topside life is as strange to me as the Dismals are to you. As I have said, the dangers to be faced here are many, and one must be ever on guard."

Bina rose and went to Climber, resting a finger lightly on his nose.

"Fever. Tell me this, Zolan. Could that flier poison as well as cut? If so, what might be the antidote for that? I used your supplies by scent and guess alone. Should I have made other choices?"

"Some creatures here carry poison in both fang and claw," our host answered, "but the urgle you call flier is not so armed. Those herbs you used were what I would have drawn upon for the same purpose."

Bina might have been reassured, but she was not finished. Now she pointed to the seated figures. "Gods, past rulers, personification of virtues— or powers of Darkness?"

Zolan did not answer at once. I thought that he sought for the words he needed.

"Lady Sabina of the Scorpys, some things are not to be spoken. I will say this: after a fashion they have a part in Dismal life, even if they are only of hard-baked clay."

"If I offend," she said quickly, "grant me pardon."

Ah, when a road is abruptly closed, it is generally because some secret must be sheltered. It would be best not to probe any further here.

"Of what manner is life above?" He changed the subject.

Could our host indeed be utterly ignorant of what chanced in Gurlyon?

We launched into history, spoke of wars, of rulers weak or forceful, recounting the unending torment of the Border and those living there. Though we did not interrupt each other, we all had our part in that telling. We had no reason to conceal from Zolan the tumult above. It was better that he should know that the upper world was a land of armed men ready for any foray.

Once he got up and went to the supplies, returning with a stoppered jug, four small bowls stacked together, and a box of dried fruit. We balanced the bowls, sipped at the liquid he had poured into them from the jug, and rested for a space.

"So." He swallowed a mouthful of the wine and spoke. "It would seem that those above know no more of peace than we do here. This hermit who you say came to the king: what part does he play?"

We told him, Cilla dwelling on the rules Forfind had given his followers and how those were used against women. Bina added proof with a swift description of that Udo Chosen, his follower, who had so broken custom. I added the fact that Udo had demanded us from our captors to answer purposes of his own.

"The hermit is said to have come from this mountain land." I delivered the most damning rumor last, watching Zolan closely as I did so. However, if he had known anything of that troublemaker, he did not show it. He made no comment concerning Udo Chosen. Instead he sat quietly, not looking to us three but rather somehow into the distance beyond us, as if occupied by thoughts of his own.

When no more questions were asked from either side, our host roused at last.

"You wish to return to that land, though it may be torn by battle?"

"It is our own," I made reply. "We know its ways and can foresee many dangers, even as you can here. There we have purpose, as you have your duties in this land we call cursed."

He was standing now. He still did not look to us but glanced again at those seated figures. "If it is indeed meant that you return, then a way will be opened."

Though he had insisted that no way existed out of the Dismals, now he seemed to be suggesting that there was. I did not push the question, for it appeared that he had understood our position and was somewhat moved by it. We must let the matter rest for now.

Bina once again brought stream water for Climber and held the bowl while he lapped.

Sabina

I HAD TENDED animals before. Though this red furred beast bore no resemblance to the sleuthhounds, still he seemed to be answering well to the same care I would have given one of those if they were injured. Zolan had recognized my healing usages, and he undoubtedly stored the supplies I had studied over. I might learn some further ministrations, if he would teach, for new skills are often developed under different circumstances.

Such were my thoughts as I made Climber as comfortable as I could.

"You know varca and thorble, quant, sizzal?"

Looking up, I shook my head. "I might well know such, but not under the names you give them."

I was all but certain he had touched my thoughts of a moment earlier. Dared I try an outright Send to make sure? No, I decided. There was no reason to let him learn any more of our Gift than he might already suspect. At the same time, I determined to indeed learn all I could without revealing too much in return.

Thus began our shaky partnership with this Lord of the Dismals. The three of us united quickly in agreement to the peace as well as we could.

Drucilla

CLIMBER HEALED SPEEDILY. Though we had no way in this mountain pocket of recognizing the passage of time, it was three sleeping-periods later that he found his feet and wavered unsteadily to stand by me, bumping his head against my shoulder. I snapped off a word, which would never have been uttered in my mother's solar, as I dropped the needle and had to search for it by running my hands over the rock floor.

Having discovered that Zolan had a supply of cured skins available, with his consent I was endeavoring to add to our supply of clothing with better-fitting garments. I kept to the same general style: long breeches and laced jerkins. However, I found a pleasure of sorts in working the various skins and choosing the colors.

While I stitched, I raised my eyes now and then to the seated ones. Zolan had never given us any real accounting of them. But I had dreamed—a dream from which Tam had shaken me awake because of my cries against the evil that was a part of it.

I stood in another cave, the floor of which was thick with fragments of fire-bitten clay. Here stood broken seats, figures partly crushed, heads snapped off, barrel bodies opened. From those jug bodies had been shaken blackened bones and stark gray ashes. This had been a place of burial once; now it was a place of terror and darkness. The evil curdled the air about, lapping at me greedily; a Shadow entity slavered for feeding, but its hunger was frustrated.

At that point, Tam had become aware that I was threatened by a peril from beyond and had intervened with Power to awaken me.

Were those two on the shelf really hollow containers, filled with the remains of dwellers in the Dismals? Did not we of the South shape coffins of another kind, though we did not place them to oversee the daily activities of the living?

There was far too much of this place we did not know. I stuck the needle almost viciously through an odd piece of near-bluish scaled material I had found and was attempting to develop into a cloak; like the skin of a serpent, the hide would shed water. Such garments would be a necessity for future explorations, for rain was now falling heavily outside the cave. We daily visited that door on the world. Three times now we had faced downpours. These skyfalls did not appear to prevent Zolan from making what must be duty visits outside; however, he did have a cloak to cover most of him, tall as he was, of the same stuff I was working on.

Even now he came splashing along the water trail to struggle out of the straps that kept a bag safely on his shoulders. Climber limped slowly over to join him and thrust a nose into the bulging top of the bag.

"Lady Sabina!" He looked at me.

I shook my head. It seemed odd to me that he was unable to tell the three of us apart. However, he had never attempted to probe, so he might not even desire to identify us closely.

"She has washed bedding. You will find her and Tamara by the fire-hole drying it."

"Later, then." He had dug into the bag to produce a packet bound up in a piece of netting, which he laid to one side. Then came something larger, wadded in a large leaf. Climber inspected it and uttered a sound rather like the beginning of a purr.

"Later," Zolan promised the beast. Next to appear was a roll of clothlike stuff, and with it in hand, he approached me.

"What think you of this?" His question held a note of boyish pride. My father's youngest squire had spoken so on the famous day of the Wiltson Hunt when luck had stood beside him and he had brought down a prize boar. Tweaking the roll, Zolan shook the contents free and held what he had to show, shoulder high, to cascade down to his soggy boots.

Fluttering out in the air was a square of—could it be *lace*?—of a size to cover a large table. I put aside my task and scrambled up to study it closer, reaching out fingers to touch and snatching them back again as speedily when I identified the material.

"Web—it is spiderweb!"

He nodded, again with that air of pride. "One as perfect as this," he declared, satisfaction filling his voice, "is seldom found!"

I glanced to his hands. He was holding the gauzy weaving by the upper corners, but it did not seem to be clinging to his fingers. If that had been wrought as a trap, as most webs were, the lines should have been sticky to effectively imprison any creature blundering into it. Surely this must have been woven by that green bag-horror we had fought, or at least one of its kin!

"Does it not stick?" I pointed to his hands, but he was actually pleating the web. No, it did not adhere, either to his flesh or its own substance where line touched line.

"Not after it is laid overnight in rain-wet sorchti leaves. Here, see for yourself." He had rerolled the filmy fiber and now tossed it to me.

Without wanting to, I caught it, finding it soft as the finest Falligan lace from Isci Port overseas. I shook the web-cloth out a little and deliberately tried to tear at one of the threads. There was no give, neither was there any parting of its fibers.

What would the court ladies—even Her Majesty—give for such veiling! I, who loved new fabrics, was quickly won. For a fleeting second or two, I held a mind-picture of a booth merchant showing such to a gathering mob.

"That is true—weaving like this might well start another war!" Once more Zolan responded to an idea that had not been spoken aloud. "I have found and preserved parts of these webs, but even I have not before seen one entire. This is the trap set in the treetops by the gorm—the bag-thing you saw die on the riverbank. Gorms can catch creatures as large as Climber and others that dwell aloft. The females are the spinners, and among those they would entrap are the much smaller males."

I did not ask the reason why they would entrap those of their own species, for I thought I knew. The way of some of our own spiders must be followed by these noisome giants: to mate with, then destroy, any unfortunate male driven by nature to seek them out.

Folding the web with care, I put it down beside my work, to catch up a piece of the bluish, scaled stuff. "No web is this, nor skin nor fur of a beast—how got you it?"

He had been lightening his bag by emptying it of more leaf-wrapped contents, but he glanced up to see what I held. For a moment he stood very still, staring at the strip.

"That is belly skin of gars—a young one. A gars . . ." Now his eyes turned to me as if he wanted very much to know my reaction to what he would say. "A gars," he began again, "is a water dweller by day and a shore hunter by night, for it produces limbs along its undersurface to aid it on land. Full-grown, its length is near that of the second shelf there—" He was pointing to the one on which much of the supplies were piled. Truly the Dismals held monsters! He must have slain this creature also—or had he, as with the web, come upon a body which had already been torn apart? I suddenly had no wish to return to my sewing.

He approached closer to my workplace. "This is also gars." He was holding now a similar scaled skin; however, the new hide was not blue-silver but rather a brilliant purple, in color like to a court robe. "This was taken from a much older male."

Dropping what he held, he groped for another scrap, then—"Wait!" He interrupted himself, sitting back on his heels. "You have the skill; perhaps you can put to good use another treasure!"

At once our host was off, heading to the other end of the cave, but he did not get as far as the fire-pit before he sought the wall to his left. How he used his hands there I could not see clearly, but he lifted out a section of what had seemed solid stone to draw forth from the opening behind it a sagging length, again wrapped in dark leaves. This he handled with a more delicate touch than he had even given the web.

It was rather an unwieldy armful, and Zolan had to struggle to keep it from dragging along the rock under foot. Then he unrolled it. I looked—and was ensorcelled as I had never been, even with the intricately woven silk from across the sea.

Color played over its surface, muted or shiningly alive. I knelt and ran my hands across the soft, unusually patterned surface. Not skin, feathers, or scales—it was more like thickly rooted fur with an upstanding nap. The background was a purplish gray, the hue of sky darkened by an approaching storm. Against this background gleamed what looked like eyes of a silvery hue, which carried a near-metallic sheen. Its texture was such as to cause one to desire to continue smoothing it without stop. I looked to Zolan for explanation.

"It is a quillian wing," he answered my unspoken question. "The air at night provides the hunting range. This is only part of a pinion."

Whatever its nature, the quillian, I knew, could not be a bird, for this substance had no kinship with feathers. Another giant insect of sorts?

Though the Lord of the Dismals had this wealth of wonders for me—and it made me start to plan what might be done to display each beauty to best advantage—so did he later empty out seeds, flower, roots, chunks of sap gum and other such products of his land before Sabina. He explained what plant or tree bore each specimen as he laid it out, also making clear what value it held for the harvester. As Sabina listened closely, so did we.

"You name this marsh lily." Bina looked down at the broad petals, white with green veins, of a bruised flower resting on her palm.

"Yes, wet your fingers; take a petal in this manner." He pulled at the blossom until, with her aid in holding it, he had it free. Dipping his prize in Climber's water bowl, he rubbed it vigorously until lather appeared and spread. At the same time, a fragrance arose. Soap, then, of a sort—and I, for one, was going to take advantage of *that* as soon as possible!

Tamara

I WATCHED ZOLAN put forth effort to teach and entertain us. The more we could learn, the better. I could well understand how he managed to entrance Cilla and Bina by his display of what most appealed to their Talents.

But did this sweet coating conceal a bitterness waiting beneath? He had spoken of taking us exploring. The rain had given an excuse to postpone that promise. Did he, or whoever stood behind him—for I was sure that one Power did so—think to lull us in this manner into an acceptance of our lot, at least for a while?

I thought of the dream that had set Cilla crying out in small gasps before I had managed to rouse her. In those few moments, as I brought her back to consciousness, I had shared a small fraction of her ordeal. That cave of the disturbed dead—surely that must lie somewhere along the cliff walls. A people had been deeply offended against by what had happened there, for death should be treated with solemn dignity.

Had it been Breakswords such as Maclan, come treasure hunting, who had caused that destruction, mistaking the coffins of another race for vessels of wealth? Like it or not, we three were of the grave violators' kin. Hostages or scapegoats—to either role we would surely answer at some future time.

Twelve

Tamara

The rain stopped at last, but not before that part of the stream running through the cave had overflowed its banks. We waded out now, with coolish water rising from knee to waist level. One advantage of our scaled clothing was that water did not penetrate it. The pack bags with which Zolan equipped us were of the same material, keeping dry the supplies whose usage he explained as he packed his own before us.

We emerged into the same pale sunlight we had earlier seen. The air about us felt dank with moisture, and strange scents wove through it. Climber still limped a little but he had sharply refused to be left behind.

Our way ran for only a short distance in the stream; then our guide waved left, using a staff he had brought to aid in climbing the bank. The water was well up to its edge, and reeds marked it with their green tips.

Accustomed as I was to rough travel, for at times I had played squire for my father, I did not see any possible break in the green forest wall. Insects danced in the turgid air around us—not the monsters we had seen, nor those Zolan had described, yet larger than the familiar ones of the outer world. However, because we had rubbed our bodies and sleeked our hair with potions Zolan offered us for protection, those would-be suckers and biters dove determinedly toward us, yet did not attack.

Three Hands for Scorpio

Again Zolan used his staff, pushing aside a thick curtain of interlocked vines to uncover a narrow path burrowing into the forest. Onto that we threaded in single file.

Climber brought up the end of our party directly behind me. I found myself playing rear guard. Looking and listening, I tried to set into memory all that might be of importance. Twice Zolan halted to point out perils. One was a cluster of scarlet flowers, its hue so brilliant that fire might be ablaze at the heart of each trumpet-shaped blossom. These grew at the very end of a vine that, for the rest of its length as far as could be seen, was bare.

As Zolan held his staff near, the ropelike growth swung forward. For a moment or two, the flowers clamped like mouths on the wood shaft, then dropped off while the vine lashed about in frenzy. On the long rod, oily moisture beaded in patches, and the wood beneath was turning yellow. He plunged the staff again and again into masses of leaves to cleanse it.

His second enemy waited at the edge of the path, which deviated to avoid the crumbling bole of a giant tree. There, growing from the rot of the wood, were what might be thick fingers of many hands, scattered in patches. Once more we stopped and he waved us back a little but not so far that we could not see his staff again in use.

Under the blows he rained on the closest cluster of finger-things, a yellowish dust spewed forth. Perhaps the current dankness of the air was what settled it quickly. The small cloud did not spread far, but coated the wood where it fell with a yellow slime, while we caught a whiff of a strong stench.

Though we went ever on guard, there were no further perils-in-wait as we proceeded. The path we followed began to rise. The tangled wall of vine dipped on either side.

My soft boot skidded a little and, regaining my balance quickly, I stooped to look. My foot had struck against something very solid, and it was all that had saved me from a fall. When the muck of fallen leaves had been scraped away, I sighted stone set flat. Having armed myself, soon after we quitted the stream, with a rough staff of my own, I dug farther to discover not just one stone block but another joined to it—and another.

Climber joined me, sniffed at the hole I had dug, and then pushed at me, plainly urging me on. I obeyed, not wanting to lose sight of the others.

I scratched away with my staff, and what I uncovered was a hidden pavement. Stone-covered roads were known in the South, and great care was taken to preserve them. The Northling tracks on the other side of the border were just that: crude trails that did not encourage travel.

Yet another scrap of mystery. I was minded to share it with my companions, but my find receded into memory soon enough as we came out of the tunnel of thick growth into the open.

Here a jumble of stones, from gravel size to boulders near the proportion and shape of a landsman's den, faced us. The ground was fairly level; I shut my eyes and opened them again, wanting to be sure I was not reading more into the site than was truth. Somehow I was sure that this had been a fort or perhaps a small settlement. Some of the larger stones had splotches, which caught the brighter sun as though shards of glass were embedded in them.

The three ahead of me had paused, and my sisters were looking back with growing impatience. I whacked at one of the glassy patches with my staff as I passed, and thereby made sure it was *not* a substance of the rock that bore it.

"What keep was this, Zolan? Who ruled it?" I asked as I came up.

"Who knows?" He shrugged. "It is very old. But, yes, it is part of a large shelter of sorts. I have dug here and there," he confessed, "being curious. But nothing has lingered through time but the stones."

"So?" I had gone to one knee and was using the stone-bladed knife issued me to pick at a glint where one of the stones lay half buried in the earth. What I freed was about the size of one of our Southern plums, and one end looked as if it had been shattered. But the rest was the texture of a carefully smoothed cabochon of precious stone.

As I rubbed the earth from it, the sunlight claimed it at once, giving a warm golden color yet not a metallic sheen. Though I had seen royal jewels aplenty, and handled some, this—mineral? metal?—was new.

"Sun stone!" Zolan looked down at my find.

"That gem is to be found here?" Again the treasure story took on more reality.

He was frowning as he stared at it closely, kneeling beside me to do so. "I have found no trace of any mine nor any stones in a rough state," he commented slowly.

"But you recognized it—gave it a name."

"I have found three of its kind—and the name is what I myself gave them."

Like my sisters, I possessed a strong interest in the lore of stones. From the time when, as a small child, I watched my mother robe for court, her jewel chest open, I have had a fascination with gems, not for their value but rather for their shape and color. And when my later studies suggested that some minerals were used for the focusing of Talents, my desire for more knowledge became a need.

This stone—if stone it was—seemed warm. I felt an odd twinge in my hand where it lay like a distilled droplet of sunlight. Then it *was* a Power stone—and how it might be used, I knew I must speedily learn.

All at once I sensed a listener-in on my mind. Instinctively, I stiffened, and my hand made a fist to conceal what I held. Again this Dismal dweller had caught my thought as though it had been a Send. I looked up to meet his eyes. He had made a Send, strange and new—but mind-speech not unlike that I had known and answered all my life.

"Power stone." He used that inner speech to confirm my belief. "It came to you, Lady Tamara. Use it well."

I had been dubious about our little expedition, yet I was certain that, in some way, I had acquired a Gift meant for me. But why? And did it come from this man I was now watching warily—or another?

Sabina

TAM DID NOT have to reassure us by any Send that what she found was indeed a prize. And that *she* had found it meant, to both Cilla and me, it was intended for her use. We did feel the bite of envy, but, knowing the nature of such Power, we also knew that to neither of us would this earthborn treasure answer. Nor did Zolan appear to dispute her ownership; rather, he started ahead again with no further word. Could we take his abrupt departure as a sign that he might covet the find?

We wove a way through the tumble of stones to learn that the territory it covered was much larger than we had first thought. When our guide called a halt, we could see a cliff wall marking the end of this section of the Dismals.

A small stretch of level pavement remained, and on this rough flooring we settled now to chew on tough smoked meat curled into rods. These we rubbed in a sweet-sour paste and took careful sips from the clay water bottles we carried.

I settled myself to look back along the way we had come. I was sure that if a careful observer stared long enough, a pattern would begin to emerge from the ruins. Finally my attention centered on one of those ripples of glass which threaded a nearby stone.

As a child, I had watched clouds to see pictures form and dissolve, one after another. Now this glitter-encrusted line before me seemed to do likewise.

First it suggested a long triangular pattern, and the word *viper* flashed into my mind. However, it did not retain that shape: instead, it shifted on the stone, the portion pointing earthward becoming more sharply visible.

I closed my eyes—the reflection from it hurt! I knew glass in many forms, but none like this. In the South, the nobility and wealthy merchants had glass in the windows of dwellings and other buildings. Finely crafted, it formed drinking vessels for royal feasts, and, backed with silver, it could picture all who stood before it. It was also fashioned into beads and ornaments, some of which were able to outshine even true gems. Women as well as men spun subtleties of such substance—

Suddenly heat beat upon me, intense as that from a furnace where glass was so wrought. I felt confined, as the heat increased until I was gasping, and my skin felt ready to crack under heat and pressure.

"Bina!"

I tried to twist free from the hold on my shoulder, for its firmness only added to my torment.

"*Bina!*"

The darkness of my captivity departed; the heat vanished. I opened my eyes to look upon only a grayish white line crooking across stone.

"Glass."

Tam looked from me to the crystal-shot boulder. "Of a sort," she agreed. "Though how it was formed, who knows." She stepped away to the side of the stone and picked at the encrusted line with her fingers. Cilla, at my other side, looked at me with concern.

"What is wrong, Bina?"

I forced a laugh. "Too much sun, I suppose—that, and far too many mysteries. I want answers."

"So do we all," declared Tam with some force.

I glanced around. Zolan appeared to have left us. But before I could comment on our host's absence, Climber's head showed at near ground level where an extra-large stone was earth-planted a little way ahead. Then Zolan reappeared, beckoning us forward.

For a short distance I felt light-headed, as if the upper part of my body was far too heavy and I might lose balance. When Cilla tried to help me, I shook my unsteady head and pushed her away, ashamed of my weakness. I continued to pick my way carefully, for I had dealt too many times with sprains and bone-breaks of others who had taken tumbles, and this ground was a maze of traps for the unwary.

The sun was well to westward when we came out of the ruins, much closer to the mountain-mark of the high cliff. Here, without any order from Zolan, Climber led the party.

His nose dropped now and then close to the ground. That very long tail lay curled up over his back, yet threatened to touch the earth. I could sense the rise of excitement in him—our four-footed companion was on the hunt. By Tam's report, he had attacked the flying monster that could have been more than a match for him. Knowing that he held such strength within himself made one uneasy.

What we did come upon was a tree trunk, its more slender top jammed into a ragged hole in the cliff well above our heads. The branches remaining were but stubs but, upon closer study, we could see that other short lengths had been inserted into the trunk to form a ladder of sorts.

Tamara

AT ZOLAN'S ORDER we shed our packs, and he tied them together with a section of rope he removed from his own. Not for the first time I was glad that we had been shorn of the full skirts to which we had been accustomed, since such a climb faced us.

As my father's sometime companion, I was more used to such activity than Cilla, or Bina, toward whom I glanced at intervals since she appeared unlike herself. However, as we approached the rude ladder more closely, I decided that it looked safe enough, even though it had been set at a steep angle. Zolan swung up by foot- and handhold with the ease of one following a well-known trail. I started after as soon as he had pulled himself through the upper crevice, leaving the rope lashed to our packs dangling behind.

He flattened himself against the right wall of the portal and pulled me through. It was a tight passage, and rough stone rasped my left arm.

I pushed on into the gloom to leave room for the others. None of the dim glow shone from the walls here, so I hesitated against venturing too far from the entrance. Our guide might know this way well enough to move on without light, but I was wary.

At last we were all aloft and had once again taken up our packs, which Zolan had pulled up. Climber had come last, again forming a rear guard, while the Protector was at the van. However, now we were leashed together by his rope, and thus, as we headed into the night, we were forced to depend entirely on his choice of path.

As the light from the cave entrance finally gave way to the swallowing dark, uneasiness grew within me. My trust began to diminish. Zolan had said nothing of our goal. Perhaps he was now intent on showing us that he had spoken the truth: that this wall-rent might seem to promise a path to the Upper World, but that the promise was false.

On impulse I brought out my find from the ruins. It was warm to my touch, but it did not give forth any radiance. Yet that warmth began to build, cool, and build again. Each time the heat increased, more of it lingered at the fading. It was following a rhythm close to that of the beating of a heart.

The guide rope suddenly pulled to the right and down!

"Take it carefully." Zolan's voice seemed to boom through the dark, and the slight pull of the cord leading us slowed.

Underfoot, our support was indeed changing, dipping a little more with each step. We had not gone far before air moved about my head and shoulders and I felt a sensation as if I had advanced from under a roof into the open.

With this feeling of being in an unconfined place came also the beginning of light, though it was a very faint glow and it came from beneath us to the right. Now I understood: we traversed a ledge with a threatening drop to one side.

Still we continued to descend as the light grew brighter. But the pace Zolan set was even slower. He did not utter a second warning; he did not have to. It was very plain that this was a place of peril.

In my palm the power gem now pulsed rapidly. I wondered if indeed it was somehow linked to my heart; yet the Power it emitted gave, strangely, a constant assurance of safety. Our progress was now hardly more than a crawl, and our guide often paused for increasingly longer halts.

The flat but inclined surface of the ledge became steps, narrow and cramped. Certainly these stairs had not been fashioned for feet such as ours. About us, the walls to our left were now covered with ragged growths of dusky, ash-covered masses of small leaves, strung like beads on garish red stems. As these began to appear, Zolan made one of his frequent nods toward this show of vegetation.

"Stay clear."

Having witnessed the unpredictability of the plant life outside, we were only too willing to follow such an order. But, even as the walls to our left supported growth, so did greenery arise on the open side of the path. These were not the trees we knew, but blackish stems as large around as two hands encircled, supporting ragged tags of thick slime.

The air about carried scents of rottenness such as could rise from growth in a stagnant pool. Suddenly one of the miserable "trees" shook violently. Zolan waved us back toward the left as a serpentlike head arose, jaws open to tear at flapping slime. The creature paid no heed to us, but plainly we should not attract its notice by any movement.

However, as the head, borne by a sinuous neck, rose higher still, I rubbed my hand, close-fisted about the stone, across my thigh. The scaled skin of the thing was clearly close kin to the substance of the breeches I had fashioned for myself. And for a flashing second I felt the rise of nausea.

At length the whole of the "tree" disappeared downwards. Very slowly our guide began to work his way along the too-narrow steps again. We must believe that, since such skin had been among the lengths gathered and preserved for future use, Zolan knew what he was about, knew enough about this monster to be able to deal with it.

I now understood, or so I thought, the reason for this journey. From the first he had assured us there was no way out of the Dismals. This day he had deliberately demonstrated native dangers, from a tuft of flowers to growths of fungi, and now to reptilian monsters.

The stairs came to an end. A crunching sounded, and occasionally a sharp crack that might indicate the breaking of one of the "trees." The stench had grown worse, and I wished heartily for one of the pomanders Cilla made so well, to relieve ugly smells.

We were looking out as if through a vast window into a cavern where swirling mist formed clouds curtaining most of the open. From here we sighted the back and tail of the snake-headed, thin-necked thing. That head and neck were supported on a bloated body, and any feet the creature might have possessed were concealed by revolting green and yellow growths.

Of a sudden there came a loud croaking noise. Zolan jerked at our guide rope and hurried ahead at the greatest speed he had yet shown, drawing us after. I glanced back to see Snakehead shifting its thick body around. A trail of mist thinned and vanished to display a second monstrous head rising a little farther on. This one was blunt and bulbous-eyed, and more than half of it was taken up by a gaping mouth rimmed with pointed fangs.

The rope twitched again as a second croaking came, loud enough to make us long to cover our ears. We were headed once more into full night. I had expected our guide, having shown us another deterrent against exploration on our own, to turn back and retrace our way, but he kept on in the dark.

A Send flashed, and we three were united. It was Bina who stated:

"That—that second thing was a *frog!*"

I was forced to agree with her identification. Almost I would swear that some sorcery of the Black Path—from the legends used to frighten children— had been wrought here: creatures we knew as harmless had counterparts in the Dismals of nightmarish proportions.

Let us get out of here, I thought. Zolan had more than made his point— I wanted no more of this place!

Still our travel through the dark continued. The gloom thickened as we moved farther from the window on the twilight-hidden swamp. The stench receded far more slowly. Had we spent all the day here? My feet began to suggest that.

By now we had come upon more stairs and were climbing again. To find safe footing meant constant shifting of feet and body, and my pack was an ever-growing burden. However, from above came the beginning of light once more.

Thirteen

Tamara

The stair again narrowed as we scraped our way up through a trap-door in the floor of a new cave. Here the like of those veins of crystal caught light that served the shelter latticed the walls, so we could see we had entered what might be the interior of a large bubble.

The walls supported no shelves or marks, nor was there any sign of permanent occupancy. Directly opposite the mouth of the well through which we had entered was a single break in a curve of wall, too well shaped to have been fashioned by nature. An arch opened, affording a view of honest twilight.

Zolan shed his pack and wordlessly headed for that opening, to be swiftly joined by Climber; then both disappeared from sight. I sought to follow, only to strike, just at the arched doorway, an obstruction. My sweeping hands discovered an invisible barrier. Neither man nor beast had been halted by this ward, but as Bina and Cilla crowded up, the obstruction, felt rather than seen, *was* present. We could no more push through it than we would have been able to breach an iron-bound door.

"Trapped!" My Send melded into identical assessments from my sisters.

We might be able to retrace our way, but for the dangers of the swamp. I stretched the fingers of my right hand, still clutching the Power stone with my left.

Power—shared, enhanced by all the energy we three could raise—

Even as I shaped the Send, I gasped and whirled half around, propelled by a potent force I could neither see nor truly measure, back against the curve of the wall.

I struck that new barrier and slipped to the cave floor.

Sabina

As TAM COLLAPSED, Cilla and I endured flows from the edges of the same Power that had sent her reeling back. The light of the crystal veins blinked out for me, and I swayed, but did not fall. Our Powers, such as they were—and none of us, I was sure, could tell how far our individual Talents extended—had been used to back Tam. However, that return surge must have been aimed mainly at her.

Slowly sight returned to me. Cilla caught at my arm. I grasped her hand and together we tottered, feeling utterly sapped of Power in body, toward Tam, who was lying still against the wall.

I had not rid myself of my pack when Zolan had shed his and, as I half fell, half settled by my sister, I dropped it free of my shoulders, tugging at its latching. Whether any of the remedies I had brought could aid Tam, I did not know—I could only try.

Cilla loosed her hold on me to draw Tam's body up a little, supporting it against her own. Tam's eyes were wide open, but unfocused, and she lay limp in Cilla's hold. Mercifully, the first cold fear that had clutched me as she fell was unfounded: she still lived.

I dug out the poor healing aids I had and tried to use them.

"She is so cold—" Cilla drew Tam into a closer embrace. "When the fire is gone—there is aching cold."

"No!" I cried out.

With Cilla's help, I managed to get Tam's mouth open a little and drop into it some of the liquid I had put together, hoping it was indeed an adequate restorative. She did swallow and, by that small response, reassured me a little.

However, she needed warmth. We, too, were shivering and my hands were growing stiff. Cilla gently rested Tam's head on her pack and, as she did, I saw one of Tam's hands slip to her side. It was curled into a fist and, when I sighted it, I was certain I knew what she held.

Cilla arose to make her way once more to the portal, where she passed her hands up and down. I knew by that gesture she discovered that the barrier was still in place.

Meanwhile, I pried Tam's clenched fingers apart. She did hold the stone from the ruins. I had no promise that what I would do might aid her; I could only hope.

As I took the strange talisman firmly into my own grasp, grateful for the warmth it held, I waved to Cilla to bring her back.

"Hold her; we can share body warmth. I will make use of this—" I showed the stone.

"What will that do?"

"I do not know," I returned truthfully. "But it is somehow bonded to Tam"—I held it between both hands now—"and is a thing of Power. She has been drained, and perhaps can be restored."

I began at Tam's head, holding the stone steady against her forehead, drawing it back and forth. Over her eyes and mouth I repeated that touch, then moved it above her throat. Without any suggestion from me, Cilla leaned over and loosened the lacings that fastened Tam's jerkin.

Across my sister's shoulders, her breasts, I drew the artifact; then I brought it to rest where I could feel a slow, weak heartbeat. There I held it. I could have shouted aloud when I felt heat spreading out from the talisman to warm her chill flesh.

"She is warmer," Cilla reported suddenly and, even as she did so, Tam sighed and her eyes closed, no longer held in that blank stare.

Though Tam now appeared to be sleeping, we did not leave her, rather settled close beside her, that our body warmth might aid in her recovery. I left the Stone lying over her heart, to ensure that any Power that might return to her through it would come directly to that seat of life.

However, now that our first fears had been somewhat stilled, we had time to consider our plight. We were indeed trapped, and to what purpose? The twilight had darkened well into true night beyond that door, which I was sure led to the outer world, if not up the interior of the cliff and to safety.

I drew one long, slow breath after another as I had been lessoned in childhood, fighting as best I could any weakening fear. When I believed I had indeed armed myself against doubt, I strove to sharpen my Talent, depleted though that Gift certainly was.

As I did so, I became aware of another reach of Power, bearing little resemblance to any I knew. Zolan, who had so effectively brought us into this captivity, had a Gift not like to ours. And a greater Talent controlled him through it—why I was so certain of this, I could not say.

"Look—" Cilla pointed to the curve of the wall above the barred exit. Her finger sketched a curling line in the air.

She might have summoned the blue fire that immediately outlined her discovery. The crystal line she indicated was only too familiar. This was closely akin to the pattern we had foolishly half stitched into being back in Grosper—like, yes, but *not* its twin. I Sent forth a questing toward the sensed Power, trying to pick up any hint of the Dark. But no warning responded. Cilla, too, appeared to have lost interest in it, for her hand dropped back, and she no longer sketched upon the air.

"It does not threaten," I observed.

"No. Perhaps we would be safer if it did," my sister returned. "Hidden dangers are far worse than those in full view. I have been thinking. . . ." She hesitated as if her thoughts imprisoned her even as this rock chamber held us three.

Drucilla

I LOOKED TO Bina, then down into Tam's face. All animation had disappeared from her expression; she might have been masked. Dared we try to reach her by Send now, would such exhaust her even further? And to use our thought-reach here—I shook my head. Bina was frowning at me.

"What are you thinking?" she asked now, her tone sharp.

"Were we somehow brought here for a purpose? And if so, what can it be? First came the pattern I dreamed." I shifted my right hand again into the fuller light and began to turn down my fingers as I counted off memories.

"That lout of a Starkadder—" she shot back acidly. "Maclan made clear that he was behind our kidnapping! Maclan it was also who dropped us into this place. Both acts run well together and fit his character. His quarrel with our father could be the root of a feud such as are common among these Northerners. But this"—she made a small wave with her own hand—"bears traces of something else."

"If," I began slowly, "Zolan could be the lost king, our presence here might serve another purpose. You with your Gift for the needle might call this a 'threading,' as though we were skeins and another's hand wrought the pattern! Our father is Lord Warden in the Border Lands. At our own court he is respected, looked upon at times as a counselor. Supposing the lost king were returned to Gurlyon, would many of his subjects welcome him?

"The great clans have been at each other's throats since the war. To have the rightful king in their control would give any chief a powerful weapon. Yet, supposing the king would appear, having been rescued by the Earl of Verset's daughters, our father could well claim what he wished for that coup—even support him with powerful voice at our own court."

Bina's frown deepened. "Do you believe then that Zolan is capable of so twisted a plot?"

"No," I answered, sure I had the right of it. "Not he, but someone else. This hermit, who has made such a stir here in the North, comes from these mountains. What he has taught is driving a wedge among the great families. Another man coming from the same direction—"

My voice trailed into silence. One of my faults has always been adding to facts the suggestion of imagination. I could well be accused of doing so now, lacking facts that should be produced to shake my air-castle of speculation.

"Does a Great One—an adept of deep Power—lie behind it all?"

Both of us stared and tensed as Tam's eyes opened and she shifted a little in our hold. She did not try to rise but looked from one to the other of us and back again. Then her hand moved to close about the gem.

"May the Greater Good reward you, sisters. You have drawn me out of the Dark into the Light again. The truth, as I would sword-swear before the queen herself and vow it before those of Talent in the Shrine wherein we serve, is this: a mind and a will are hidden here, and their purpose means trouble for all we cherish."

Her tone was akin to one used in reading from the Sacred Book of Sartha, for awe and belief lay at its core.

I wet my lips with tongue-tip. Perhaps she might now answer certain questions.

"Does Zolan alone work this?" Even as I spoke, I was inwardly assured that my theory was not the truth.

Tam's masklike look did not soften. "No." She did not add anything to that bald negative.

It was Bina who broke the short silence. "Then we still do not know our enemy, and attack could come from any direction." Her free hand, the mate of which rested on Tam's shoulder, tightened into a fist.

Tam did not answer. She might have been giving, by silence alone, her agreement to Bina's statement. However, she now shook off our support and sat up, holding the talisman gem beneath her chin. A glow was rising from it to paint her jaw, shine on her mouth.

"The fact remains," Bina said, a bit sourly, "that we must get out of here."

Her voice was harsh with frustration, an emotion felt by all of us, as strongly as though we shared a Send.

I looked again at the lines on the wall facing me. Designs, drawings—I blinked. For an instant I saw the pattern I feared as clearly as if it were limned on a sheet of patterning-paper and laid on a worktable. Bina's pack—she carried her improvised healing materials with her. . . .

Reaching out, I dragged the thick bag to me, loosened the closing tags. What I sought was fortunately at the top since Bina herself had been rummaging inside for what might help in Tam's recovery.

A mat of fibers, clotted together, came to hand. I did not look up but continued to rummage beneath that first find.

"You have a distillation akin to velle water?" I demanded, bringing out next a netting bag, which enclosed a thick-sided stoppered jug.

"You hold what you seek," she returned. "What would you do?"

"This potion may be of aid." Whether I would make matters better or bring further trouble on us, I had no idea. Yet so strongly had a suggestion come to the front of my mind that I could not resist it.

Rising with the fiber mat in one hand and the bagged bottle in the other, I walked toward the wall on the right of the archway. The barrier, as I had hoped, did not prevent movement in that area; it evidently stood only across the opening to prevent passage out.

I wetted the mat with liquid from the bottle and set to work. The glassy veins were raised a little above the surface of the surrounding rock. I rubbed them with care; my supplies were limited, and I could afford no waste. I did not attempt to coat the shining line from one end to the other, sure I did not have sufficient supply of the velle for that. I had to content myself with cutting across the scrolling at intervals.

No fire blazed here, but now the scent of burning arose, carrying with it the suggestion of spices, an under-smell of something charring. It heartened me to see that, when my hand arose from each application of the liquid, the glass appeared cracked, eaten away.

As I brushed, I chanted, hardly above a whisper. Before I had attacked the design for the third time, the words I used for my petition were echoed by both Bina and Tam.

The pattern I followed dimmed first at each spot I anointed; then the glass itself flaked away. When I had dealt with the mineral trails that bordered the door to the right, I swung back to avoid any touch with the invisible barrier and went to do the same with the left-hand side.

Now the bottle had to be shaken to produce its final few drops. I feared the liquid would not last to complete the action. Whether it served to destroy more than just the wall design, I would not know until I finished.

I realized that the glow arising from the crystal lines was ebbing, even from the portions my efforts had not touched. This chamber—it was too well-shaped to be considered a cave—was steadily darkening.

Then Tam arose to stand beside me, her low chant stronger in my ears. She had formed a cup with both of her hands and she now held them out so that the gem-light guided me to the last of my scrubbing. I feared a second attack, such as the assault we had earlier faced, and when that did not come, I could only believe that my actions had achieved nothing.

We three stood shoulder to shoulder before the archway. Only bits of dimmed and cloudy crystal were visible here and there where the scrollwork had shone. However, that these pieces of pattern held any Power now we could hardly believe.

Any danger that might linger must be mine alone. I tossed the wet fiber mass, the empty bottle, from me and took a determined step forward, my hand stretched out.

Out and out—my fingers encountered nothing. I took another step, a longer one, forward. Again, nothing. Then my hand was under the archway. We were free!

"Yes!" I swung around to face Tam and Bina. I spun away again to sweep both hands back and forth, meeting no obstruction this time.

I was drained from the use of Talent, yet I had no wish to spend one moment more in this stone cell. Nor did I know if my attempt at Ward destruction would continue to work. Was an alarm now ringing somewhere in the Dismals to alert the setter of this trap?

Stooping, we took up our packs. Tam halted abruptly at the one Zolan had discarded when he had so abruptly left us. With Bina's swiftly proffered aid, she dragged it directly before the portal, and together they booted it through.

We were out in the open night. Before us stretched a wide section of ledge. No trees grew here, so moonlight fully bathed us. Tam's talisman, too, continued to glow brightly, banishing much of the surrounding dark.

At first we could not see any way over. A cautious exploration of the edge of the rock shelf revealed only a descent as sharp as that down which we had been initially lowered. And we were not at the real top of the cliff, either. That towered above us, slanting perilously outward, and its dizzy backward-bending offered no possible foot- or handhold. Had we won our way into the open, only to be held in a prison of another kind?

"Rope—" Tam turned to the pack Zolan had shouldered.

Tamara

I PULLED AT the loose tangle of thick cord that had been bound to the pack when Bina and I had shoved it through the opening. What use it might have now, I did not yet know, but it was the best tool I could think of.

"It cannot be long enough," Bina protested. Cilla had dropped down, using her own supply sack as a backrest.

I was aware that her opening of the door had depleted her; I also knew that I was far from restored from the backlash of force encountered in my own adventure. All the same, I was sure that we had precious little time. Our escape must have been felt by whoever set the Ward within—breakage of a binding-spell can always warn the one who placed it. Without doubt, a search would be mounted for us, so if we got no farther while we could, it would mean swift end to our hard-won liberty.

Cilla's eyes, I could see, were closed. Roused now, she could do little to help herself. I made my hands into fists to still their shaking as best I could.

Zolan and Climber had gone this way, and that length of rope had been discarded as if our host had no use for it. Neither he nor the beast from the Dismals had been waiting for us. Thus there *was* a way either down or up.

I swayed as I stood there. The Dark—that Night of Nothingness my sisters had drawn me from—seemed to be lapping over the rim of the ledge to threaten me. I was forced to lower myself to the gritty rock as Cilla had done before me.

Fourteen

Sabina

Tam and Cilla lay comatose on the ledge. Any further action must now be mine. First I squatted down opposite them and raided my supplies. I began by chewing, as a cow might a cud, a mouthful of dried trail meat. I could so nourish myself and explore for them at the same time.

Once more I crept carefully to the outer rim of the ledge, lying flat to get as far as was prudent. Though the moonlight made measurement difficult, I believed that we were perched far above the ground, which sloped away from the foot of the cliff.

A number of vines hung below, some reaching well above the earth where they were rooted. We had been shown two perils of the dense forest that shot a thick green tongue close to the cliff base. What dangerous surprises those upward-thrusting plants might produce we had no way of knowing.

The nearest one appeared to cling firmly to the rock for support. I needed better light to see clearly. Now I arose and moved to the section of wall to the left of the archway.

I could indeed get a clearer view of the cliff here, but the swell of its surface directly above discouraged any attempt to climb. If Zolan had been able to go there, he had used some method no longer available.

Still I continued to skirt the wall, my eyes searching anything above my reach. If only I knew more! If only the Powers we had uncovered here had been manifest when we had been able to ask aid from my mother or Duty!

It was scent that revealed the secret. Acuity of smell is one of a healer's most valued skills, as sickness can many times be detected by some odor given off by a patient. Medicaments too are often sorted by scent. Equally, though, this sensitivity can be a burden in places of strong reeks. Thus, according to training, healers spend as little time as possible where that sense may be nearly overpowered.

When I had attended Climber, I had learned his personal scent, covered as it had been by the blood of his wounds and a lesser odor, doubtless from the monstrous attacker. However, during the time he had been in my care, I had registered another scent—not only of healing-salves but also the cachet of the animal himself.

I moved closer to the wall. I might well have just overturned a flask of some potent liquid. Animals can produce such "markers" during their travels, to set signals along their ways, to signify their gender, to offer challenges. These scents are much stronger than the usual odor given off by a furred traveler.

Climber! Though I could not be truly sure of the identity of the beast that marked this particular stretch of stone, I felt my guess was correct. Zolan's companion had chosen to spray this area of cliff and not too long ago.

Why just here? There might be many reasons and some beyond human ken. However, some things render themselves more discernible to touch than sight, especially at night. Straining my arm upward as far as I could reach, I drew fingertips down the cliff surface. Aside from weather pittings I felt nothing. If any structure therein, whether portal or stairway, had been concealed by Warding, I could not sense it.

I located a damp spot, oily to the touch. The rightness of my guess was beyond doubt—the stone had been marked, and very profusely. Now I looked along to my left. Why should the animal set a mark if this place were not path or boundary?

Clouds scudded across the moon. Light was limited again. Only a black shadow at my feet caught my eye before darkness really closed in. I stooped to explore it with a hand.

This was no rope I grasped, but neither did a vine bear scales. Only some protection of the Great One saved me as the "vine" suddenly flipped over in my hold. Instinctively I cracked it against the stone and flung the limp body from me, hardly able to believe I had been so unwary. A snake of sorts, perhaps so well matching a vine in its coloration as to fool its prey. I took a small step backward, but my foot hit a rough place and I lost my balance as the ledge shifted beneath me.

I fell on my back, momentarily as helpless as an overturned beetle. The moon was now completely veiled, and I dared not struggle to sit up, so close was I to the precipice.

Neither of the sleepers stirred until a squall rose from the ocean of shadow below, and brought a drowsy mutter from one of my sisters. A light floated up from those wooded depths. It leveled out a little above the ledge, then zigzagged its way toward us. No chance it was Zolan or Climber— neither could travel the air in such a fashion.

I levered myself up and scurried back to our impromptu camp, rousing Cilla and Tam with an urgent Send. A buzzing sounded, louder by far than any normal insect call. Darkness only intensified the feeling of danger.

"What is it?" The demand from Tam's direction was sharp with fear.

"A flier—?" Cilla answered hesitantly.

A flier indeed, yet not, I was certain, of the same breed that had slain the spider-thing. I could trace outlines just enough to tell that the newcomer must be insectile and I stooped, running my hands along the surface of the ledge, seeking, for lack of any other defense, a stone lying there. If we were to attempt to use the Talent, so soon after drawing deeply upon it, we could leave ourselves totally weaponless.

The thing did not aim directly at us, as I had expected. On our feet now, we retreated, still facing outward until the cliff backed us. The light-bearing air creature moved to the right, slowed, then alighted. As far as I could determine, it had come to rest against the cliff wall not far from where Climber had left his mark. A change had occurred there: in the growing dark I could see a bright cluster of small light-specks fanning outward.

We had won into a semicave through a well-like entrance; here now was a similar fissure in the ledge. Our visitor left its perch. With a fluttering of wings, it descended to the break. Its head bobbed up and down as might a tool wielded with precision. A series of clicks sounded, suggesting that its actions were loosing debris into the hole. At last, rather clumsily, it sought to face the cliff again.

Its two forefeet were clamped, as well as I could judge, on either side of the bedewed wall, while its head, pear-shaped and crowned with whipping antennae, rested over the stain. By its movement, which I could only half see, I thought it might be tonguing—if lick it could—the "marker." Whatever it did strengthened the scent I had detected earlier. It had no interest in us; the stony cliff held its whole attention.

We gathered together. Swiftly, by Send, I outlined my exploration. The hole drew us but we must contain our impatience until the creature with the curious taste had departed.

Time stretched out. The first pallor of dawn streaked the sky, illuminating our visitor more clearly. It possessed a rounded ball of a belly and lower body, a very slender rod of waist and beyond, a much smaller ball from which extended two very thin upper legs, one on either side, with thicker ones flanking them below. The lower pair folded to peak joints well above its upper portion. The head was very small compared to the rest, and neither eyes nor mouth could be discerned. However, a pair of furred antennae beat ceaselessly on the cliff.

With the increasing light of day, we could clearly see the opening on the ledge. Why we had not discovered signs of this during first careful inspection, I could only wonder. Had a Ward indeed been set, one that had been banished by the coming of the flyer? Or had my touch broken it earlier without my knowledge or any planned attempt at doing so? That did not matter now—what was important was its existence.

I pushed past Cilla toward the cliff wall. When would an end come to the winged thing's nuzzling of the tainted rock? I leaned against the cliff, fingers working. A blast of the Power that had served us before might clear our way. My fingers twisted open; then, by force of will, I curled them palmward. This was like being caught up in a dream—such a dream as I had long feared might be a key to unlock a portion of the mind better kept under control.

Now that I sighted the night creature more clearly, my curiosity grew. The flier had made no move against us, and to kill where no attack was threatened was against all we had been taught. A ruthless use of Power was a step down the Dark Path.

I flexed fingers once more. The sense of immediacy that had bullied us since Zolan and his beast left us was with me again. Almost I could hear—or was it feel?—a sharp voice repeating, "Cilla, Cilla!" as I had often been summoned when too long at a project.

The eater—or licker—raised its head at last. Its antennae were now scraping the edge of the fissure. Proceeding out on the ledge, it turned its body, the lower part of which now appeared very swollen, and backed once more toward the crevice.

That huge abdomen, its light dimmed to a faint gleam, seemed to contract and expand several times. From beneath the rounded bottom fell a green orb about the size of a ball of wool prepared for the weaver. Then one of the back legs kicked, and the ball rolled to the edge and fell into the well-crack. Six more of what I now recognized as eggs followed to disappear so. Its duty to the species done, the creature spread its wings and rose gracefully from the ledge to fly toward the forest from which it had come.

Perhaps imprudently, we felt sure that our problem had been offered a solution. We emptied Zolan's pack, dividing its contents among us. I brought out the small stone knife and began sawing the lacing of the bag in such a way that I soon had a long strip of well-cured hide. This I rolled and fit into the top of my carrier. Though I had no really workable tools, I was not minded to waste anything now.

The sun was well up when we agreed we were ready to go and approached the opening through which the eggs had rolled. Somehow we were not really surprised to discover rough hand- and footholds descending along one wall to a lighted space below. I held out a hand to test if this possible way of escape held Wards. I was not alone in doing so. As I took this precaution, Tam and Bina did likewise.

No barrier rose against us. Tam swung over and made use of the aid offered by the niches. She had not reslung her pack, but left it above where Bina knotted all three together with the rope we had earlier found inadequate.

Bina waved to me to follow Tam when a signal came from below that our sister had safely reached bottom. I set myself to a slow descent, testing each hold as I went; I have never found myself at ease with heights.

Bina lowered our supply-sacks to us. With more light I looked up to see if the eggs had found a resting place. From this point they could be seen on the wall at about my height. They had lost some of their roundness and appeared to have become plastered to the stone.

"This place," I said slowly, "did not show when we first searched the ledge. Was it Warded? If so, what destroyed the Ward?"

Bina looked at the right hand she held up into the morning light. "Perhaps any such barrier was destroyed by my discovery of Climber's 'mark.'

Who knows? How greatly are the Dismals guarded—and by whom?" We could make no answer to that.

Not too far away, a stream gurgled out between two wide slabs of rock. Toward that we veered, realizing acutely just how long it had been since we had slaked our thirst. We refilled our water skins and set about to see more of what lay around us, seeking any visible trail we could follow.

We soon emerged into the open before a thick wall of trees and discovered a carpet of long springy grass. For some reason, the urge for action that had driven us lifted from me. I commented on that discovery, only to be assured by Tam and Bina that they also shared my sense of relief. We did not, however, quite relax our vigilance, remembering the unknown perils that might be concealed by the giant vegetation.

Soon Tam discovered a sign, which we agreed was probably left as a trail marker. It lay along the bottom of the cliff and ahead of that the way appeared open, unchoked by tree or vine, bush or rock. It was a stone, wider at bottom than top, standing upright. Along one side were markings, half erased at places. These carvings bore close likeness to some found on the walls of Zolan's cave fortress.

We gnawed at the hard rations we carried. The salty taste of the meat sticks overrode the sweetness of the clumps of what must be dried fruit. It became harder and harder to think of shouldering our packs and getting to our feet to push on. Instead, I sat watching the flow of the stream, noting the fleeting shadows below the surface that suggested some sort of aquatic life.

Tamara

AFTERWARD I KNEW right well what had drained from us our will to travel. We were being lulled as weary children might be quieted to take a nap. Except—

The pouch at my belt that held the light-gem suddenly shattered my sleepy contentment with a burst of warmth, though I was not aroused to the point of uneasiness. Overhead the sun no longer shone so directly, and tree shadows crept towards our halting place.

For a moment or two the strange shapes cast by the trees held my still-drowsy attention. Then—I must have cried out as I grabbed the top of the gem bag, jerking it away from close contact with my body, though my hands were not safe from that blast either. Fire had blazed from it—yet not any fire such as sprang from wood offering comfort and service. This, instead, took the place of a rousing war-horn and jerked me to my feet. Bina and Cilla blinked up at me.

I had no time to alert them. That was denied me as if they were warded by a power as strong as any my mother and Duty working together could raise.

All contentment disappeared. I wheeled to face the post of stone. I was summoned, my body controlled by the will of another. And, for this moment at least, I was powerless to fight its urging.

Past the carved stone I moved, and, as I put it behind me, Bina and Cilla were—gone! I was alone. Suddenly my mind was whelmed by a tide of memories that flooded in, carefully sorted and drawn from my past.

Afraid? Yes, I, Tamara of the House of Scorpy, was afraid. Still, that emotion was deadened. I was very aware of all about me, but it was as if I were viewing a series of pictures, seeing things not a part of my real life. My pace was now near a trot as the compulsion on me tightened.

The bright, intense colors, the sharpness of tree and leaf, began to dull. Some of the drabness of the stone to my right seeped out to cloud my path. Yet, in an odd way, as all I passed seemed to fade, within me grew a sharpness of other sight. Did I "see" what did not exist? There was no way I might prove or disprove that. However, I was aware of figures who might have risen out of ground as growing vegetation, or else were released by curdling pillars of the very air.

They lacked my height, being instead short-limbed, the flesh and bones of their extremities heavy and stumpy. The trunks of their bodies were overthick, their shoulders very wide. And—they had no faces! No feature existed above the spread of those shoulders. Glints of color, which might have issued from gems, a suggestion of shadowy garments. Not beasts—of a certainty, not of clean animal-kind—rather, these were beings apart.

The North was rich with strange stories of things no one of our day had ever seen: dwellers in mountains and hills, who often teased and tweaked mankind for their own entertainment. I thought now, when I caught a clear look at this company matching pace with me, that I did recognize some as emerging out of one such tale.

Save for an area about ten paces around me, I could no longer see anything clearly. Somehow, though, I was not fearful anymore but increasingly impatient. I progressed toward some goal of immense importance. I *wanted,* pressed by all the emotion in me, to arrive. That need became a punishing lash to set me into a run with no care for the way beneath me or any difficulty awaiting me ahead.

Sabina

CILLA HAD SEIZED my hand with crushing force as Tam left us. First there was a very dim shining about our sister's body, ever moving with her, becoming brighter and brighter. At the same moment the Power that held her reached out also for us. It was a force we could feel against our skin, taste, hear—sometimes as a humming, at others like a call just beyond our ability to capture with ears.

This near-music did not warn us against following—it urged us to action, and we must needs follow. With our packs and Tam's bag, which we carried in turns, we could not match her speed, and she was soon out of sight. However, that tie binding us together from birth held tightly. She was, we knew, ahead, and we hurried along her trail.

Later we caught sight of—Tam? Could we be sure that speeding column of light was she? We could. The time that passed could no longer be reckoned in precise measure. Our sister continued to hasten away from us at an ever-increasing speed. We struggled to keep up as best we could.

Fifteen

Sabina

We tried, first singly, then together, to reach Tam by Send. What we met was a barrier, but not one of Tam's raising. We had discovered long ago among ourselves that no mind-message propelled by strong purpose sent by any one of us could be refused by the others. However, I began to wonder if, since she had found the talisman, Tam had won to a new level of skill.

The blanketing forest never reached quite to the cliff. For that we could only be glad, though in this open we might be easily sighted by a prowler within the edge of the green to our left. Also, at times, Cilla and I had to slow and pick a cautious way across stone and gravel fallen earlier from above; but such obstacles did not appear to slow Tam, who was so far ahead that a curve to the left hid her from sight.

"She—" Cilla spoke with a discernible tremor in her voice. "Could she be possessed?"

She was putting into words my own growing fear. We had believed ourselves armored by the personal Wardings which we had carefully renewed at intervals since traveling north. However, that had not saved us from being drugged, nor had it won us our freedom from Maclan or stood against all that had happened in the Upper World—perils against which the spell was supposed to guard us. In fact, we knew very little, until exposed to it, what might chance here.

"Yes, it is possible." I could make no other answer to Cilla's question. Then I began to delve into my memory for what I knew about signs of possession.

Such displacement of one soul by another had been known in the past. Twice in fingers' count of centuries an accusation of that foul practice had been raised against families who exhibited Talent. From our first coming north, we had been warned against any open display of our Gifts for, in this land, ignorance and fear had brought punishment and even death to innocents accused of misuse of Power.

Still, what we knew might only be the outermost fringe of the whole truth. Too, the Dismals appeared to follow another law. Zolan—? No. Somehow I clung to the belief that, highly gifted as he appeared, he was not in control. The unknown in this place was powerful enough to engender profound fear.

"Look!" We had paused to exchange the extra burden of Tam's pack. Cilla caught at my shoulder, pulled me around as she pointed with her other hand.

Tam had slackened speed. We could see that the pillar of light, which we had come to accept as our sister in this place, had halted before the cliff. Rising behind her was what could only be a structure of some sort, though it was difficult to make out any details. Between us and the—building?—the air was murky, almost as if fog surged in waves.

I admitted to myself that I wanted to go no further. However, those who can summon Powers dare not yield to fear. Surrender, even in a small measure, ever opens a way for the Dark to rend and destroy. This had been our teaching since the Talent first stirred in us.

So I hefted the extra sack and stumbled forward, Cilla flanking me, pace for pace. Tam remained still in sight, now unmoving. Our boots, in spite of their many layers of thick lining, had been badly worn. As I took a forward step my foot came down on a sharp stone, sending me off balance. Striving to keep to my feet, I spun sideways, to fall heavily on more punishing gravel. I could not stifle my cry as more pain sliced through me, but my own cry was lost.

"No! No!" Cilla screamed. "Tam—Tam—we come!"

I pulled myself upright. The light that was Tam—but this could not happen! Power—yes, Power gathered here, a mind-might that was not ours. Nor could I feel any trace of my sister's Talent, if she were struggling against the alien force. Tam was being absorbed by the cliff facing her. No opening could be detected there—she was simply being drawn *in through* the stone, and in the space of two breaths she was gone. Cilla collapsed beside me and hammered her fists against the ground where we now crouched.

"Send!" she shrieked an order. "Merge and *Send!*"

We Merged, tried in every way we knew to raise a silent shout, calling on all our Talent. We broadcast our message—and that rebounded, the energy returning even as the Power had flashed back at Tam when we had fought to pierce the barrier in the cave. There was no reaching our sister.

We scrambled up, abandoning our packs, and hastened back along the trail to the point where we were sure we had last seen her. We even lunged against the wall, beating at it with our fists until sense returned and we knew that, for now, we must admit defeat. But one battle lost did not mean that our warfare was ended.

Tamara

THAT SHADOWY CREW I had sensed keeping me company was gone. Their disappearance was like having chill water flung in my face; I was aroused. Stone walled the way ahead of me, but I had no command over my body's action now. In a step or so I was going to flatten myself against that barrier. When we had attempted to leave the prison cave, there was a Warding, which could not be seen. Here was quite the opposite. I did not smash against the rock as I expected, I simply passed through it, realizing in the doing that I was triumphing over another unseen barrier. Yet no planned and successful ploy of mine brought me through, for my body still refused any orders I gave it. The will of another drew me.

I was walked at a brisk step down the middle of a hallway or tunnel. The glow from the stone let me see that there were no openings on either side. The walls also emitted light enough to show me, in time to slip sideways and avoid it, a length of battered armor and a huddle of dull bone and blackened flesh. Such sad relics might well give dire warning of what awaited here.

Yet, to my utter surprise, that grisly array brought a kind of laughter from me. The weapon I carried inside me was not a mere length of well-honed steel, nor a snaplock. I was more and more certain that the same was true of the unknown adversary ahead.

He or she could possess my body and draw me to action, true; yet my mind remained my own. I dared not, however, seek in any way to discover how free, or just what Power I could summon. It was better that I play a waiting game, for I thereby made sure to waste no energy before being called to risk all.

The apparently endless tunnel made a sharp turn left and now slanted upward at a gentle slope. Not too far ahead there appeared a suggestion of a doorway in a partition blocking off half the hallway. Hitherto, except for the skeleton which might have been set as a warning, the floor of the passage could have been swept free and bare within the hour. No dust lay here, where the accumulation of ages might be expected.

That condition changed abruptly. Fanning out from the doorless portal was debris, like to the wrack left on a storm-pounded seashore. I saw broken pottery, shards lying thickly among layers of what did seem like dust, save that it was dull blue in color. I avoided a large fragment that lay in enough light where it might have been easily viewed. I would have paused to examine it, only the will that impelled me would not allow it. Yet I was certain it could only be half of a pointed head such as was worn by one of the ancient guardian figures in Zolan's cave.

More fragments of pottery crumbled under my feet as I passed through the doorway. I clenched my hands at my breast, and the warmth of my gem battled the chill that assaulted me now.

Places exist where monstrous acts have been committed in the past. For one with the Talent, to venture to such a place awakens echoes of feelings, once human and now as shattered as the figures lying about me. Pain, loss, then rage so blistering it was like an actual torch held against the flesh—the frustrated fury of the helpless void of defense.

So intense were those emotions that I swayed, keeping my feet only with difficulty as I paced down this room bored out of rock. Benches were smashed, their occupants reduced to shards and strewn afar. Parts of figures and—something else! One of the statues, not totally destroyed, lay on its side. It was hollow—and inside still remained broken bones and more of the blue dust.

A place of death! Even as many of our people were buried in shrines, or in coffins laid in hallowed ground, here those of another race, after being given to a purifying fire, had been placed in these jars.

Once arranged in dignity, they had met with some disaster which had reduced them to dishonored dust. Was this desecration, perhaps, the result of a treasure hunt by Breakswords from the land above?

Those misty figures that had matched step with me earlier did not reappear. I believed, though, that they had strong ties with the disaster. Another opening was visible ahead, but that exit was netted across with visible cords of—*light*! The force possessing me weakened, until at last I could stand fast, resist the urge that still pulled me forward, but only feebly now.

I had to take a stand in this strange push-pull of will against will. And I chose to put my objection into words.

"I am here by your desire," I said loudly, speaking firmly as if I had been summoned to answer to some charge before the queen's own court. "I am Tamara of the House of Scorpy." I gave my right name; now, by the laws of Power, I could demand the same revelation from this Other.

I waited, but no answer returned, by sound or Send. I therefore changed to ritual. Our Talents might not be the same, yet like Laws of Light rule all Powers.

"By sky and by earth,
By starlight and sunlight,
By water and fire.
By heart and by hand,
May Those Above Ward me
With swords of truth,
Shields of pure deeds,
For by them I exist.
Stand, Great Ones, witness—
Ashlot, Mori, Branu,
Have here my hailing!"

I was moved then to raise the gemstone on my open palm. My answer came in the snapping of those lines of light that had closed the way before me. The compulsion that had forced me to action was truly gone. I could have turned, I knew, and retraced my way. But by my own will

I had bound myself to see this venture through, and my direction must be forward.

Still holding the gem as a lamp, I went on.

Sabina

NO OPENING EXISTED in the cliff that we could either feel or see. We were sure that Tam had indeed been possessed, taken—but to where? We had traveled the circles of the Great Light, but only with our mother to hand, traversing them only within a dedicated Shrine.

Weak with fatigue, burdened with fear, we sat on the ground. Cilla began to cry softly, not from any apprehension but because of our loss and her inability to see ahead in any fashion.

She leaned forward a little to pick up a sliver of stone, one end of which was pointed. Having turned it around several times, she set the sharp tip to a hands-wide space of earth from which she had swept gravel.

"By sky and by earth
By starlight and sunlight,
By water and fire,
By heart and by hand—"

As Cilla drew those ancient symbols, she gave each the ritual call to life.

The point now rested on a space free from any debris. She might be answered or she might not. It was ever so, for great labors go forward in another time and place, and such deeds still have their roots in our world. Only by Power would any interested in us reply, if such a Being deemed us worth the effort.

Our time, and the time in that Otherwhere, is not reckoned the same. We might wait only a slight movement of a clock hand—or it might be days—or never, should our plea go unanswered.

Cilla closed her eyes, but she remained alert and kept the stone pen held ready. Suddenly it began to move. No words, no archaic pattern grew. Instead—I hunched nearer, leaning as close to that patch of earth as I could.

"Yagargy!" I identified the leaf outline Cilla's tool sketched with such care.

Her hand fell against her knee as if all its strength had drained into the wavering lines. Cilla opened her eyes to look.

"Yagargy," she echoed. "The Power plays with us."

Her voice was bitter. I swallowed, tasting the vileness of risen bile. Yagargy was a weapon of the Dark Ones. It bound its user to a captivity from which no freedom could ever be won. Wherever it was found in our homeland it was destroyed by fire, and any person debased enough to use it was considered already dead. The offender would be placed into a cage for all to see, while water and food were withheld until the hapless one died and his—or her—body was disposed of as foul waste.

Such doom was the worst sentence that could be given in our land; however, it was pronounced for good reason. Those enslaved by yagargy became totally the creatures of the Dark. Some said that they were indeed dead, though their bodies still walked and talked, for that which was their innermost essence was gone.

Every practitioner of herb-craft knew that poison well, even as they also knew the signs of an addict. In the end it was always a healer's sworn evidence that condemned those so evilly indulging themselves. For the evidence of partaking of the drug, whether as juice, leaf, or powdered root, was that the user was suddenly endowed with Talent—Talent and an uncontrollable appetite for Power.

"I did not summon the Dark—" Cilla struck her stone stylus through the center of the crude drawing. "It is this accursed place!" Her head twisted from side to side, as if she would see where stood Evil to be faced.

However, it was true that she *had* used a proper Calling. Had I not echoed it with her? Those of the Light could not call upon some aspect of the Dark by uttering a petition sealed to the Light. So there must be some deeper meaning to what we had both seen. Tam—no! That I would not believe. We would have known from the very beginning if our sister had been tainted, for our Talent would also have been crippled, being three in one as we were.

Suddenly I scrambled to my feet—my bag of medicaments had been left when I had fallen. Pain lanced up my leg from where it gnawed into my foot. The discomfort slowed me down, but did not stop me.

I returned, dragging the supply-sack behind, having to free it with fierce tugs when now and then it caught on stones. Cilla was on her feet, one tattered boot grinding into the picture-space as if she feared that devilish plant depicted there would root and sprout at any moment.

She looked at my burden as I lurched into the place before the cliff.

"There is no antidote for yagargy; you know that well." She wore a sullen scowl, and anger smoldered in the eyes that met mine.

I had none of the innocent and helpful growing things I had known from early childhood. What lay in pouches in my pack were ones Zolan had indicated as useful. However, his explanations had been scanty and few, since little time had been given for such lessons. Several of my gleanings I had recognized as being perhaps of the same family as the heal-herbs native to the sane world above the Dismals. Still, I had only our host's limited identifications to guide me.

Spreading this supply before me now, I picked up each small packet in turn, squeezing a little, then sniffing, tapping memory a word at a time as a basis for my guess. During this inspection, I took time to shed my torn boot and grease the hurt taken during my tumble.

Cilla stared for a short space, saying nothing more, her mind closed to any Send as she watched me. Then she busied herself with that length of cord we had saved out of Zolan's pack.

I finished with my doctoring, put aside singly the powders and salves that were useless for what I would do. My mind flinched away from the final act, but my will held.

It was twilight; we paused to eat from our small store of rations, drink from our waterskins. I had reached the last of my herbs, and Cilla, making good use of the time, had cobbled patches for my boots, or I might never have hoped to continue.

Opening the flap of the last packet, I again used the skill of scent. Rare perfumes aplenty sweeten the world. Some are born of flowers, others of pressed bark or crushed leaves; still others are wrung from seeds, dried fruit. I drew a deep breath once, then another.

"Bina!" Cilla was beside me. Her crying of my name dragged me back into that place between stone and forest.

I blinked. The hour between dusk and true dark encouraged shadows to spread. However, my sight was as clear as it might be at noontide.

Cilla's face was so close to mine that her breath touched my cheek. Then the perfume seemed to reach her. Raising her hand, she struck me full across the face, her expression one of open horror.

"Yagargy!" She snatched at the small bag, but I jerked it out of reach. She did not try to rise but scrambled backward, still facing me.

"No!" I returned. "Listen!"

I tried to add more meaning with a Send, only to meet a closed mind. Her hand had tightened now about a stone with jagged edges, and I knew she would use it as a weapon unless I could make her understand.

"Cilla—yes, this seems to be yagargy, yet it is not the plant we know. Zolan swore to me when I found it that it is used in this place because it beckons to Power, but that how one intends to use that Power makes the difference. Now we have no other recourse. If Tam has truly been possessed, she can only be freed by such force as we have never called upon before.

"You called upon the Light." I held up the pouch. "This was the answer given. I caught no stench of Darkness; our Wards did not quake. That Power of Light to which we were sworn to at our birthing answered—"

Her face twisted. "Bina, already Evil works upon you!"

I gave a sigh. What must be done, I would do—and now.

"Great One." I did not speak to Cilla but tilted my head to view the sky, marveling a little, for never before had I seen the coming of stars so clearly.

I placed the small parcel on the ground where Cilla had stamped flat the remains of her drawing.

"Great One," I began again, "Queen of Day and Night, Dealer in birth and death, do I now offer a bitter end to life, or do I wield a right weapon in Your Service?"

I no longer watched my sister but kept my gaze fixed on the herb-bag. All things were possible to the Great One, yes, but would She deign to respond?

After a long moment, movement began in the packet. I saw a red stalk emerge from the hide, covered with a mixture of seeds and leaf fragments. It spiraled upward until it stood more than a hand's breadth above its rooting. That stem writhed and bulged, to bring forth thread-thin branches, each growing thicker by a breath. The branches leaved, bore flowers of the same vibrant red. The growth now resembled in miniature the warning pictures of yagargy. Then—

Those flowers, which hung like drops of fresh blood, were not withering or ready to fall; rather they were blanching, purifying to a glorious white. As they paled so, perfume filled the air.

A sob arose, aching in my throat. I did not hesitate but reached out.

Sixteen

Tamara

Three strides I took through that once-Warded doorway. Around me the light from the gem formed a dense haze. In the beginning I could not see far beyond its limits, just enough to assure me I was no longer in a hall but rather in a chamber of some size. Something of the rage that had been fed to me earlier in the place of destruction stirred. This was an effort on the part of the unknown Power, I believed, to make me feel inferior. For every trial I had passed, another would rise.

I halted, encased in my cocoon of light. I waited.

"Lady Tamara—" No Send, but rather a voice. And one I knew. Had *Zolan* been the one playing this game?

I did not answer, nor did I try to find him by the Talent. However, I was almost instantly sure of something—he was not alone. The other presence could only be sensed. Still I waited.

"Sorceress—" Still his voice but, again, another's words.

I returned no sign that they had been heard; instead, I raised the gem to my lips. I did not think the words but spoke them as if they were for the talisman and none other.

"Heart and hand
At Thy command,
Raise my sword
Of tongue, not steel.
In Thy shrine I bend the knee."

Though I spoke hardly above the faintest of whispers, my chant sounded as clear as if I sang it from a mountaintop. The haze was no longer quiescent. It moved as might a breeze-borne mist, reaching farther out, then thinning ever more until it was gone.

Facing me was a dais of stone centered by two benches twin to those supporting the jar people. One was occupied by another jar figure whose ball-prison showed no sign of life, yet vitality was there. To the right stood Zolan.

I gave no greeting, merely stared at the jug coffin on the bench.

Climber, his rich coat shining like a jewel (though I could see no source of luminesce save the talisman), flowed about the dais to stand beside the Protector. He turned great golden eyes upon me.

"Sorceress." A Send, that, yet none of Zolan's projecting.

For a moment I thought I could see features form in scant lines on the ball-head.

"I am no sorceress," I returned, keeping my voice as barren of feeling as I could. "I am of the House of Scorpy and am Talented as their women are."

Ball Head considered my answer; then she surprised me utterly with a second mind-message.

"In the Name of Varch, Keeper of the Gate—begone!"

That order held no meaning for me, though the name she called upon stabbed like a dagger-thrust of Darkness. Zolan stirred, looking to the enthroned one as if he would protest.

I offered no attack in return for, above all, I needed to *know,* to assess what had entrapped me.

Another period of silence ensued; then came yet a third Send. I was instantly on guard. The message was foreign to what I knew and trusted. It did not translate into words but strove to place me again under compulsion.

I moved the gem from my lips to my forehead. All my life I had been aware of those points of my person upon which a Ward must be locked.

The protection I wore had been battered and thinned by whatever Maclan had used to take me, but it was still in place. Now it swelled, strengthened, and I was shielded as if by a battle lord's body-armor.

The Send was ended. After a moment, Zolan moved a step or two away from the dais and turned fully to face me, his hands up a little as if he protested.

"Pharsali means no harm." He spoke soothingly as he might to a child. "Great evil has been done here. Those of your kind ravaged, killed. And before that—" He glanced over his shoulder to the seated figure as if asking permission.

"Before that," he began again, "Another made a pact with the Dark, which threatens not only Those Waiting but your own kin."

He paused for an answer.

"I am listening," I replied tersely.

So he served as a voice for the faceless thing baked of clay, and listen I did.

What I heard then was as mystifying as a tale translated from a strange tongue, dealing with a life whose like was hard for my breed to imagine. Still, that the account was accepted as truth by both Pharsali and Zolan I understood. The truth—as they knew it.

So long ago that my people had not yet come into this land—so far back, indeed, that they even preceded the small dark ones who came before us—this race, who carefully preserved their remains in creations of their hands, traveled by some unexplained means hither. When I learned this, I wondered whether they might have come from one of the other layers of existence, which we of the Power are aware of but do not try to visit.

The Jar Folk were in flight from enemies of their own kind, for there was a system of belief rising among them that many of the people, including those who came to dwell in the Dismals, thought to be evil. At the death of their physical forms, their personalities could continue to exist; among them, however, had been born a cult teaching that, if they wished, they might take over another body. At least one subject race was available that could be used to supply new vessels of life.

Thus arose conflict and the dispersal of many of their clans or nations. How this particular group had come to the Dismals was not revealed.

Once in this below-the-surface world, they discovered that theirs had been a bad choice. Fatal plagues struck, and thus was created the company of Seated Ones. However, the portions of being that were their essences remained. They strove to enhance their Power until they were able to venture out in spirit to explore, to learn. With this mode of existence most were content. Centuries passed, and the Jar People watched with interest as the native life of the upper world changed. They themselves continued to live by their oaths, observing only, and taking no hand in affairs not their own.

Until—Zolan, before my eyes, cringed as though a feeling of guilt had dealt him a pang.

Until our host's own arrival, an event whose occurrence he could not recall. His memory ran no further back than his being in this same cave while Pharsali had soothed him and taught him how to survive, for he had been a small child.

All the alien folk, but especially the Jar female, had instructed as well as guided him. But Tharn—Zolan nodded toward the empty bench that shared the dais with that of the round-headed one. He stopped short, and his hands clenched, then opened again.

Tharn, who was co-leader of the Jar People, made an evil choice. When Zolan became a young man, Tharn decided that he himself would leave the Dismals and visit the outer world. He tried to force his spirit into the boy's body and was defeated; however, neither could he be destroyed, and save for setting fresh Wards upon him, his own folk could not control him. His will was strong; he waited.

Then his questing spirit discovered another Uplander, a near-insane hermit. By dreams, the Jar leader drew the man to him and transferred into his chosen vessel before the others could prevent it.

At that time, Pharsali had joined temporarily with Zolan to spy out some disturbances in the far reaches of the Dismals where an entrance might exist that those above could use to descend—an event the Jar People had long feared as they had watched the actions of the natives. However, their ability to explore in spirit-essence was sharply limited. Pharsali, whose power was equal to Tharn's, could range no farther than the rest. The body carrying Tharn soon passed out of reach.

Before the twisted leader, in the body of the hermit, had departed, he had destroyed those of the outer cave, thereby making sure that he need no longer fear their interference. For, evicted from their "bodies," they had no power to oppose him.

Thus Zolan had become Pharsali's only hope of preventing an evil fate for those above. The destroyed jars I had seen held only a portion of the group that had immigrated to our world. And among the others waited those who shared Tharn's desire for a new body and a life in the upper lands. Though Zolan was wholly of Pharsali's training, even he could not be dispatched above to follow the Dark Mage, since Tharn's far greater Power could find him only too easily.

Now my thoughts struck through to Pharsali. I was aware of the touch of the alien female, but it did not threaten.

"This hermit—Tharn, as you name him—has won the interest of the king, is a member of the court. He has gathered more than one kind of Power to wield."

The Protector and Pharsali were both silent for a long moment. At last came a Send from the Jar woman, not any communication from Zolan.

"We sensed you and yours early when you were brought here as captives. We knew that you were unlike those who came seeking treasure; Tharn sent one party to so indulge its greed, but the land itself rose in defense."

"Thus," my Send interrupted her, "we were brought here by *your* will! You also made sure that we were removed from the aid coming after us."

"You would have died!" Zolan broke in heatedly. "That offspring of a vorpe had a dagger ready for your throats and would have wielded it, had it not been suggested to him by Power that he entrust you instead into the— care—of this land."

I licked my lips. So we *had* been a part of another's schemes all along. I no longer doubted at all that the favor of our fortune rested with the Ball Head. Nor could I deny that Maclan would have found it far less trouble to have us dead. But worse fates existed than death. I thought that I could guess what was coming next.

"You want my body, so you can hunt down this traitor of yours!"

Ball Head remained silent, but I had aroused Zolan to action. He moved between me and the creature on the dais as if to protect her from me. Even as I had felt that emotion in the cave of breakage, so now I could sense rage rising in him, tightly controlled but growing ever stronger as his eyes met mine.

Once again, as in that place, the heat of his anger appeared subject to the Jar woman. She might have curbed a hound slavering for a kill.

"Not so!"

The Send was not abrasive, as it might have been, yet it still gave me an odd feeling of guilt, and I hurried to strengthen *my* anger by remembering all that had occurred to us since we had come into the Dismals. I no longer needed evidence—I knew. We had been tried as a warrior tries an un-known blade before going into battle, a rider puts a horse through paces before adding it to his stable.

"Do we have a choice?" I had followed that thought to the final question.

"Wait to see what we shall ask of you. You have declared that you three are daughters of a leader of forces above. Should he not be warned?"

This Pharsali was clever to tug the thread of feeling that awakened our sense of duty. If all I had heard here was the truth—and the Talent judged it so—then, indeed, the Lord Warden must learn what the Dark threatened.

"Can you open the way out for us?"

Ball Head did not nod, but in a way I half thought I saw that movement from the faceless female.

"For you—and for him." There was no pointing at Zolan, yet plainly he was the one she meant.

Now he spun halfway around, his body stiffly tense, to face her fully. I sensed no eagerness in him for such a venture but felt, instead, a speedy denial.

Ignoring him, she continued. "Our fosterling now needs those who will care for him in your world, even as we have tended him in this. You will be his guides, as he has led you in this place of our exile."

She spoke the bald truth. Should Zolan appear in the land above without any companion or aid, he could well be deemed defective in mind, or even demonic in those places where Tharn now wore a stolen body.

"I would see my sisters," I Sent back. "I do not speak alone." However, my mind was already busy trying to look ahead at what might await us in our own level of the world.

Drucilla

BINA WAS GOING to do it! I bit at my knuckles as I watched her. So many times I had observed her busied so, ready to hand her this or that ingredi-ent as she asked for it. But this—this mass of green and red, which had grown out of the earth I had drawn upon—this was a thing of death, a growth no healer should touch.

I glanced from Bina to the wall, grayish in the moonlight. Tam—Tam had passed through that barrier as if it did not exist. *Tam—?* I Sent, to be met with a silence much deeper than any my sister had ever raised. Tam possessed, Tam held by the conniving of an unknown Other! I realized that a little of what peril the future held was a loss of our sister. The rending away of an arm or leg would be far less crippling to us.

Bina straightened, her hands now holding a sap-wet mass of flower and stem crushed together. For a moment she simply sat looking at the wall. Then she raised her right hand to her lips and mouthed a small amount, at the same time silently holding out the mess to me.

I shrank from what I must do. But without Tam, without Bina, I would be as lost, as lifeless, as a leaf whirled away by an autumn wind.

Scooping out a laden fingerful of the mixture, I chewed it hesitantly. The taste was sharp as relish used on the meat of midwinter to cover evidence of age, but it was not unpleasant. I swallowed.

I kept my eyes on the cliff while Bina and I knit threads of Power together. Never had it come so easily without effort. That facility gave me a heady feeling—why had I hesitated? This Power—to hold it—to make it work for my purpose—this was always *meant to be!*

Suddenly we were standing before the face of the cliff—I was not aware that I had even risen. Power—Bina was one with me, and I did not hold back. Now the entwined cord of our Talent, throbbing in rhythm with the beating of my heart, was hurled at the rock to cling and crawl, a visibly gleaming thread against what seemed solid stone.

This was what I was intended for. Why had I been denied such inner strength? That rock—one moment it was intact, the next it had vanished. A portal, filled with darkness that appeared to churn, waited before us. We took the way that had opened before us.

No light shone here. We went forward with care, my left hand in Bina's right, our unengaged fingers slipping along each wall. The faint radiance from outside lasted no more than four or five paces. No sound broke the silence.

"No." Bina stopped, held me anchored. I could feel each of her motions now by the smallest displacement of air. Our senses were keener, clearer.

Then Bina lifted up a questing hand, and a short burst of blue radiance broke forth. From her fingertips the light spread until she might have been holding five short candles.

Sabina

I WAS CONSTRAINED to call up a measure of Power, since we could not go blindfolded into this place. However, the force I summoned was not for slaying, and I kept it at the lowest use of energy I could. Thus, when we saw death lying at our feet a little later, we were able to avoid those poor remains, and when we won into the place of breaking, we made no misstep. Here our pace was like striving to walk against a heavy current, so often did we stagger, fighting for every step we won forward.

Fear, and, stronger still, rage—those emotions tore at us as if they would feed upon our bodies. We felt the quiver of our Wards, for those barriers had not been set to contend with such forces as this.

We saw another door to the chamber, and we headed towards it. I felt a greater impact of Power. Determined not to waste any of my own strength, I allowed the glory-glow I had summoned to die. However, there was illumination ahead—not the blue fire we knew but rather a yellowish glow such as might mark weak sunlight.

Thus we went on and came into another chamber. Within that room stood Tam, unmarked, appearing as we had seen her always when preparing to face some trial of strength or courage. Fronting her was Zolan, Climber close by his knee, and behind him a dais supporting two familiar benches. Only one was occupied by a clay figure, a statue with a round head.

Before we could Send, a message came—not from Tam, who held her jewel before her, and not from Zolan. It was alien, like a piece of writing from some foreign land, requiring all one's wits to make sense of it.

"Welcome to you, Lady Sabina, Lady Drucilla. As has the Lady Tamara, you have proven your Talent."

"Did I not say"—Tam's Send came at once—"that we three are as one? Certainly if I won here, then they would come also. It is their turn now to hear what you would have of us."

Again, that Send, which became clearer and clearer the longer we received it, gave the history of the Jar People (so we have come to call them, as their name for themselves was never told us). At the same time we understood what this Pharsali would have of us. As we compared it to what we already knew, it made sense.

We were offered escape from the Dismals, for, in spite of all Zolan had reported, there *was* a way out. Then we would be in Gurlyon again. I did not use Send, rather open speech, to raise protest.

"When we reach the Upper Land, we shall be in a place which has been disputed many times over. However, we are weaponless, and clothing such as ours could bring trouble from any who sight us." My jerkin and trousers did not seem strange to me here, but I could foresee how any rider coming upon us, whether Breaksword or a follower sworn to some reiver lord, would straightway take us into custody. Unless our newly strengthened Power could be a defense? But, long ago, we had sworn an unbreakable oath against using our Talent for that purpose. Sword, snaplock and the weapons of human time and place could be used, not those of the Power—except against Dark Ones.

Both Tam and Cilla assented to that Send aimed impartially at the two before us. Where could we possibly find what we must have: clothing and accoutrements that would arouse no unwanted interest?

"Those who descended to our world to reap and ravage"—again the alien Send, hot with the same intensity of emotion we had encountered in the chamber of destruction—"stayed for a space. They came laden, for they had been raiding above, and what they had taken still lies in their old camp. It may serve."

I wondered. If it were true that we had been drawn to the Dismals by the will of Ball Head, then perhaps others had been similarly beckoned to this place. But why and how would Breakswords be summoned to plunder and destroy? If this Pharsali could read minds—and I was sure that she could, for as I framed the thought I had felt a discernible touch against my inward shield—then she was not going to give any answer to my suspicion.

So it remained that Zolan was to be sent into the Upper Lands under our guidance and care. Breakswords and Border raidings aside, that challenge should be trouble enough! I did not look forward to such a journey with complete confidence, either in the actions of the three of us, or his reaction to Gurlyon.

Seventeen

Sabina

Those who had come seeking the "treasure" of the Dismals had not attempted to conceal the entrance they had discovered. Though when they had returned to that site, they had found no exit to use. Rotting rope lay in coils at the foot of the cliff, but how the Dismal-dwellers had betrayed the invaders could not be discerned.

Bones, a pile of rusted metal breastplates, and several dented steel bonnets lay with the tangled rope. These grisly trophies lay heaped about another object—a long, hook-ended stick of a nonhuman limb, which stood in their midst as if to mark a field of defeat. If one surveyed the scene more closely, the marks of attack by monsters were clearly visible.

We had no desire to put name to any of the slain Breakswords and for the present we avoided the battlefield. However, as one, we turned on Zolan. We had been promised a campsite for the plundering, but nothing lying here was of value to us.

Tam, however, suddenly left my side and made for the heap of gear on the ground, then swooped, as a hawk stoops on her prey, to arise with a sword in her hand. The blade was dulled but intact.

Our host was only moments behind her. He had found a snaplock, but that was unusable, the damp having rendered it so. Hurling it to one side, he pushed a little farther into the pile. Though he found another sword, it was also useless—the blade ended a short length beyond the hilt in a jagged break.

Though every inch of me sickened at the thought of such delving, I forced myself to hunt also. Cilla was the last to join us and she wore a mask of disgust.

In the end we freed three swords and four daggers, which were sound. Tam stood wielding the blade she had first discovered, her body following through the movements of practice. She was obviously caught by memories of Grosper and our life there.

I wanted to hurl back into the tangle of rope the dagger I held. It was a vile-looking weapon: both edges of the blade appeared deliberately serrated, to deliver the worst of wounds. The hilt was made of horn, and the knife had known so much use that this blade-holder was worn smooth, save for where a leather strip, now green with mold, wrapped it.

But such war-spoils were not what we had come to seek. I looked to where Zolan stood, awkwardly swinging another sword, his actions making it plain he had no training in the art of arms.

"This is no camp," I stated sternly.

He had caught the point of the sword between two rocks so it twisted out of his grip, the clatter of its fall bringing attention also from Tam and Cilla. Seeming deaf to my complaint, he got the blade back in his hand before he looked up.

"Up there—" He pointed to the cliff with his upraised chin, keeping both hands upon his weapon, lest he lose it again. "There lies the way." His head inclined to the left.

Directly before us the cliff wall was bare but, some paces away, it was cloaked in a heavy growth of vine. We could see, through gaps in the leaves here and there, that the anchoring stems indeed were thick. Yet the invaders had chosen to anchor their ropes about these growths, which in the end had somehow betrayed them.

I edged around the nearest vine and came to stand by the base of what might be a natural ladder. But I had no desire to try its strength—this lower land had shown too many perils for us to risk committing ourselves in overhaste to such a climb.

However, there was one among us who had no second thoughts about the matter. Climber, who had waited to one side as we plundered the battlefield, near hurled himself past me, to spring some distance up from the ground. Half hidden by tattered leaves, he found firm foothold and proceeded upward, making good speed.

In only a short time, his red fur tunneled out of the upper reaches of the vines, and he found a grasp on the stone easily enough to pull himself over the edge of the cliff. He had not arrived out in the Upper World, though, but had merely come to a ledge. It was wide enough, so that he could pass out of sight, then, on turning, look down at us again.

A faint Send came from him, an urging for us to follow.

With a gagging distaste, I set the dagger in my belt, feeling that I had taken on a touch of evil, as I began to search for handholds in the leaf-curtained vines.

My climb was both awkward and slow, however I found no looseness of vine or indwelling creature to fear. As Zolan's companion had done, I pulled myself over the ledge to lie panting for a moment while the beast's tongue flicked across my cheek.

The vine was shaking—someone had followed me. On hands and knees I crawled away and for the first time saw that this spot was closely akin to the one we had found earlier. The ledge was deeper than one might guess from below.

Not too far from me lay blackened stone bearing signs of past fires, and piled against the cliff were bags and bundles. This must be the camp we sought.

I made no move to investigate by myself but, a moment later, Tam was with me. After her came Zolan, and last of all Cilla. I was trying to understand how and why the Breakswords had chosen this site.

Tamara

It was good to stand armed properly once more. The hilt of the blade I had found was firm in my hand as I breathed deeply. I had not realized how the lack of customary weapons would be so frustrating. Zolan had never known such skill. That would be another problem we must solve, but it could wait.

Almost as one, the three of us turned to the gear piled along the cliff. Never knowing what we might be forced to handle in the future, we did not slash the ropes that held the bundles and bags, but worked patiently at the knots to free the contents.

Indeed the Breakswords had made a profitable raid! They certainly had not plundered a mere tower hold—they must instead have taken some helpless merchant. The prize was sober clothing and, though the garments were of dull shades and plain of adornment, the stuff was honest wool and recently woven. Such would not betray us to any we would meet.

"New made," Cilla commented as she stroked the folds of a sturdy gray cloak.

"Merchant's trade goods," I returned firmly. "Fortune has dealt well with us! A chapman can travel in a small party without attracting too much attention, so we might well pass with little notice."

Bina shook her head. "But without mounts and pack ponies, are we to drag our wealth along the ground?"

I laughed. "Bina, you have ever been the practical one! Yes, animals we must have—"

There came a sharp hissing sound from above. Glancing up, we saw that Climber had reached the top of the outer cliff. We looked to Zolan for interpretation. He laid his sword carefully on the ledge and, giving us no explanation, set himself to another laborious climb. If he had possessed the clawed feet of his beast, he might have made a faster job of the journey. We watched him go at a creep, testing and retesting each hold before trusting to it.

Until we knew more, we had no desire to follow. However, we set aside exploration of the packs but rather sat with our heads at a painful angle to watch him. I caught up a handful of grit that some past wind had deposited in a place between two packs and began to rub it along the spotted blade.

I had not known how deeply I had missed weapons until I once more held a sword hilt in my hand. Yes—I had drawn upon the Power, yet I had always been aware that true control of that was a chancy thing. Steel, though, was a tool I could be sure of.

But I nearly dropped the weapon when I was hailed by a Send I knew by now, only that alien shading did not accompany it.

"Up!" Zolan made an order of that.

We were in no way in a hurry to obey but lingered to roll the plunder back into the covering that had protected it.

"*Up!*" A shade of anger darkened the message.

Zolan had always curbed any emotion he might feel, except when Climber had been injured, but not this time. Was he threatened by some danger?

The cat-creature had swung into sight again and was descending with the same skill that he had used to go aloft. We had moved to cliffside and I, for one, was trying to make out handholds. However, our red-coated fellow traveler did not even look at us. Determinedly he made for the booty, set his needle-tipped teeth in a rope end, then leaped back and began to climb again, trailing the rope behind. Once more he disappeared over the rock edge above and was gone.

The rope flapped against the stone wall behind him, gave a short tug upward and settled again.

"Rope!" The message of the Send was no longer "*up,*" but it was easy enough to understand. We need not fear trusting ourselves to those shallow, sometimes only fingertip holds Climber and Zolan had used—we would also have this support.

The thick cord was still twitching, and I guessed that Zolan was making fast the other end as swiftly as he could. I looked to Bina and Cilla, made my sword tight as possible without proper sheath, and reached for the rope that at last had stopped swinging.

As I climbed, I marveled that Zolan had made his ascent without a rope. I considered that I was well trained in the martial arts and that I subdued once and for all the uneasiness with heights that I had fought desperately when younger, yet I had the feeling that some force in this place, albeit one weak enough to be withstood, had pressed against me all the way. A near-dissipated Warding? I fought down that first flicker of fear and, with my hands on the rope and the toes of my boots searching for chinks in the wall, I continued.

From above a hand reached down. Steely as a chain it closed about my wrist and, in a breath or two, I was drawn painfully over a rocky edge, feeling my clothing tear.

Now two hands were set on my shoulders, lifting the forepart of my body to drag me along. My sight had blurred, and I felt suddenly so weak that I lay flat where I had been dropped, able only to shift my head to one side, so that I did not rest facedown.

I could do no more than lie there panting. A short while later I heard sounds behind me, surely announcing the arrival of one of my sisters. I tried a mind-message and met only confusion.

Weaker and weaker I grew. I attempted to draw on Power, however, not only did nothing answer but clouding of mind now joined diminished sight. Even as I had been thrust here, so another compulsion arose—one that strove to push me backward. Yet I would not yield until darkness fell, perhaps to enclose me forever.

Drucilla

THE ROPE AND the rock that faced me I could no longer resist, nor did I really wish to. Tam had gone and then Bina. The rope pulled taut, and I judged that an order to be followed.

As I fought my way upward I realized I was meeting opposition from without—a challenge set not against the body but rather the Talent. It was surely a Ward and, though nowhere near as strong as those we had found elsewhere in the Dismals, it still tried to repel me, so that I had to put forth twice the effort I might have used. I began to mutter my desire for aid.

Several days had elapsed between our meeting with the Jugged One and the making of this climb. I did not think that Pharsali intended us to shrink from what we did now. Perhaps Wards grew weaker with the passage of time, and this might be old by human reckoning, nonetheless a force so used might have been partly the reason for the carnage to be seen on the floor of the world below.

It grew necessary for me to pause longer and longer in my search for toeholds as I proceded. Without the rope I could not have done it at all. However, I was aware of what lay about me when Zolan reached to draw me onto level ground. The air was much cooler and I was shivering, regretting that good cloak I had left behind; but with his help, I was able to totter over and drop down beside my sisters.

Tam had managed to lever herself up straight-armed, though she was blinking oddly and showed no sign of recognizing me. Bina was twisting back and forth as if to bring herself also into sitting position.

Having made sure of us, Zolan stood a little away on a plateau that stretched for what might be leagues beyond toward distant mountains.

I could not see what had caught his attention, but he suddenly began to stride away from where we were clustered.

We watched as our guide continued to grow smaller before our eyes. By the sun, the time must have been well past the midpoint of the day. This place held no cave or other shelter, and the wind freshened to roughen our skin; however, no one suggested returning down that rigorous climb to raid the loot on the ledge-camp for other clothing.

Tam got to her feet and Climber raised his head from his paws. She made no move to push past him but shuffled instead to the rope, which lay slack across the mixture of rock and sun-baked earth. She stooped, caught at the cord, and tugged. The far end did not come free; it appeared to be securely anchored.

As if she were too tired to return the few steps to us, she sat down there. The front of both her jerkin and her leggings were scraped, and small tears showed in the fabric, yet she made no effort to examine them. Zolan was no longer in sight. We might attempt to follow, save that none of us three had the strength for such action.

Bina did not get to her feet, but she moved to face us at the rim of the Dismals. She was frowning.

"The other side—" She spoke as if assuring herself of the accuracy of a memory. "Maclan dropped us from the other side. Must we get all the way around the Dismals?"

I found that possibility too overwhelming to answer at once. She was right, our enemies' approach had been from the east, not the west. But such concerns did not seem to matter anymore; I, for one, could stir for no action whatever. The thought of having to tramp forward for an unknown number of leagues, guided by the dizzying edge of the canyon rim, was too exhausting a prospect for me to consider at present.

That Ward, for force-barrier it must have been, still possessed enough power to limit us. I was cold, hungry, and thirsty. The answers for all of those wants lay below. Perhaps this was not the route Pharsali had promised us. We *were* out of the Dismals, yes, but were still almost as helpless as we had been when we were sent there. Zolan had gone off. If he had spoken the truth, he was as ignorant of the land that stretched about us as we had been of his world.

Tam looked out over the country where our host had disappeared. Once more she grasped the rope and gave a sharp tug; this time, though, it did not come free here where its end was twined around two large stones pushed together.

"We cannot go down again," I protested. "The Ward is not exhausted but we are."

Bina nodded. "That is so."

Tam turned to face us squarely. "Now we ought not to attempt it, no, yet it must be done. Without supplies and warmer clothing it is useless to—"

She stopped nearly in midword. We felt it, too—a pull, a compulsion. Oddly, it brought no fear but rather a sensation of expectation totally free of any emotion but a feeling of goodwill.

We moved together, though none of us rose to our feet. Now we were crouched shoulder to shoulder, hand clasping hand, and waiting—

This was unlike anything I had felt—we had felt—before. I tried to sift the feeling, believing it could not be intended for me. It radiated warmth, not for the body but the mind. Someone—or thing—wished me well but also desired my presence. I looked at Bina and to Cilla. They were watching the land, whose openness was broken only by clumps of trees here and there.

Climber was on his feet again, his head up. He gave a cry that was neither yelp nor purr, yet no challenge.

"Zolan!"

I was sure I was right. Then I saw distant movement. We sat, still hand-linked, waiting. Out among the sparse stands of trees, the sprouting grass of late spring, shadows began to move. No, not shadows—solid forms, and they were coming at such a good pace that they grew quickly before our eyes.

"Horses!" I cried aloud.

At the front of the small herd there was a mounted figure. Zolan, it must be the man from the Dismals, but how—?

That compulsion now centered upon the rider and the animals which followed him. The mounts looked unlike the horses I had ridden; then I understood. Though there were indeed three or four taller animals among them, Zolan was astride the bare back of one of several small, tough ponies, such as had been known and cherished centuries long in Gurlyon for their versatility.

In a moment they were level with us. Zolan slipped from his seat, turning to draw one hand down the nose of his mount before he faced us.

Though none of them appeared tired, neither did any stray, but remained in an uncertain half-circle.

Zolan still did not address us. Instead he looked to Climber, and I felt the brush of that alien Send. The red-coated beast walked toward the man slowly. Some of the ponies snorted and backed a little, but not one bolted. Climber reached the horse Zolan still kept hold of by the ragged mane, matted with leaf fragments and a twist of vine.

Talents—! This was true Talent, but it was not one we shared. I had heard of horsetalkers, men who could walk out to even a nervous stallion or battle destrier and, within moments, establish bond. Perhaps that was how, originally, a fierce hunter such as Climber had become his companion.

I was on my feet now, walking toward him. This pocket-sized herd was not from any proud stable—the closer I drew, the more visible that fact became. They were of the wild, untended by any currycomb, perhaps never having felt the weight of a saddle.

Eighteen

Sabina

So Zolan performed an act of Power which answered our most pressing problem. The herd he had found and ensorcelled spread out a little to graze, pawing at the dry winter grass, seeking to uncover the new growth still low to the ground. Zolan appeared unaffected by the energy-leaching barrier that had tested us so severely, but then he had also walked through the one in the cave, which had been an iron wall as far as we were concerned. When Tam spoke of the difficulty we had in passing this Ward, he only shrugged. Nor did he give any explanation of how and where he had discovered the horses and ponies. He made no effort now to keep them within our reach, but rather set about at once to retrieve the plunder from below.

We would have joined, although reluctantly, in the effort, but he waved us away, even as he readied for what we opined was a descent as dangerous as the climb had been. Climber flashed down at twice the man's speed, though Zolan seemed well fitted for what he must do. We tossed the free end of the rope over the edge at his call and waited until it twitched, whereupon we labored to draw it up, discovering that we must work together to raise the two bundles it held.

Though in spring the days had begun to lengthen, twilight was drawing in, and we could not continue in the dark. After we had untied the fourth load and dropped the rope once more, there came no further signals; instead Climber joined us. Lashed to the red fur of his back was a small bundle, which he brought directly to me.

He sat there staring up into my face, and I received a fleeting mind-picture of the waterfall in Zolan's cave. The suggestion was both plain and effective—I was so dry I could scarcely gather enough moisture in my mouth to swallow. My hands had been busy, and I was now holding the contents of the bag he had brought me: four waterskins, flat and dry.

Climber's tongue lolled out. Seeing that I was watching him, he rose and turned. As I gazed at him, he looked over his shoulder. I took the hint.

Tam and Cilla were at the cliff edge watching Zolan's ascent. I nodded to Climber, and he trotted off with me moving slowly and weakly in his wake. By my calculation we headed north. As we moved out, I began to hear bird cries; a moment later my fogged mind and muffled senses connected to give me an answer. Months before, as the pitiless Gurlyon winter approached, I had heard such vocal flocks flying south in gatherings so vast they could not be numbered. Now they must be on their way back to their summer range.

Can the human nose, so inferior to that of animals, pick up the scent of water? I was certain now that I moved towards that life-giving source, and my pace quickened as my body's demands overcame my weariness. We were a good distance away from the cliff, and the way was dipping gradually lower so that I did not have to look for hand- and toeholds as I moved. Below stood trees, of the sort that did not shed in winter but held their dark needlelike foliage all year long. They raggedly surrounded a circular pond of respectable size.

I lifted my cupped hands a little later, to relish a draught of cool water. I gulped and sputtered as it drained down my chin and throat. Then my father's warning surfaced in my mind: *Drink sparingly at first, if you have been long thirsty.* But simply to sit there and allow the water to trickle through my fingers, watch the migrating birds float and wade a little distance away, and to take a sip now and then was blessedly renewing. For a time, I forgot all else.

Climber came to nudge against me, taking the edge of one of the waterskins and tugging it away. I roused myself and set about filling them; it was near dark now, and guilt spurred me on. When the bags were bulging,

I shouldered the straps while Climber waited impatiently for me a little way along the return trail.

Drucilla

THERE APPEARED TO be no end to Zolan's energy; perhaps our erstwhile host was better able to call on his own sense of Power than we could now do with ours. He pulled and positioned the larger bundles we had drawn up the cliff into an uneven circle. The cloak I had wished for lay now about my shoulders, and Bina had given me some crumpled leaves to rub between my rope-burned palms.

She had returned, before the light failed, with news of nearby water, and four skins of it burdening her back. What food supplies the unfortunate merchant and his attackers had left were no longer fit for use. But Climber had brought in a grass-runner, while Zolan supplied some roots to bury under the coals of the fire, above which chunks of meat seared on sharpened sticks.

Tam's hands were surely as painful as mine, but she was still hard at work. She had hacked off another thick lock of her hair with the dulled sword and now strove to knot it into a small bag. Muffled exclamations of frustration and anger burst from her from time to time, but she persevered, hunched close to the fire to catch the best light.

Zolan subsided at last on the far side of the fire to sit staring into it intently, as if reading some important message in the flames. He had tied back his hair with a twist of grass, and now, in addition to raw scratches on his bare arms, I could see a long scrape down his left cheek.

We had reached our present campsite, true—but where would we go from here? I closed my eyes and tried to picture the markings on the maps I had indifferently scanned back in Grosper. Grosper! A Send—could we reach our mother from here, now that we were safely past any of the confining Wards of the Dismals?

And how much Power might we now call upon? I knew that the balance of Talent could have been changed by our drawing so heavily upon it in the immediate past. I opened my eyes to look into the flames. Then I remembered the gem Tam had found in the ruins. A caller—it might prove just such an energy magnifier. Silently I relayed my thoughts to both my sisters.

"Yes," Tam was the first to respond, also by Send. Perhaps her thoughts followed my own. As Bina agreed, Tam put her hand within her jerkin and drew it forth closed but with golden light gleaming between the fingers.

"Whom do you call?" Zolan used voice instead of mind-speech. Was the nature of his response evidence that the Power he held had been lessened by his coming into the Upper World?

"We seek our mother," I returned.

With the care of one handling a fragile treasure, Tam laid the gem on the ground and we moved together, forming a circle around it with clasped hands.

Eyes closed, I faced darkness from which I began to form an image of my mother as she often appeared, seated at work, her desk before her spread with the reports she read to such good purpose. Just so—yes, she was sitting in the high-backed and cushioned chair she often preferred, fine satin skirts outspread to prevent creasing (Mother tolerated no disorder in garments). Her face grew larger as if I were approaching ever closer.

Now I was able to sense that strength feeding into me readily and swiftly from Tam and Bina. Perhaps because I had suggested this course of action, so I was the first to essay the contact. Approaching me came a sense of rising heat, not to burn but to warm, to cherish, as Mother might reach out comforting arms to encircle us all.

I was—in! Fearing every moment I might lose that tenuous touch, I mind-spoke swiftly. I wasted no time in description but relayed only the most crucial facts: that we were now free, that we moved once more in the Upper World (though we were not sure where), and that we carried news of great import. I used my words as I might threads, stitching with them a tapestry or working a needed banner for imminent battle.

I felt as breathless as if I had been shouting that curtailed report aloud. Then came a reply:

"*Head South if you can. We are at war—Gurlyon struggles within. We shall come—*"

It was a firm promise, standing as a sworn oath. I had not been aware of the weight lying on me until I was freed of it. Sighing, I looked to Tam and then Bina. Both of them nodded. We three might be separated in body from our mother, but we had been reunited with her in spirit and might henceforth draw upon that link for support. All at once I was very sleepy. Together, side by side so we touched, we curled together. Tam had taken the gem up again and placed it where it rested on her breast to yield heat under the cloaks we had drawn over us. Out in the world, a world familiar to us if no longer safe, we finally knew a measure of peace. And, at that moment of rapidly approaching slumber, Zolan was no longer a part of it.

Tamara

ALL AT ONCE hunger pinched my middle, and I awoke. The fire was dead, but light surrounded us, a glow that rose from neither flames nor from the gem. I instantly put my hand forth to search for the jewel from the world below, fearing that it might have disappeared during the night. My fingers touched it and, brushing aside the cloak, I clasped that strange find. Its glow was gone; it was only a dullish oval. Dead? Had my uses of it destroyed the Power within, or could it not display life for long outside the Dismals?

Not too far away, chunks of roasted meat, still twig-impaled, rested on a small square of hide. Beside them lay roots that had burst their outer charred skins in places and now emitted white puffs. Seeing those offerings, I was distracted from concern over the stone and drawn back to the necessity of food.

Food—had I Sent that word? I was not sure. However, a stirring began around me; Cilla and Bina were sitting up, rubbing their eyes. I glanced across the fire-pit. There was no sign of Zolan nor Climber, whom I had last seen seated close to the man. A second search showed me that we were, for the moment, alone.

Bina reached for one of the water bags and held it up, setting its spout to her lips with one hand and working its cap loose with the other. As she drank, Cilla lifted one of the roots.

After one bite, she grimaced. "Cold," she announced, eyeing the tuber dispiritedly. But she did not stop eating.

So we broke our fast for the first time back in our own world. That feeling of freedom and rightness continued in me even as I also chewed the cold and tasteless fare. Since arising, we had seen no sign of Zolan and Climber—they might have returned down the cliff. On impulse, I stood to look over the piles of bags towards the plains.

If Zolan had left us, the horsetalker had not taken his herd with him: one horse and several ponies yet stood at graze.

"He is gone."

Bina stood beside me.

"Do we wait, search, or go on our own?"

My sister posed well the questions from which we must choose answers. I watched the small group of mounts. Used as I was to horses, I had no belief in my ability to render them as biddable as had Zolan. There was nothing about their uncared-for hides to even suggest they were tamed, trained mounts. They did not show signs of any ranch. But how had these steeds survived so long if they were indeed the animals the reivers had left? From the remains of that battle we had found at the bottom of the cliff in the Dismals, years—a number of them—must have passed since the raiders had gone treasure hunting. Were those I now watched the offspring of the mounts and burden-beasts that had been left to wander free after that conflict? The matter, however, meant little now.

"Let us search for him." Cilla had joined us.

It was true that we had been able to contact our mother, but our Talents were not the same as Zolan's. Still, this answer was the best any one of us could offer now. Again we encircled the gem, but we had no more than settled around it when Cilla shook her head. "Mother was already bonded to us. Zolan is not."

She rose and walked around the fire-blackened spot to the other side of our rough camp where we had last seen him. There she stood, looking intently at the place where he had lain.

Drucilla

IF ONE PERSON is not bonded to another by blood or close kinship, then in order to reach him or her by mind-speech, a Sender must have an object recently touched by the one sought. I knelt, stared down; I might have been trying to count every fragment of gravel and earth. The bed-place showed evidence that someone had lain there, and for time enough to impress the surface; however, such traces did not hold enough Power for my purpose. I plucked a pinch, a very dusty scrap, of red hair from the ground. Not

Zolan's—the tuft must have come from Climber's hide. Could the man be reached through the beast?

It was true that the animal of the Dismals could communicate with Zolan, but the cat-creature's Send was either too low or too alien to clearly reach us, and we had never been able to receive any but the faintest sense that it even existed. Still I held my find carefully as I continued to search. At last I was forced to accept that the bed held nothing more for me to find.

When I showed the fur-scrap, I expected disappointment; however, to my surprise, neither of my sisters greeted my find so. Tam motioned to the gem she had set out once more on the ground. With care, lest I lose one of the hairs, I placed them on and about the talisman. We closed the circle, seated ourselves as we had the night before, and made ready.

Many rules governed the use of Talent. Since I had found the hairs, I must initiate the Send, even as I had when we quested for Mother. Again, as had been the case with our call to her, Climber's image was easy to draw upon the dark curtain of the inner mind.

We could not guess what form a beast-bound Send should take; it might be that Climber's lack of speech might be an insurmountable barrier. I eyed the mind-picture I had raised.

"*Come back—bring Zolan.*" Words—those simple phrases and the feeling of need—were all I could project. "*Come back—bring Zo—*"

I was interrupted by a Send so powerful that it might have been a physical blow.

"*I come!*"

"That was not Climber!" Bina exclaimed.

In spite of the fact that it had been somewhat accented, as if our spoken language had been shaped by a foreign tongue, the message had come without doubt from Zolan.

We did not attempt to reach either of the roamers again. Instead we busied ourselves with a further examination of the contents of the plunder bags.

"Those robbers helped themselves to some burgher's well-stocked pack train," Tam commented.

She was right. What we shook out in the way of clothing were, in spite of long-set creases, trews, shirts, and jackets of sturdy stuff and good honest make. I pulled free a second bundle to discover women's garments of only slightly less durable manufacture. Woolen, these were—no satins or tafties of Southern gentlewoman's wear. But the necks of two of the gowns were edged with embroidered patterns, simply yet carefully done. A third dress, without any decoration, might have been intended for a personal serving maid.

The goods-pack held two petticoats, but four chemises, the latter with narrow lace binding about the trim. I held one up, only to find that the looted merchant must have dealt with customers shorter and stouter than the likes of us.

We measured our newfound wardrobe against our bodies and made the decision that we would not discard our reptilian Dismals garb but would pull this more acceptably feminine gear over it. Our appearance would be that of trampers—those who beg their way and have no fixed dwelling-place. Such vagabonds had come and gone at Grosper for as long as we had been there.

We were still poking about the bags when we heard a whinny and looked up quickly to see Zolan, mounted, Climber running beside him as he rode towards our camp at a gallop. Within a short distance he pulled up, to sit looking as if he had never seen us before.

The ill-fitting clothes evidently served to disguise us. I remembered our condition of undress at our first meeting and felt the blood rise to my face. A moment later our host smiled. I did not know whether he was minded or not to laugh at the appearance we offered.

"Ladies." He sketched an informal bow from his seat on the horse, which was tossing its head in display; it had been fitted with an improvised bit and bridle. "I see that you are minded to be on your way."

"We have had news of aid from the South," Tam answered. "The sooner we start, the shorter will be the journey."

Zolan's smile faded; his face became blank.

"Just so." He slipped from his mount and tossed the extra-long reins to Climber as if this action had been long in use between them.

Again we worked, breaking off our labors only long enough to eat. Zolan had brought back with him more roots to be roasted. They were easier to chew and swallow when hot but were undoubtedly not as good as the fare to be had in even some of Alsonia's humble taverns.

When we finished with the packs, selecting what to take with us to present the likeness of traders, it was too late in the day for us to start out. We had even come upon some small trinkets that might gain us entry at a keep, should we be invited into such a dwelling.

I welcomed an object that was, to me, a treasure: a wooden case in the form of an acorn, which protected a number of coarse needles and a couple of skeins of heavy thread. We each had a cloak and wool cap that could be pulled down far enough to hide our ears and our long hair, the remainder of which would be hidden under our cloak-collars.

"No!" Tam flicked the skirt of her dress about, frowning heavily at the sight of reptile-skin leggings that still showed beneath. The dress that had fallen to her share, when we had cast lots for the clothes, was even shorter than those Bina and I were wearing—after a fashion. *"No!"* she repeated even louder.

She tugged and pulled at the clothing that was never meant for the use she demanded from it. Standing once more in only the garb of the Dismals, she reached for a set of trews, which slid easily over the skin breeches. Her choice of a shirt and then a jacket somehow did suit her. Only her long braid remained, and she lifted that plait now in her hand as if she weighed it.

Swinging around, Tam pointed to the dagger I still carried, though I wanted no part of such a weapon. She held the braid straight up and as far away from her head as she could.

"Cut it!" she ordered aloud in a tone that left me to understand that she would hear none of the arguments ready on my lips.

When I did not move at once, she let the plait drop and put hand to her sword hilt, though she must know that a blade so dull would not serve for a cosmetic operation.

Reluctantly I did as she wished. When I had sawed through that luxuriant twining of never trimmed locks, she snatched it from me and stuffed it into her shirtfront.

"So be it!" she snapped. "Let us ride."

Nineteen

Tamara

Ride we did not, until shortly after dawn. Zolan and Climber had brought in the remainder of the horses and ponies. Three more of the mounts had saddles improvised with materials from the bags as well as bridles woven by Zolan, doubtless products of his day apart.

He drew us, one by one, to a horse and obviously Sent some introduction or order to the animal, giving us also a name he must have selected for each beast.

I was glad that I had chosen not to wear skirts, as we must ride astride on such unfamiliar and surely untrained steeds, and women's garb made a knee grip difficult. The horse he had apportioned to me was a mare, certainly not of high breeding and rather the worse for her wild life, as well. Her rough coat was gray, and her ragged mane held a sprinkling of burrs.

We had already packed what gear we had onto the stoutest-looking ponies. Those impromptu pack-beasts were roped together in a long string and led by each of us, turn and turn about.

Our first goal was the pond Bina had discovered. There we made sure that the water bags were well filled and that the animals drank. No food remained on which we might break our fasting, and we knew we must acquire provisions of some sort as early and as well as we could.

It was a good morning, somewhat warmer than we had experienced since leaving the Dismals. Our way south led not directly to the mountains ahead but rather towards a point to our right, but for a while our path paralleled the clifftop. There Climber disappeared. We were passing a stand of trees at the time, and that copse was well behind us when he returned. In his jaws was clamped a game bird of the breed often served on the table at Grosper. Though one fowl would not go far for four of us, Zolan dismounted to solemnly receive this gift, which he proceeded to secure by tying its feet to the pack-roping on the nearest pony. He made much of Climber, pulling his small ears gently and running fingers through the thick fur.

I do not know how Zolan was able to measure time, but at intervals he would bring the whole party to a halt, have us dismount and breathe the animals. I took the chance at each of these stops to work upon what I had started earlier. From my shorn hair I had at last netted a miniature sack into which I could fit the gem out of the ruins. To that talisman bag I added a small braid by way of chain, so that the packet might hang about my neck. The stone was dull; I might have exhausted whatever power it had by overuse. Still it was truly a treasure—one Mother must see and examine.

Dusk had not yet fallen when Zolan called an end to the day's journeying. We had angled even farther from the mountains, though the land was not very flat. During the afternoon, Climber had added to our larder another bird and a plump ground leaper unwise in venturing far from its burrow.

We did not string a rope to tie the horses, as was the custom for travelers. Instead, as each mount and pony was relieved of its burden, it was allowed to simply move off, Zolan giving no heed to its straying.

We found water at the campsite, a wide and shallow brook into which our animals waded as they drank. We washed our faces, scrubbing our hands with leaves pulled from waterside plants. Bina gave a little cry of recognition and harvested a small growth of cress, sharing the leaves out carefully with us all.

We had eaten, not enough to satisfy but at least better fare than the day before. Since we were far less tired than we had been the previous evening, we lingered by the fire Zolan had started, oddly, with the rubbing of a stick by a small stone—or was that only a gesture to conceal some use of his Talent?

At the same time, it became evident that our companion out of the Dismals wanted something from us: information. He began with a series of questions; he might have been compiling the list for some while.

The inquiries he made were intended to give him some idea of the Upper Land and those dwelling there. We answered each in turn carefully, trying to be as usefully informative as we could. The unhappy situation along the Border was fairly easy to outline; after all, we had lived with the results of that conflict for years. Our father's wardship we made plain, along with the influence he wielded, both in the North and at home. Lastly, we explained to our best ability the disturbed state of Gurlyon, ending with the story of the lost young king.

Bina it was who faced him squarely when the tale was ended, with a question from us all:

"Are *you* Gerrit?"

He said nothing for a moment but simply stared at us where we sat across the fire from him in our usual position.

"Well, are you?" Cilla finally demanded.

He did not lower his eyes. "No!" he said sharply.

I entered the game. "If you are, then you may expect double danger ahead. He who now sits upon the throne is in the process of striving to overthrow the rule of the older clan chiefs. It is he who welcomed this priest from the Yakins, whom you say is no Speaker for the Light but a force of Evil. Mother has warned that Gurlyon is in a state of war—not against the South this time but clan against clan, even as was so in the far-back time of Munstrater when Lasseran and Borkley made a pact and brought Gurlyon to heel. The royal line has been broken twice since then, always to the harm of Gurlyon and its people."

Zolan's face had become masklike, as we had seen it before when he was not minded to share his thoughts. He stood up, and the ill-fitting clothing he wore seemed transformed into a regal robe as he delivered a true courtier's bow.

"My thanks to you, ladies. At least I have new facts to think upon which may help me in the future. Rest you well; I go to check on the mounts." He bowed again and left us.

"Is he, or is he not, the lost king?" mused Bina.

"He has courtly manners," suggested Cilla.

"Which he could," I replied, "have learned elsewhere than at court. It may well be that he was young enough to forget his life in the Upper World but that Pharsali's training readied him instead to be a king of Gurlyon."

As I lay in the nest of grass I had pulled for a bed and tugged my cloak over me, I wondered what snarl would tangle this skein of the World-Weavers ere we all reached our journey's end. I fully expected to dream, but I brought no memory of night-visions back with me into wakefulness when we roused in the morning.

I sat up, still yawning, to see Zolan a little away from our camp. With sword in hand, he was striving to follow a pattern of attack—at least, I *thought* it was attack—and making a very poor show of armsmanship.

He might resent any word from me; however, if one wears a sword, one must be prepared to use it. Gurlys, who were trained from the time they could stand and hold a hilt tightly, might not all be masters of the blade, but the poorest of instruction exceeded none at all. Was it now my duty to offer a child's weapon-training? To any of my own people, such an offer would have been insulting, but then they would have no need of it. I could not let our host be butchered just because words from me might injure his pride.

Glad that I had no skirts to impede me, I stepped fully into his sight, my own sword in my hand. As I thought he would do, he stopped short in his awkward posturing and stood panting, set-faced and offering me no welcome.

Planting my swordpoint in the earth, I set both hands on the hilt. The stance I copied from Markand, who had given me training. It was a posture of his I had come to dread, since such attention always meant he was going to speak of some error of mine with blistering heat. Perhaps I assumed my role too well, for Zolan retreated and started to return his weapon to the sheath he had fashioned to hold it. Still, I knew I must warn him that ignorance of his weapon might mean speedy death. Unless he summoned up Talent—a tactic that would lead to cries of witchcraft and perhaps fiery death at the stake.

"I was lessoned young," I said. "My father ordered that we be taught to use weapons when we were still children. The folk whom you must meet to fulfill your promise to Pharsali, those of gentle blood, and others, are so instructed as well. The Gurlys are quick to take offense, especially when they are drunk—a common state for many of them. When the 'lifewater' flows freely, they pick quarrels, which can only be settled by bloodletting."

I paused. He had halted in his withdrawal and seemed to be listening thoughtfully. Send touched me.

"*Show, do not tell, sister.*" Cilla stepped up beside me.

She had never shown any pleasure in martial art, but now she did something I never thought to see—she unfastened the cumbersome dress, let it fall to the ground, and overstepped its folds. I did not need another mind-touch to know what she planned.

"By favor," I asked him carefully, "give your blade to Cilla. Let us show how such weapon work is done."

He visibly hesitated, but my concern had evidently made its point. Advancing, he gripped the blade of the old weapon, then held out its hilt to Cilla. Following her example, I shed my disguise also.

We sketched the grave and graceful salute of those who would meet blade to blade. Then we set to. The clothes from the Dismals were much akin to our usual practice garments and, after a few moments of limbering up, we were at our mock conflict in earnest.

This play-war was akin to returning to some long-loved but nigh-forgotten place for me. The ring of blades was sweeter in my ears than the finest court music, and my feet moved as they might serve me in one of the formal dances there.

Cilla was good—she could not help but be, after the training she had. But her lessons had never become a real part of her as they had with me. At length I tried a thrust I had proudly learned only a short time before this whole strange adventure had begun, and her blade was neatly out of her hand.

"Well done!"

I swung around then to face Zolan yet again. He stared at me, at Cilla's sword lying on the ground, then back to me, before he said: "Such mastery takes time to acquire."

"Yes. But if you will wear a sword, you can be readily forced to use it." Frankly, at that moment I had no idea how we were to solve this problem. Even if we could meet with those whom Mother had said were on their way to us, the distance they must cover might mean days of travel ahead. More troubling still was the plan for Zolan to seek out the Gurlyon court, where the king prided himself on his knowledge of military art, and those wishing to curry favor with him must be apt with the sword. If by chance the Gurly ruler showed interest in Zolan, he would find faults aplenty in the newcomer. Somehow I had not foreseen this problem when I had so quickly accepted the Jug Woman's mission.

Zolan stepped past me and picked up the weapon Cilla had dropped, to stand looking at the discolored blade as if he wished to imprint the sight of it deeply in his memory. As he slipped it back into its makeshift sheath, his lips were a tight line. Then he looked up.

"My ignorance being so great, what is left to me?" His question held no note of self-pity but showed a bald acceptance of fact. "This?" He held up his hand, palm out and fingertips well separated in the manner we used when readying ourselves to call on Power.

I shook my head, but before I could answer, Bina did it for me.

"Such Power is also a danger," she replied as she helped Cilla fasten her dress once more. "Dark magic leads its user straight into the fire. And these Gurlys, for the most part, fear any with the Talent. Your quarry would be quick to name you Dark One and raise the land against you."

He folded his arms. "Do you tell me, then, that my sworn journey is fruitless?"

"No, for are we not sworn also to the same? Scorpy word is not broken," I said, knowing that I spoke the truth. We were as pent in his difficulties as he was.

"We"—Bina spoke slowly, as if not quite sure which word would be the next one out of her lips—"must play the game of a Misrule."

Zolan looked blank, as well he might, but we fastened at once on her meaning. In Alsonia at Midwinter Day, there was always feasting, and for that day all rank and rule was forgot. One of the waiting-maids became queen when she plucked a silver ring from the morn-cake; servants became masters until the coming of night. And all revelers used imagination to the full in inventing a disguise of strange clothing. One person might be an animal, another a character from some story, but, whatever the mask and costume chosen, during those hours each was required to act as he, she—or it—appeared. Sometimes overzealous playacting led to trouble; however, our gracious queen had done much to refine manners since coming to the throne.

"What would you devise?" Bina looked to Cilla, who had always been the most creative one of us. Several times in the past she had taken prizes for costumes for the Midwinter Day festivals.

Wiping sweat from her forehead with her sleeve, she moved to stand directly in front of Zolan, surveying him from head to foot and back again with an intense scrutiny.

"Can you mask?" she asked at last.

"Mask?" he echoed.

"Thus." Again we must instruct our onetime teacher with "show," not "tell."

Cilla appeared to have drawn up over her face an ever-thickening veil. For a moment or two, the shadowy stuff hung firmly in place, then it grew thinner. Cilla's features remained but she was no longer our sister—instead, our great-aunt Drucilla stood there, plainly ill-pleased at the position in which she found herself.

Zolan stared.

"Great-aunt Drucilla," she said. "You see, boy, it is not in the least difficult. Simply draw upon the Talent you were given. Take someone you know well, summon a projection of that person, then hold fast the mask that comes. It must be renewed from time to time, but you need only call upon it when truly necessary. Do you understand?"

"Yes." If he did understand, he obviously was not entirely certain. It was Bina who pointed out the weak spot in what we had hoped was a strong answer for our needs.

"Zolan, how many like yourself and us do you know?"

Suddenly he grinned as if he had at last found a key to what we were suggesting. His face became expressionless. A puff of mist gathered beneath his chin, journeyed slowly upward even as the one Cilla had summoned did for her. So, even if his Talent was different, still he could achieve like results. But, having heard Bina, we were alert to learn what would emerge from behind the transforming fog.

Fade it did. We stood stock-still, though we should have suspected what was coming. Cilla was confronting herself—a little taller, to be sure, and possessing a somewhat odd figure, but at least wearing the proper features.

"Thus?" Zolan asked, his voice suspiciously meek.

Great-aunt Drucilla's brows grew, producing some more new, if small, wrinkles.

"Do not jest, boy. If you cannot do it, why not just say so?"

The fourth sister disappeared. Zolan was frowning too. "I have no other guides."

"Yet you did not fail, either," Cilla said, allowing Great-aunt Drucilla to withdraw also. "Thus—you *can* mask, if you wish."

He shrugged. "Well, I will have no need of such mummery if we do not ride on—the morning is well spent."

Drucilla

FOLLOWING THE SAME action as the day before we at last continued on our way. No talk broke the silence among us; we—at least we Scorpys—were still striving to solve the problem Zolan presented. Though we were very used to him, it was far from difficult to realize how any Gurly of this waste-land would see him as a very strange traveler, one to be mentioned as soon as any honest man was again with his fellows.

My sisters have always credited me with being able to provide unusual clothing and oversee effective costumes for the festival. Now, however, we needed another person to provide an outward seeming for Zolan to copy, and perhaps I had at last met with an exercise in disguise I could not solve.

The clothing he had taken from the peddler's pack covered him in a lumpy fashion that did nothing to alter his upright posture. His skin was still far too pale for any wayfarer, though that condition could be corrected, and his hair might be trimmed as Tam's had been to the general length common for a male. No, the safest guise of all was the mask, but he must have a model for that—to really summon a disguise that would hold, the summoner must be very well acquainted with the model.

We had started our day's journey late and kept our pace slow. Our noon halt was late, as well, and it was also mealless. Climber had again added leapers to the burden of one of the ponies, yet Zolan built no fire. However, we did not rebuke him for such privation, since we had ridden over fresh tracks—those of cattle, probably the small and dangerous black ones of the mountains.

An inspection of the tracks also showed impressions made by unshod horses; we might be viewing what had betrayed a raider. For the Gurlys not only raided across the Border but also refined their skills by preying upon strangers in the highlands where the rumored barbaric old clans were thought to have headquarters. Thus a raid in this part of Gurlyon was a distinct feat of daring.

The last such outlaws we wanted to meet were Reivers of this part of the land. When we passed our warning on to Zolan he accepted it, turning more to the left, since the track seemed to be angling west.

Our animals were faring better than we. Unless we had better fortune, we might soon be faint enough to tumble off our mounts, too weak to go farther.

It was then that Climber came shooting towards us, his scarlet coat like a flame. Zolan signaled a stop and waited for his bond-beast to arrive. Having exchanged a Send, which was still unreadable as far as we were concerned, he shared Climber's report with us.

"There are buildings beyond—some have been half destroyed by fire. Climber found no life in the place. Let us scout and discover what we can."

Reivers was my unspoken thought. If a holding had been attacked, it might well be that only death remained. However, a faint chance existed that we might find supplies. Zolan went from horse to pony to horse, gazing intently into the eyes of each. The ponies were freed of the lead ropes but not unburdened until after Zolan's beast had led us to a dip in the ground. In that sheltered cup they scattered to graze.

We three, working as one, set Wards which would keep out other folk, should strays still roam the land from the herding party we believed had been responsible for a raid. Once the barriers had been raised and secured we joined Climber.

The countryside was far less level here, though the rises were not of great height. We took advantage of every chance for cover; the three of us also strove to sense out any other presence. We had often done this before from mere curiosity and had had no results; we followed the same pattern now. Climber would have to serve as advance scout.

Suddenly I sniffed. Something was, or had been, burning not too many hours before. A brisk breeze blew into our faces bearing that scent. Belly down, we crawled up the nearest slope to see what lay on the other side.

Twenty

Drucilla

Many tales are told concerning the vicious cruelty of raiders. I myself had tended survivors of such attacks who had been brought to Grosper in the past. However, no previous experience prepared me for such devastation. What I now saw was a horror greater than any I had ever dreamed.

The place of destruction was no shepherd's cot but a tower keep of some size. Trails of dark smoke threaded groggily upward to taint the sky. Bodies lay here and there, undoubtedly those of the inhabitants, as the raiders would have taken their dead with them if they had been beaten off. Certainly what we could see did not suggest that this struggle had ended in victory for the defenders of the keep.

I noted Climber picking his way toward the disaster. Though we had seen no signs of life, the beast from the Dismals advanced cautiously, using bushes for a blind here and there, and stopping to scent the acrid air. He reached the level land of the settlement, where stood the burnt-out remains of huts. Again for a space of time he simply stood as if now his ears and nose would serve him best.

Zolan made no comment but simply launched himself downhill. Within a step or so he commenced running swiftly until he skidded to a stop in earth loosened by churning hooves. Only then did he look up to wave us on.

Tam was the first on her feet, and Bina was nearly as quick to follow. I, however, longed to turn in the other direction. What profit could there be in searching such bloodied chaos? Though hunger was a constant pain, surely those who had looted here had either carried off all supplies or wasted them past use. I had no choice but to follow, but I did so at a slower pace.

Tamara

HAND TO SWORD, I joined Zolan and was the first of us three to reach him. The stench of smoke and other odors I would rather not identify set me coughing. We were on a track—it could not be termed road—leading directly to the keep. Facing each other across this rough way, the wreckage of two huts lay mounded to our right and left.

Faceup beside one of these small dwellings, a woman lay stripped of clothing, her arms pulled up above her head and lashed to the broken haft of a small spear. Beneath her, the ground had been recently readied for planting. Beyond her body was that of a boy, treated in like manner, showing many stab wounds.

I made the Sign of Calling the Great One, not only for the peace of the suffering but that those who had used them so might be summoned to full justice.

We moved on as Bina and Cilla joined us. Bina gave one quick glance and also made the Sign. Cilla copied it without looking.

Those two were not all the dead, merely the first. Indeed, so often were we confronted from either side by such scenes that they lost the power to shock, only to sicken those who looked upon them. Here Evil had been given rein, so fully that Fear could well follow.

The door to the wall surrounding the tower keep was gone but, where one would expect remnants of a broken barrier, none such existed. From the complete absence of any torn hasps or fragments of wood, no portal might have ever been mounted here. The strangeness of that empty frame made me reach out and clutch Zolan's arm, bringing him also to a stop.

Some trick of Talent? I studied all three sides of the opening in the stone wall. The edges bore a rim of dirty yellow around their perimeter. Now another harsh, biting odor intruded strongly on my senses. I loosed my hold on Zolan and inched forward. This—I had heard rumors of this use of Power but never had seen evidence of its reality.

Here was legend come to life. I looked around. Another broken lance lay not too far away. Fetching it, I pushed forward. With the splinter-headed weapon held in front of me, I drew the shaft up, down, and around the three sides of the doorway, being careful not to touch the yellowed edges.

"What would you do?" Zolan demanded.

I used the spear to indicate the nearest length of yellow line. "When a raid comes, a door of wood may be beaten in, or set aflame, if the defenders are unable to pick off their attackers by arrow. That was not what befell in this place. Old Lore teachers that some of the Talented of ancient times had other weapons unknown to us. I think a siege-engine of Power might have been used here. We must all keep well away from those lines when we go in."

I was not sure that I wished to enter at all, and I could sense that Bina and certainly Cilla thought such action highly dangerous. Zolan, though, was not to be deterred from his quest. Having regarded me searchingly for a second or two, he marched on through the break left by the missing gate. A sense of responsibility sent me after him. It was true that he was Talented, but what had been wrought here was of the Upper Land and not the Dismals and might therefore be the product of Power alien to all he knew. At least I had *heard* of such a weapon, while he did not recognize it; thus it must be of this world.

Contrary to what we might have expected, the strip of land about the base of the tower was not near filled with bodies. Several corpses, however, lay in line with the missing gate, and these folk had not been killed by steel or snaplock ball. Their bodies lay in positions that made us sure they had died in great pain and terror, yet we saw no outward signs of wounds.

The door of the keep itself had not been made to vanish by some spell as had the outer portal; here an improvised battering ram, still lying to one side, had been brought to bear. Perhaps if the other weapon had been born of Power, it had been exhausted in a single use.

We explored. Death reigned everywhere, from the bodies of a pair of sleuthhounds trained for defense to the pitiful small form of a cradled baby in the great hall. She who had been doubtless its mother lay naked and savaged beside it. Again we called down the Peace of the Great One and could only believe that all within these walls were now safe at rest within the ever-living Light.

Trying to close our minds to the slaughter, we made our way to where the storerooms must be. Since winter was only a short time behind us, and the first crops were yet to be harvested—many not even showing above the soil—supplies would be few, and perhaps all had been taken by the raiders. Still, through some strange quirk of fortune, we did find fruit, very dry, and also the hard kernels of dashen. We stored all we discovered in hide bags that were stacked nearby, perhaps the same in which those supplies had been brought.

Bina went exploring in another room off the kitchen, crunching through the debris of broken pipkins and battered pans. She, too, made use of a bag, filling it with what she found in the stillroom.

And it was she who made another surprising discovery.

Sabina

THE STORES IN the stillroom had been little disturbed; even wax-stopped crocks stood uncracked and sealed. I made quick choices of what we might need the most, glad to be once more in the company of herbs that I knew well.

I had cleared one shelf of small jars, all labeled (which was a boon), when I noted that the section of shelves themselves seemed to be pulled away from the wall at one end. Removing the few containers still left on these, I tugged at the entire storage area. It appeared to be firmly fixed; however, when I gave a hard pull, it grated towards me.

Darkness lay beyond, not only honest night, but—I reeled back, too shaken to do more than cling to the wooden boards. I had been assaulted by a heavy pall of pure evil which enwrapped me as might a net meant to capture. Choking, I fought to draw in a full breath.

I heard, dimly, the voice of Tam, but even a Send was beyond me now. Then an arm slid about my body, and I was drawn back. My hold on the shelves being broken, I stood only by the aid of him who held me; a moment later, I was swung about, and Cilla came to give me support.

A sudden blaze of light leaped up, and the darkness was broken. In Tam's hands her talisman was glowing ever stronger. Zolan reached for her but she had already found the hidden opening and, as her hand lifted higher to give a view of what lay ahead, he was still a step away.

We could now see into that chamber as if the most brilliant of suns shone through the stone. The space which the shelves had concealed was hardly more than a cupboard. Yet it held an occupant. Propped back against the wall stood the severely emaciated body of a male. It was robed in the fashion of the priestly garb worn by Udo the Chosen. And crowning that corpse—I heard Cilla's scream, felt the sway of her body against mine. The light wavered, and Tam uttered a word that was half defiant cry, half curse.

Skeleton hands clutched the throat of the man—his own. His face was only a charred patched of flesh against bone. And—

Cilla had hidden her head against my shoulder. Not loosing my hold on her, I Sent: *"Tam—Power for Tam!"*

We linked, found Tam, linked again. But Zolan had already shouldered our sister aside. He now faced the horror straight on, and his hand came up.

The back of his hand was towards me, but I was sure I had seen something cupped in the palm. He spoke no audible word of ritual or command, yet a burst of light flared forth. A movement stirred the stagnant air of the cupboard as if barely visible waves rose and fell—green light pressing forward against roiling dark.

The oppressive presence of Evil that had sapped my strength vanished. It had affected Cilla also and perhaps Tam, though she had not wavered to confront it, doubtless drawing extra energy from the talisman. In fact, I felt as renewed as if by a night of deep and healing slumber.

Against the wall still huddled the figure in the vestments of the Chosen. Now, however, it began to slide downward against the stone. We watched. As the body reached the floor, Zolan approached it.

With his padded boot he toed the thing, and at the same time he leaned forward to pick something from the floor. Whatever he had used to clear our surroundings had disappeared—If he *had* wielded any instrument of Power, what he held now was a rod perhaps slightly less in length than his forearm. Taking this wand in both hands, he snapped it in two, casting the pieces down on the body. Then he retreated from the space and, without a word, pushed until the shelves were back in place, no edge jutting out to betray their secret. Only when this action was completed did he speak.

"It is well that I have come forth. The Evil One has launched his war."

"The robed one was the renegade of the Dismals?" Tam asked.

"No, but what was used here was a weapon of Dismals Power. It seems, however, that he could not control it properly and that what he had summoned returned upon him full force."

Such a backwash of force we could comprehend. The Talented were taught from the time they could understand that to loose Power they could not completely command was to lay themselves open to the very weapon they attempted to use.

"Those attacking here," Tam said slowly, "possessed a Talent weapon also, but that, I believe, was, long ago, one of our own—"

"Which means"—Zolan's face was grimly set—"Tharn has established contact with someone or something of this land. He has either made common cause with a Talented Gurly or has stolen learning from the past."

I wished to shout a denial of such reasoning; however, it was all too logical. Now Cilla, moving in my hold to face the others, added to Zolan's theory with more somber reasoning. "Those who murdered, took this holding—if they still have the weapon which they used to destroy the wall gate—" She choked on the word "gate" as if its very naming called up sick fear.

Tamara

I WAS PUTTING my sun-warm stone, for so it felt, back into my pouch. Perhaps we had come into a state of arrogance because of the Talent and the abilities we were all sure had been added to our inborn force during our time in the Dismals. The source of the Power these raiders wielded might well be found in a search of such libraries as our grand dames and Great-aunt Drucilla kept. I, for instance, would not have possessed that scrap of recollection regarding the gate if I had not read or heard of such barriers in the past. However, its true nature and how best to deal with it remained unknown.

But our father and mother were on their way—

Mother! I caught instantly at that questing tendril of thought. Almost as speedily, Cilla and Bina were with me in mind as well as in body. However, before I could tell Zolan what must be done, Climber hurtled in, dashed forward, and reared up to thud paws on his chosen human at waist height. His rush sent Zolan crashing back against the shelves, and pots went flying.

Zolan dropped to his knees so that his eyes met Climber's straight on. Silent communication lasted but a moment; then he jumped to his feet and headed for the kitchen.

"A survivor!" he said. That amazing news brought us at a run behind him.

Climber led the way with Zolan on his heels. Through the kitchen, again scattering debris and raising dust, the bond-beast passed the stairs leading above to reach a place where he brushed the floor vigorously with a paw. Though it was too dark to really see, my mind went instantly to the idea of a trapdoor. Such underground storages were often used for prisoners. Had some unhappy soul been half buried here while the hold of the keep was occupied by the enemy?

"Candle—lamp—" Bina turned back toward the kitchen, but I swung out the gem, which now gave a faint radiance. Cradling it between my palms, I centered Power on it. The glow increased to light as would a breath-fanned torch.

Zolan was kneeling by the edge of what was indeed a trapdoor. As soon as he could see, he hammered back the bolt and then was around the door and pulling at an iron loop in its top, clearly intended for access.

"What be going on?" demanded a voice out of the depths. "Old Raven-Eye come into his wits again? Best be using that eye of his to look for Ichon's banner—"

Bina came up with a coil of rope in one hand and a lanthorn to add to the light. Zolan caught at the sturdy cord and started back to the stairs to make one end fast. I leaned over the edge of the trapdoor to view the unfortunate imprisoned below.

I looked into the face of a heavily bearded man.

"Who are you, wench? Or is Ichon taken to letting his get ride a-reiving, be they man or maid?"

I drew a deep breath. "The keep has been taken. We are all who are left of a merchant's train. We thought your hold slaughtered to a man—"

He was silent for a long moment and then struck the near wall of the cell-like space in which he had been held. From his lips came the greatest number of powerful oaths I had ever heard loosed at one time. Then Zolan was pushing me to one side and tossing down part of the coiled rope so that it struck the face of the prisoner and silenced him.

Thus we came to face Lolart Boartusked, once Guard Sergeant of Frosmoor. The minute the prisoner was wholly out of the makeshift cell, he threw the rope from him, struck Zolan with a mighty fist, sending the man from the Dismals staggering, and raced up the staircase.

We wasted no time in following, though Bina had lagged behind with her bag of plunder. By the time we reached the great hall, we heard such a bellow of rage as seemed likely to shake the rest of the walls down upon us.

The guard sergeant came back into the hall, staggering like one who had taken a mortal wound. Above that heavy bush of a beard, his weather-beaten skin was a sickly gray. Wavering on his feet, he stood staring at us, plainly suffering from such a shock as to near destroy his wits.

"All—all o' 'em—her ladyship—th' wee 'un." He glanced at the corner where the woman lay by the cradle. "Where's Ichon?" He did not seem to be asking that question of us. Instead he turned away, lurching toward a dais at the other end of the hall. The room was a rough miniature effort to copy a chamber of state.

For the first time we saw—for we had been only too eager not to view closely the dead upon our coming—that someone was sitting there. He might have been first watching the massacre, then waiting for us.

Lolart was off again, heading for the watcher. When a step from the dais, he stopped short to beat with clenched hands at the air above his head, screaming such a cry as might have been uttered from a prison pit of eternal darkness.

Though we were sure that the evidence of another horrible act waited on that throne, the four of us were drawn after him, for to view the tragedy ourselves might be an inescapable duty.

Sabina

MY LEFT HAND in Cilla's and my right held by Tam, I went, drained of all will—I could not turn away, as more than half of me urged. I have seen death before, even death by violence; but what faced us now was over-laden with Evil such as I had not met since Zolan had forced open the cell in the wall.

The man who was bound to the chair—for it was a man, though the mutilation that had been performed on the body had nearly erased any sign of gender—was tall and broad shouldered. A blood-fringed strand of hair, stuck to the back of the chair, had been white, but he could not have been much older than my father. Someone had thrown part of a cloak about him; however, that garment served very little to hide what had been done here.

Cilla pulled loose from my hold and ran. From the distance, I could hear the racking violence of attempts to vomit, though she must certainly have little food left within her. I swallowed and swallowed again, clapping my hands across my mouth.

We come of a fighting line for many generations. But this was not warfare—it was brutalization beyond reckoning. There are those who delight in the torment of their kind. If any such twisted souls reveal their natures in our father's command, he straightway rooted them out. If they had already given way to base instincts, they were condemned out of hand; otherwise, he sent them under guard to the Black Isle to live or die among their own kind.

The monsters who had been at their beastly work here should be slain when taken. Reivers such as Maclan had already been judged and condemned and would have died within an hour of their capture, but this atrocity was worse than any the Breaksword had ever been accused of.

Zolan laid a hand on Lolart's shoulder. Again the huge man swung a fist, but this time Zolan ducked and avoided the blow. When he stood up again, he showed no anger.

"Was he"—the man from the Dismals made a gesture at the mangled body in the chair—"your lord?"

The guard was shaking; an icy wind might have whipped about him. He swallowed visibly several times before he spoke.

"This be Ichon Raven-Eye of the Marshurs, own brother to Hughes, their chief. He be one of the great ones in Gurlyon. They who dared this— they will pay mightily—"

Suddenly he reached out and, before Zolan was aware of what he would do, he gave a mighty pull on the ancient sword and tore it from the flimsy sheath Zolan had made. Turning again to face the body, he sank to his knees, holding out the blade.

"Thus do I swear, that under sun, under moon, under star, I shall seek, my lord. You shall look upon heads, count hands of those who raised steel against you. Blood debt will be fully paid."

And we who were watching knew well that such an oath would be kept while life remained in the sergeant's great body.

Twenty-one

Sabina

We had turned to a grisly labor as the sun fled. We would have needed a full company to have adequately cleared that holding of the dead and seen them to proper burial, but here were neither time nor numbers enough to accomplish that. Few enemy bodies were found; perhaps the raiders had taken them away. We strove to give the fallen defenders what honor we could. The sum of those was few in number—certainly not the tally of a full garrison. It was full dark when those we could find lay in rows in the great hall.

Lord and lady were wrapped in the richest fabrics we were able to discover, though that stuff had been wantonly rent and was sadly damaged. With the cradle between them, the two were laid in state on the dais.

Lolart worked a little apart and, from his muttering, it was plain that he was addressing some of the dead. We could not distinguish more than a word or two of his mumbling, and I wondered if his wits had indeed been turned by what had happened here. Why he had been in a cell when we found him we did not learn; indeed, at that time, he had not even given us his name.

Dark as it was now, we would not remain in a place so haunted by Evil. My sisters and I were constantly communicating, not to each other but to the Powers unseen that reigned in another place. Our clothing and hands were stained with blood. I had raided my herb pack to pass out handfuls of dried leaf-bits, which we each chewed until our jaws ached. The virtue of that herb was to divorce the mind somewhat from a laboring body. Tam had also brought out her jewel. Not only did it furnish a modicum of light but added to our feeling that a curtain of Power hung between us and the dead.

Lolart leaned against the wall; it was evident that even the great strength of the old campaigner had been sorely taxed by our labors. Zolan's hand fell on the burly soldier's shoulder, and the man from the Dismals spoke with more than a shade of compassion in his voice.

"This place is no longer for the living, guardsman. Come with us—we have a camp a little way from here."

The other might not have heard him; still, when Zolan tightened his hold and drew him along, he stumbled forward without protest. I tugged at my bag of medicaments. Tam and Cilla carried the bulk of our finds between them while Zolan shouldered the rest. Climber had disappeared; perhaps he had gone hunting.

We returned to the shallow valley where we had left the horses and pack-ponies and established a camp.

Drucilla

WE KINDLED A small fire between two rocks, hoping that they would prevent any light from escaping that pockmark of a valley. We washed many times in the brook that trickled through our campsite, yet I still seemed to feel the crusted blood gloving my hands. I kept stretching my fingers, rubbing them together.

"They must be warned—" I Sent. We had not been discussing Mother and Father, but my thoughts had come to dwell more and more with them.

Bina was seeing to the leapers Climber had caught. I, who had thought I could never bear to look upon food again, was ready to tear at the meat that now dripped steaming fat into the fire.

Tam had dropped beside me. Once more she drew the gem from its hair bag.

"Yes," she replied aloud.

Bina turned away from the fire and came to join us. Zolan was a distance away, seated by the silent, blank-eyed guardsman. Likely Lolart saw neither us nor the present scene at all but only what lay behind.

On Tam's flattened palm rested the glowing stone. I placed my hand on her supporting arm, and Bina grasped her other hand. We closed our eyes. Zolan would know we were Sending but we could not ask him for support, since his Power differed too greatly.

We searched, casting our collective thought far abroad. Without warning, I was seized with an amazing force that swelled within me, arching my body in its intensity. I knew my sisters shared it. Truly, even in the short space since we had last so pooled our Power, some greater strength had grown.

Our Send speared out like a consciously aimed weapon. It struck against a barrier; however, we did not recoil or relax but continued to thrust until— *Through! Through!* We could have shouted that aloud. ·

The barrier suddenly gave way, and we were indeed safely inside. What we could sense now was Mother's own Ward and, in a fraction of a breath, that also was gone. Swiftly we united behind Tam, who told our bleak story is as few words as possible, and ended by warning that such Evil was free to raid elsewhere. In return, we received a certain ritual with instructions to use it. Then came silence.

Tam remained still, but her hand now held the gem against her forehead. I got to my feet and moved to Zolan and the guard.

"Further Warding is needed, for it is still two days or more before we can meet with those from Grosper. Our mother has also revealed that the followers of Forfind have risen and that the king has either become one of them or else is held prisoner."

I saw the armsman blink. He might have been waking from a troubled sleep. The blink led to a glare turned fully on me.

"Devil—true devil!" he spat. "Such witch-work is why—"

"Condemn us later," I interrupted. "Warding we must have at once."

"Warding?" he repeated.

Zolan caught the soldier by the arm. "Up with you, man. This must be done—and now!"

Lolart allowed himself to be drawn along to where my sisters waited; then Zolan brought him into a circle with us. The glow from Tam's jewel gave us what light we needed. It was Tam who spoke now and directly to the armsman.

"What we do is for protection. Those who wrought that bloodletting at the keep depend upon more than sword, spear, and snaplock."

As though grudging this truth, Lolart jerked his head toward Zolan. "So he has told me."

"Give me your name," Tam ordered, "for true names must be used now."

"I be Lolart Boartusked of Ichon's kin. Would you call for a guard upon what cannot be seen?"

"Just so, Lolart. Let us now form a circle."

Zolan suddenly produced from the inside of his tattered shirt a clenched hand. As he slowly spread his fingers he looked at Tam.

"There are Talents and Talents," he said. "They may not be of the same calling, but if they are of the Light, they are linked together, even as the Evil now come into this land can call upon the Darkness inherent here to join forces. Therefore, let our speech be voiced together."

On his palm lay a strange object that appeared to be a slender tube of bone. It did not glow, as did Tam's treasure, but it possessed a curious ability to draw the onlooker's attention as if at any moment it might alter shape.

Tam's hand with the gem swung in the direction of what he displayed. I flinched, for within me stirred such an energy as could have brought me to my knees. Then it was gone. No threat could be felt in its inroad, only promise.

"Let it be done," said Tam swiftly. "Take hands—"

Though she and Zolan were only partly united, we were indeed linked. The armsman was seated between Bina and Zolan; I was joined to Bina, and Tam also held to me. Tam began to speak the ritual, and Bina and I followed; Zolan and Lolart came a little behind as both echoed us.

"I, Tamara of the Scorpys, ask the Boon of Shaft Ward, with these others. We go to battle Dark and Night, Evil and Might. Let the Shield promised to those who believe in Light close about us at this saying."

I followed with my name and the exact words of that ritual. Then Bina spoke. More slowly, as if striving to match the exact words, followed Lolart, and at last Zolan. In only a short while we were finished, and what might follow we truly did not know.

An arrow of blazing light shot up from Tam's hand to meet with another from Zolan's. One shaft was green, the other golden. They met, wreathed together, and formed a hoop that spread until it was larger than our circle.

Once complete, it descended, passing from air to ground before it vanished. Within that space, I had a vision of a wall of swords between us and the outer night, and I breathed thanks to the Giver of Talents.

Our circle broke apart, and hunger was again upon us, the pain worse for the scent of the cooking meat. With no speech, we ate a small portion each of leaper. However, this time it was made more palatable by the addition of one of the herbs Bina had brought. Lolart also knocked the wax stopper from one of the smaller pots, and we used our fingers to gouge out dollops of berry jam, sourish but satisfying.

When we had done, Zolan spoke to the armsman.

"You have a story, friend. What enemy did you have, and what brought their fury on your hold?"

Lolart gazed into the dying fire as he spoke.

"Lord Ichon was my milk brother—my mam nursed us both, as we were born on the same day and the Lady Penthea was ailing. He was always wise beyond his years, and in time he was made First Kin, by Marshur choice, to young Gerrit, the king who vanished. The king was journeying to the Guardian Shrine for the final blessing of his mother, but Ichon remained behind as he had been hurt when a boar charged his horse during a hunt."

Lolart raised his hand and absently stroked his bearded chin, as if his words had awakened some memory.

"Thus," he continued, "Ichon was not with Gerrit when the king was attacked and taken. An outcry was raised, though, and Ichon was accused of knowing where the king might be. He took the Sword Oath against three champions, but Truth was his shield and he defeated them all.

"However, he would live no more with those of the court, for he thought that some did in truth know where the king was. Thus he came here to this outpost and served Gurlyon well, for he wiped out five invasions of the mountain people during his years as lord of Frosmoor."

The guardsman's honest face darkened as his tale continued. "Some time ago, we heard of this Devil Lover from the mountains—and all we could learn was ill. Lord Ichon was summoned to a meeting at Kingsburke when it became plain that the Dark One had Arvor's ear and favor. It would seem, Ichon said when he returned to hold his own council, that the king strove to make the false priest a tool against the lords from whom he wanted free. Ichon would have none of this fight, for it might turn kin against kin. Thus he ordered that we of the clan should hold apart.

"Five, six days ago"—Lolart look down at his hands, as if needing to tell the days on his fingers—"there came that—" He fell now into the coarse speech typical of a soldier. Zolan touched his arm warningly, and his head snapped up.

"Your pardon, Wisewoman! That—messenger of the demon came." Now his hand went to his throat, and he pulled from hiding within his buff coat a medal swinging on a thong. "This luck-piece was given me by one of your sort—Wisewoman Osira, who lives by the Goddess Pillars near Redmont. She told me to wear it ever, and it would keep me safe."

Tam held out her jewel. Its gold glow became, for a breath or two, a soft blue, and we made gestures of reverence at this new emblem of the Great One.

"Well—" Once more the guardsman looked down at the medal he had left hanging in view. "She had the right of it." His voice carried a note of bitterness. "Because of this talisman, I did not change." Again he paused.

"Change?" Zolan encouraged him to continue.

"The folk at Frosmoor—they began to change as soon as the messenger was taken to Ichon. All were bowing—even the guard!—and speaking him fair. Ichon ordered drink for him. That devil-spawn then said as how he was sent by Arvor himself. Starkadder and Riffler had at last shown themselves to be traitors, and Starkadder had sent out a call to the Southerners to come. He had a sealed message that swore this for truth.

"But Ichon—he was not yet bewitched by the messenger. He called for council, and the kin house-heads, they urged sending the king a force. I spoke last of all. I was fair angered by their coat turning, so I demanded that we at least talk more of it. Then—"

Lolart's voice shook; his hand again nervously stroked the left side of his chin. "Then he—my milk brother—he went mad. He ordered me taken to the dark hold, to be left there until I came to my senses. So it was done. It was you who brought me forth to see blood and death—and the end of our clan. I am Breaksword now. If I had not spoken out, I might have been able to make a stand. Only a third or less of those who should have held Frosmoor were among the dead—the rest are gone!"

Zolan moved, and the hand that had cradled his talisman reached out once more to clasp Lolart's arm. The armsman had been shaking, but under that grasp his shoulders stilled as the man from the Dismals spoke.

"Your choice was the one any man of honor would have made. Do not blame yourself. It is plain that your lord and those at Frosmoor were indeed ensorcelled, yet that spell must have been broken in some manner, or they would not have fought at the last."

As he finished, Tam added an assurance from us. "Do not call yourself Breaksword, Lolart Boartusked, for have you not taken oath in blood to bring your lord's murderers to justice? It may hap that we can give you the means of keeping that vow. Those who come to meet us have a wish as great as yours to rid this land of Evil, though we are none of us native here. Ride with us."

When the old campaigner raised his head, I could see the moisture on his beard and other tears still gathered in his eyes.

"You speak well, my lady," he said. "I am a man of weapons, though I lack them now. Yet I will not turn from the road once my feet are set upon it."

Thus our force of four became an army of five.

It was late when at last we did our best to get some sleep. However, in spite of the horror that lay behind us, I did not dream darkly. A nightvision came, yes, but the feeling it brought me was one of mission and promise. I stood in a hall not that of Frosmoor. A swirl of many colors wreathed me, and I sensed human movement around me, as well, yet I could not see any who caused it. Still I was certain that I walked among a strange and unknown company.

Then the looping of tinted light parted, and a woman came through. She was no beauty by the standards of the world I knew, yet her appearance had a quality that drew attention and held it firmly.

In her hands, clasped before her breast, she held a rod, and up and down that wand rippled the same rainbow of hues that formed the mist. For a scant breath I took in her bearing and burden, and then I knew whom I fronted: no woman who yet lived, but a consciousness now tied by will to a jug in a distant cave.

"*The renegade of our people gathers strength,*" Pharsali's Send reached me. "*He will seek a change of body soon. Be you and yours prepared that he does not take what he would have.*"

The mist concealed the Jar Woman from me, and darkness and peace descended once more. I felt chilled from more than the night wind's creeping under my cloak, so I roused somewhat. Near me someone stirred restlessly, then settled as I did also.

Sabina

CILLA LAY STILL sleeping when we roused shortly after dawn. The sense of safety that had settled upon us from the Ward Mother suggested remained about us. I shook my sister gently until she opened her eyes and stared at me as if expecting someone else in my place. She followed me to the brook to wash face and hands as Tam joined us.

"I dreamed," Cilla said suddenly.

"How could you escape it?" I returned. Cilla had had many dreams, and her night-seeings, which were always vivid, sometimes heralded in part future action.

Without answering my comment directly, she began to tell her dream. Tam stopped trying to bring order to her short hair and listened.

" 'Change to another body'?" she repeated slowly. "Could such a deed be done without permission of the rightful occupant of that body?"

We all shivered at that thought. If Tharn had somehow developed more Power, would he be able to perform such a spirit-rape? And whose was to be the body? These Gurlys raised no Wards. Ichon and his people had been led to their own deaths—of that we were certain, having heard Lolart's story. The old soldier was a man of greater perception than he appeared.

"Perhaps King Arvor." Tam voiced the worst possibility, and her hands closed convulsively on her hair-bag. "We must ride—now!"

We did not have much to break our fast, only some of the musty meal made into a paste with brook water. Once more I doled out the Power herb mixture, though we could not long continue to use it, since too much would befuddle our thinking.

We had but four mounts to five riders. However, Lolart refused the offer of ride-and-tie that Tam suggested. This was a system conserving energy for man and mount. One person rode ahead and tied the steed, while the other followed on foot and mounted in his stead until it was tie-time again. Zolan, at whose ability with horses we had continued to marvel, made the offer a second time, only to be refused. Instead, Lolart took over the lead of the pack-ponies and departed with a stride that did not put him and the train too far behind.

The day wore on. We had filled our water skins before setting out, as well as eating our meager meal. But our repeated uses of the Power herb mixture gave me times of giddy-headedness, and I locked my fingers in the edge of the blanket serving me as a saddle to secure balance. Luckily we kept to a pace hardly more than a walk.

If there were any other keeps hereabouts, we did not sight them. Climber no longer scouted before us, nor did he hunt this day. He had returned earlier from some venture limping on three paws. Zolan had drawn a long barbed burr from between two of the beast's toes, and I had applied such salve as I could to draw out any poison. Thereafter he shared transportation with his bond-mate, resting across the lap of the rider. When this proved impractical, Zolan rode back for one of the ponies and returned to us, installing the hunter on a pad instead of the bags that had hung on the pack-animal.

We each took turn scouting ahead. On my third stint at that duty, I saw the scavenger birds. They were cawing raucously and circling overhead. I could guess all too readily what had brought them, and I searched the ground ahead as well as I could by sight of bodily eyes alone. Their would-be prey was quickly located, for it was still moving: someone, either man or woman, was dragging along the ground a short distance ahead with visible effort. I would have ridden forward to aid but, though I had little liking for fighting, my father had trained us in tactics as well as weapons-play, and I knew that what I now saw might well be the bait in a trap.

Yet I discovered that I could not simply ride back, for should that one who yet fought for life lie still, the rapacious flock would be on their intended meal instantly. Even as I made my choice, a corbie, well-known as an enemy to any weak and wounded thing, launched itself downward. I saw an arm weakly upraised, then the limb crumpling as that defensive gesture failed.

The bird dodged the blow easily, then wheeled and returned, settling. Very faintly I heard a cry of fear and pain. I urged my horse forward.

As I drew level with the bird and its victim, I loosed my cloak and pulled it free. Two more eaters-of-death had landed. The mare threw up her head and neighed a challenge, but the scavengers did not rise. I whirled the cloak as a fowl-catcher would wield his net, and the birds circling low sheered away.

Then I was off my mount, beside the body that lay facedown. A raven sitting on the head, face turned from me, showed an open beak, threatening. Again I swept out the cloak, and the black scavenger rose sullenly to avoid the flapping cloth. I saw no sign of the other two birds I who had also descended.

I dropped the cloak over the crawler, to give some cover if the carrion-feeders thought to attack again, wishing vainly for a proven snaplock. If I had been sure that no one lurked in hiding, I would have shouted; instead I Sent and was instantly answered. Until the others arrived, I would play sentry here.

Twenty-two

Sabina

Now a change began in that ever-growing flock of birds overhead. Only a few ravens wheeled above; more of the dark cloud were larger raptors—direhawks, those killers of the weak among the sheep flocks. Among them wheeled a sprinkling of other scavengers I had never seen before, with red-wattled heads bare of feather. They flew ever closer and bolder, and the thought came to me that they might have been set to this attack by some reason greater than any normal hunger.

Suddenly I felt a sharp stab of pain where my neck joined my shoulder. Without thinking, I used my hand to discover the source, and I cried out at the hurt as instantly my fingers, too, were torn. I pulled it back into my line of sight, burdened by an unfamiliar weight, and felt the thrust again. It was not a large raptor that attacked but a small bird, its claws set deeply into my wrist, that was striking furiously with a wickedly pointed beak between my fingers, tearing the flesh there.

Again I screamed. The meat-eater showed no fear; rather it raised a dripping bill, its eyes promising worse horror as I struck at it with my free hand. Fingers closed on feathers at the back of its head. I had to tear it loose, and I felt flesh rip away with it as I pulled.

Wings swished above; claws caught in my cap, by chance alone skimming past hair. The bird I had captured made no effort to escape but continued to attack, though my grip held. I twisted frantically, using both hands now, and finally felt the thing's neck snap. As I hurled the small corpse from me, I stumbled over the body beneath the cloak and fell across it. A second scavenger that had been ripping the wool of that garment raised its head to squawk.

My fall brought a muffled groan from the one who lay under me, and I hurriedly rolled aside. The shrouded form moved, the cloak bunching as I fought to regain my feet. Three more of the feathered devil-creatures were spiraling down on me now.

Without a weapon I could not hope to defend myself. My only chance—and it was a very slim one—lay in the hope that my companions were not too far behind. For now, I swiftly lay down beside the stranger, pulling the cloak to cover both of us.

The motion rolled the body onto its side against mine so I could see that I fronted a man. And bloodstained, cut, and torn as his face was, I knew him instantly.

"*Rogher!*"

It was my father's squire.

Tamara

BINA'S SEND HAD speeded up our pace. We passed quickly over one of the rolling hills. Now we could hear cries sounding like one rusty blade drawn across another and spied an undulating blanket of birds that were tearing a moving heap on the ground.

Zolan matched my speed on seeing that horror, and he caught at my rein when I would have dashed down the slope.

"No!"

I aimed a blow at him. Bina was under that cloak—her pain and fear beat at me, and at this moment I shared all she was suffering.

However, Zolan held to the grip that had stopped me. At the same time, he answered the clamor of the birds. With his free hand, he held his bone-tube to his lips, blowing through it as if it were a whistle.

He gave a second blast, even more shrill than the first. The screams of the birds suddenly ceased. Two and three, then four and five, they took to the air again. At length the heaving bundle on the ground was free, for all its tormentors had returned aloft.

Now, however, having formed a smoky smudge on the sky, they headed towards us. My mare screamed in fear and tried to rear as I struggled to keep my seat. For a third time Zolan used his whistle. Amazingly, that night-blot of wings did not fly straight at us but rather past, still keeping in a flock, heading westward.

As soon as I was sure that this flight pattern was not some ploy to attack us from another direction, I was on my way. Zolan no longer tried to restrain me but followed fast. I did not call aloud to Bina, I Sent.

The cloak, now little more than a fringe of tatters, was flung aside, and our sister, her face showing a scoring across one cheek that dripped blood, watched me come. She did not get to her feet but remained where she was, with the head of the wayfarer resting in her lap.

I dismounted swiftly and hurried to her side. Her horse had disappeared; doubtless the terrified beast had fled. She shifted a little, as I joined her, to show more clearly the face of the one she supported. Seeing him, a vast fear awoke in me. Such scavengers regarded eyes as a delicacy. If they had struck at his head—

He still wore his buff coat. It was torn and caked with earth as if he had reached here by crawling. A freely bleeding gash gaped below one eye—*below*, not through it, praise the Great One! One leg also lay at an unnatural angle and, as Bina shifted a little, he groaned.

Rogher opened his eyes and looked up at the one who held him. "Lady Sabina—" He moved his head a little to see me, and a confused frown crossed his face. With my cropped hair and men's clothing he did not know me for a moment. Then he actually grinned:

"Lady Tamara—what game play you now?"

Some of the tension eased. "Rogher, our mother, father—?"

"Behind me—half day, perhaps. I rode out—scouting. My horse—"

He made as if to sit up but fell back.

"Mallord is not here," I said, needing to know more.

"He—stumbled," he continued in a halting voice, "fell, like one—bullet struck."

"Then came the birds?"

I was startled. Zolan had appeared behind me silently to ask that question.

"Yes." The squire frowned, seeming to disbelieve his own memory. "They—*rained* down as if a black cloud shook them loose. My Mallord—"

His horse had been a cherished friend. Rogher had raised the mount himself from a foal and trained it, and astride it, had twice won races.

"Those accursed things went for him first. I—I crawled—to where there were some rocks—and they could not get at me."

Zolan loosed one of the water bags from his saddle and brought it, approaching with care against any spillage. Bina drew Rogher farther up against her shoulder. As our father's man drank in small sips, Cilla and Lolart joined us.

The armsman looked down at the squire.

" 'Tis out of nature," he said.

"The birds?" I caught his meaning.

"Aye. There was ravens, but with them enemies to their kind—rawheads, strike-bills, and other death-eaters. Suchlike do not company together. This be known."

Zolan, meanwhile, had gone over to Bina's mount, who had returned with sweat visible on her hide. He drew his hands down on either side of the head she lowered to him, and I saw her shivers lessen. Then he unbound the bag in which Bina carried her remedies and brought it back to us. As Cilla and I turned to take up the duties Bina usually held, tending both her and Rogher, he looked to Lolart.

"So those birds are never seen together? Then some mighty reason must have made them flock in company for attack this time."

Lolart was quick to catch the thought behind the statement. More grimace than frown now distorted what we could see of his face.

"Someone is dealing with deep Dark Powers."

Zolan nodded. "That much is manifest."

Now he turned to me. "The Warding—it did not hold to protect Lady Sabina, or did it?"

Bina looked up as I drew a strip of torn cloth from Frosmoor's spoilage to bandage her hand. "It—it did not!" Fear could be plainly heard in her tone.

I sat back on my heels to consider this new danger. Then our sister spoke again in a calmer voice:

"Or did it?" She reached out her unbandaged hand and tugged at the slashed-to-fringes edge of the torn cloak. "I killed that bird; we survived. Perhaps the Warding kept the fliers from feasting. It is strong, yes, but what it stood against was—and is—more powerful still." She addressed Zolan rather than me, and he watched the sky now, looking away from her.

"Could those battle-birds have been called from the Dismals?" I demanded.

"Yes." He added nothing to that single word.

Lolart stared at us both. Though he asked no question, I took Zolan's brevity of speech as a warning and inquired no further.

Now a decision had to be made. Rogher had not only suffered tearing from bird beak and claw but he had also broken his leg, probably when his mount fell. Bina, with our help, set the break, which was luckily a clean one. She then bound it with two lengths of wood cut from a sapling Lolart had found. However, the squire refused the herb she offered to ease his pain.

"We know now what will happen next," he said. "I would not be muzzy-minded if another attack comes."

I reached over and drew the dagger Bina carried. A small ritual needed to be done to put Rogher under the protection of the Warding, if that barrier would guard; since the strike of the birds against Bina I could not be sure. I pricked my finger deeply with the point of the old weapon, and a bead of blood issued forth.

Placing the now-bleeding finger to our patient's lips, I ordered him to suck and swallow. Trusting in his knowledge of us from of old, he obeyed. This act of Power would temporarily tie him to our company by blood, and the Ward would draw him in also.

Now we lacked two mounts for our party, but Rogher could neither ride nor walk. So we made ready to camp close by, the squire being sure that the party from Grosper was not too distant. I knew that Mother would be able to pick up our presence without need for any Send, and to use such a Calling now, in the presence of the Dark Force that had summoned the birds, might betray us at once.

Cilla stewed a mixture of coarse meal and herbs over a small fire, and Lolart, with a well-thrown stone, brought down another leaper. Not to be outdone in the kill by any mere two-legs, Climber mastered his limp long enough to catch a second grass-bounder, a reckless young one.

After we had eaten, the old soldier spoke. "I ride scout." The words were a statement, not a question. He rose and started toward the place where the horses grazed.

"No—" I stepped into his way. "Would you stir about and so give the Power that wants us another chance?"

"You said that we were under the Light's protection, Lady Tamara." Again he stroked his cheek where the beard covered it, almost as if he unconsciously traced an old scar.

"If we stay together, yes," I returned. Now I questioned Zolan. "Do you not agree?"

The man from the Dismals nodded. He had made no explanation of his own part in banishing the birds—if the vicious fliers *had* been birds—and I had no right to ask for what he did not offer on his own.

Lolart stirred restlessly. I knew he wanted to do what he, as an experienced armsman, believed was right, instead of sitting here to wait for what might come to him and us.

Diplomatically, Zolan assigned both the guard and himself employment. "We shall bring up the ponies; then let us see what is of true worth among the goods we carry. Our plan of playing traders may not come to pass, and we must not keep useless burdens on the animals."

I took my turn beside Rogher while the rest of our party once more opened the bags and sorted through the loot of that long-ago raid, Zolan explaining to Lolart its source. Pain still showed in the squire's eyes. He began to talk feverishly, telling me all that had happened after it was learned we had vanished from Grosper.

"My lord—he had the ice-anger on him. He told the clan chiefs that, unless they aided in a search for you, he would believe the deed was a plot hatched amongst them all.

"Chief Starkadder—he made his son speak out before the company, then he drove away that Udo Chosen. He said the priest was a demon follower and the cause of what his son had done. And that lout's summoning, through Udo, of Maclan to do the actual taking was a cause of even greater rage to my lord."

"The men of Grosper came with sleuthhounds, and we went on the track, but not before my lord sent a message to King Arvor, which warned him of what such a threat to the Lord Warden might lead our queen to do. Then our lord came back—and he was a man locked within himself, letting no one learn his thoughts. Our lady sent one messenger to the nearest guard and another to the Green Grove. She stayed apart for a whole day and, when she returned, she said that you all still lived but that some Power alien to hers raised barriers between you.

"News came to us from Kingsburke that fighting had begun there. The Chosen had taken over, and their leader had made Arvor prisoner. Most of the clans then set upon them. Men babbled of monsters and such mad notions, and we could get no true news of what was happening in that place. But both our lord and lady said a task awaited that must needs be done, and so we came riding."

He ended, flushed and panting. I held the water bag for him to drink. Before it was more than midday by the sun, he was raving and had to be restrained, the fever leading him to believe that Father had summoned him and he must go. Lolart lent his strength to keep the squire from a struggle which might have undone Bina's tending, and she pressed a mass of wet, torn leaves against the bandages on his face until he lapsed into unconsciousness.

We strove to pile scoured-up turf and earth into walls of a sort; then Zolan used cloth drawn from among the loot to fashion a shade over Rogher. We saw no more birds, not even any of the hawks common to the air in these parts. Climber kept licking at his thorn-stabbed foot until at last he joined Zolan, who at intervals checked on the horses and draft ponies.

Waiting was far worse than traveling. No Send came to us, and we were certain that this in itself was a warning against trying to reach those from Grosper. Lolart, meanwhile, was busy with a hide thong he had sawed from one of the burden bags—a difficult job with only one of our rusted daggers to aid. At last he began searching about in the earth disturbed for our wall-building to produce five pebbles. We saw that he had now armed himself with a sling such as shepherds sometimes used, and he began to employ it at once. Five pebbles he released from the whirling hide loop, then retrieved them and tried again. His aim grew better with each throw, and I, intrigued, reached for another piece of hide to cut a strip of my own. A sling would be a new weapon for me but a weapon nonetheless.

Sabina

I LAID THE cooling pad once more on Rogher's face. My other hand, thick and clumsy with bandages, was useless when I tried to move my fingers. The strange lack of feeling raised wariness in me. Beaks and claws had torn my flesh, yes, and I had not suffered such wounds before. Only now our own herbs, gathered and mixed to the best of my supplies and knowledge, had brought no lessening of pain. And when I had last viewed Rogher's face, I discovered that the puffiness that had half blinded him had spread.

Had we both received some venom into our wounds? How greatly I longed for access to my own store of drugs, and to those books compiled from the learning of generations before me! Now, as I cradled my wounded hand against my breast, I knew what I must do. I looked to Cilla, and she read in that gesture what I wanted and came at once to sit beside me.

"I must go Deep," I told her in a whisper.

"To show yourself to—*them*?"

"Yes—and with no one to follow," I answered. Once before in my life I had tried this inward journey, but Mother and Duty had both held me then with Power.

Cilla continued to regard me, her lips pressed together. She laid a hand on my knee, but I shook my head. No company, no. I dared not make too great a stir in the force. We might not be as well Warded as we thought— did not pain eat at me now?

Slowly Cilla shook her head, but she withdrew her hand as she realized that this was my will and that I believed it necessary.

Closing my eyes, I pictured my heart beating, began to slow its steady pumping. Then around me, with the inner Sight, I raised walls on either side to serve as barriers. Down that open path between them, "I"—that which was my essence, for in truth my body had released me—traveled.

I stood now in a vast space wherein were crowded multiple boxes: some narrow, some deep, but each with a sliding panel set into the side facing me. Slashes of color marked every container, symbols I could not translate as I paced along. If what I sought was stored here, I would know it.

Along one aisle I had come, and now I started down its neighbor. What I used for organs of sight within this place were beginning to dim. Yet I kept on and on. How long had I been searching? I could not tell, for time in the Deep Place cannot be reckoned.

Then one color flashed out more strongly, and I sped towards it. Green—the color of growing things, of natural life in my own time and place. The guarding panel slid to the side with no need of my touch. It was old, very old, of that I was sure. And within—

I was never to see the contents wholly, for at that moment the scene that lay about me shivered, shook, and—

Drucilla

I watched Bina go into the Deep. What she faced now was death of body. Her form was already flaccid, and I caught her as she fell backwards to make sure that she was safely lowered. Her skin was pale under fainter brown painted by the sun. When I took her uninjured hand, it was limp and cold.

"What does she?" Tam pulled away from her employment, stood over us. With both hands raised to her head, her face a mask of horror, she fell to her knees beside us. "She is gone!"

"She searches for knowledge she believes she must have," I answered dully, "in the Deeps." I knew what Tam meant, though I had not ventured to confirm her condition for myself; Bina was no longer one who shared life closely with us.

"We must give her a guard on that road!"

I slapped down Tam's hand. "You dare not follow—her Deeps are not yours."

Even though we had been tied from birth, that was the truth. Certain memories are not ours to comb; they may lie far back in time and belong to one person alone. To gain knowledge from them, the searcher must turn to the All-Memory, which is of the spirit, not the body. Yet this is a matter of great danger, for the seeker may be trapped by some event of peril in the past and unable to win free. If the diver has none to tug her back from the wonders of those Deeps to the surface of physical life, then—

Tamara

I snatched Bina's hand from out of Cilla's grip and held it in both of mine. It was cold—so very cold! Had what she sought been learned just at the point of death? I refused utterly to believe that. All at once, though I had not tried the way of the Deep, I flushed into the open a memory of my own. Within a moment I had ducked my head, and the bagged stone from the ruins slid down my breast. Placing Bina's hand by her side, I freed that gem and gazed into its heart.

A change commenced in its radiance; I felt it begin to warm. Cilla had watched me closely. Now she drew aside that rag of dress Bina wore and unlatched the top of the reptilian vest. I laid the ever-warm stone over my sister's heart. Did that center of life still beat? By the mercy of the Great One, it might, though I could not yet be sure.

Sabina

SUDDENLY I FELT both heat and light, but both assaulted me—these forces were meant as weapons, not for nurturing. I was Sabina of the Scorpys—I tried to cling to that identity, even as I became aware that I was in a place and time I could not remember, and one where fear held me in thrall.

I was somewhere in the open—this I understood; also, I was captive. I had held out very long—too long to suit those who had taken me prisoner. More and more my sight cleared. I seemed to stand on a place much higher than those before me, for I looked down on a gathering of figures, all of whom wore drab-colored robes with hoods drawn up to hide faces.

From them issued a droning chant in which I could distinguish no separate words. I felt now the pressure of real chains about my wrists, though I did not look down to see those restraints. A similar band was tight about my waist also, and it anchored me past any real movement.

Then the throng before me parted, and down that open way came—

Once more, darkness closed in and, welcoming an escape, I allowed myself to be borne away.

Twenty-three

Drucilla

The twilight had closed about us. Bina lay quiescent. She still lived—barely; I believed that Tam's gem kept her with us by some fragile thread. We had tried time and time again to reach her, drawing on those new energies we had developed in the Dismals—to no avail. Now and then we looked to Rogher, who was in little better case than our sister. The squire was very flushed, burning with fever; perhaps the raptors had had envenomed claws.

We could only keep on with Bina's treatment and change the pads on Rogher's face. We also stripped the bandages from our sister's hand, to find it swollen into puffiness, the skin tight and shiny. This we treated with the same herbs she had chosen for Rogher.

Lolart and Zolan came and went, seeing to the animals and fetching more water, but they did not venture far. We choked down the water-soaked grain from Frosmoor, but neither of our charges could be offered that lumpy, musty fare.

Twice the man from the Dismals stooped to look at Bina and the squire, but he said nothing. When he came the third time, Tam had surrendered Bina into my hold, working the stiff fingers that had been crooked around the gem.

She looked up at Zolan. "Have you seen this condition before?" She demanded harshly.

"Yes—the wounds hold venom of some sort." He drew out the words slowly as if he dreaded them.

I bit my lip. Could one of the horrors from the Dismals have been summoned to join the flock of carrion birds?

"For some poisons, an antidote may be found," Tam declared, scrambling to her feet. My arms tightened about Bina. Yes, certain venoms could be overcome, but others—

All at once I felt the familiar mind-touch of a Send. For the first time in hours, I knew a surge of hope. Those we awaited were near.

I continued to hold Bina, but Tam was already at the wall of our camp and over it with a leap, Climber running beside her. Now I too could hear, in the quiet of nightfall, the thud of hooves and a jumble of raised voices. Those we awaited had come.

Time became a patchwork of colors and cries. Strong comforting hands rested on my shoulder, and the protective sense that always marked the presence of Father enfolded me like a warm cloak. Presently Duty and Mother gently took Bina from me.

It was as if a heavy burden slid from our shoulders to be taken up by others. I tried to watch what Mother and Duty would do to rouse my sister and deal with Rogher's wound. Instead, I found myself treated as another charge or a child, being gathered up in Father's arms, carried to where pallet-places had been arranged on the ground. As I lay there, I saw him bring Tam also, then place her beside me before he touched both of our foreheads and bade us sleep.

Tamara

I AM NOT A great dreamer; Cilla is our farer into other planes of consciousness. Yet I saw before me a door and knew that it was for me to move beyond it in search. It was a strange place I entered—one that had never known peace. The Power that abided here was not an active force; rather, it manifested as a brooding sense of negation. Life as I knew it was denied in this domain. Trees, warped of limb, grew as if in hopeless anguish. The light was a forbidding yellow miasma, eloquent of a diseased origin. Underfoot lay slime that gave off a foul stench like the battleground of the monsters in the Dismals. A bitter moaning of pain and sorrow came to my ears, faint as a cry of the wind, though no air stirred.

That this was a place of endings I understood. I also realized that to remain here meant being absorbed into a living death, far worse than any clean slaying. Still I could not retreat.

One of the twisted trees grew ahead—a sapling. Before my eyes it writhed, not as if to free its roots from the earth but rather to further distort and torment the branches. Pain arose in me. This was a call to action; the tree and its agony filled me with a need to break the spell of deathly lethargy that lay upon this sad land.

I set hand on its branches, tried to hold them firm against the Power that wrought against them. My fingers sank into slime. Fetid puffs of air followed—perhaps an invisible living thing breathed into my face. Then something brushed against my legs. I looked down and beheld a vine, moving like a serpent, striving to bind me.

The touch of that climbing, clinging growth was filthy, bringing such a feeling of defilement that I cried aloud, but still I fought the Evil will that tormented the tree. Burying my clawed fingers deep in what I could see, I gave a sharp backward pull. Fierce opposition met my act, and then I felt the shock of a great ripping. The branch within my reach straightened again; the leaves, which were curling and beginning to yellow, moved. Suddenly, framed in those life-regaining limbs, I found myself looking—into Bina's face! Her eyes were closed, and her forehead was furrowed with pain. Swiftly I tore at a second branch—and still another. My legs were clamped tightly together by the rapidly growing vine, but I dared not spare the time or attention to rid myself of it. The tree limbs no longer displayed my sister's face, but the sapling itself now was rocking, seeming to offer those branches directly to my hands.

An instant later, the young tree was gone, and Bina, her eyes still fast shut, stood there. Her left hand nursed her wounded right one against her breast. About the two of us a nightmare forest grew in a moment, its branches and vines closing in. I coughed, my eyes tearing, for the stench of the air grew thicker, bitter as acid to burn the skin, choke the throat.

Now a stronger threshing began in the moving foliage. Bright against the dry dullness of leaf and vine flared redness, as if fire were coming. Climber! His pointed teeth tore at the growth striving to encompass us as he launched himself, his great claws extended to bring down the vines.

I stumbled toward Bina as he cut through some of the growth that sought to chain me, half expecting that I would find myself clutching air, my sister merely a spirit. Blessedly, I grasped firm flesh and held to it. For the first time—I might, like Bina, have been shaking off the grip of the Dark Power that stifled our Talent in this land—I cried aloud:

"In the Name of the Great One!"

My one arm about Bina held her tight; now I freed the other. As I brought up my right hand before what lurked among the trees, I straightened a forefinger and shouted aloud:

"By Earth and Water,
Sky and Fire,
Flesh and Spirit,
Time and Space,
Be my sword within my hand!"

Those words were not born of any ritual I had been taught, yet I felt no surprise when forth from my palm shot a light shaped as a sword. My hand closed, and within it I felt the hilt of a weapon. Straightway my body reacted, and I thrust as if I displayed my skill in a hall of arms.

My attack was met! The blade that crossed mine was less brilliant than the one the Talent had given, being in color a rusty red. Along its edges pulsated faint lines of what appeared to be bloody mist.

I pushed Bina behind me. Climber reappeared and pressed against her, on guard. Turning back, I saw that gore-wreathed weapon still swinging back and forth. Did my invisible opponent seek me so, or were those gestures made as a warning, meant to strike terror into a faint heart?

It made no matter. I stepped forward again and deliberately engaged the blade. Now I was only aware of the battle; my surroundings had narrowed to the meeting of the swords. All the past years of training flowed into my shoulder, arm, and hand. Thus—and so—and now *this way*—

My opponent seemed tireless, yet I myself had not yet been hard pressed. So far I was at ease, playing the role of one who tested the weapon-craft of another.

I tried certain tricks of a master-at-arms, yet none succeeded. Thus I knew that the foe who engaged me had been well schooled in swordplay. Sometimes I thought I half glimpsed a shadow body, but each time I strove to touch that phantom figure, I failed.

Well schooled in swordplay? Not so—this was a master, a warrior who could well have fronted my father to win!

I retreated, knowing that I was beginning to tire. Now that dancing point boldly followed me into the open where Climber had cleared a space. The blade swung, though no hand held it.

Was I overconfident in my skill? However, having challenged, I was certain I must see this engagement to the end. That spirit-sword still pursued me, or—did it? For the space of one deep breath, I saw no blade but a branch stripped of twig and leaf. If that was the nature of my opponent's weapon, why, a fighter did not set point against branch but did—*this!*

My sword swung away from that branch, then swept back as might an ax, striking as close to the supposed hilt of the other blade as it could.

A shrill scream split the murky air. My blade passed through that shaft of bloody light. I could see no sign that my stroke had done any harm, but I was certain that this was the tactic to be used.

Now I stooped a fraction and struck again—upwards. The other weapon moved sluggishly; it could not fully escape me. *Up*—one light beam visibly penetrated the other, to emerge on the far side.

The other sword shivered, wavered. Speedily I struck again, downward from the left to catch the blood-hued blade. Another scream, a gurgling cry; then the red weapon shot toward me, not thrust but hurled.

Before I could dodge it, its edge passed over my shoulder. Pain seared along my cheek, sending such agony through my whole body that I fell forward. Still I clung enough to my purpose that I held my own light-shaft up to meet the dark creature I could hear but not see.

A cry burst from my unseen enemy, then died to a croak. Before me, headless, flopped a black-feathered bird. At the same instant, it—and I— were swept away from that hellish landscape. I think I cried, *"Bina!"* but there was no answer.

Drucilla

THE THRASHING OF Tam's body roused me. My father and mother were bending over to press her back onto the pallet. Night's dark had closed about us, yet there was a fire nearby. It leaped a little as it was once more fed by one of our Grosper men.

Without warning, Tam's body went limp. She breathed in harsh rasps as she might have done after a fast bout in the arms hall.

My mother looked to my father.

"Did you witness that?"

"Yes. Though who or what she fought, I could not see."

"It was a barrow-wight! What has come upon us, Desmond? Old Dark things are awakening—or being summoned!"

Tam sighed and opened her eyes. "Bina!" she cried weakly, struggling to get up.

"All is well now with the Lady Sabina." Duty came into the firelight. "Your talisman, Lady Tamara, is a mighty one. It works in no fashion we have learned, but it can be used to potent purpose."

She opened her hand, and the object she held glinted gold.

Rogher had slipped into a healing slumber. Tam and I were roused, and Zolan was then summoned to give the tale of the Dismals: what abided there still and what had come forth from it to stir up old evil in Gurlyon.

It took us until nearly dawn to finish the telling of our adventures and to answer questions. I saw Father studying Zolan closely. The Lord Verset, well remembered for his service at Erseway, might have seen young King Gerrit after that battle. Verset had been in command of part of the occupying force, though they had not been stationed long at Kingsburke. Was he now of the same mind as we had been at times—guessing that Gerrit had come out of the Dismals with us? However, he neither spoke of the lost king nor asked Zolan for another name.

We did not ride on in the morning but later. We had rations to strengthen us, and Mother and Duty had also shared out proper clothing from their supplies, so that we once more went garbed as was suitable for our rank. Duty clicked her tongue reprovingly when she viewed Tam's shorn hair; other changes might not show so openly, but we were well aware of them. We had not been children in years when we had been tossed into this venture, and it had not lasted long, though a year seemed to have passed. But it had added far more than the time of one sun-circle to our experience and had moved us out of the last days of innocence into independence.

This I realized very well when Mother came to me as I stroked the divided skirt of my riding clothes; the clean fragrance of the smooth cloth was a pleasure I relished greatly. We had bathed at a pond, shadowed by Duty as if we were hardly out of leading-strings. Hair and bodies had been washed several times over with flower-scented soap of my own making—a luxury I hardly remembered. Tam twisted a scarf around her still-damp locks.

Duty had inspected closely our scaled clothing from the Dismals, shaking her head and pursing her lips many times over. I believe that, after removing the gems that had secured it on us, she would have thrown it into the camp refuse-heap to be buried, had we not prevented her from doing so.

Mother inspected with greater interest what we discarded, fingering the vest I had laid aside. "Snake?" she asked.

"Perhaps. I am not sure. These are of Zolan's making; he gave them to us. Strange beasts aplenty—and creatures of our world grown to monstrous size—live in that land."

"It would seem so. . . ." Mother spoke as if she had been distracted in midthought. Suddenly her hand swept up, and her fingers might have turned to candles. The spurt of blue flame at their nail-tips dimmed quickly to only a faint glimmer of fire.

I did not think—I moved. My own hand answered hers in the same gesture; five flames atop my own fingers flared—but died.

"So that is the way of it," she observed. "And have you slain beast—or man?"

I shook my head furiously, dropped the hand that had betrayed my difference back onto my knee.

"Be sure you speak the truth," Mother cautioned, her hand still raised, the nails yet rimmed with sparks. "If you use Power without careful thought, the Talent will lose luster."

Again I gave that gesture of negation. "I have used my Talent to open passages through the Wards of other people, and for no other purpose."

"This Zolan—has he ever spoken of the past?"

"He has told us only that, having been lowered into the Dismals by those who wished to see the last of him, he was taken into fosterage by her of the Jug."

"King Arvor has been seized by the demon priest. Starkadder, or any other clan which has risen against the Chosen, would be quick to hail this stranger as their missing king, knowing that such a claim would draw many of the small neutral clans to his banner."

That was the truth. But would Zolan play such a game? He had taken oath to act against the Evil; might he believe that victory would be assured by entering this battle on the opposing side?

As if my unspoken question had been a summons, Zolan came bearing down on us, Climber limping beside him. Climber—had the cat-creature dreamed, in his own fashion, to be so drawn into that dark vision of Tam's in the struggle for Bina?

The red beast left Zolan's side and moved straight to Mother, his golden orbs of eyes regarding her. They watched each other thus eye to eye, neither apparently aware that Zolan had also joined us.

Then Mother did something that astounded me: setting her hands together at lip level, she bowed her head. It was a greeting such as she would give to a Wise One of higher rank than herself, owning a Talent foreign to her own, perhaps, but certainly bestowed by the Light.

Now I was aware of a Send, though I could not read it. Zolan took another step and rested his hand on Climber's head. It was plain that he understood much better than Tam and I what was in progress.

Climber's rich red fur stirred, rose, formed a glowing mist about his body. I felt the pressure of great effort. Then that soft radiance subsided but lapped about him, so that all we saw now was a misty pillar.

Mother did not turn to Tam but held out a hand in her direction.

"The focus stone—"

Tam hesitated for only a moment before she turned the gem out of the hair-pocket she had woven and placed it into Mother's waiting hand.

For a time, Mother sat with the gem cupped by her palm. She might have been holding a pen or an artist's brush when her hand again moved swiftly, lines of gold following those sweeps. Now she rose to her feet as the lines coalesced into a pattern that I found at first hard to distinguish, well practiced as I was in design.

I blinked and stared, did both again—and then it was finished. A body was outlined in that red mist; a ball that served as a head nodded forward.

Mother had ended her drawing. Instead, she thrust the stone forward in the direction of the sphere. Gem touched mist, was engulfed.

We had been four humans, and a beast from the Dismals; now we were five. The being that now fronted Mother bore some resemblance to a small woman. A robe of the same red as Climber's fur covered her closely below her breasts, which were made more prominent by a drapery of jeweled chains. About her short neck was set a collar of flashing stones that fitted tightly. The back of her ball-head was covered by short, red, silky hair much like fur, while her eyes were slightly protuberant yellowish orbs. As soon as she became fully visible, her ring-bedecked fingers went into motion.

I caught my breath. Two of those signs I knew—and they were repeated by my mother.

"Welcome, sister-in-spirit," was our dame's greeting.

"You have cast rare cublings, sister," returned the woman. "They have shown me that this land, though barbarous, indeed holds true wisdom to be met."

"There is wisdom—and unwisdom," Mother replied. "It would seem that some kin of yours has turned the Life Mirror towards darkness."

"What tree, however hale, has never grown a worm-eaten branch? Still, the evil that has been done must now be righted. Zolan—"

At the sound of his name, the man from the Dismals drew closer.

"This one will trim that rotten limb—he is oathed to do so, sister. Take him to where the king sits in council and leave him then to his task. It is also certain that Evil has called upon Evil, for the Dark Forces in your world have been summoned and have answered. Those who now bend to the Shadows from the earliest days of your people can be faced only by ones with Talent native to this time and place. Only thus may this ill be met."

The woman-cat-beast accepted my mother's consent. Once more the borrowed body and features blurred, mist thickened and swirled into nothingness, and Climber sat staring straight ahead as if he had been ensorcelled. But then, perhaps, he had.

Twenty-four

Tamara

Climber kept his place before Mother. None of us spoke; the questions we longed to ask made us tense. However, only Mother could answer them, and she must do so in her own time and by her own choice.

She looked to Climber and smiled.

"Very good," she said softly, just as in the past she had applauded some demonstration of the Talent performed by the three of us. Leaning forward, she smoothed his head and scratched behind his ears. His long red tongue curled out about her wrist; then he stood up and limped away. Without any comment, Zolan followed him.

Mother now looked to her hand, on which rested the gem. Its pure gold was dimmed as if part of its alien life had drained away. She held it toward me and I took it up; in my hand, although dulled, it was warm. I stowed it quickly in the hair bag.

"So be it," she said softly, like one making a vow. "So shall it be." Then she looked from me to Cilla and back again and spoke with a tone in her voice I had never heard before. "The doing of that which we must now do will be hard, bitter. Those with Talents must answer when a need arises."

This should have been a time of rejoicing, since we were free and reunited with those we loved. I swallowed and tasted bitterness indeed, as if I had mouthed saubun berries before they were ripe.

She looked away across a desolate land. My eyes followed hers—why had all the vibrant life been leached out of meadow, hill, copse, in this fashion? The answer came from within me, and it was one I had to accept. Our beloved home had become a place accursed, and so it would remain unless we spent all our energy to cleanse it.

"Well?"

We tensed. Father stood there, hands on his hips. He raised his head a little and drew in a deep breath, striving, it would seem, to catch some scent carried by a rising wind.

"Not so," Mother answered. "The old wild Talents have been freed. Again shall the Shadow Hounds lead the faceless Hunter, and the Green Ones walk the forest. The Wards have been broken here in Gurlyon, and no Warden can repair those quickly or with ease; the Wild Folk acknowledge no border drawn by men, for they belong to all the land. And evil ones among our own kind—they whose hands drip blood and who find their pleasure in acts of the Dark—are also gathering. No, it is not well, but an ill time for us all, Desmond."

"Yet shall not the Light also raise its Talent?" he asked slowly. "For that is the way of all balance. And against those who are men ready to pledge their service to the Demon One, we can also use steel."

Steel, indeed—his hand swept forward so that the weak sun over us now shone on his naked sword. Within me, I sensed that my weapon, too, rested ready.

Since we could now neither turn back from the way to Kingsburke nor detach any of the guards, thereby weakening our small force even more, Rogher had to accompany us. Duty set her jaw and, resolute as her name, took over his care.

Through the rest of the day and night that followed, we were at her beck and call. Potions were brewed, and he swallowed them under her piercing eye. Duty was not to be gainsaid. She and Mother had uncovered his leg and, though the wrapping and the supporting splints remained in place, they used their hands for massage of a kind. As they worked, they uttered spells in the Old Speech that was heard on this island before our own people first landed on its shores.

Bina worked to loosen the bandage on her hand as we told her of the scene with Climber. The skin was less red, and the puffiness was reduced. I used the gem to speed her body's repair of itself. After first drawing it back and forth across the wounds, I told Bina to hold it above the limb, while all three of us pictured the torn flesh healed, the hand and its fingers useful once more.

We saw no more this day of Zolan or of Lolart, nor did Climber come to the fire when darkness fell. We tried hard to put from mind all the ill news we had heard and to concentrate on healing. We were aware that Duty and Mother had renewed the Warding that encircled the camp.

"See—" Bina held forth her hand, palm up, to me. I took the stone she offered before she turned her fingers over. Then I bit back an intake of breath. True, her skin bore no more streaks of the angry red that betokened poison. But the sealed pinkish seams where the wounds had been, and the ridges that had formed between her fingers where the flesh had been torn, would disfigure her hand for the rest of her days.

She was smiling as she caressed that scarred and coarsened surface, but her eyes were heavy with tears. "By so much—or little—have we won, sisters. Let my maiming be an omen for all to come."

By dawn Rogher was also restored. The rough brace that had been fashioned for his leg was greatly shortened to enable him to ride. And the wound on his face, like the tears in Bina's hand, was sealed with a new-grown scar. Unlike our sister, however, he would doubtless wear that badge of an encounter with our foe as did many armsmen: as a near mark of beauty.

We did not move out until after nooning and then in such order as our father decided. Our own horses, together with the spare mounts usually brought along for travelers in unknown territory, were enough to provide for us all.

None denied that I ride behind Father. His squire was left to Duty's eagle-eyed company, wherein were also Bina, Cilla, and our mother. Once more our party had gone through a Warding ceremony. In addition, the soldiers rode well weaponed, with no peace ties in use, such as were normally adopted when crossing the border into another sovereign country.

The country still bore a faded look, but I did not think it was as empty as its wanhope appearance suggested. I kept turning my head from side to side, for the feeling that we were watched never left me. Two scouts rode ahead and two behind to assure we were not indeed followed.

We were well beyond the end of the Dismals now, so that when we angled west we had no sight of that strange slash in the land. Zolan kept much to himself and the company of Climber. However, Father often paid no attention to his reserve but continued to ask questions, none of which dealt with the Jugged People but rather with the other inhabitants of the World Below.

Zolan could not escape without seeming antagonistic and sooner or later would yield to Father's curiosity with some tale of the giant creatures— insect, animal, or reptile—with which he had himself had to deal.

I noticed that our erstwhile host no longer wore the sword we had taken from the field of massacre; nor did he bear, to outer appearance, any weapon at all. Fortunately, no move was made among the troop, as the custom was, to test a newcomer for what he might offer in offense or defense.

Now I became aware of another change in the world about us. No leaper exploded from the surrounding brush; no hawk coasted in the air above. Indeed, save for our own company, no life showed about us. As twilight closed in, our forward scouts waited in a place they had chosen for a camp.

They reported a keep not too far ahead where people worked in newly plowed fields. Father had summoned Lolart to ask what he knew about the land. He reported that the Gurly named the keep Rossard, and stated that its lord had been friend to the folk of Frosmoor. With our troop's First Sergeant, Gorfund, the guardsman rode on to give warning of what disaster had wasted his own home and to discover what he could about the temper of those we might encounter ahead.

As we established our camp and the night gathered the dark about us, I grew more uneasy. Our chosen site had protection, both from armsmen at sentry and the strongest Ward that could be set. Yet I could not rid myself of an ever-strengthening conviction we had been detected and were awaited.

Sabina

I COULD NOT restrain myself from often rubbing my hand. Some tenderness still lingered between my fingers, and the scars I would ever wear, like Remembrance rings, though I did not need such memorial jewelry to recall what had happened. Rogher was drooping in the saddle, and two of Father's men lowered him onto a pallet that had already been spread for his ease.

As the squire subsided on a camp-bed, his gaze touched me.

"May the Winds of Callon be ever at your back, Lady Sabina." He raised a hand to the scar that tautened the flesh of his cheek.

"And at yours, Rogher," I returned. "We shall need any aid we can find in days to come." Callon's winds—the breath of flowers, of full and generous life, of promise—yes, we might well beseech the Powers whose gift they were to breathe them on us all.

His blessing gave my thoughts another angle. Callon was our peace, our future home—or so those of the Shrine had vowed—and their teaching was never questioned. Together with Tam and Cilla, I had been First Named within those walls.

Callon was the dwelling-place of the Messengers of Light. It was also, however, a guardhouse of sorts, for warnings could be sensed or dreamed there. Dreams . . . Quickly and resolutely I pushed the thought of night-visions from me. I had heard and pondered Tam's account of how she had found me on another plane of being; by her description of the horrors that flourished there, it must have been a lower one. But of that sending-forth of my spirit I could remember nothing.

To have a portion of memory sliced away—I shivered. Those of the Talent feared any attack that could lessen their inner powers. Was I the less now that the poison of the enemy had ravaged me?

I moved a little away from Rogher and the fire, which was, as always, the center of the camp. Our scouts had selected a place shielded by several monolithic rocks: standing stones. Such structures were also known in Alsonia. Most were thought to have designated the meeting places of the Early Ones. Our mother and Duty had tested those that surrounded us before we settled in, to report them clean of sorcery.

My back was against one of the rough pillars. My Talent raised me no warning of any trouble here but, to be doubly sure, I fumbled in the pocket-pouch on my belt to bring forth a much-folded square of cloth. From it arose the scent of mingled herbs—a defense of Duty's fashioning, and a mighty one. With this barrier laid across my face and beneath my nose, I need fear no assault though dreams.

Now I tucked it, half folded again, into the front of my riding coat. Leaning my head back against the supporting stone, I closed my eyes.

Though I was usually ready to perform camp tasks, this evening I felt no urge to render service in that way.

I cannot truly remember when I became aware of the new sound. My head had turned so that my ear pressed almost painfully against the rough surface. Very faint, very far—was it indeed a sound or rhythm, that of a drum whose beat matched the throb of my heart. Though I did not move my head, I searched about me for a stone, my hands catching in winter-killed grass and uncovering new growth underneath. Grass—earth—neither was of any use for my present purpose.

With our new clothing had come the always-familiar bosom knives. I drew mine now. Setting the hilt close to the monolith, I tapped the stone with as little sound as I could manage, using the same rhythm. If it were only a fleeting return of some happening in the far past—the scholars in Alsonia had used such a method to draw upon history—then I would have no reply. But if it were a summons—

The Wild Talents had been aroused from a long sleep. Was I now engaged in gaining the attention of a much older Power forgotten by humans? Alarmed at my action, I discovered I had to use actual force to separate the hilt and the hand that held it from the stone. Cilla came up to me just as I sundered that hold.

Swiftly she dropped to her knees to catch my hand with both of hers. Then she leaned forward and set her ear also to the stone. I was certain that that faint thudding was growing in strength. It no longer followed my heartbeat but was slower, heavier.

"Mother—Duty—"

I knew what she meant—we must warn the others. Yet when I tried to pull myself away from the pillar I had thought a mere backrest for a tired traveler, strove to get to my feet, I found I was no longer free. Near panicked, I tried to call out—and discovered that I could not raise a sound. Ensorcellment! It had caught me, fool that I was.

Drucilla

By a sudden flare of the firelight I could mark Bina's struggle. Now I pulled away from her stone, fearing that I, too, might be entrapped. Mercifully, I was free. However, when I had released my sister's hand, she once more returned to pounding the pillar of rock and, though her body writhed and she even bent far over enough to set teeth to her wrist, she could not escape.

I must get help—put out a Send to Mother, Duty—but when I strove to fit words together, I discovered that, like Bina's hand, my inner voice would not obey me. I felt a rush of fear. What had caught us? The thing was within the circle of our own Ward. It had not stormed that barrier; instead, we had caged it with us.

A dark figure loomed over us—Zolan! Desperately, I framed a mute message for help.

The man from the Dismals pulled me away from Bina, yet he did not reach for her but rather knelt and set both palms flat against the pillar.

He was making a sound so low I had to struggle to hear it—humming, or a singsonging of strange words that were meaningless to me. The knife fell from my sister's hand. Her mouth twisted in pain as she grasped her scarred fingers and drew them protectingly close to her breast.

Slowly Zolan drew his hands, held apart, down the stone wall; he appeared to be outlining something there. Mother came up, stood watching for a moment or so, and then shook her head vigorously as Duty joined her. I had lost all touch with the camp at large. Only the five of us and the stone existed in this night-dark world.

The lines Zolan had drawn on the stone were as sharply clear as if he had sketched them on a white surface with a stick of charcoal. Now we could see, short, bulky, and still shadowy, a Thing standing on two feet and possessing two hands. Zolan drew back, no longer touching the rocky surface, but the creature pictured on it continued to gather more substance, become clearer.

This being I knew. The man from the Dismals might have copied, from one of the crumbling skin-leaves of the oldest records of the Scorpys, such a human body. The head was out of proportion to the rest of the figure, much larger than was natural—if it could be said that anything was natural about this mockery of man. Huge eyes stared blankly from under great furry brushes of brows, which were kept apart by a jutting nose crooking forward. The mouth was all but hidden beneath this hook, while the chin possessed an unnaturally square line. Above sprouted a thatch of head covering, so coarse it stood up in spikes.

It was a Frush: underground dweller, sly deceiver, toller of the benighted venturing into its territory. Wise folk of the old days strove to strike a bargain with a Frush, if it appeared near any cot, lest gardens be stripped of growth, cows dried of milk, or horses and ponies ridden to exhaustion during the night. More than a hundred tales of Frushes existed in those ancient chronicles, most dealing with how they harassed, and bested, mankind. They were allied to neither the Light nor the Dark, and would serve no Power by their own will.

The creature had real eyes now, and those orbs glinted as they surveyed Zolan. Thick lips, nearly scraping its nose-tip, parted, and it growled.

Zolan's hum had not stopped but had grown louder and now became words.

> *"Varsh, Larsh, Ceder, Sim,*
> *Landor, Trie, Magar, Rin.*
> *Snople, Yaple, Vinder, Dot,*
> *Ragour, Papah, Anlee, Mot!"*

It was nonsense—a child's counting-out rhyme. Still, it appeared to have a meaning for the Frush. It hunched and looked as if it were going to break from the stone, to throw itself at Zolan. Yet it did not burst free.

Zolan groped in the grass, never taking his eyes from the creature. Keeping it chained, perhaps by that steady stare, he held up Bina's knife in both hands. A quick move of the knife brought up a glowing bubble of blood on a free finger.

Though the Frush twisted and tried to duck, Zolan was able to flip the drop with the point of the dagger directly at it. I saw the red spatter appear between the Frush's eyes. Its mouth opened as if it bellowed, though no sound reached us.

Without turning his head, Zolan spoke to Mother.

"Lady Sorceress, what geas would you have me set on this one?"

She answered promptly. "To watch and wait, to serve as eyes in light and dark."

"So be it." Zolan lifted the dagger and lightly touched the semblance of those pouting lips in the stone. "What is your name, Frush?"

The thing struggled, and the eyes glared. Then the lips shaped one word, which, though it sounded very faint and far away, we yet heard.

"Titoo."

"Titoo, I hold you by your name. You will watch and wait, serve us with your eyes, until the hour when I give you back that name."

Again the Frush howled, but this time we heard it, and it was deafening. So loud was the roar of rage that the very stone appeared to tremble, as into the ground supporting it, the Frush melted and was gone.

Feet came pounding up. That last manifestation of Power must have aroused all the camp. Zolan tendered the knife to Bina, sucking the bloody tip of his finger. Duty planted herself directly before him. We had seen the expression she now wore many times in our childhood.

"What are you?" she demanded sternly. "You dare to blood-tie one of the Wild Ones? No good can come of this!"

"There are Talents and Powers, Wisewife. Yours were fostered in this world; mine were strengthened elsewhere. I deal with earth, and the creatures of earth."

I heard Duty draw a deep breath. For the first time in my life she showed surprise and, when she made answer, it was in a different tone of voice.

"So be it, Warlock."

He shook his head. "I am no warlock; I dance not to a tune that may sweep my feet down the Left-hand Path. I claim nothing but that which is my own."

Zolan turned away but in doing so he came face-to-face with Mother, who stepped quickly before him.

"Do not"—she spoke in warning, I understood, and not in command—"draw to yourself some Power you cannot face."

He bowed to her with a courtier's grace. "Lady, to this battle I am new. What I can do to further our cause, I will, but I shall take no reckless chances."

Thus it was that Zolan broke a little from his shell, leaving us to reconsider him.

Tamara

HAVING TRAILED FATHER in his circuit of our camp, I did not witness Zolan's meeting with the Wild Magic, but I was made quickly aware of what had happened. It took either a very reckless or very confident one to deal with such Power. Our knowledge of Wild Magic was slim, though it is supposedly inborn with a user as is the Talent. I had heard that, from time to time, a few who can deal with it come forth. Unlike sorcery, however, it cannot be learned, nor does it grow with training—it simply *is*. Nor, as far as we Scorpys knew, are its limits measurable. It is rooted in an age far past.

Tales told by the firelight are rich with unicorns, hopwits of the household, willights who dance in the swamps, wolfweres, willow-women, and a wealth of other children of the Wilding Way. Other, Darker, offspring the Old Magic bears: boogels, barrow-wights, volies, and grossmiths. Winter's tales, all of them. Yet—if Frushes lived and could be put under the command of mortals, then surely all the fears of childhood were real and able to confront one.

How narrow our life had been! Even though we had relished our Power—our very small Power—it had been contained by ignorance. If Wild Magic had been loosed, then in truth, all Gurlyon was flooded and what we could not see might press us from every side.

I began to search memory for all I had ever learned from the old tales concerning possible defenses. Cold iron was one. Most of our party went clad in steel bonnets, breastplates, and carried that metal in their swords. But one of the strongest weapons on the other side was the art of shapeshifting. Those of the Wild who were true weres could walk in company with us and not be detected. Or rather, they could be discovered by the proper Talents, but with none of the Old Ones could one ever trust outward appearances. Certain herbs had virtue against them—Bina had grown rowan and holly, ivy and fearnot. I gave a small start—had I really heard that? A tinkle of laughter had answered my memory-combing! I closed my eyes determinedly. If Zolan could deal with Wild Magic, so would we also. Or was I again thinking too highly of Scorpy skill?

Twenty-five

Drucilla

I awoke in the morning to feel softness and warmth against me. To my surprise, Climber had apparently shared my bed for at least part of the night. Perhaps, though I had not been conscious of his presence, it had been that which had kept away any troubling dream.

The sun was no herald to awaken this day; instead, one of the thick and ghostly mists for which Gurlyon is infamous blanked out most of the camp beyond the half shelter where we had slept. I noted Mother combing her hair prior to braiding it into a traveling net, and Duty tying the ribbons of her cap firmly under her chin.

Climber yawned widely, nosing against me until I scratched his ears. He then gave me a hearty shove with his shoulder, confirming his faint Send that suggested it was high time to break our fast.

He had never before sought out any of us—Zolan was his bond-mate. What did it mean that he had now come to me?

It was not until I was ready to take the trail, hair braided tight, be-scarfed, and jacketed, that I finally left the shelter, my sisters ready to follow.

Father made his way toward us, grim of face. He greeted us with no usual wish for a good day and a fair ride. Well aware that such words in this hour would be empty form, we were not surprised when he launched into speech as if we had continued with him all night.

"Your friend"—he must have seen Climber, for he spoke directly to me—"has disappeared."

I was not only startled but felt a sudden prick of fear. The Wild Magic and the Frush Zolan had placed under bond posed ever-present perils. The man from the Dismals might have meddled too far with a Power he was untrained to handle. However, I could not be sure of that, for certainly our instruction in the use of the Talent had not been shared; his gifts must have been fostered by the Jugged Woman.

But Climber—certainly the cat-creature could find Zolan, if he were still to be found. I opened my mouth to say so but was cut short when the Send came. Father also caught that mind-message and whirled around, snatching a battle whistle from his waist sash. One shrill blast would alert all within hearing, even if they were mist-blinded.

A suggestion of Evil that had moved through the night now slunk through the dulled air, its Power not only encircling our camp but perhaps also casting out a loop toward the keep we had so carefully avoided. The Lord Warden responded, but his Send went unanswered.

"Climber—use Climber as a focus!" I cried. Without being urged, the beast moved to Father's side.

With one hand on the scarlet creature's head, he followed my suggestion. It was a clear message, emphatic as a battle-cry. *"Where is Zolan?"* Father shouted silently. *"How many raiders are advancing?"*

The answer, when it came, was so unlikely that it might have been shaped to deceive us.

"One"—the next few words made the odd reply clear—*"a gray robe."*

I needed to hear no more. "He means one of the Chosen. It was thus at Frosmoor—the Gray Robe was the bringer of sorcery."

Frosmoor, where the keep and clan lord had fostered the Chosen—though where that false priest had, in the end, been riven by his own power. Was the same trick to be tried again? But Lolart had ridden to warn the folk of the keep we were skirting—unless, as before, the forces of the Dark had a means of silencing him.

My thoughts must have been charged by Power without my summoning it, forming a Send, for an answer came.

"This time the bait is known for what it is. I bring him in; Ward yourselves well."

Father nodded as if Zolan stood before him. He touched Climber's head. "Ride guard for him, good beast."

Having been so dismissed, Climber whisked into the grayness and was gone. We made our preparations. There was no breaking of camp; our party did not wish to be mist-bewildered and to go astray attempting to meet with Zolan. Instead, more wood was fed to the fire; then, under Gorfund's orders, most of the troop concealed themselves. It was good strategy that only a fraction of our force should be evident.

We readied ourselves for a little drama of sorts. Mother and Duty weakened our Wards, for those spirit-shields, at full strength, would be at once detected by the Chosen; of that we were certain. Once he had been brought in, the barriers could be reinforced, but if possible he must believe our Talent less than it was. With the priests of the Left-hand Path, any small show of a Gift on our part would be dismissed as Wisewife trickery used to amaze simple villagers.

We had not long to wait when the mist rippled and we heard a ringing challenge from one of the sentries. Father stood unflinching to the fore, flanked by six armsmen at guard. The mist appeared to grow thicker at one point. We easily sensed what approached—the chill foulness had in no way been disguised. Either this servant of the Jug Demon had never learned concealment or else he scorned our protections.

Zolan drove before him another horse on which was seated a robed and cowled figure, hands tied behind him. His face was so deeply shadowed by the hood that we could see no features. However, Zolan pressed his mount up beside the other to pull that head-covering sharply away.

The man was already known to us—this was Udo, the first of his kind we had met. His face was bleached white with anger, and he spat out a stream of filth together with garbled words in a strange tongue; but he halted abruptly as Zolan raised his hand, leaned over, and slapped him hard across the mouth.

"Sassssss!" The snakelike sibilance Udo used in reply showed that he was not to be deterred from sound, at least. Then a man no longer sat on the horse. In his place crouched low a creature with scales, long stiff bristles for hair, too many limbs, and glaring eyes.

Mother's light laughter came almost as a greater shock than this meta-morphosis. A moment later Father joined his mirth to hers.

Without knowing our Talents, Udo had seen fit to try thus to impress and frighten us. Mother nodded to Tam, who raised a hand and flicked two fingers together. Udo in his own form appeared again, and his rage, if possible, grew worse at this failure.

Father spoke first. "This be no time for games. What do you here, Chosen?"

For once Udo was silent, though his eyes held tiny yellow fires—unclean lamps for any human to display in those windows of the soul.

"I have asked a question, robed one. What bloodletting will you be about?"

Udo allowed himself a sneer. "Lord Warden, your warrant does not run here, as you will discover. Had you any wit, you would head for the Border—with those whores and witches you company with." He glanced in our direction, then back to Father. Now he turned his gaze upward as if he could see a sun instead of the netting of mist.

"His Majesty the king will within this very hour bring you and yours to a Horning. Then all hands will be raised against you."

I sensed a stir among the armsmen present. If Udo spoke the truth, we had been formally outlawed, and we would thus be unable to safely reach Kingsburke without fighting through—we would be like mice attempting to enter a trap.

"Have him down and search him," Father ordered. He must have remembered that the other Chosen had carried strange aids to his Talent to use against Frosmoor.

Gorfund started forward, but Zolan had already carried out part of the order, sliding from his own saddle to pull Udo roughly from his. Though the Dark priest kicked out and strove to free himself, he found it useless to struggle.

"Toy of Pharsali." Udo spat directly into the younger man's face. "I know from what you came and to what you shall soon return. Do not think you can best Lord Tharn!"

Without warning, a snarl sounded, and Udo screeched in pain. From out of the curling mist Climber had appeared, to sink knifelike fangs into Udo's leg.

In an instant Sergeant Gorfund grasped the Chosen and Zolan stood free. The bond-beast also released his hold but did not retreat. All about us the mist continued to thicken. Tam reached for the bag she now wore in full sight and spilled the talisman into her hand.

A golden ray shot up from it, cutting through the webs of fog that had settled in to blind us. Udo gave a cry of surprise and fear, then went limp in the sergeant's hold. His eyes were fixed on the gem, and his mouth fell open a little.

Search him Gorfund did, Udo offering no resistance; all his attention was for the stone Tam continued to hold. She moved forward a pace or two. He would have shrunk away, but he was bound by armsmen the sergeant had summoned. Gorfund himself brought Father what he found strapped to the False One's waist beneath his robe, as well as the contents of a belt pouch.

As he passed Tam, a flame shot from her hand to the end of the tube-shaped object that had been drawn from under the Chosen's robe. Gorfund gave a shriek as the cylinder spun from his hold to roll near Father's boots, where it proceeded to burst into flame. Udo gave a final wail and crumpled to the ground, where he lay motionless.

The sergeant stamped at the burning rod and he, too, cried out. He jumped back and continued to stamp and scrub his feet into the turf as if his boots had suddenly been set afire.

Zolan unhooked a canteen from his saddle and straightway dashed its contents onto the small fringe of flames. An oily greenish smoke answered, reeking like a week-old battlefield.

Sabina

I WATCHED THE wretched Chosen lying still and began to wonder if Tam's weapon out of the Dismals indeed possessed fatal Power. Father now held the pouch taken from Udo, who offered no opposition, being effectively bound under the sergeant's supervision.

We removed ourselves to a place under the partial cover of a thickly woven square of cloth of the kind used to shelter troops in the field. The mist was now fast becoming rain. We sat on mats as one of the armsmen brought a small brazier to provide some warmth and a spicy smoke to quell the lingering stench of the now-charred rod.

Tam still held her talisman in sight, and Udo, parceled like a bale of trade goods, was stretched out before Father and Mother. The Chosen lived, at least, for his eyes were open, fixed on his captors as his lips stripped back in a grimace of hate.

Mother leaned forward a fraction to sketch a symbol in the air. Udo squirmed at that, trying to roll away, only to be pushed back in place by Zolan. Unless he had been Warded by a Power far greater than any we knew, he must now respond with the truth as he saw and heard it.

"You were bound for Rossard." That statement—no question—came abruptly from Father.

Udo's head twisted on his shoulders; his teeth clamped on his lips, then opened to show bloody marks. However, an answer was wrung from him.

"Orders—"

"Whose?" Father could be as terse as the Chosen.

"Those of the Voice of Tharn," came the second forced admission.

"*Vislaf ci rorble*—" Zolan spoke as he held up his hand with an instrument I saw was a whistle. To these words, the Chosen simply looked bemused, as he might if hearing only the garbled sounds we did.

"*Star!*" The single word carried the force of an order.

When Udo continued in his attitude of rebellion, Zolan gave what could only be a sigh of relief and settled back a little.

"This one is an underling, Lord Warden," he reported.

"What did you think him to be?" asked Mother.

The man from the Dismals did not speak at once. He appeared to weigh one answer against another; Mother's invocation of the truth-urge might have touched him also.

"One truly born Evil," he returned soberly.

Turning to Father, he added, "Your pardon for my interruption, Lord Warden, but there was a need—a strong need—to learn what rank this one holds among our unknown foes."

"So be it." Father nodded. "And listen well, Zolan: should you hear aught from this so-called Chosen that needs further explanation, speak freely. Now then"—once more he addressed Udo—"these orders were of what nature?"

"To see that Rossard lay open to raiders."

"As Frosmoor was laid bare to them?" asked Mother.

"Yes—"

He had said only that one word when I tensed. The soldiers had used two of the stone pillars in this circle for the stretching of our temporary shelter from the steady downpour, and my place was close to one of those. I now caught the throbbing beat I had heard before. The Wild Power was astir! Zolan leaped to his feet, hunching so as not to take our roofing with him.

Perhaps Udo had summoned help, though we had not heard or sensed any exertion of Talent; he had assuredly made no Send.

Zolan crowded past me, his hand out to the rocky pillar. He gestured me back.

Astonishment erased Udo's sneer. That Zolan had recognized the source of what was coming was a surprise bordering on a blow to him.

At this second manifestation of the Untamed Power, the man from the Dismals did nothing to summon the Frush or whatever else might materialize. Drawing out once more the focus of his Gift, he tapped it against the rock in a distinct pattern. This time, all that grew out of the column was the head of the Frush. It snarled, the huge fleshy lips twisted—an ugly sight. However, if it were displaying rage against Zolan, it could do no more than make a child's boogel-face.

Udo jerked, trying to move into a better position to face the thing from underground. It saw the false religion plainly now, and those lips gibbered, almost as if it begged help from one expected to offer aid.

Zolan had stepped back a little so they could see each other clearly, Frush and Chosen. Another despairing cry, and Udo's head fell back again as his eyes closed.

The priest's pate had been shaven except for a ridge of locks that spilled in all directions. Zolan stooped and, catching at that unkempt crest, yanked the head up again with force enough to bring the Chosen to his feet.

"*Saray u Sal!*" he ordered.

The head on the column pursed lips and spat. Something that was not liquid hit the earth at Zolan's feet, moved sharply kneed legs, spread wings. Before it could take to the air, however, he stamped it flat.

With one hand still holding Udo's head off the ground, he shaped a symbol in the air with the other. His answer was a second insect from the Earthborn's mouth, a missile that once more fell short. But Zolan had established a bond-tie with the Frush only the night before, so his control should be fresh and strong—how had it been so far broken?

"*Soz!*" Udo no longer tried to free himself by shaking his head; rather, he was grinning.

I could hear Duty to my far right reciting a Ward-spell.

Zolan was blank of feature, relinquishing his hold and allowing Udo's head to thud back to the ground. The man from the Dismals turned his back on the Chosen to fully face the stone. Raising his hand, much as he had done to silence the Chosen earlier, he struck out at the Frush, though in gesture only, his fingers never touching the rock.

"*Sssaar—*" His voice became a hiss worthy of one of the great reptiles of the Dismals.

The Frush must have been ready to spit out another flying thing, but none appeared; instead, the bulbous lips came together with an impotent smacking sound. Then the creature spoke, though its words themselves were spat:

"*Get you—get you—promise to get you!*"

The curse was as clear as any human could have uttered. Above the mouth, the eyes appeared ready to bulge entirely free of their sockets.

Zolan poked a single finger at those eyes, the one from which he had drawn the blood the night before. The Frush fought to free its head, so forcibly that the pillar rocked. The man from the Dismals stood unmoving, silent. At length the head slumped forward a fraction, and a loud, frenzied panting marked the end of the creature's struggle. Zolan relaxed a bit, once more intent on Udo.

"*Sar!*" He repeated to the Chosen the same word he had used with the Frush.

Udo, in spite of his bonds, fought to move, to retreat from Zolan. His face was a dusky gray, and saliva dribbled from the corner of his mouth.

Zolan spoke again a single word—"Talk!"

And talk the Chosen did.

Drucilla

THE DIFFERENCE WAS manifest now—the Zolan we had known in the Dismals had vanished, and in his place now walked this figure of Power. Did the woman of the Jugged Folk feed into him in some manner extra force to enhance the Talent that must be his birthright? Or did the strengthening come to him as it did to us: the more he called upon what lay within him, the stronger he became?

Bina caught my hand; our Talents united and held. Then we reached for Tam, to find her—Warded! This was something so out of our triple nature that it daunted us. The Power-stone in her hand—could that talisman have placed a barrier about her? No, we were Tamara, Sabina, and Drucilla of the Scorpys, and no breakage could cleave us one from the other—never!

For the moment we did not try again. My arm brushed against the Frush's pillar. I felt its rage, then—I *knew!* This was what it wanted, that monster imprisoned in the stone: to separate us. Perhaps it had not tried to come at Udo's call—this might have been its foul purpose all along.

"Bina!" I Sent in ever-growing fear, and once more met—Warding. I shook the arm I held. No one was watching us. Udo was the center of attention; he was spilling out much we had to know. But to me this was far more urgent. Wild Magic—we had ever been warned against contact with the Power no mortal could tame. Our people were too far removed from the early earth-bonded folk to understand it well.

"*Bina! Tam!*" I tried again. Then, in spite of knowing the importance of the interrogation she was absorbed in hearing, I silently cried, "*Mother!*"

She made no answer, though she turned her head and looked in my direction. Perhaps she had indeed sensed my cry for help, yet she gave no outer sign that she had done so.

Twenty-six

*** *

Sabina

Cilla's eyes were wide, and her breathing quickened. Fear hung like an almost visible cloud about her. She clutched at me, her hold on my arm tightening until I could feel the cut of her nails as she drew closer. I might have offered the only safety in her world.

Those around us were so intent on their questioning of Udo that they paid no heed to us. Cilla's voice came as a thin whisper, which I heard only because I centered wholly on her now.

"I cannot Send!"

Instantly I focused my inner strength and attempted a mental message, only to batter against an impenetrable barrier. No mind meeting was possible with Cilla. I next Sent an alarm to Tam, but was met again with utter, unbroken silence.

Somehow, without planning to do so, we had retreated from the group about the captive priest, though the stone holding the Frush was near, at arm's reach.

The creature's head was still bent forward. It might have been utterly cowed by Zolan's handling, but I was aware that the closest eye, large and protruding, had swiveled in our direction. It knew, I was sure, what had happened to us.

Cilla straightened, though she still kept a hold on me. She too was now staring at the head in the stone.

"It acts." She kept to a whisper.

Not being able to Send was for us to suddenly be reft of an eye, an ear, a limb—a maiming of mind far greater than the most grievous wound.

"*Mother!*" I thought-hailed with all my might. I faced her where she stood between Father and Zolan, her attention fixed on Udo.

Nothing—silence—loss—

"*Tam!*" Surely some vestige of our birth-bond remained to Talent-touch, but again—emptiness.

"*Duty*—" I tried my last recourse. Duty had once seemed all-knowing, and she had been the one to keep us ever busied with learning and exercising our Gift. "*Duty!*" Had I done as I wished, I would have screamed her name.

The Wisewife stood a little apart and did not appear as interested in the questioning as the others. Instead she was staring at the head on the stone. Her lips moved constantly, and I was sure she was bespelling the Wild One with all her strength.

Cilla broke away from me, moving with purpose, her target the stone. As she approached that plinth, the Frush lifted its head to face her. The thick, puffy lips shaped a grin.

My sister had been the one of us three who most disliked any dispute. Now her face was set in an expressionless mask. She raised her right hand, fingers wrapped about the hilt of a knife. A blade, for this sort of work? One could not fight sorcery with a mundane weapon! Then I remembered: the Wild Magic had its own laws. For some attacks, the very touch of iron was enough to defeat the purpose. I drew my dagger, a woman's constant companion in this dire country. It was not only the best that could be shaped by Father's smith, a master of his craft, but into it were bound certain Powers of our own.

What progressed with the prisoner and those around him vanished from my mind as I matched step with Cilla. She now stood before the head—and its mouth no longer grinned. My sister had become a stranger. The closed mask did not alter as she held her dagger higher.

"*Iron, cold iron,*" she intoned. The phrase might have come from a bardic lay. If a stone head could flinch without a body of flesh to support it, that of the Frush did so now.

"Eyes for seeing," Cilla continued in that same emotionless voice. She advanced the point of the blade slowly. The head twisted, but found no escape.

Then I was seized by the shoulder, pushed aside so brusquely that I might have fallen, had not another steadied me. Zolan caught Cilla's arm even as she prepared to strike the Frush's right eye.

She snarled like a sleuthhound and hissed not unlike Climber, without looking at the one who tried to stop her. Lightning quick, she used a trick of arms taught us long ago, switching the dagger to her left hand.

However, Zolan was able to move more quickly, and his hand came down edgewise on her wrist with a force hard enough that we could hear the sound made by the blow. Dropping the weapon, she gave a cry of rage and whirled about to try to vent her anger on him, but he held her fast.

My rage flamed to match hers, when I heard the Frush give a snorting laugh.

"What chances?" Mother closed up beside Zolan.

Cilla answered. The white mask of her face now flushed red. I had never seen her is such a rage.

"This *thing* from the depths"—she nodded toward the Frush—"has used its tricks on us. We are now mind-mute!" Her elbow drove into Zolan's stomach and he rocked back with a hissing breath. "They fear iron, these Wild Ones—do not all the old legends tell us that? Let it feel the kiss of iron, then, until it thinks better of such fiendish games!"

Zolan actually laid hands on her again and shook her.

"Would you finish us all?" he demanded.

Suddenly I felt a sensation of force bearing down on my head, a weight so painful that I also dropped my weapon, to clutch my skull in both hands. I clamped my jaws to silence a gasp of agony. Had that crushing pressure been a Send? If so—

"I told you—" Cilla's voice grew more shrill. "I am locked out—or in, Bina is also, and maybe Tam—"

"It is so." Tam cut in from beside me now.

"What games are played here?" Father's voice was harsh.

"No game." Mother was the first to answer. "It is true; our daughters are thought-blocked."

Father turned to Zolan. "You controlled this creature, or made it seem that you did. How is it that he could build such a barrier?" His face became a mask, as Cilla's had, and he regarded the man from the Dismals as if they two were alone in the world. However, Mother moved up beside him.

"Iron," she said slowly. "Duty—"

"Milady," Duty answered briskly.

"What says *Malichor Sum Magnia* concerning iron?"

"That the Wild Ones cannot abide it," replied the Wisewife promptly. "When we of the Upper World first laid hands upon the metal, wrought and wielded it for a weapon, those of the Deep Forests and Outer Lands fled."

Cilla continued to watch the Frush. " 'Twould seem," she said between clenched teeth, "that they did not flee far enough!"

Mother looked directly at Zolan though she said nothing, unless she used Send between them alone. Father nodded; then he moved so quickly and skillfully that he had Zolan's hands pinioned behind his back before he could react.

Zolan was helpless in that grip and, after a moment ceased to struggle. Still he gave warning.

"Think well of what you would do! Milady Sorceress, Lord Warden, would you throw open a gate to a Power you have no hope of controlling?"

Once more I saw the oily, thick-lipped grin on the face of the Frush.

I reached within myself, tried to summon Power as I had in the Dismals—hands out, fingers flexed. A warmth began to rise, yes, but not as strongly as before. I might have returned to the days of my early childhood when I first understood that I possessed Powers and must learn how to control them.

"This Frush," Mother said, "is, or was, blood-bound to your service. Is it by *your* will then, that our daughters are parted each from her sisters?"

"You have heard, milady," the man from the Dismals responded, "what this Udo has spilled forth. Blood-binding, as powerful as that may be, cannot hold entirely against a great Power of the Dark. This Old One"—he nodded toward the Frush—"was without doubt already bonded to him of the Jar Folk I was sent to hunt. When Udo came hither, unknowing that we had already tapped Earth Power, he tried to summoned a creature he believed in his own master's employ. This one came to serve as best it could."

"And," Mother spoke clearly, "such service seemed to be whatever might be done to weaken us most."

Father released his hold on Zolan. "Duty?" Even as we had earlier, the Lord Warden now called upon her.

The Wisewife moved to the pillar encasing the Frush; then she stooped and caught up the dagger Cilla had been forced to drop. This she held high before the Earth Child. Its head came up, yellow eyes following the rise of the blade. Zolan stirred as if to stop her, but Father dropped hand to his shoulder and held him fast.

Duty did not aim the sharp point at the face as Cilla had done; rather, she tapped the stone with it, immediately under the chin of the Frush. A squall burst from its mouth. The greenish teeth it showed gnashed in fear and rage.

"You of the Old Ones," Duty addressed the creature, "do what must be done—break the spell!" Leaning a little forward she no longer tapped but drew the dagger point down the stone.

"*Yaaaough!*" A second screech. The stone rocked but did not fall.

"No!" Zolan's cry was almost as loud as the Frush's. "He is a focus—a focus only."

Duty did not turn her head, but the hand holding the dagger lowered.

"*Land and sea,*
False and true,
Sun and moon,
Fire and water."

With each word, she signed the air with a key gesture to Power. Once more the knife fell to the ground. Her hands now arose breast high, the fingers pointing outward. Her lips moved soundlessly, for the force she called upon now must not be named aloud.

From the top of the pillar a blue line of fire ascended and formed a circle, and that ring of radiance, with the plinth at its core, began to descend. The Frush ground the back of its head against the stone as it strove to see. The light did not pass over it; instead, it circled three times about the pillar just above the Earth-Born's head, then halted to form a band of blue about the gray rise of the stone. The head twitched and fought at what held it, and greenish matter oozed from the eyes to run down the hairy cheeks as though the creature shed tears.

Finally Duty turned to face Father and Mother.

"It is true. The Frush is merely a bow, serving to loose the arrow of another."

Cilla made again for the pillar, her hand balled into a fist. She was sobbing with fury, a feeling I shared, for our hearts could touch even if our minds might not.

This time it was Duty who stopped her, by turning around and flicking a finger in the air. The blue circle puffed into a mist, and that cloud, in turn, also descended.

"To your own place, go!" ordered the Wisewife.

The mist vanished, and so did the head.

Tamara

MY HAND CLUTCHED the hair-bag as I watched Duty banish the Frush. Cilla was weeping openly now. We might be no longer thought-tied, but I could sense that her tears came from rage, not fear or self-pity. I shared, too, her revulsion for being in a world void of our sisterly mind-speech, if we could not break the barriers dividing us from each other.

Duty came away from the stone and beckoned me. Together, we returned to where Udo still rolled, frantically trying to free himself while attention was off him. His head was as high as he could raise it. When he sighted us, his grimace of anger and terror broke for a moment, and he laughed.

"So, hag," he yelled between bursts of raucous mirth, "you've met a master!"

"Who is that master?" I dared to raise my voice.

His head turned a fraction, but before he could answer—if he would have done so—Zolan appeared at his other side.

"Tharn." It was the man from the Dismals who replied.

Now Udo's head turned violently in his direction and his eyes narrowed. Though he had been driven to answer all of Father's and Mother's questions, much of his rebellious spirit now appeared to be returning.

"If you know, whelp of Pharsali, then why ask?"

But Duty now took a hand. She leaned far over until she forced him to look her straight in the eye.

Even through my mind-barrier I could feel the force she used and I knew that Mother also fed it. Suddenly the false priest's face went slack, his mouth fell open and his eyes rolled up to show only the whites, as his head thudded back to the ground. Without looking up, Duty gestured to me.

"The stone from the Cursed Land," she ordered.

I went to stand beside her. She looked up.

"Battle is coming—"

Did I hear her say that, or was the thought mine alone? I looked to the captive. He shriveled, his grayish skin taking on a warm hue like well-baked clay. In the wink of an eye, he became She who dwelt in a jug hidden in a cave leagues away: The matriarch of the Jar People.

"*Let me in!*" Her silent demand was sharp as a blow.

I obeyed—at that moment I could not do otherwise. However, she did not replace my spirit in my body, as she said Tharn had done with the hermit—I could still feel the rasp of the hair-bag against my skin as I loosed its strings and took the gem into my hands. I knew its warmth; now it blazed.

Compelled by that alien will, my hand stretched out directly above Udo's head. And abruptly what lay within those fingers that I moved back and forth in a small circle was no longer my gem but a small pointed ball such as served to head some of those intact jugs I had seen.

I met with instant opposition; my fingers twitched. I strove to summon Power and could not. The sweep halted, and my hand's direction reversed as if I must uncoil all the rings I had already sketched on the air. Out of nowhere came a weightless spear of—smoke? shadow?—like a long black finger. It touched upon the back of my hand, and I was released to begin the circling once more.

Dimly aware that Pharsali's fingers held my own, feeling a pain as though those ghostly digits were claws, I continued.

The end came, suddenly as the snapping of a twig. Light, golden light flared up. I swayed, enfeebled as one long bound would be when her bindings were suddenly cut.

When I could see again, my own fingers, holding merely the gem, rested quietly on my knee. Clinging to the back of my hand appeared to be the mysterious wand I had seen Zolan use, but even as I glimpsed it, that weapon of Power vanished.

No one, fleshed or unfleshed, gave orders now; however, I was sure what must be done. I raised the gem and pressed it for a long moment to my forehead between my eyes, knowing that it could serve as the key to unlock my prison. Swiftly I was on my feet.

Even as I had made the gesture on myself, I repeated it on Cilla, then

Bina. We three might have been completely alone, I was so focused on them.

"*Free!*" The Send united from both of them was a soundless shout.

We gathered in a threefold embrace. But as we emerged from a place of seeming deathly cold into warm life again, another in the camp passed indeed into the Endless Night.

"He is dead." Duty stood by Udo.

"He was possessed by an eating Power." Zolan's hand was empty, his talisman once more in hiding.

"And we," Mother said, "have thrown down a gauntlet. Perhaps too soon."

At Duty's suggestion the body of the Gray Robe was carried well away from the standing stones before the armsmen buried it. We had planned to make an early start, but it was well past noon as we broke our fast before proceeding on.

Climber, who I now realized had vanished during our ordeal, appeared only as we rode forth. He made an exaggerated curve to avoid passing close to Duty as he came to pad along beside Zolan's mount.

We had gone but a short distance at a pace modified for Rogher. The squire managed to sit a saddle, once he had been aided, with some effort, to mount. The whistled signal of a scout from some distance ahead slowed us more as Father signaled a halt to await the report.

We were, the scout told his commander, about to meet others—a party from the keep Lolart had ridden to warn were on their way. The old soldier's arrival at Rossard had come hard on the heels of a hunting party who had returned to tell of Frosmoor's fate. It was well that Lolart was known to the keep lord, or he might have met his end then and there. We needed to kindle no beacon fire to assemble, for, on learning of Father's approaching troop, the folk of Rossard were eager to ride and join us, seeking to balance blood-scores.

So, before the sun moved very far on its downward path, a motley band of riders—in vast contrast to our disciplined armsmen—joined us, Father greeting them gratefully. The newcomers had news of Kingsburke, mainly that the Starkadders and the Raghnells had fought a battle in the streets of that city, where new monsters appeared at nightfall out of nowhere to attack both sides, wreaking a great slaughter. No one had heard of the king in days, and some thought him dead.

Thus encouraged we continued our march northwest. Again we camped at the coming of night and, together with Mother and Duty, we laid Wards. Those Gurlys who had merged their forces with ours looked askance but remained silent. Zolan did not join us, nor did he even give sign that he knew what we were about. I felt an uneasiness at his behavior.

Our present Binding was set against all evil but pointed to no one kind. True, the man from the Dismals had shown some ability to control Wild Magic, but our recent experiences gave evidence that the Wards we had always trusted were not so strong as we believed when we were confronting an unknown and—to us—alien Power. Indeed, Duty and Mother added more elements to our ritual. For my part I openly bore the golden gem for whatever it might do to strengthen those vital barriers.

Twenty-seven

Sabina

*Z*olan came to our fire as Duty shared out provisions, but he took a position outside the circle that included our family and the Gurly lord with two of his principal followers. I watched the man from the Dismals carefully, not paying much attention to the talk, which was mainly an exchange of rumors ensuing in the chaos that Gurlyon had become. Perhaps because I was so intent I noticed that Zolan was also being covertly eyed by one of the party from Rossard.

The stranger was close to Zolan's age, yet obviously well seasoned to warfare, for he wore, in a backsheath, the longsword of an earlier time with an unusually ornate hilt. An antiquated mail shirt also covered his wide shoulders and broad chest, and his long, sandy red hair caught in its links now and then. The metal garment appeared a most uncomfortable piece of gear even for protection.

I tried now to remember his name as presented by the clan lord: Fergal? Fergus? I was not sure. He was pleasant of feature in a rather barbaric way, and clean shaven as was Zolan. Beardless—now I looked at our companion in the adventures of months past. In all our traveling, I had never seen Zolan shave, yet he showed no growth of facial hair. For some reason, until this moment, that lack had not occurred to me.

Cilla had often worked with my stores back at Grosper, combining and refining herb juices and extracts. Some years back she had produced a cream, nicely scented, which would sweep hair from the arms, leaving them smooth. I had no reason to understand why this observation, so far removed from our present troubles, made such an impression on me, except in our present company smooth cheeks were nonexistent for males. I also knew that youths preferred a good sprouting of face hair.

"So be it." Father nodded to the Gurly lord, his slightly louder tone breaking my train of thought. "We shall scout."

Uneasy curiosity continued to prick me even as I settled for the night, Cilla and Tam beyond me. However, for some reason I did not share the oddity I had discovered with either of them.

Sleep did not come quickly though I sought it even by the mind control I had learned from childhood. Too much had happened this day. Also, I was puzzled. It was true that we rode now into unseen danger, whose nature we did not understand, yet the purpose which had brought my father and mother into the war-swept North to Kingsburke set me to pondering. We had believed that they had come to seek us—well, we were united again. Nonetheless, we were still pushing on deeper into Gurlyon. Was it only because of Zolan's need to confront the Dark? Or—

I lay very quiet, staring up at the tent covering, and shivered. Never could I forget the horror of the silence the dimming of our shared Talent had forced upon me. What if we were all bound by some some unknown geas and were being forced, unknowingly, to serve as pieces in another's twisted game?

A slight stir broke the night silence outside—some sleeper shifting position? We three lay nearest the opening on the side of the improvised shelter. A fleeting thought crossed my mind: would I *ever* rest in a proper bed with stout walls, well guarded, standing between me and the perils lurking so plentifully in the outer world?

I near cried aloud. Dim, far away, yet within my reach sounded a murmur. A Send I could not quite receive? Climber! The cat-creature was only a shadow creeping, belly flat to the ground. I smelled the scent of his fur—a strange odor pungent as crushed leaves, sharp as his teeth. Then his breath blew softly against my face, strong, too, but right for his kind—that of a carnivorous beast.

That Zolan's companion had come with a purpose was certain, only

I had no knowledge of beast-tongues. Making an effort, I strove to project a mind-message. What reached me in reply was a need for my attendance on some task—and immediately.

Tam and Cilla were breathing evenly. I was aware of their deep slumber— they might be caught in a pleasant net of the Dream World. I edged off our shared pallet with infinite care. Why it was so needful to prevent their knowing what I did, I could not say, but I felt intensely that it was necessary.

Then I crawled forth, flattened as best I could, from under the shelter. Climber retreated before me, moving backward and keeping close watch on me. I saw the sentry, and I paused. Though my every move seemed to rustle loudly, he did not look in my direction.

Zolan had never shared our shelter on the off-side where Rogher rested, nor was he near my parents. Instead, he found a place of his own, companioned only by Climber, outside. It was toward that shadowed spot the beast now urged me. Then all at once Climber stopped short and hissed, warning me to pause too.

Voices—very low but, by some chance audible, though they were the merest whispers.

"My lord king—do you not know me? My mother was your nurse; we were milk-brothers—"

"You are mistaken!" This was certainly Zolan and he was angry.

"King Gerrit, do you not bear on your shoulder the Mark of the Eagle? I did see that when we bathed at the pool this night, just as I saw it when Wisewife Nolwen set it upon your skin. It was the sign proper for the blood son of the king.

"I am not the one you seek!" Almost a hint of fear struggled with the rage now. "I am Zolan and I come from the Dismals. Do not make more of me! This is my warning, Fergal of Wild Cat."

A choking noise, then Fergal spoke again.

"What did you? You took away my breath!"

"And I can as easily take away your tongue!" Zolan's anger was in full spate now. "I am *not* a king, nor will you shout abroad such a falsehood. I am one of Power—no one, and nothing, else—and I have been set upon a task. That truth is all that exists."

"Stand by your 'truth' then." An equal anger sounded in the Wild Cat's voice. "You have doubtless lived too long with these Southerners and now they use you to their purpose. It was often said that they stole you away, and that legend has at last been proven. Fear not—who wants a turncoat for a ruler? I was foster brother to Gerrit when he knew truth and fair dealing—and what country truly owned him."

Suddenly I felt of a vast surge of alien Power, a force that was neither of the Light nor the Dark. Only the edge of its outflow may have touched me, but my body recoiled as if in answer to a monster blast of winter stormwind.

What had Zolan done? I was certain that he had raised that Power. We had accepted our companion as being a follower of the Light, but could we be sure of anything about him? That Fergal was certain of his being Gerrit, I could well accept, even though Zolan rode now with the Lord Warden from the South. The rumor long believed by the Gurlys, that their boy king had been a prisoner in Alsonia—would seem at last to be proven true. And the return of their long-lost ruler would be enough to unite the clans to turn southward in invasion.

A shadow passed from behind a pile of equipment and supplies beside our shelter. The moon was cloud-bitten tonight, but I was able to mark the hilt of the back-sheathed sword. Fergal was returning to where the arms-men rested. Climber pressed against my thigh, and I reached down to draw my hand through the thick fur of his head. Then he, too, was gone. Why had the beast summoned me? To be a witness to Zolan's strong denial of any other identity?

What I had heard I must share as soon as possible with Father. In the past, when pressing need arose, we could Send to him. His was a lesser Talent than our own, but such Gift as he possessed had been honed by years of his union with Mother.

I cast forth my mind-message, felt it enter his thoughts. For a moment, I stood on a hillside looking down at a sunlit valley, a place of peace and rest. Then that vision broke and was gone, and I knew that Father's dream, too, had been broken.

Swiftly I reported what had been overheard. There was no reason for me to add the danger of what might come of Fergal's revelation, for he would think of that at once.

"Well done," came his answer, almost as strongly as if Tam or Cilla replied. And the compliment, for its very rarity, I would treasure even above the words of my sisters.

Tamara

THE GRAY OF near dawn hung over us when we roused. Our camp was quick in its action as it prepared to move out.

"What's to do?" I demanded of Bina, who was braiding her hair tightly for the day's riding.

"Trouble," she answered shortly.

Then a Send came. After hearing what had happened in the night, I stood amazed. It was Cilla who at once pounced upon the question that mattered most to us.

"Why did we, too, not awake?"

Why not indeed? Always, before lately, it had been true that any thought or action that caught the attention of one of us became instantly a matter for all three. Bina looked from me to Cilla and back again.

"I do not know," she replied slowly, spacing the words. Apparently the oddity of this situation had not occurred to her.

A breaking of our communication—a muting, a silencing! The fear implanted by the Frush stirred again. Swiftly I Sent to Cilla and Bina, then to Duty, who was packing some of our mother's possessions.

All those so thought-touched answered, Duty turning to look at us even as her reassuring silent reply came. So we had *not* again been rendered helpless—at least so far.

Bina spoke of the wave of strong Power that had ended Zolan's meeting with Fergal and the way it had swept past her. Had being brushed by that force kept her from us? No, she had been able to focus and reach Father. But the fact that we were now dealing with a Power we neither knew nor understood was a new peril added as a bead on the thread of the many we already wore.

I saw Zolan at the other side of the camp for only a moment. He was saddling his horse, and Climber was a bright patch of scarlet beside him. He seemed unaware of our coming forth to take wedges of journey-bread from the stores and to pick up the saddle water bags that had been filled the night before. Nor, as we rode forth, did the man from the Dismals make an attempt to engage either Cilla or myself, Bina having joined Duty to see how Rogher fared. Father, Mother, and Gorfund stayed deep in conversation, while the keep lord and his men grouped more closely together than the day before, though a little apart from us. Our scouts had departed early as was the custom.

On impulse I urged my mount forward beside that of Zolan.

"A day more," I observed, "and we raise Kingsburke. 'Tis the second-largest city of Gurlyon—only the port Varbruke being larger." I spoke as I would to a visitor knowing nothing of the territory. Was that not what Zolan presented himself as being?

"You have been there before, Lady Tamara?"

"Once, seasons ago when we first came North and our father needed to present his warrant to King Arvor. Kingsburke was all new and strange to us and we found much in that city of interest, for it is unlike our own queen's court in Alsonia."

"Arvor—what manner of man is he?"

I noted that he did not use any honorifics in mentioning the ruler. That omission might well betray him if he repeated his question to a native of Gurlyon.

"His Majesty is young and well versed in arms. Two seasons ago he led an army to beat off raiders from overseas and won. Ten of the raiders' ships were burned to the waterline and the men left from their crews now labor in chains. 'Tis also said that he pushes against the clan chiefs who placed him on the throne and would be rid of them, and that is why he favors the Chosen."

"It is also said," our companion added conversationally, "that he has disappeared. The kings of this land, it would seem, have a habit of doing that." Zolan was watching me with care. Did he believe he could read in my face how much I knew?

"Yes," I agreed brightly. "And now," I continued brashly, "they may think that Father returns with a new king—"

"And whom does the Lord Warden support?"

"Since you are the only stranger and not one with the Southerners, they may just hail you."

To my surprise Zolan grinned widely. "I fear they are going to be disappointed. I may be several things"—his tone became serious—"but I am not one to welcome Tharn, no matter what guise he wears. The ways of courts are not for me. What I do may well lift trouble from this country rather than split it with fighting clan chiefs shouting slogans at one another. The farther I ride from my own land, the more I long for its peace."

From the close of this speech, our companion rode quiet, and I forbore to break that silence. I was, however, sure of one thing: Gerrit might be thought to ride with us, but Zolan chose in no way to assume the identity of the lost boy king. However, though he did not elect that role, might not others make the decision for him?

The scouts did the best they could to guide us along a way to avoid any keep or village, though the latter mainly huddled around such a fortified hold. However, the closer we came to Kingsburke, the more difficult this became. Finally we had no choice save to take what passed as the main highway, though it was as badly rutted as the road about Grosper.

Drucilla

TAM HAD SPENT the morning riding with Zolan, Bina and Duty with Rogher. I had started alone, but someone came up beside me. I recognized Fergal, he who claimed to be Gerrit's milk-brother. He inclined his head in the formal manner of the Gurlys, but appeared to have little time for flowery speech commonly used to address a woman of rank in Alsonia.

"Your servant, my lady." The Wild Cat did use the Border speech and not the Gurly dialect, though I would have understood that also. "You have passed along many hard trials."

He wanted something of me, and I was eager to know just what.

"You have the right of that, sir. Taken by black sorcery, we were thrown into the Dismals. It would seem that that land is used to hide the evidence of Breaksword raids."

"True, Lady Drucilla. We hope the king will raise the Standard, calling upon all true men to root out these raiders. Too long have they been free to do as was done at Frosmoor."

Momentarily I was overwhelmed by the memory of the rapine that had been wrought there. I hesitated, then decided it might be well to aid our own cause, for words, too, could be weapons.

"Those at Frosmoor were betrayed by a Chosen. Even if those Gray Robes do not command troops they can turn the minds of clansmen to murder."

"As they have!" Fergal was silent for a time, but he did not leave his place;

his mount still matched pace with mine. When he spoke again, he had changed the subject.

"Lady Drucilla, what know you of the Dismals?"

"Little enough," I answered, though, as with the recollection of the ruined keep, the nightmare memory of the World Below flooded my mind like a full Send. "Those who took us were not able to deliver the three of us to the one who paid them; they had been warned that Father and his troop rode hot-tod behind. Thus we were lowered into that place and left. It is a strange land quite unlike this Upper World as if it were no part of it. And it holds many perils—"

"Yet it also holds people," Fergal observed. "This stranger who rides with you makes no secret that he comes from there."

"That is so." I did not expand my answer. "Our imprisonment in the Dismals seems, as I said, to be a common ploy of the Breakswords."

"Did many survive, then? Our tales tell only of those who tried on their own to discover what lies below, never to return. Men speak of treasure to be found in the Under Land."

I turned quickly to a half lie. "We did not seek for riches but a way to the Upper World again. We found that at last where some who had come, perhaps in search of wealth, had died—and not easily. But their ropes served us."

"If such a way out existed for you, lady, could it not serve others also?"

What was this clansman searching for? In an instant he made it plain.

"Those who were also dropped there and survived—are there many such?"

I shook my head. "We saw only bones. I think that most of the Breakswords' victims were flung from above, rather than lowered, as were we."

"Zolan was lowered, then; so—those who had taken him did not want him quickly dead?" Fergal's eyes held an almost feverish gleam.

"We have not asked him concerning his past. To us, he was a savior, protecting us from the monsters, for night-frights indeed walk by day in that place: the legends speak the truth. Zolan says that he is of the Dismals and we accept that."

"And if he is not, does he have clan-kin above to rejoice if he returns?"

"Ask that of him. I am not his voice."

At this terse answer, the Wild Cat appeared to make up his mind to tell me all. "Lady Drucilla, it is my mind that you company with our true king—Gerrit, who disappeared as a child long ago. A heavy hand is now needed, a ruler who is apart from all clan ties. Such a leader could free Gurlyon from the black Power that spins its evil webs in Kingsburke."

I turned my head to face him squarly.

"Clansman, this is no affair of mine, or Father's, or Alsonia's. It is against that Darkness alone that we ride, since we are Scorpys and have birth-given Talents. We have always served the Light and now that Power calls."

"These Talents, lady—are they a burden or a gift?"

I had no time to reply to that. A flash of red shot past my horse, sending it rearing, so that I had to summon all my skill to bring it under control again. The clansman had tried to catch my bridle, but my mount already answered to me again. Now I could spare attention for what had occurred. Climber had stopped where Tam and Zolan rode ahead. Now they also came to a halt.

A Send reached me: Tam's. *"Ambush ahead!"*

Two snaplocks rode in holsters on either side of my saddle horn. I gathered the reins in my left hand and reached with the right for one of the pistols.

"Ambush!" I cried to the clansman. He did not reach for his huge sword but rather drew a double-barreled snaplock of his own from under his cloak.

This was level land, and much of it had been cleared. However, ahead of us the poorly surfaced road wound between two hills of some size. Fortifications, towers and walls, rose on both—the first defenses of Kingsburke. That an ambush could be set this close, under the very eyes of the garrison there, was an exceedingly bad sign.

Our father, together with Captain Tweder, came pounding back from the van, Mother so close behind that her mount was nearly nosing the tail of his. She beckoned to Tam and me and we saw Bina pushing up from the rear.

If an ambush had been laid, then where could it lie in concealment? I wondered. No thickets of brush or trees grew here, no walls except those ringing the forest above. The woods above—! Were the soldiers stationed there watching for our party particularly, or was Kingsburke now under siege, with armsmen posted in the forts and under command to destroy any who might come to the aid of the city?

Under Father's orders we retreated, but carefully, facing always in the direction from which attack might come. Still no movement was to be seen about either of the watchtowers, nor along their walls. But more sinister yet was another absence: above those fortifications, no royal Standard flew. Who now held the King's Towers?

Twenty-eight

Tamara

"A test," Mother said.

The clan lord and his three lieutenants (Fergal was not counted among them, I noted) were frowning. Several shuffled their feet as if anxious to leave and pursue some other plan.

"A heavy and hard one," Father returned.

What she outlined as our next move seemed only reasonable; even a wreaking with the aid of Power at such times had been rumored to have excellent results in the past. But the Gurlys had no tradition of Talent use and might find this nearly unbelievable.

The three of us, as well as Duty, and—somewhat to my surprise—a newcomer to the troop whom I did not know, were among those Mother had summoned. Then came Father and—Zolan as if he would try this game. I was still partnered by the man from the Dismals, though I was certain he had not been included in the chosen group.

Our snaplocks were returned to their holsters. The coming conflict would be a very different kind of battle—one in which, to judge by their growing scowls, the clansmen had no faith. I fastened the gem from the World Below to my head just above and between my eyes. It was already warming.

"A march by?" Captain Tweder asked.

"The clansmen," Mother replied.

The chief stared at her. Behind him, one of his men spat on the ground, his opinion of this uncanny business given wetly.

Perhaps because of the struggle with the Frush, the chief did not refuse. So march before us he and his men did, slowly, to enable us to survey them one by one. Then they moved away, leaving us, we hoped, with faces and forms safe listed in our memories.

The scout, left to watch the towers, returned with the information that nothing was yet to be seen about either fortification. His relief went forward to replace him there.

Mother looked to Zolan. "Do you understand what we would do?"

"Yes." His reply was curt.

"Then," she spoke to the rest of us, "let us begin."

Thus, shaping with our combined Talents, we raised both a seeming troop of Alsonians and a gathering of Gurly clansmen to march along the road we had left. Stronger and more detailed the unpeople became as we enhanced the Sends that gave them substance. As the Lord Warden's flag appeared to whip in the wind above their line, they took on the look of armsmen parading in review for a dignitary the queen would honor.

We braced ourselves against the steady drain of Power, but no member of the ghostly band we summoned showed any sign of weakening. On and on down the road they marched as we stood on a rise behind them.

Now fleshly clansmen of the North came into sight, dust rising about the feet of their small wiry horses. I realized that the road must be made to seem disturbed about the feet of our troop, as well, or this travesty would be quickly exposed for what it was. The Gurlys were noted for keen sight and ever-ready suspicion.

The warmth against my forehead approached the point of burning, but I needed all the help the jewel could give me. Abruptly the drain I had set myself to ignore lessened, and I knew at once what was to be done. Keeping my eyes on the marchers, I allowed myself to answer. My hand swung out to clasp another's, one that bore hard and callused fingers. There was no need to turn my head and thus risk breaking control of the spirit-soldiers; I was well aware that I was now united with Zolan. My Power had touched his before but never so deeply; nevertheless, the gem I wore made this melding of Talents, though so dissimilar, easy.

A skirmishing party broke from the mimic troop, which had now arrived within arrow-shot of the towers. That move was born of Father's knowledge of battle strategy. No move had yet been made by those who must wait in ambush, but I was sure that the report of our beast-scout had been true.

The soldiers forming the van slowed. Now a man spurred forward— again Father's addition to the illusion we held with all our might. And that move set the fire to the fuse.

Not only did a shower of arrows skim down in a deadly cloud from archers rising above the walls, but more armsmen poured, seemingly out of the ground itself, to strike like a spear point at our troop!

I do not know how great an effort it was for the others to change the projections we controlled, but I funneled much of my energy into letting men and horses fall, pincushioned with arrows; then I had to hold them still in sight as dead on the ground.

Suddenly a new force entered the battle. From the tower on the rise that faced us burst—a monster. I had always shrunk in fear from the sight of the giant insects that rendered the Dismals so deadly. This creature seemed one of those, like to that flier set to feed upon the spider in the nightmare skirmish we had witnessed. Borne upon huge beating wings, it rose aloft to swoop down upon the tangle of men and illusions below.

Now clansmen were running—not those shadows we strove to hold the seeming of but our enemy's soldiers; they must have discovered that they aimed at illusions alone. The huge flier swung low, lower, and seized one of the fleeing troop.

Even at this remove from the struggle, I could hear his screams. If the flier was part of the ambush, having somehow been summoned from the Dismals, it was turning on those it was meant to serve. As suddenly as the thing struck, however, I understood. The winged monster was born from Zolan's Power—and who better to produce such a menace?

Well into the air it had lifted when its prey twisted to fall free. The flier flapped low again, hunting for another victim. I could hear cries from the force drawn up behind us. Though they could not view the combat, they had been able to sight the creature and what it bore.

"Now!" Father's hand swept down in the agreed-upon signal.

The flesh-and-blood troop, already in formation, moved out. Father mounted the horse brought to him by an armsman on the run and joined those already thundering along the road.

We continued to feed our mock army, though we would not be able to do so much longer. The pain that had arisen to beat in my temples was shared, I knew, by all the rest of our company.

Still the flier swooped, this time at the walls of the tower where the archers were stationed. More soldiers attempted to flee; two fell over the edge of the parapet to the ground below.

Our living troops and the Gurly clansmen were closing fast. At last Mother gave the signal releasing us from the strain of holding the illusion. I wilted to the ground. With the end of my need for keeping our phantasms intact, I was as empty as a spirits-crock after a feasting. It was too much effort to keep my eyes open, almost too much to keep breathing.

Drucilla

NIGHT SKY CURVED over me. The stars framed there were very bright—brighter, I thought bemusedly, than I had ever seen them before.

"Cilla!"

Now I saw no stars but rather a dim face that could be my own in a mirror.

"Bina?"

She was tugging at me, and I obeyed by sitting up. I sensed others stirring about me. I shook my head—what had happened? My whole body ached, and it took a great effort for me to move.

"Come." Again Bina pulled at me.

Come—where? And why?

"You must get to a horse," she continued as I yielded to her, somehow standing again. I heard a snorting nearby and smelled horses, yes.

Not really understanding how I got there, I found myself in a saddle. My mount bore both bridle and reins, but it now moved under the control of someone walking by its head. All I could do was to cling to its coarse mane and strive to keep myself upright. Luckily we were advancing at little more than a walk.

Though the main focus of my attention was our dreamlike progress, memory began to stir. The bushy-bearded face of a Gurly kept forming in front of my own as if he strode backward before me. Then I saw a man with a scar-twisted lip, and beside him a boy with a straggle of face hair. Northerners, all of them.

My grip on the mane tightened as realization dawned. Those three—they were Patterns! To create the form of something living or unliving, one must first fashion a Pattern; that was a task I had performed many times over. As if a door had been flung open in my mind, I remembered: we had Patterned a war-troop of our own folk, and a riding of Gurly clansmen. That act must have been a success, or surely we would not now be free.

"Bina?" There was no need for whispering as I had just done—or was there?

It was not my sister who answered but the one who led my horse.

"The Lady Sabina, milady, has gone to see the squire, who is hurt."

"And you are—?" I prompted.

"Ison of Scorpy-Alt, out of the Southern Isles," the man answered. "I have come into the company of the Lord Warden with a message from the queen, and I am to ride with his troop for a space."

I sat up a little straighter and loosed my right-handed hold in the dark to reach the nearer snaplock, which a brush with my knee told me was slung at the saddle horn. A sect of Clan Scorpy dwelt in the Sea Islands, right enough; however, neither Father nor Mother had mentioned this distant kinsman. I had dealt with illusion this day to such a point that I was suspicious.

Then I remembered how we had gathered our own living band before engaging the enemy—if one might call dispatching shadows launching weapons. A stranger had been with us—young, he was, and wearing the buff coat and breastplate of a trooper. On sudden impulse, I loosed a Send, then grabbed again at my horsehair anchor as I nearly reeled off my mount.

"You—Read?"

I trembled as an answer was returned—not with the clarity of one from my sisters or Mother, but still plain.

"I Read, yes. I have the Talent."

Very seldom was Reading a masculine gift. Our father had it in part, and it was said that his brother who died of the wasting illness had been Gifted with even more.

"I am your cousin—son to Magus Scorpy—"

Magus had been Father's other brother. He had chosen to serve Alsonia at sea and had died at the moment of victory in the great engagement with sea-slavers in the Southern waters.

"Welcome, Kinsman." I spoke aloud, too drained to maintain mind-link. "Tell me, how went the battle?"

I heard a chuckle out of the dark rising above the sound of horse hooves and the thud of marching feet.

"I believe they are running still. That dragon certainly shook them in their boots!"

"Dragon?" I was momentarily bewildered. "Oh, the winged one—Zolan must have woven that illusion. Such horrors are to be found in the Dismals, as we can testify. Then those who lay in wait for us were all defeated?"

"It would seem so. Our people hold both towers now. The Gurlys who were taken report that much trouble is afoot in Kingsburke. My Lord Warden is questioning them."

Ison continued with the news. A number of the soldiers from both towers had fled. Several bodies had been left behind to mark their encounter with an enemy who had never been truly there; some of the clansmen appeared to have died from sheer fear. The right-hand tower would shelter our family with more than half of our troop as a garrison, while the Northern clansmen held the other.

"It is plain," my escort concluded, "that the Gurlys do not find themselves wishing to be too near to us. And perhaps the Lord Warden is just as well satisfied to have it so."

The night seemed very long. Much as I wanted to know more about this newfound cousin, I found it a strain to talk; I think I dozed at times. Ison seemed content to lead the horse. If he had lent Talent energy to our deception, then apparently he had not been as drained by the effort as we.

I roused at the blast of a snaplock out in the night, swiftly followed by a Send:

"*Lady Drucilla!*" Reins slapped across my wrists and, without completely realizing what I did, I clutched at them. "*Can you manage?*"

A shout—another. A second pistol shot—this one louder. Instinctively I took control of my mount.

"*Yes,*" I Sent back, then felt, rather than saw, Cousin Ison move away.

Tamara

I still wore the gem from the ruins bound to my forehead as we rode through the night. It had been the surge of heat from the stone that had fully aroused me. Then came the flash of a snaplock cutting the dark before me, bringing my hand to grip a similar weapon. A second shot followed. I was riding in company, but I could distinguish neither the nature of my companions nor the source of the pistol report.

"*Aahh!*"

The new noise was not a cry of pain but the cry of defiance a warrior might give when an expected action was to hand. Now, too, there came light of a sort, neither hot torch nor cooler moonlight. A globe of yellow, a sickly hue, appeared close to the ground, a little to one side of the track along which we rode.

Globe? No, the sphere was fast assuming a different form, lengthening into a shaft like a spear held upright. Changing again, it shaped itself swiftly into the likeness of an armsman, though not as tall as most in the troop. The soldier-image stood unmoving as we advanced towards it.

Whoever rode matching pace with my mount pushed ahead and away from me. Against the unhealthy glow, he was only a shadow. Then a shout broke the night again, and my companion dropped to the ground before the light.

"*Vos!*" A word, this time, but who of the troop had half screamed it I could not have said. Someone barked an order, and the sounds of hooves ceased. I had already brought my horse to a halt.

Power was in play here, but not mine nor my sisters', and certainly not Mother's or Duty's. This Talent was Zolan's, for, as much as by his voice, I could now identify his distinctive Gift in action.

The evilly glowing form did not match him in either height or human features. Instead, Zolan now faced one of the squarish Jug bodies, but with visible features on the ball head. However, that shape was continuing to change, becoming less squat and thick-limbed.

At the same time, I was aware that I had been netted in just such ensorcellement as we had ourselves used earlier. This apparition had no real substance! As I drew nearer, a second sharp thrust of light came, not shooting from the thing before Zolan but springing from my gem.

The beam struck over Zolan's shoulder straight at his challenger. The stranger threw up arms far too long to match its stature and began to beat at the air before the man from the Dismals. The shadow-creature was trying to reach our companion, but however madly its long and massive arms battered, they were rebuffed by a shield they could not breach.

The Jug-warrior crouched and hurled itself at Zolan, only to rebound.

I could now see the features on the head ball clearly: eyes that were dark pits holding a yellow spark in their depths, a nose as sharp as a bill of a raptor above a parody of human lips that moved, dribbling dark moisture. As if unconsciously obeying an order, I swung my head in the thing's direction. The gem with its radiance moved in answer, to center upon the middle of the alien face.

"*Vos!*" Again the strange word—a name?—spoken by Zolan. From my position behind him, I could not see what he was doing, but the apparition gave ground. The light of my jewel followed it until the apparition flickered, broke into yellow fragments, and disappeared.

I remember but little of the rest of our journey. Mother rode beside me and now and then put out a hand, feeding me from her own inner strength. The pain that had come with the awakening of my stone held me, dulling all other perceptions.

Sabina

IT WAS EVIDENT that an attack had been made upon some portion of our company. I could easily sense that the battle was a matter of Power, but, because it occurred farther ahead in the troop, I could investigate no further unless I called upon the Talent. I heard mutterings among those close to me, but I could spare no attention to translating them, for I now used a Send to Cilla and to Tam. Cilla replied clearly at once, but Tam's answer came haltingly, and with it Mother's assurance that the danger was past.

Not long afterward, we swung from the road we had followed with such care and the horses began to climb. The heavy darkness that had hung about us through this journey—perhaps in itself a lesser assault of the enemy—held unbroken until a torch blazed ahead. Shortly thereafter, we passed between thick walls into the inner court of one of the two towers.

A relief that, oddly, took the form of a feeling of pressure relaxing followed our passage through the gate and our sight of the wall about us, its sturdy, well-set stone rising for three stories. Here were more than torches to drive back the dark—several lanterns had been lit. With a sense of profound gratitude, I dismounted.

For the remainder of this night, at least, we would shelter behind stout walls and under a solid roof. Darkness, within and without, had been banished for a time, and we could rest.

Drucilla

WE BEDDED DOWN at one end of the hall on the second level of the tower. I obediently drank from a flask Duty urged upon me and passed it on to Tam. So far, my warrior-sister had said nothing of the skirmish of Power that had occurred along the line of march, but she sat with our mother's arm about her for a while. Then she seemed to rouse and pulled the gem off her forehead. Her cropped hair swung free as she shook her head vigorously, and we could see a dark bruise between and above her eyes. Duty hurried to spread ointment on the mark.

That Tam had once more met opposition or threat from the enemy, we were sure. However, for the first time in our lives, we did not press her for an explanation but were content to watch Mother settle her for the remainder of the night. She pulled up a cloak over Tam before moving the lantern away so that it would not shine in her face. Before she slept, though, our sister first made sure of the jewel from the Dismals, dropping its cord once more over her head.

Was Tam somehow loosening the threefold bond that had always been our strength? That talisman from the ruins—did it threaten our oneness? I stared at the ceiling above, trying somehow to fasten my attention firmly on its boards, to force myself out of the present entirely.

One by one, I summoned memories, not of Grosper but of a far less imposing dwelling and the sights and smells that went with it. I saw fields of grass and pastures where cattle grazed, heard flights of doves, felt the pleasant weight in my arms of Quinnie, cat matriarch of the house we had once called home. Why, two of her kittens were sleeping in the folds of the scarf I had just discarded. . . .

A hand touched my forehead gently.

"Sleep, my dear Cilla."

Yes, I was small and wrapped in warm love again, back home in my own land.

Twenty-nine

Tamara

A violent storm awoke me. Though thick walls kept its blasts from us, the rage of the winds was beyond anything I had ever known. I shivered, pulling closer the cloak that wrapped me.

But the tumult of the wind was not the only sound disturbing the night's peace, I thought as I sat up, holding my aching head. I was also hearing voices, faint but hot with violent anger, threatening. Yet I could distinguish no real words in the bursts of growls and shouts.

The light of a single lantern across the chamber did little to illuminate my surroundings. I counted the mounds on the floor and numbered four: Bina, Cilla, Mother, Duty, all of whom lay silent and unmoving. None of them had summoned me. Had the "voices" been merely the storm-winds venting their rage into the arrow-slits in the tower walls?

But no—I caught movement in the far reaches of the hall. How I was able to see motion through the heavy shadow and dark I did not know, but that this was truly important I was very sure. Trying not to disturb those about me, I got to my feet.

The movement was stilled now, but need had not released its hold on me. If I made any sound as I moved, the storm covered it. The darkness was almost palpable; I edged forward with hands outstretched, as if expecting to encounter a barrier. We had set Wards in this place prior to retiring, but those barriers were of a nature I could understand and pass if I would.

Now I became aware of a faint graying in the dark ahead. Using this lessening of the gloom as a guide, I soon discovered the bottom step of a stair that must lead to the next floor of the tower. I could not have turned back even if I wanted to; as though I were under Father's orders, I began to climb.

As I ascended, the pallid light grew stronger. I reached the next floor where I could make out several long guns, each braced by a small square of window, their heavy barrels set to fire through those ports. However, the light I had seen, which was quite visible now, shone downward from above another stair. These steps could only lead to the roof, and who would dare venture out onto a flooring of rain-slick stone in the midst of such violent weather? For the first time I questioned where my curiosity was leading, or what might control me.

My pause, though, was only a brief one. I came to the foot of the stairs to look up. If the next level held an opening to the roof, it had certainly not been broached, or the fearsome wind would now be prying with rude fingers at my night-garb. I climbed.

Thus I entered a much smaller space, one that must crown the tower. Lying on the floor at the head of the stair was a rod, from which came the limited glow of light. At each of the four sides of this space, a window was set into the wall. Three of these were shuttered, but the fourth framed a square of the night. It also admitted sound: the howl of the wind, the clamor of the voices I thought I could hear borne upon it. Yet no wind-force reached this place through that window!

Before it stood Zolan, his back to me, as unmoving as one of the well-trained guards before the Alsonian palace. Crouched before him, front paws on the inner window sill, was Climber, his attention also fixed on what lay without.

Neither of them showed any awareness of my presence. I left the stairwell to step behind Zolan, striving to discover what that stone frame held to inspire such interest. It puzzled me intensely that no storm-blast blew through the opening.

The tempest raging outside was no uproar of our world's winds, I straightway realized. Beyond the window spun a whirling, lashing fury, visible in itself. The unnatural storm needed no trees or other solid forms against which to display its power, yet, weirdly, it had not come within the outer wall about the tower.

And that maelstrom itself held movement. Ships? But ships were of the sea; none swam the waves of the air! Nor were these objects like any seagoing vessels of my knowledge. Each was shaped not unlike a huge rod tapered at both ends and outlined with red-orange light. After a moment's observation, I realized that they were engaging in some form of combat. Lines of fire shot from one vessel, aimed at another. Suddenly one of the airships broke apart and fell earthward.

"Yes—so!"

In spite of the uproar of the eerie wind I was able to hear Zolan's words.

"This is of the past." He continued as if carrying on a conversation, yet I was somehow sure he remained unaware of my coming. "It is buried centuries deep, finished. Nor shall Dobulgar rise again."

The combat in the clouds had ceased, but I hardly noticed, for in that instant I myself fell under attack. The living heart of Tamara Scorpy was assaulted, an unseen entity striving to quench my inner core of life as a lantern might be extinguished.

I knew in the same moment that I could not escape, nor even survive except by summoning all the Power I could draw upon to hold fast. Zolan spun about as I swayed from side to side. His arms went about me, and I was held fast as his lips met mine—not in a show of passion but in a sharing of energy.

Power—eagerly, hungrily, I drew it in, and still the exchange continued. This was no longer my own fight—my body had become a battlefield on which two opposing forces contended while my soul was merely a bystander. The invader, whoever or whatever it was, no longer tried to bend me to its will but turned instead on Zolan with fierce intensity.

However, it had not utterly overwhelmed my defenses, and now I strove to raise such a shield as I could for Zolan's aid. How long did we wrestle with the Dark before allies arrived to lend aid in the fight? I never knew. Dimly I became aware of the approach of unity and determination. Bina and Cilla—Mother, Duty—they had ascended into the tower and joined our eldritch encounter! I now held all the forces of an army within me— one such as I was sure the intruder had never engaged before. Then a new, less-powerful strain of Talent arrived at that moment, approaching timidly but certain of what must be done. Still Zolan and I stood lip to lip, and the invisible war within me reached the point of slashing, tearing pain as if my body were being torn apart.

Sabina

WE CROWDED TOGETHER in our desperate need to ascend the tower stairs, jostling against each other in our haste to climb. We found Tam standing encircled by Zolan's arms, her lips pressed tightly to his. Outside the open window behind them, streaks of raw color were bursting back and forth across the sky. Without any word from Tam, I moved to her back and placed my hands upon her shoulders. A moment later Cilla joined herself to me in like manner.

What we two had, we speedily offered our beleaguered sister: energy born of Cilla's Talent united with mine and poured through me to Tam. I became aware that a beam of light had formed about the two before us. Then, as a spear might be aimed by a warrior, that shaft shot out through the window.

More and more Power surged through the channel of my body into Tam. The ray of luminance broadened and continued to bore outward. The turmoil outside grew worse and worse, and I had to close my eyes against the whorls of blistering color.

Green and blue in that aerial weaving darkened to red, the raw crimson of blood. The stain might not have entered to touch my body, but pain thrilled in my every sinew. Still I clung tightly to Tam, as did Cilla and those behind her.

It was Zolan who, never loosing his hold on my sister, moved. Drawing away from the window, he took all of us with him. The pulsating scarlet outside had moved toward the tower and now appeared to touch the very frame of the opening. Without hearing any order, but simply feeling a demand I could not leave unanswered, I struggled to increase the flow of Power in spite of my pain. Around the ragged edge of my thrust came a whole entwined wave of force from Cilla and the others—our final great effort.

The light outside was bulging inward, swelling like an overloaded waterskin being forced through too small an opening. Then it burst to spit forth a body. In that instant, our connecting Power was severed. I crashed to the floor as Cilla struck me from behind, and Tam, released by Zolan, crumpled against me.

The blood-glow vanished and, in its absence, we were blinded for a few breaths. When we could see again, Zolan was standing over a man whom another Power had used the scarlet light to deliver.

Rolling forward until his body struck the wall under the open window, the newcomer began scrabbling against the stone in an effort to hoist himself to its sill. Now Zolan moved, as well, catching the stranger around the neck to drag him back. And the man from the Dismals was not the only one in action, for Ison, the Scorpy who claimed kinship with us, thrust his way past him to slam shut the shutters, submerging the room in darkness. We could still hear the fight but could see none of it.

"*Yya werli cvorg!*"

That cry did not come from Zolan. The words were strange and without meaning to me, yet they seemed harsh, even—evil. At least they carried a chilling sense of sheer horror.

Around Tam grew a radiance we had witnessed before—one that promised aid: the gemstone had surged to life, and it brightened ever stronger. At last we could see Zolan clearly. But, though we might have expected the new arrival to be another of the ball-headed folk, the man he was now choking into silence appeared to have no relationship to the people of the Dismals. Rather, he was a young Gurly, more richly dressed than a clansman.

"*Aid me!*" The stranger managed a strangled cry. "I am your king! This madman—"

He got no further as Zolan, abandoning his throat-hold, swung up a fist that connected with the point of the clansman's chin. Under the force of that blow, the intruder reeled back, striking the edge of the closed shutter. The thud of his head against the wall was loud enough to be clearly heard.

Zolan at once stepped forward to stand over the limp body of the stranger, wavering a little and breathing in great gulps. Ison Scorpy dropped to his knees, setting his fingers to the side of the bruised throat.

"Still alive," he announced, then turned his head to look up at Zolan. "Who is he?"

Tamara

BUT NO ANSWER came. I raised my head from Bina's shoulder with some difficulty. Any weakness I had ever felt before at a draining of the Power had been nothing compared with this.

"He said—king." I looked to Zolan, not to the body crumpled on the floor. A king was reported to be captive in Gurlyon, yes—but there might be two rulers now.

Zolan made no move to examine the body Ison was straightening out. Climber came out from the shadows, sniffed at the inert man, and lifted his lip in a silent snarl. The beast had expressed his opinion of the man, and it was a low one, no matter what his rank.

Mother came into view from behind me, her hands resting on my shoulders. She had sent into and through me many of those wracking waves of Power.

"This is King Arvor," she said, not in accusation but in recognition. Yet her attention was for Zolan, not for the unconscious stranger. After a pause, in which the man from the Dismals made no answer, she spoke again:

"Is this the king?"

That she would ask such a question when she had already answered it made no sense. I straightened. The glow from my talisman appeared to keep rhythm with her labored breathing.

"What is he"—I flung out toward the body the hand holding the gem— "flesh or spirit?"

Zolan, who had paid no attention to our mother, stared at me sharply for a second and then gave a guarded look at his recent opponent.

"Who knows?"

But our mother was not to be denied. She gestured at Arvor.

"You drew him here—"

Zolan denied that statement at once. "He was sent."

"So . . ." Apparently she was able to accept this reply. I was thinking far more clearly now. We had heard that the king was reported missing, that the Chosen from the mountains remained in Kingsburke. If Arvor had been a prisoner, and that renegade from the Jar Folk did possess great power, he could well have planted the ruler among us now as a weapon of his own.

Now Mother addressed Ison rather than Zolan.

"Ask my Lord Warden to come—" she began, but she had gotten no further when Bina and I were gently pushed to one side, and Father stood there.

"What chances?" he demanded of Mother. "Even the troop is near ready to flee. Men have been struck down by the Power that raged here!"

He did not wait for an answer but took another step forward to look down on Arvor. The king moaned and made a weak gesture toward his head. I moved the gem at once so that its still-growing light more fully illuminated him.

"King Arvor!" Our father looked directly to Zolan. "How came he here? Was he with the tower garrison but did not flee?"

Ison spoke. "The Power brought him, Lord Warden." He pointed to the window. "Through that—in a blaze of flame!"

Father's thoughts kept pace with Mother's. "Was he drawn by you? For what purpose?" he demanded.

Zolan gave a sigh, and his hands went out in a gesture of helplessness as he made the same answer: "He was Sent!"

The radiance of my jewel made very plain the expression of our father's face. Familiar as he was with the force that fueled our Talents, there were some displays of that Power he would not accept without more explanation.

I was on my feet now, though I still held the talisman so that its radiance touched the king. He was showing more signs of returning consciousness, turning his head as if to avoid as much of the eye-smiting light as he could.

I faced Zolan squarely, and my words came evenly and with emphasis.

"Is this one indeed our enemy?"

Slowly our companion shook his head. "Not now—"

The man on the floor suddenly sat upright. He stared at us, his eyes fastening on each in turn before passing to the next one. Fear shadowed his eyes and furrowed his face. Then Ison stepped back, and the king looked beyond him.

"How—how came I here?" His voice was unsteady. "I was with the Chosen while he told me what was happening in the streets—that monsters had been summoned by those accursed Southerners whose unholy Power killed and yet could not be quenched."

Suddenly his eyes fixed again on Father.

"Damned dealers with the Dark!" His voice had risen to a scream. Then such a stream of obscenity aimed at Father, Mother, and finally at us burst forth to taint the air as I had never thought to hear from the lips of any man of gentle birth.

Ison moved. The sound of his hand striking the other's mouth was near as loud as the vomit of word-filth ended by that blow.

Father stood over the king, shouldering Ison to one side.

"King or not, youngling, you will keep a clean tongue in your head. I shall forget this, since it would seem you have been a victim of another's Power. Your advisor is Chosen, yes, but by the Dark. With some foul intent he has sent you hither. If you know that purpose, you would do very well to state it now."

His face twisted in rage, Arvor spat, and the moisture spattered on Father's buff coat. Ison's hand lifted to strike a second time, but Father shook his head.

Now Duty came into the full light and stooped a little to stare into the king's hot eyes. Before he could pull away, she laid fingers on his forehead. He was instantly still, his gaze caught and held by her.

After what seemed a very long pause, his face relaxed. The Wisewife's fingers moved back and forth, and I realized what she did. Just so had she brought all of us at times to calm and peace when something had gone very wrong with our lives. I remembered sitting once under a wind-twisted tree as a child, holding in my hands a fallen nest with three dead baby birds, my eyes painful from crying. It had been Duty who had comforted me then by the same gentle use of Power.

I was not surprised to see the king's eyes close, his body slump back to the floor; Duty had given him the Dreamless Sleep. Now she spoke to our mother.

"This one has been possessed without his consent."

She stated what was the greatest of crimes to those with Talent: the seizure of another's soul, the very atrocity that had set the woman of the Jugged Ones against the lord of her own kind.

But the Wisewife was continuing. "Even though this was done against his will, a channel has been opened, and at any moment he can again be invaded."

Zolan moved for the first time. "This body housed its own spirit before Tharn came," he informed us grimly. "The true Arvor was held captive by those who would use him as a tool—"

"—But when you seized him here in the tower, the hold of the Gray Robe was broken!" I burst in.

"Yes," our companion nodded. "It was then that the evil Power that had banished the king's soul was broken; but Arvor's body had already given house-room to the Dark One, and taken the taint of his nature, and so the king appeared to change.

"Even now, though the Jugged One's gateway has been closed"—the man from the Dismals sighed as though from the depths of great weariness—"we still face great trouble. We cannot keep the king as prisoner—the clansmen will come over from the other tower sooner or later."

Mother spoke then, not to our father but as if she were voicing some thoughts aloud the better to study them.

"Shall we work the memory change?"

Alteration of the mind of any man or woman, even an enemy, was another act that was dubious in the eyes of the Talented; however, it was not totally forbidden, though it was only undertaken when no other choice was left.

Duty did not look away from the sleeper, but she answered, "We may be too drained. It would be better to wait—"

A rousing cry from without interrupted her, followed by other sounds that reached us even through the tower's thick walls and shutters.

"By the Waning Moon!" Father pushed aside Ison and reopened the window. Leaning a little over the sill, he looked down at the courtyard. Then he whirled about.

"How long will this one sleep, dame?"

"I cannot say. He has been weakened by"—she paused, and her mouth twisted as though she would spit forth as foulness her next words—"what he has undergone."

"So be it." Father's face was grim. "Listen well, all of you. This shall be our tale: Those we drove from this watchtower were not in truth Arvor's men—the greater part of them served the One we now hunt. We found the king here, bound, a prisoner, reserved for some hideous fate by the Chosen and his followers. He had also been kept under control by means of some potion. He has now been freed by us, and we shall guard him on his way to return to Kingsburke. If you"—he spoke now to Mother—"can implant at least a portion of false memory, let the story run as I have said."

Father then gestured to Ison and, after a pause, to Zolan. "Now we go to see what manner of trouble lies below."

He did not leave at the close of this speech, for he also had orders for the three of us. "All know that you gave strength to summon the shadow army. Tam, hide that talisman of yours. Bina, Cilla, get you below with your sister and appear very weak. It shall be given out that you and Zolan protected the king with your Talent or the Chosen leader would have struck him dead rather than let it be known that that false priest deals in soul-rape that is far worse than murder. Let us to this wreaking straightway. It may be that we shall have to bring the clan chief and some of his leaders here to see the king. If you continue to hold him as he is now, all the better, Duty."

During this speech, he had approached the stairwell. Now, without any addition to his last orders, he was over its edge and gone, both Ison and Zolan close behind him. We were left guardians of the Gurly king.

Thirty

⋆⋆⋆

Sabina

We did not move out of the watchtower for Kingsburke. King Arvor was carried to the lower floor, still limp in deep sleep, to be bedded next to Rogher.

Within a very short time clansmen came to view their ruler, filling by the chamber. We had made ourselves very visible as concerned attendants, although we ourselves would have liked to share the king's slumbers. With Duty I had sought out the quarters of the healer to make inroads on the supplies stored there, providing support for us all.

Sitting down at last I crushed a palm full of leaves and drew deep breaths of the invigorating scent. While I was thus employed, Tam and Cilla busied themselves putting our own gear in order.

There were many measuring glances cast in our direction as the Gurlys came to view King Arvor, some I thought *too* searching. Though the story Father had so swiftly crafted did hold together, a number of questions obviously remained.

It was a day of heavy clouds; the ravishing colors seemed to have burnt all the heavens, leaving only ashes. Just before day the warn fires at the top of each defense tower had been lit and remained unthreatened by wind or rain.

Also messengers had ridden out and we caught enough snatches of the visitors' words to realize that now a full clan call had gone forth in the king's name. Our own troop took no part in this. Nor did we see Father again soon. It was plain that he was very willing to allow the Gurlys to handle this business.

At length Mother summoned Tam and Duty. Together they left the hall for one of the small rooms, which provided privacy for the officers. They had not been in that small chamber long before a faint glow, pulsating with limited Power, suggested that Tam was calling upon her talisman.

Tamara

MOTHER PULLED A flat pillow from a bunk to the floor where she had already seated herself, motioning us to join her. With the pillow as a less-than-firm base, she flattened it further with the force of both hands, setting upon it a large disk of finely burnished silver.

I recognized a tool she used but seldom—a seeing mirror. It had in the past been exposed to several baths of Power. However, as far as I knew, it had never been taken out of Mother's most private workroom before. To call upon such aid would alert any Power source within leagues of its use. Still, our presence here now had been well established by the events of the night. Why hide now?

"Let the light of the talisman be the sun above," she said. Her hands were on either side of the disk. Energy would flow from flesh and bone to activate the seeing.

I steadied the gem above. The glow did not give off heat this time, only the light. Duty was singsonging words of summoning.

The disk came alight. Even the plate grew larger until we looked through what might be a window taller and wider than any in the walls about us. What we clearly saw now was a section of cobbled street. Stone buildings loomed high on one side but on the other side there was a stretch of open ground. A more intent study told me that this was the very heart of Kingsburke and facing us some distance across the open ground was the palace of the Gurly kings.

I had seen that only once before when we, as the family of the Lord Warden, had gathered there to be presented to the king. That had been a number of years ago when we sisters were children, the king hardly any older, and most of our attention had been for the dignitaries participating in the ceremony. The court was so unlike that of our own land, so lacking in rich furnishings, brightly garbed courtiers, that we had spent most of the time exchanging Sends of opinion. So far had my thoughts delved into the past that I was sharply snatched into the present by movement on the seeing disk.

Men, some still wearing uniforms and helmets, women, and children, some in their mothers' arms, were retreating backward into the open space. It was as if they were being helplessly herded by some implacable enemy.

Then that which had so cowed them appeared, not only from the direction from which they had come but crawling, hopping, striding also from the opposite side. I gasped, but my hand did not shake. The gem continued to provide steady light.

There were Gurlys among the newcomers, yes. But we saw only a sprinkling of such normality. The rest—

The monsters of the Dismals were nothing compared to those gathering under our gaze. There appeared to be no winged killers, but reptilian ones abounded. And leading them, things that were neither beasts nor men, for which I could find no name.

"Wild Ones!" Duty identified the company.

The group of city people tightened into a smaller and smaller space. Again those threatening them began to move, now neither forward nor backward but circling the humans, until little space remained between prey and predators.

One of the horrors whipped out a tentacle whose tip wrapped about an infant at its mother's breast and jerked the child loose, flipping it into the air. The baby fell among the creatures and disappeared. Her mouth torn wide in what must have been a racking scream, the mother flung herself forward. Monsters and half-men opened ranks, and the maddened woman plunged on, not to be seen again.

I cried out in horror and rage, but I also felt a whiplash of fear. Duty's hand shot out to steady my wrist, which had begun to shake. Another of those to be seen in the mirror was taken, to serve as—amusement? *food?*

"We must aid them!" I broke the silence with that cry. "What more will chance—"

Duty opened her wrist grip into a flat hand and struck hard fingers bruisingly across my lips. I stiffened and tried to master my shivering, while she, with a glance at me of solemn warning, drew herself closer to the disc.

Now the Wisewife lowered an object over the mirror: a short pendant of crystal, pointed at both ends, and dangling from a silver chain. Deep inside the jewel, colors swirled swiftly to birth and as quickly died. Slowly the pointer began to descend towards the plate, swaying so that first one end, then the other, pointed at the disc.

During the gradual lowering of the talisman, another of the Kingsburke folk was seized by the tentacled member of the Wild army. One tip of the crystal was pointed down now, and it remained in that position until it touched the surface of the disc—precisely where the attacking horror tightened its coils.

The jewel produced a distinct sound as its tip touched the disc. Instantly, we were engulfed in roaring as of a storm-wind and heat fourfold greater than the hottest midsummer day. We cowered, even as the people of the city had cringed before the monsters, deafened, blinded, and burning as if our skin was being seared from our bones.

I could hear Duty's voice shrilling higher and higher. My hand holding the jewel dropped nerveless to my knee; I felt but I could not see. Then, though unconscious of doing so, I forced my hand up again until the gem touched my forehead between my closed eyes. Once more it was hot with energy, hotter even than the air about us.

"Evo! Evo!"

"Old Ones, loose hold!"

Duty's voice rose ever stronger and louder. I opened my eyes. My head must have been bowed, for the first thing I saw clearly was the disc. No longer did it shine—across it spattered a black stain, a blot which, the longer I regarded it, looked more and more like the outline of one of the monsters.

Mother straightened. She spread open her hands, and I could now see that some of the Dark taint also discolored her palms. Not knowing whether my action would prove an answer, I speedily drew the gem across her blackened flesh.

I saw her bite her lip as if to stifle a cry, but the stain vanished, and her skin showed unmarked and clean again. Duty, meanwhile, had snatched the crystal pointer away from the seeing disc. What she held now was only a shriveled cord dangling a lump of foggy slag in place of the clear pendant.

"So—be—it!" Mother intoned slowly. "We must fight on *their* chosen ground, not ours."

Duty stood up. Dropping the chain and its blob of melted crystal to the floor, she set her booted foot firmly upon it to grind what remained into a powder.

"I was a fool." The Wisewife's lips curved downward in a sour droop.

Mother shook her head. "No," she countered, "it is best to know what strength stands against us. But an end must be made, and soon. We are those best fitted to oppose the Dark—and its weapons. That truth cannot be denied."

Drucilla

MOTHER, DUTY, AND Tam came out of the small chamber to which they had earlier withdrawn. It was obvious to our eyes that they had undergone some arduous ordeal. However, before we could discover what had happened, the king stirred on his improvised bed and sat up. His blue eyes no longer showed any mental dullness, nor did any physical weakness linger to impair him. He looked towards Mother and spoke.

"Lady Sorceress, you dabble in a potent Power!"

His voice, curt and commanding, was as different from that we had heard earlier as were those now-piercing eyes. To the implied challenge, however, Mother made quiet and calm reply.

"I and mine do not 'dabble,' Your Majesty. Within this land, however, dwell other wielders of Talent who are doing so. The Powers of the Wild Earth such as have never been put under restraint are now manifesting themselves, seizing whom they will of your people—the folk to whom you owe protection and succor. You have opened a door to the Dark, and all will be lost if that is not again closed fast."

Arvor's lips were pulled tightly across his teeth as he stared back at her, and now his voice sounded like a beast's growl.

"Woman, you forget yourself—"

If he would have delivered a further rebuke, he had no chance, for Tam interrupted.

"We have forgotten nothing, Your Majesty. Scarcely a day ago we saved your body for you!"

"You speak nonsense," he retorted angrily. Rising swiftly to his feet, he gestured at himself. "This is my body, right enough—how have you saved it? Body and spirit are one and the same!"

"Are they?" Tam demanded. "How came you to this defense tower? Did you ride hither with your men? If so, then"—she gestured to the hall about us—"where stand your guards, your close clan chieftains? Do you see them?"

He frowned, his thick brows almost meeting above his nose. "I was—" he began, then hesitated. "Yes!" His tone became more forceful. "I was in my chamber in the palace. The Chosen came to me that we might find a way to fight the monsters, and—" Arvor fell suddenly silent, and the shadow of fear crossed his face.

"He took my hand," the young ruler continued laboriously, as if pulling word after stubborn word from his memory, "and then I was on the floor, and I was fighting."

"But you remember nothing that happened between," Tam persisted.

Mother and Duty stood silent, withdrawing a little, shrewdly leaving Tam in command.

The king's scowl was heavy, and his face was growing increasingly flushed. Suddenly he turned away. Yet he could not win free of us, for I stepped before him and barred his retreat, as would a guard.

"Your Majesty"—I spoke with little respect in my tone—"you have been ensorcelled, and you are at present free only by our efforts. The Dark has taken you once. If you do not face that fact and ready yourself to do battle, why, then—" I raised my hands and shrugged in a gesture of defeat.

"Witches—all of you!" Arvor was nearly shouting now, his wrath once more heated to the boil it had reached the night before.

But we had forgotten Duty. The Wisewife who now stepped before the raging youth was implacable, a personification of her name, prepared to list his shortcomings aloud, shame him before all the company.

Suddenly I caught a scent I knew well. So sharp was it that I swallowed hurriedly as my eyes began to water. With no fear of reprisal, Duty hurled a lump of herbs that had the appearance of a well-chewed cud into the king's face.

His head snapped back; then he stood blinking as the small wad slipped down his chin to the floor. When he spoke to Duty, he might have been a small boy longing to appease a stern guardian.

"I have done nothing wrong, Feemie. Truly I have not!"

Duty nodded. "No, you have not, Arvor. But if you do not listen, you may. Do you wish the Evil Ones to hide beneath your bed tonight?"

He actually looked stricken. "No-ooo!" he cried in a rising wail.

She nodded again. "Very well. You are king now, Arvor—remember that well. You must lead the clansmen, but you must also listen to those who know what you truly face and are able to guide you." She paused, then snapped her fingers in his face.

The bewildered youth raised his hand uncertainly to brush it across his eyes. A moment later, he shook his head and blinked at our old nurse, whom he had thought his own.

"Feemie—you are not Feemie!"

"No," she agreed calmly. "Feemie has long rested at peace with herself and her world. But her care yet abides, and the life-lessons she gave you remain. You have followed a willful path into a tangle of Evil, and now you must cut your way out. Heed well."

His attention fixed firmly on Duty, the king listened. She spoke simply and clearly, detailing what we had learned in the Dismals and explaining what we faced now. When she had finished, he drew a deep breath; his right hand groped at his side for a sword he did not wear. But he asked no questions.

Then he looked from his new teacher to Mother.

"Gracious lady, I have spoken foully. If you will forgive my words—"

Mother inclined her head. "It is done, Your Majesty, and already forgotten. We must allow no division to come between us, for by the sowing of such discord does the Dark Power reap a harvest of lives. What lies before us now is far deadlier than any war, and in that conflict you may well again serve as the weapon this lord of the Left-hand Path seeks. What we can do in protection for you and for all our forces, we shall; yet our enemy has raised the ancient powers of the land, against which we are often impotent. We cannot cry victory until he is utterly destroyed."

"What I am empowered to do, that I shall do," he replied with the solemnity of an oath.

Thus the king joined forces with us. Throughout the day and much of the next night, meetings were held with the clan chiefs who had answered the Gathering-signal of the tower fires, and messages were sent forth by those already assembled. Father and his officers attended these war-meets, and there was much coming and going of soldiery in the hall.

We withdrew to quarters in the room above to hold our own strategy discussion. The second clan force to ride in had had among them a long-bearded, green-caped man who climbed the stairs to join us.

By the heavy golden pendant lying on his breast and the massive signet on his right thumb, he was one long in service of the Light. However, those adornments were not truly needed to identify him, for his Power flowed palpably before him as he came.

Mother arose to greet him with such deference as she would our queen. He, in turn, held out his ringed hand for her to lay fingers on, as if they were priest and priestess in the same shrine and therefore of equal standing.

"May your Light shine, Brother," she said.

"As may yours, Sister. You have come a hard and long way in the service of the Great One." The Lightwielder made a gesture of benediction that included myself and my sisters as he said, "May the Power bless you all."

Having been made known to this newcomer—Arthter by name—we settled ourselves once again, and Mother took up our tale, even as Duty had earlier for the king. The Shrine Speaker saved his questions until she was done. Then he centered on the three of us, had us each in turn tell of the Dismals, then of the woman of the Jugged Folk and the task she had laid upon us.

Arthter asked to see Tam's gem but, though he looked at the stone, he would not touch it.

"Lady Tamara, you hold a treasure; therefore, you also will have much asked of you," he said quietly. "Guard it well, for its like has not been seen in this land, North or South." Then he addressed Mother.

"So this foul soul has tampered with the forbidden gate, and the Wild Magic comes to his call. However, it may be that we have been given more knowledge of the ways of the Old Ones than he knows. For the Green Power is of the heart of the land itself, and we are also the earth's children, though of another breed. I must speak now with Zolan."

That statement was not quite an order, but I felt at once the Power gathering for a potent Send. Earlier Zolan had been with the armsmen below, though he kept well to the rear of Father's group, as if he wished to escape notice as much as possible.

Mother cast forth a mind-message. Within a few moments, we heard quick steps on the stair, and the man from the Dismals came among us. The Shrine Dweller did not speak at once, nor did Zolan break the silence. I grew uneasy, for the two men almost appeared for a moment to confront each other in the manner of undeclared enemies.

Arthter at last held out his beringed hand. Zolan still hesitated, then finally extended his own so that they touched palm to palm.

"*Var si dun*—" Our companion's voice was hardly above a whisper, but it was very firm.

Arthter clapped his hands together and then held them out a little, palms down. "*Thirtam,*" he replied.

Zolan's mask broke as he responded eagerly to the other.

"Ask!" he fairly cried. "That which I have will be given."

Thus was our company increased by one, and though I had visited the Shrine many times with Mother, some of the matters that were discussed now were as far in advance of my training as if I were still a novice petitioner, unvowed to the Light.

"We face a battle of spirit as well as steel," Zolan said at length. "The soul of the hermit that was driven from his natural body may well have ceased to exist; therefore it cannot be summoned back. The absence of that spirit weakens us, as the hermit's desire for what is his own could add mightily to our strength. We must also remember that Tharn himself has no refuge if he is deprived of the body he now inhabits, for the clay vessel that held his essence in the Dismals has been destroyed. Desperation will thus arm him to the fullest extent."

He hesitated before adding, "He took the king once; he may try again. A second possession may be even easier to achieve. Therefore Arvor must be Warded as completely as may be achieved."

"And as soon as possible," Mother added. "It remains to be seen if we are able to go up against Wild Magic, which is not of the Light."

"Yet neither," Arthter interjected as she paused, "is it of the Dark—it is a Power that chooses its own way. But whatever tactics of the Talent we would employ, we must move as soon as possible—and not with the armsmen."

As he made that very definite statement, he turned to regard Bina and me. Swinging his chain of office well to one side, he delved into the breast-fold of his cape to bring into view a roll of cured skin. This cylinder he carefully unrolled. It was a map, a very old one—indeed, the outlines upon it were so dim that it must needs be held close for eyes to see them at all.

Tam caught my thought and held her gem down to those faint tracings.

Arthter rose, pushing back towards the wall the bedroll that had been his seat. Wordlessly the rest of us did likewise until we had won a free space on the floor. When that area, circular in shape, had been cleared, he came to my side.

Again the Shrine Servant reached under his green garment and this time brought forth a slender rod of strange wood, green also, but with dots of gold undulating over it. With this wand, he pointed to portions of the map, at the same time giving me instructions.

"Lady Drucilla, copy these as carefully as can be done on the floor here and now."

Mother's Send came quickly: *"Do your best, daughter."*

I knelt beside Tam who held the Dismals jewel. The light grew ever stronger as she fed it Power. Taking Arthter's rod, Sabina began to transfer to the old wood flooring those parts of the map he had indicated. I knew the picture now for what surely was—a section of Kingsburke.

Thirty-one

★
★ ★

Tamara

Wind whistled about us, burdened with the stench released by violent death. Fear, rage, and pain tainted the air almost as thickly, as well as other emotions I could not determine.

Bina, Cilla, and I stood together, as did Mother and Ison. Zolan held himself a little apart, just as he had remained aloof from Father's forces, though Climber sat beside him. The focus of our company, its core, was Arthter, Duty at his right hand.

I kept my eyes fixed on the two of them, not daring to look about, though I was sure I knew where we were. The buildings of Kingsburke walled us in, and beneath our boots we could feel the earth of the open space before the palace. Cilla's hand gripped tightly the rod with which she had drawn a map of this place on the floor of the defense tower.

I was not even sure that we existed as more than wisps of identity, delivered here by such high Power as only the greatest of adepts could summon. We had been in the tower, and now we were in the city—that was all I could swear to. Still, none of the storm clouds of raging color surrounded us such as had heralded the arrival of Arvor.

The gray of early dawn gave us a measure of light. Light—I fixed my gaze upon the gem I held with all the focus I could summon. It was as cold now as any dew-wet stone, seemingly dead. Had the Power that had transported us here burnt it out?

The foulness, rising from the lifeless things lying on the cobbles, continued to intensify until it choked our nostrils and throats, and the aura of terror and suffering grew more oppressive with it.

"Ready—" The adept did not turn to address any of our group, but his tone alerted us. Bina's hand was on me, catching mine in her hold, as she linked also with Cilla. We were tightly three in one again, and so we would be—we *must* be—until the end came, one way or another. And our joining was but the beginning of a melding with the others that increased steadily in strength.

As yet there was no opposition; Kingsburke might be a long-deserted ruin. We felt a pulsation, like the beating of a great heart. Then we sensed a Gathering begin.

Four streets fed into the blood-spattered square, one at each corner. Movement was commencing on each, and it was easy to sense, though none of us looked to see what advanced. Instead, the palace looming before us held our attention.

It must have begun as a defensive castle, that pile, for some of its stones were dark with age, while others, marking later additions, were lighter. Wide steps led up to a door so large that a full company of armsmen might enter it four abreast.

The vast door had the sheen of metal under the strengthening glow of approaching day. It was shut, and we saw no sign of guards on duty.

"*Hicar vorlun tee.*
Iscar, wun, inze . . ."

The ancient words rolled easily from the combined tongues of Duty and Arthter. I had thought I knew our old nurse well, but this seeress was strange, her Gifts beyond those we three had ever learned or practiced.

The largely unseen motion down the streets was increasing, a darkness rising with the light. Its flow was now edging out into the square. Yet, strangely, the sickening stench that had plagued us was now being overlaid by cleaner odors. I felt no breeze, but I smelled the scent of herbs and other healing, growing things; of earth freshly plowed after rain; of pine; and of flowers—not the blossoms tamed for a garden but rather the shy ones that hid themselves in the wild places.

"*Evo—EVO!*" That cry voiced no threat, no order, rather a welcoming hail.

The things that had poured in from the streets like a fourfold tide did not advance farther into the open square but clustered together. Even now I could not look directly at them. Surely if they were the monsters I had seen in Mother's viewing mirror, we were now nearly surrounded by danger. Yet we were held in this place.

"*Sansong, Lare*"—Duty and Arthter again mingled voices.

Zolan strode forward, one hand resting on Climber's head. His head tilted back a fraction as he shouted: "*Strength to strength, Dealer-in-Death!*"

He was not greeting the Wild Ones as I was sure the Wisewife and the adept did, but rather addressing the door.

From the two side streets that paralleled the palace now trooped forth beings whose like I had only seen pictured in books of ancient legends. A great bear shambled on its hind legs behind the much smaller form of a girl, her greenish white hair by turns hidden, then revealed, by a gold veil that floated about her. Coming to meet them from the opposite side of the open space was an armored figure, his war-gear that of an ancient time. Drifting from his closed helm like a plume was a vine studded with small flowers. With him strode a massive cat wearing a gemmed chain that gleamed through long neck fur—not a collar of service but a decoration of honor.

Others came into sight, two by two, each different from the others of their company. Here were none of the monsters we had seen; rather, all these beings had the appearance of those able to walk in the Light without fear. I understood then that even the Wild Magic had its good and evil and that its followers had—as did we—a choice of two paths to follow.

None of us greeted the newcomers, nor did any of them look to us. However, Duty and Arthter moved forward a step or so. Behind them Mother, myself, and my sisters did likewise. Zolan showed no interest in either our group or the Children of Earth. He stood now at the foot of the stairs leading to the palace door.

"*In the name of the Nine Daughters of Lazar, by the Blood of the Sooks, and by the Kinship of the Last Ship, Tharn—let it be decided between us, here and now, in this place. Dishonored bones cry out!*"

I could not see the object he held, but he hurled it. The missile struck against the steely surface, to be answered by a reverberation such as a mighty blow would waken from a great drum.

"Come forth!"

Metal rasped, grating over stone. Slowly that barrier opened. None of the daylight penetrated within; the portal was only a wide aperture filled with the black of a moonless, starless night.

Then that darkness was pushed aside like a curtain, and a single figure appeared.

Sabina

I GASPED, AND my hold on the hands of Tam and Cilla tightened. Before us stood neither a hermit nor a human with the stature and presence of an adept—even a Dark one. This was indeed an enemy, but not the one we expected—it was Maclan, wearing the smile of the successful hunter planting a triumphant boot on the carcass of a fresh-killed stag after a royal hunt.

He laughed as he raised a hand to beckon Zolan forward. Just so he had behaved when we lay captive. And suddenly I was healed, not only by my own anger but by that which overflowed from Tam and Cilla. I dropped linkage with my sisters; my fingers curled, then straightened to curl again. Within the flesh, the heat of Power was rising. The old rules could not hold now—we were entitled to our vengeance. This time the predator would face no helpless prey!

Maclan/Tharn addressed Zolan. "Pharsali favors me," he observed, eyeing our companion. "She sends me her treasure: the fool! Yes, I have taken another body. This husk"—he shivered affectedly to draw attention to the stolen form he wore—"is wanting in some ways. Yours is more to my taste, youngling. Do not think you can deny me this time, even backed by these cringing Light-lickers you dare to mistakenly depend upon."

He extended both hands and gestured imperiously. "Come, you believer in Power, and discover what it may truly be."

Zolan remained exactly where he was; however, he swayed in his struggle to hold his ground, and the outmost cord of the flung noose of force he dodged touched us.

I did not deny I had been wrong. As a man would change his garments or assume armor to work his purpose, this Tharn from the Dismals now wore the body of Maclan the Breaksword. For a brief instant I wondered what had chanced with the true Reiver.

Then we three became one again: Tam became me, and became Cilla, as I became each of them. During our sharing, however, unlike the possession performed by the Evil One, our bodies remained our own. We sharpened our Talent, fastened our attention once more on the one before the door. His smile faded, and I could see his lips beginning to shape words unheard. Much of what had been Maclan was gone. Force boiled in that stolen body, as the renegade from the Dismals grew ever stronger, calling down Power into himself that he did not yet wish to use.

Whatever spells he might be muttering were completely drowned out by a great coughing cry. Climber had reared onto his hind legs, in that posture almost matching Zolan in height. His long tail lashed out like a fiery war banner.

Zolan caught at the roll of thick fur and flesh at the animal's neck. The cat-creature tried to turn his head, snapping vainly at the air, but he was unable to reach the restraining hand.

He-who-was-not-Maclan advanced a step forward and laughed again.

"You remember, do you, Lebrek?" he shouted jeeringly. "Yes, I see you have not forgotten!"

Climber roared and twisted, fought for freedom. Zolan was manifestly struggling hard to keep his hold.

"Loose him, youngling, if you wish!"

Zolan had now embraced the beast that was still on hind legs.

"Like to like!" Maclan nodded encouragingly, beckoning once more.

Climber grew still; however, Zolan did not loose his hold.

"You test my patience." The Dark One's grin disappeared, and his right hand came up. Save for a forefinger, it was curled into a fist.

We were one, united in what we would do. Tam swung up in turn her own left hand, the light of the gem glowing between her fingers.

Maclan pointed directly at the two below him, and from the tip of his forefinger speared greenish flame. It met the beam Tam had loosed—met it, and sprayed back to engulf the fisted hand.

"*Yaaah!*" he screamed, the throat-tearing sound no part of any spell but an animal scream of pure torment. His arm dropped back to his side, and even from this distance we could plainly see blackened flesh.

He took a stride to the very edge of the top step. Now whatever was clothed in the Breaksword's body turned to us.

Drucilla

THE FACE OF our enemy twisted, and he flung both arms above his head as if to seize a storm and pull it down upon us. And indeed he might have done so, for suddenly the sunlight was gone, darkness descended, and thunder rolled. Then a flash like lightning struck. Again, as she had forestalled the green ray, Tam swept high into the air the gem to deflect that lance of light. This time, however, no beam answered from her weapon, but a curling strand of golden fog that spread about our company.

I saw Zolan's hands moving in slow gestures, graceful as a Shrine dancer's at the time of the Turn of the Wheel, summoning the New Year's birth.

Lightning flashed again, struck the slow movement of the fog, and was hurled back once more. From the two companies of the Earth Ones rose shooting stars of blue, vivid as the skies of high summer. The Wild Ones had raised their own shelter!

Then, in a single moment, the battle was done, and we stood before the palace as we had before. Zolan turned his head, looking not at us but to Duty and Arthter. I felt the touch of a Send, but its message was not one I could translate.

Without a word, our companion ascended the steps, Climber at his side. None of us tried to stop him. Maclan's arms dropped to his sides, and I saw the fingers on his unharmed hand crook possessively, as might the claws of a raptor settling upon its prey.

Then a tremendous outpouring of Power was loosed, its waves flooding over us like the surge of a river in full spring spate. Tam still held fast to the gem, but its light had died. In that instant, I realized what was happening as clearly as if Zolan had shouted it aloud to us all—he was giving the Dark One what he most wanted: a body!

How our companion had been overcome I could not guess, but I knew that we had to make our own attack, raise all the Light we could to thwart this new soul-theft. The three of us broke linkage. Tam nursed the gem, and Mother stepped into Bina's path. I, however, slid to the other side so that no one stood ahead of me any longer.

I did not step, rather half threw myself forward. Both my hands closed about Climber's tail; then I was up on the lowest of the stairs that led to the door. My act, futile as it might be, served to attract Maclan's notice. As he glanced in my direction, Zolan reached the topmost step.

Maclan brought his hand down toward me, and I crumpled as though he had struck a physical blow. Then Zolan made his final move. He did not use fists but closed his hands on the Dark Lord's shoulders and pulled him forward into the same restraining embrace he had used on Climber.

Maclan's broken teeth showed in a wolf's grin. In turn, he wrapped his own arms around Zolan, and the two grappled weirdly together, motionless and in utter silence. About the frozen figures hung an uncanny radiance, a light forged of Darkness—I could find no other words to describe it.

Into me flowed a new wave of Power so great it doubled me over, set me gasping. All sense of identity was swept away from me as its intensity mounted—I was merely a conduit for its swift-rising force.

Terrifying though the feeling was, however, I knew that not only was it born of Talent but wielded by one in the service of the Light. But it was also unfamiliar and, because I could not flow easily with its pattern of Power, painful. Indeed, with its second surge, I felt as though a blazing liquid fire had been poured into me. And I could not escape—even the right of refusal to submit was raped away, leaving me only a weapon for another's use. A weapon, or—a mirror like Mother's, but for alien eyes?

I could still see what lay about me—I was yet held captive where I had gone to crouch. Zolan and Maclan stood locked fast, no movement even of breathing visible in their statuelike pose.

Up built the force. Now I was half-blinded by light—a rainbow radiance of many colors. Some shafts of this luminance stabbed toward the figures on the steps from behind me, others from either side. My breath came in great gasps—this light also had weight, and I was being crushed!

Now the two by the palace door began to sway; then out of that black-mouthed portal arced a vast limb of scaled skin. What appeared to be the body of a giant serpent reached for Zolan, then twisted viciously in the air.

A streak of red, Climber flashed forward, setting jaws on that roll of scale-sheathed flesh. But, though he brought the first monster down, it was only the advance guard of the Dark's forces. Things that had no place in any world we knew began to pour from the opening.

Again an agonizing pain, which I now sensed was anger in my possessor, ripped through me, aimed at the silent combatants above. At the same moment, the Wild Ones took up the battle against the nightmare creatures, an Evil they knew. Struck by the massed Power of the Green Magic, the horrors began to glow; then, one by one, they burst. However, the men, who seemed locked indissolubly together, remained as they stood.

The entity that had taken me over now set its will even more firmly upon me. I received no orders; I was simply used. Now, though I did not stand, I was urged to drag myself upward, step after step.

Climber, having no more monsters to harry, was circling the two; but, strive as he might to find an opening for another attack, Maclan and Zolan seemed Warded, untouchable.

Haltingly I lifted my hand, the same one with which I had struck my own opening blow in this war. My fingers, worked by another's will, clawed the air; there, clutching at a substance unseen, they worked it into an object visible. I now held a dagger of light. And suddenly, with the making of that knife, I knew the one who had made her weapon of *me*—indeed, I had once dream-met her. Pharsali!

Drawing all my last strength, the Jug Woman used my hand to hurl her gift—but not at the Dark Lord—at Zolan! The force-blade struck him full in the back, pierced through clothing and flesh, and disappeared from view.

What had I done?

Light, gold as the glow from Tam's gem, flared, enclosed the men and the beast beside them in a cylinder of brilliance. I crumpled onto the step, though I sensed I had not yet been released.

Out of that column of radiance fell a body; at least, the object had a human outline. Then the light-cylinder melted downward and puddled on the stone, where it was swallowed. Zolan swayed, eyes closed. But—was he still the companion we had known, or had the Evil One accomplished his will? For there was something about the man from the Dismals—

My suspicion was dashed away by the wave of joy that now filled me, but, while I felt it, it was not my emotion. She of the cave of jars was rejoicing, calling on deities who were not mine, while my eyes wept, torn by her fierce pride and joy. The truth was plain: Zolan, too, wore a body not his by birth—he was Pharsali's son.

Tamara

IN ALL OUR years of life, in any experience of knowledge gained, Talent shared, or testing endured, never had we encountered such a trial for body and soul as this. Cradling the gem in my two hands, Bina moving shoulder to shoulder with me, I hastened toward the stairs.

The last of the Dark things was being dispersed by the Wild Ones, and now those conquerors, too, were winking out of sight. The Green Folk could have been only images wrought by our own need and fear. Mother, Duty, and the Northern adept still stood together, but they seemed unharmed and we were not concerned for them. Cilla lay facedown, unmoving, on the palace steps, Climber limp beside her. Zolan knelt by Maclan, who appeared pale and drawn as if he had passed through some deadly illness.

Without rising to his feet, the man from the Dismals turned and mind-spoke. His Send was plain, but it held no heat of victory.

"Tharn—is—gone." The words were spaced well apart, spoken through nearly overwhelming fatigue.

We reached Cilla at the same time he slipped down to the step where she lay. Bina, her healer's instincts taking over, had already lifted our sister's head. No recognition showed in her open eyes.

I was shoved aside; Mother had come, as had Duty.

Together they eased Cilla over onto her back. With a frown, Mother shook her head at Zolan, warning him to remain in place, but neither she nor the Wisewife paid him any further heed.

Instead, Mother appeared to speak, and anger flared in her voice as she spoke.

"Break—*break link,* I order you! You have achieved what you would do, Woman of the Jars—now release my daughter!"

She drew Cilla's head against her breast, and I saw tears begin to gather in my sister's open eyes, then trickle down. Bina's hand fell upon my shoulder—arose—the gem was cool against my forehead. My whole body was taken by a shudder so powerful it shook Mother as well.

"It is finished," I said slowly in a whisper to be heard because a vast silence enclosed us.

And so it was.

An Ending–?

⋆⋆⋆

Tamara

The combined forces led by the Lord Warden and the highest-ranking chiefs of the assembled clans arrived together, having fought a skirmish with the remnants of the rebellion. The king was under surveillance, for Fergal's story had had an effect not only on his own clan leader but several others, all of high standing. Nor was it forgotten that Arvor had welcomed and supported Chosen Forfind in the beginning.

Our own party had made its way from the now-loathsome square into the palace and sought an inner room. We did not carefully note its location, nor do I remember much of that search for shelter, for we were all drooping and eager only to discover places on a carpeted floor. There sleep that was close to a swoon overtook us.

Sabina

No DREAMS CAME to trouble me. When I became aware of low voices again, though not words, I stretched out a little to ease an aching leg. I sensed warmth and a weight there, then I felt a damp tongue rasp over my arm, further arousing me. Opening my eyes, I saw lamplight—and looked upon Climber resting against me, his eyes regarding me strangely.

Emptiness was what I felt the most. Uneasiness arose as I put name to the feeling. What had passed away—or, worse, had been wrung out of me in time just past?

As I had done in the past when I awakened from some disturbing dream, I turned to the oldest and surest companionship I knew.

"Tam? Cilla?" At least there was no difficulty in my Send.

"Bina!" A unison cry; I had reached them both. The root of my fear was stricken, then died completely. The Talent remained to us! Once more our world shrank, tightened to hold only us three. We moved to cling together. So assured, we at last attended to what lay about us.

The room we had come into was a large chamber in which great lamps hung at intervals along the wall. At the far end of its expanse stood a dais and, on it, the Throne of the North.

Below that raised platform an argument was in progress. To one side we saw Zolan, and across from him Arvor. A little apart stood a number of the clan lords—among them Starkadder and others whose badges stated that their families had been involved in the past in the making of kings.

Drucilla

I WATCHED ZOLAN closely. The strangeness I had earlier sensed in him was stronger. He was—what? Not of humankind; perhaps not as far removed as the great spiders of the Dismals were from those lesser spinners who wove their traps in our world, yet no true kin to us. Now he glanced toward the clan lords. Fergal started forward, but Zolan shook his head.

"You know the truth, but once more I shall tell you: I am not of your kind. This shell"—he drew his hands down his body—"is merely what I wear that I might serve those who are left of our people. Years agone, a young male child whom some of your folk would have forced to their own service was banished to the Dismals to shift the balance of power in favor of one clan. He had been used so hardly—think well on this, my lords— that he no longer thought—he only feared. He sickened—"

Climber trotted forward, then stood up on his hind legs and nudged

Zolan with his muzzle. The man who was from, and of, the Dismals stroked his head. Then he continued. "This very one, this hero of great courage, has chosen to live in a beast's skin that he might serve his lady. He found the boy, brought him to Pharsali. She knew the child was dying. In her sorrow and her love, she was moved to violate an ancient taboo, and into his body—the form of the youth you knew as Gerrit—she sent the spirit of her own son.

"I am not of your blood. The lady sent me to deal with the one who would have made of your land a place of Always Dark, who slew and slew, and dyed your ways in blood. With the aid of those of an Old Learning, I have done as she has sworn me to do—Tharn is dead. The task is yours to cleanse the stains he has left.

"I say to you that I go now to my own place."

Tamara

HE DELIVERED THAT message with conviction, and he spoke with the force of truth.

Now a stir began among the Gurlys, and one of the clansmen raised a voice, but not in denial. Arthter had silently gone forward. Now he faced the company.

"Starkadder, Raghnell, Merven, Drafford, Wallingsor, Quain." The adept addressed the chiefs who stood before him, though from his lips the roll call of names had the sound, and force, of an incantation. "You know me and the truth I am sworn to speak, so hear me now and cast any doubt from your minds. This Evil was not of our world, and it has been dispatched to the judgment of its gods. Which of you can now stand forth and say that Zolan shall not return to those of his kin? Raise your voice, if you will—"

Utter silence.

"It is well!" His voice was that of a Speaker of Laws passing a decree.

Not only did Arthter smooth the way back to the Dismals for Zolan by this intercession, he also chose to ride with him. And our companion welcomed him, speaking (we suspected) not only for himself but also by the favor of the Lady of the Jars.

When Zolan was preparing to ride out later, I went to him with the gem out of the ruins and offered it to him, saying: "This is of your heritage, not mine. Let it return to its own land and people."

But not only did he refuse to take the stone, he gave me—no, us three—another gift of perhaps greater value.

"Lady Tamara, this jewel was freely given to you by our Old Ones. Keep it always, and may it serve you well again." He closed my hand around the talisman, which glowed warmly in response to the double touch. Gazing at my fingers, seemingly lit with the hidden fire they held, he then said: "This gem seems a fitting emblem of the Power you wield—you, and the two who share your mighty birth-bond. Indeed, so greatly have the three of you wrought in this war that the hero-singers will remember you three long after the flesh now alive, and"—his tone grew momentarily quieter—"the clay of the jars that holds my people has returned to the dust.

"However"—now Zolan's voice rose until it rang like a war-trumpet through the hall of the kings—"I doubt not that, in the meanwhile, the battle-cry of *Three Hands for Scorpio!* will summon many to the banner of the Light."

Then he was gone, back to his own place as we must return to ours; and whether he spoke in the spirit of true prophecy in that hour of parting was left ours to determine.

THUS WE SAW an end to this dark venture. When we had arrived back in Grosper, we found a message from Her Gracious Majesty summoning us to court that she might learn from us the whole of what happened.

Now we put an end to our tale.

Tamara of Verset
Sabina of Verset
Drucilla of Verset

[Small sheet of parchment found in the records of Alsonia]

I, Drucilla of Verset, need to make certain the following information survives. Her Majesty, it seems, would have us back in Alsonia for another reason. She wishes to ensure that the Talent will, for centuries ahead, make safe her kingdom and has, to further its perpetuation, selected certain husbands for us. She had already sent Ison to join our forces for this reason, as though he were the soup course that heralds a full feast! But no one can choose a mate for another, and, if we are too straitly constrained, we know a land to the north that has long provided a haven for renegades and adventurers and may welcome us—that place of wonders, the Dismals.

ABOUT THE AUTHOR

For more than fifty years, Andre Norton, "one of the most distinguished living SF and fantasy writers" (*Booklist*), has been penning bestselling novels that have earned her a unique place in the hearts and minds of millions of readers worldwide. She has been honored with a Life Achievement Award by the World Fantasy Convention and with the Grand Master Nebula Award by her peers in the Science Fiction Writers of America. Works set in her fabled *Witch World,* as well as others, such as *The Time Traders, Solar Queen,* and *Beast Master* series, to name but a few in her great oeuvre, have made her "one of the most popular authors of our time" (*Publishers Weekly*). She lives in Murfreesboro, Tennessee. More can be learned about Miss Norton's work at www.andre-norton.org.